Praise for Cold Rock River

"A powerful story of family, love, and loss that will keep you up into the wee hours. Absolutely wonderful! Beautifully told and straight from the heart of an exquisitely talented writer."

— New York Times BEST-SELLING AUTHOR DOROTHEA BENTON FRANK

"Jackie Lee Miles brings her rich talent to a higher level. The journey of two young brides . . . from sensitive adolescence to women of substance . . . makes for a very fine recipe."

—EMMY-WINNING CREATOR OF THE WALTONS, BEST-SELLING AUTHOR, AND AWARD-WINNING SCREENWRITER EARL HAMNER

"A compelling story you won't want to miss! Well told and deeply true to its time and place."

—NEW YORK TIMES BEST-SELLING AUTHOR HAYWOOD SMITH, AUTHOR OF THE RED HAT CLUB AND THE RED HAT CLUB RIDES AGAIN

"Warm, fresh, funny—the characters leap off the page! Miles is a fascinating new voice in Southern fiction. Readers will rejoice."

—KARIN GILLESPIE, AUTHOR OF DOLLAR DAZE, BET YOUR BOTTOM DOLLAR, AND A DOLLAR SHORT

"*Cold Rock River* is an absolute gem! Filled with humor; sometimes subtle, sometimes out-and-out hysterical."

—ANN KEMPNER FISHER, EDITOR OF B.O.O.B.S.: A BUNCH OF OUTRAGEOUS BREAST-CANCER SURVIVORS SHARE THEIR STORIES OF COURAGE, HOPE AND HEALING

"Jackie Lee Miles is a wise and perceptive writer with a keen understanding of human frailties."

—JULIE CANNON, AUTHOR OF TRUELOVE & HOMEGROWN TOMATOES, 'MATER BISCUIT, AND THOSE PEARLY GATES

Praise for Jackie Lee Miles's Roseflower Creek

"Once you start you will not stop until the last gripping page. The lyric prose will thrill you, the story is unforgettable, and the characters will stay with you forever."

—WILLIAM DIEHL, AUTHOR OF *PRIMAL FEAR* AND *EUREKA*

"*Roseflower Creek* is a compelling, fast-paced narrative that captivates from the first page to the last. It is beautifully written and sensitively told. Don't miss it!"

——*NEW YORK TIMES* BEST-SELLING AUTHOR HAYWOOD SMITH, AUTHOR OF *THE RED HAT CLUB* AND *THE RED HAT CLUB RIDES AGAIN*

"Lori Jean will jam her thumbprint into your heart forever!"

—CARMEN AGRA DEEDY, CHILDREN'S BOOK AUTHOR AND COMMENTATOR ON NATIONAL PUBLIC RADIO'S *ALL THINGS CONSIDERED*

"I may be through with this book, but [it] will never be through with me."

—BARRY FARBER, NATIONALLY SYNDICATED RADIO TALK-SHOW HOST

"Jackie Lee Miles writes with rare simplicity and grace, telling Lori Jean's story in a voice as pure as new milk and as genuine as a child's smile. Like Lori Jean, this small, delicate novel has a very large soul."

—R. ROBIN MCDONALD, AUTHOR OF *SECRETS NEVER LIE* AND *BLACK WIDOW*

"A powerful, extraordinary novel. The characters haunt the reader long after the last page is turned."

—EARL HAMNER, CREATOR OF *THE WALTONS*

Cold Rock River

a novel by

Jackie Lee Miles

CUMBERLAND HOUSE
NASHVILLE, TENNESSEE

COLD ROCK RIVER
PUBLISHED BY CUMBERLAND HOUSE PUBLISHING
431 Harding Industrial Drive
Nashville, Tennessee 37211

Cover design: Unlikely Suburban Design
Text design: Mary Sanford

Library of Congress Cataloging-in-Publication Data
Miles, Jackie Lee (Jacquelyn L.), 1947–
  Cold Rock River : a novel / by Jackie Lee Miles.
    p. cm.
  ISBN-13: 978-1-58182-570-1 (hardcover : alk. paper)
  ISBN-10: 1-58182-570-6 (hardcover : alk. paper)
  ISBN-13: 978-1-58182-668-5 (paperback : alk. paper)
  ISBN-10: 1-58182-668-0 (paperback : alk. paper)
  1. United States—History—1961–1969—Fiction. 2. Teenage pregnancy—Alabama—Fiction. 3. Teenage girls—Alabama—Fiction. 4. United States—His-tory—1849–1877—Fiction. 5. Women slaves—Alabama—Fiction. 6. Family secrets—Fiction. I. Title.
  PS3613.I53C65 2006
  813'.6—dc22
                                                                    2006020514

Printed in Canada
1 2 3 4 5 6 7—14 13 12 11 10 09 08

To the many people that grace my life:

My husband, Robert, who is everything; my parents, Cliff and Lois Lee, who taught me to climb mountains one step at a time; my sisters, Sandi, Barbara, Vicki, and Lori, who promptly made molehills out of those mountains; Shannon, dear daughter, who brings such joy, and her husband, Corey, who is simply the finest son-in-law God ever created; Brett and Alana, dearest son and daughter-in-law, your own love story humbles Adie's; Isabel, precious granddaughter—you are my heart—what delight to watch you grow! Rebekah, friend extraordinaire, who reminds me when the going gets tough to always get together; the Dixie Divas, book-writing belles and comrades, how grand it is to tour with you! And especially to my readers: much joy for your journey.

Above all, to the man upstairs—everything is for you.

Acknowledgments

My deepest gratitude to Ron Pitkin, president of Cumberland House Publishing, who placed this book on the page: You are a dear, dear man. Thank you for believing in me.

Special thanks to the Cumberland House staff—especially to my editor, Mary Sanford: You're brilliant! You made a difficult task possible. To Stacie Bauerle: Thank you for your attention to detail! And to Teresa Wright: You do so much and stay ever humble.

Best regards to Ann Kempner Fisher, dear friend, editor, and all-around-wonderful person. Without you, it'd be hard to write. Your words, though not always what I *want* to hear, are always what I *need* to hear—and the ones I love best are, "You wrote yourself into a corner? Big deal—write yourself back out!"

Many thanks also to Marjory Wentworth, South Carolina Poet Laureate and gifted publicist. How blessed I am to have found you. And all my thanks to Jim Hubbard of Worry Free PC, who performed miracles when my hard drive crashed. Without your expertise I'd be living in an institution. I hope you win the lottery.

There are so many more that I should thank, and dearly want to thank, but I have no more room to do so. Y'all know who you are. Forgive me, each and everyone. I love you bunches.

Cold Rock River

chapter one

I WAS FIVE THAT SPRING Annie choked on a jelly bean. She was twenty months old; she wasn't supposed to have any. Mama made that quite clear. Sadly, I wasn't a child that minded well, so I gave Annie one anyway. I figured she ought to taste how good they were. I figured wrong.

Annie choked *bad* on that jelly bean, and her face turned blue. And Mama wasn't home. She'd gone to Calhoun to sell her prized jams; sold twelve jars of her double-lemon marmalade. Imagine that; there's Mama, waving folks over to get a sample of her jam—selling her heart out—and *all the while* Annie's choking to death.

My pa slapped Annie on her back; smacked her hard with the side of his hand, right between her shoulder blades. Pa had hands the size of skillets. He smacked her twice, but it didn't do any good—might of made it worse. Annie stopped making those sucking sounds like she did when her face turned colors, and her body went limp and her pretty blue eyes just rolled up and disappeared right inside her cute little head.

My older sisters, Rebecca and Clarissa—twin girls Mama had two years before she had me—got on their knees and prayed like preachers. They asked God not to take Annie from us. I didn't get on my knees. I watched Pa beat on Annie instead. It was more interesting. I didn't have anything against praying, mind you. We did it all the time in Sunday school and I knew most of the prayers they taught by heart, except for *The Lord's Prayer*, and I was working on that.

"She can't die," I said. "She's in *our* family." It made perfect sense to me at the time.

"Oh hush, you ninny," Rebecca said. "You don't know nothing."

"Help us pray, Adie," Clarissa said.

I wasn't worried. I knew Annie couldn't die. Bad things like that only happened to strangers. The proof arrived daily in the newspaper Pa buried his face in. Mama had hers in the Bible or a cookbook, the hands on the clock determining which one. While she stirred the pot and touted miracles, he turned the pages and spouted mayhem.

"She can't *die*," I shouted, stomping my feet, trying to get their attention.

Rebecca and Clarissa kept praying, and Pa kept pounding—his eyes big as mixing bowls. I started wailing. Pa dangled Annie upside down by her feet and ran with her like that all the way next door to Miz Patterson's. She wasn't home. She'd gone to Clarkston to see her grandbabies. She went every Friday; stayed the whole day—took me with her sometimes. She and her daughter Delores would sit on the front porch and sip iced tea and rock themselves dizzy while they watched Delores's kids—mostly boys—wrestle on the dirt ground that used to have grass. I wanted to tell Pa, but he ran out the door before I had a chance to. I chased after him but couldn't catch up; he was running two-forty.

"Call an ambulance, Rebecca!" he shouted. Annie was flopping like a rag doll washed one time too many.

"Miz Patterson!" Pa's voice sounded like the low keys on a piano when he talked and when he bellowed it got deep as a pipe organ that had a bad cold. Miz Patterson was as close as we ever came to a neighborhood nurse. Everybody went to her house when they needed doc-

toring. There was a path to her door on account of it. She didn't
charge anything for her kindness. People gave her what they could; a
cup of sugar, a few eggs, maybe a pound cake made with real butter.
Bernice Harper gave her a banana crème pie when her son Willie fell
over the handle bars of his bike and nearly bit his tongue off. After
that, whenever I thought about Miz Patterson, that's what was on my
mind. So, my pa's running over to her place, Annie's choking, and I'm
thinking about that creamy slice of pie she gave me.

Pa ran back with Annie still hanging upside down. His face
looked like a bear had scared him and his eyes agreed. At that tender
age, I didn't know there was a word for that look—my father was *terrified*. It certainly got my mind off that pie. Rebecca was on the big
black phone with the operator trying to explain where Route 3, Box
949 was.

"Well, it's in Cold Rock, but it's not on a street, ma'am," she said.
"It's on a route! Ain't you ever hear of a route? Who hired you anyway?" Rebecca yelled. "Our baby Annie's dying. Get us a ambulance
here, you ninny!"

Pa heard it all and realized help was not coming anytime soon.
The look on his face got worse. His eyes were crazed as a horse that's
been spooked by a snake. It scared me plenty. I dropped to my knees.

"*Pleasegodpleasegodpleasegodpleasegod* . . ." I chanted sing-song, staring at Annie draped over Pa's arm. She was limp as a stuffed toy that
had lost all its filling.

Pa stuck his thumb backwards down Annie's throat. I remember
being comforted by the fact it wasn't me. Pa's big thumb stuck backwards down Annie's throat looked like a terrible way to die. But what
do you know? That jelly bean popped right up out of her mouth! It
spewed out with a bunch of vomit and splattered all over Mama's
clean linoleum floor. Annie started coughing real hard and crying. Pa
said, "Sssshhhhh, you're okay, baby. S'gonna be alright, now. Daddy's
got ya." He hugged her to his chest and patted her softly on the
back—like she was a China doll and would break—which I thought

was very strange, seeing as he nearly pounded her to death when she was choking. Pa bent his head forward and buried his nose in her blonde curls. His shoulder muscles started dancing with each other.

"Pa's crying," Rebecca whispered.

"Don't cry, Pa!" Clarissa said and ran over and wrapped herself around one of his legs. He reached down with his free hand and rubbed her head, but his shoulders never stopped moving. That started Clarissa wailing, which got me upset, seeing as she was the one I favored. I ran over and hugged her.

Annie struggled to get free from Pa's arms. He eased her down, then wiped his face with the big kerchief he always kept in his back pocket. Clarissa stepped back and looked up at him while Annie toddled about. Pa was taller than a cornstalk with legs as skinny as stilts. He reached down and dried Clarissa's eyes. She was hiccupping and sucking her breath in and out. I rubbed her backside while Pa steadied Annie on her feet.

"No need crying over sorry milk," I said, and "Pretty is when pretty does," and "Do like you said and not like I do." I had the words a bit mixed up and most of their meanings were lost to me, but I liked how they sounded whenever Mama said them, and I was desperate to comfort Clarissa. There was something about the way she cried that day that made me think—if she kept it up—I might stop breathing.

"It's okay, 'Niss," I said. "See?" I pointed to Annie wobbling across the floor. "Her face ain't purple and her eyes ain't lost in her head no more." Clarissa looked up to where I was pointing, and Pa let go of her. I heard the air rush out of his chest. He sat down on our old maroon sofa and pulled a pack of Camels out of his shirt pocket. He tapped the bottom, pulled one loose, and slipped it into his mouth. Mama always said Pa's hands were steady as rain, but when he flicked open his lighter they were bobbing like a fishing line with a bite on one end. It was the Zippo Mama gave him. He spun the wheel with his thumb, and a flame shot high into the air. Pa turned the lighter over, slipped his nail into a tiny groove on the head of a small screw, and twisted. Like magic the flame settled back down. He tilted his chin sideways, leaned forward, aimed the tip of cigarette into the fire, and sucked inward. I watched as the smoke curled into the tail of a cat, zigzagged upward and outward, then disappeared.

"This the *only other* thing should be lighting your fire, hon,'" Mama said when he opened the shiny red box it came in one Christmas. They both laughed.

"They have dumb jokes, don't they?" Clarissa said, and I nodded.

"You don't neither one of you know nothing," Rebecca butted in. "You're the dumb ones."

Pa carried that lighter from then on. It had a shiny gold eagle on it that faded over time, but he said he would no more replace it than he would one of us. If he was up and dressed, we knew that lighter was in his back pocket. He had a habit of taking it out and snapping the top open and closed till it drove Mama batty, but we weren't allowed to touch it.

"Could burn the house down with this thing," he told us.

"I'm gonna burn you down, you don't put it away and stop that racket," Mama said. Then something bad happened between them, and Mama took back the lighter. We never saw it again.

That day Annie choked, though, Pa still had it. He lit two Camels up, one right after the other, but he kept his eyes glued to Annie. She waddled over to where that jellybean lay in the middle of all that vomit, snatched it up, and aimed it straight for her mouth. Rebecca grabbed hold of her and slapped it out her hand. Annie let out a howl like she always did when she didn't get what she wanted.

"Clarissa! You and Adie clean up that mess," Rebecca said. Me and Clarissa were used to her bossing us around since Mama usually left Rebecca in charge and her standard warning was to mind her or else. Most of the time I did like she said, but I wondered why Clarissa did. They were the same age, except Mama said Rebecca came out first and was three minutes older.

"Three minutes—that hardly counts!" I informed Mama and nearly got my head knocked off.

"Clarissa doesn't have to mind you," I told Rebecca during another moment of defiance. "You're not her boss; she's the same age as you."

"Hush, you little brat," Rebecca said, "and you do like you're told 'fore I tell Ma you been sassing me while she's gone. You won't get no supper." Mama was making macaroni and cheese, my favorite, so I immediately grew contrite, behaving like an absolute angel for the rest of the day. Don't ask me why, but Clarissa always behaved, no matter what. Not me. It all depended on what was being offered for dinner. For instance, I hated cabbage. But Rebecca didn't know it. I kept it to myself, and when I wanted to sass her good, I picked those nights so I'd get sent to bed early. It was a good deal for me. I didn't have to do any dishes, I didn't have to eat that darn cabbage that tasted so awful, and I got to lie in bed and read books for hours with no one pestering me.

"You take that sassy mouth of yours to bed, missy," Mama would say. "Won't be no supper for you tonight. I'm making corn beef and cabbage, too." I'd hang my head down and look real sad while I climbed the stairs that led to the bedroom we girls shared. It was next to Annie's—which was really just a little sewing alcove that barely held her crib and a changing table. Mama and Papa had the bedroom downstairs. It faced the train tracks. Mama said the trains lulled her to sleep. But poor Pa, when the whistles blew in the night, he'd jump out of bed thinking it was the alarm clock. Took quite a few of them pesky wake-ups before he stopped getting dressed for work in the middle of the night.

"I got to go in early enough as it is," Pa announced loud enough that the neighbors would hear, if we'd had any. He repaired the machines over at the poultry plant. "I don't need no dress rehearsals at three a.m. What the hell they put them dang tracks next to the house for?"

"Charlie, them tracks was here first!" Mama said. "Now shush and go back to sleep. You forget I'm up same time as you? Who do you think fixes your lunchbox, the fairy lunchbox fixer?" By then we were all awake. Eventually, Pa adjusted to the shrill blast of the whistles as the night trains sailed through Cold Rock.

As for me, I liked lying in bed and hearing the trains rumble past in the dark. On hot nights when the air was too thick to breathe, I'd settle in next to the windowsill, my knees resting on my pillow, my head cradled in my arms. In the fall there was a cool breeze when the cold winds blew down from the mountain. But the nights I remember best were the muggy ones when I couldn't sleep, when the sheets were damp with sweat from Clarissa and Rebecca and me being scrunched too close together in the double bed. Pa had promised to build a bed for me and Clarissa that would fit under the eave, with a trundle bed that would slide out from beneath it. He never got around to it. The sticky bedcovers woke me before the train whistle ever got a chance. I'd kneel at the windowsill while the cicadas held their evening concert. A single magnolia tree rested at the side of the clapboard house. When the wind blew just right, its fragrance drifted into the room, rich and heavy as any treasure, and if I inhaled deeply, its sweet, musky scent made me dizzy. When I felt reckless, I kept breathing it in until my knees grew weak and I'd sink, half delirious, into the pillow parked on the floor. There, I watched the lights from the caboose twinkle past, pretending I was on it, headed to China or Africa or South America to be a missionary, like the women who visited us at Christ the King Holiness Church when they needed more money to carry on their services. Later when I found it took more than trains to get them to where they were going, I dreamt of planes and boats and anything that traveled to distant lands. I was going places; I was going to see the world. My dreams got bigger and brighter with each passing year. Then I met Buck.

But for the time being, seeing as I had the entire world laid out for me up in that little bedroom crouched under the eave of our house, what with my books and the night trains and the future I painted, I planned out most of the times I wasn't going to mind Rebecca and did it on a regular basis. I got out of doing a lot of dishes, and I ended up with much prettier hands than Rebecca. Hers were already beginning to look like Mama's.

Of course, all that misbehaving made me the black sheep of the family. I was always in trouble. I got extra skinny, too, since I missed more suppers than I ate, but I was the best-read one of the bunch. It's a wonder not one of them ever caught on.

"Girls, you stay off that sleep porch till it's time for lights down," Ma would tell Rebecca and Clarissa. "Teach her a thing or two about minding." Clarissa was always quite sorrowful for me—she had such a tender heart. I could have told her Rebecca and Mama were just playing into my hands, but I knew she'd let it slip, so I didn't. Not until we were grown. Then we laughed on it good, even Rebecca. But the day Annie choked was no laughing matter.

We found out later that what Pa did—stuck his thumb down Annie's throat—is the worst thing to do when someone's choking. Well, Pa didn't know that. He did what he thought he had to, and it saved Annie's life. When Mama got home she hugged every one of us and said, "*Well*, sometimes the worst thing turns out to be the best thing."

Too bad it didn't work out like that the next time Annie needed help. We'd gone up Cold Rock Mountain to fish and swim like we did many Sundays when the weather was nice. What happened changed all of us. But Uncle Burleigh said, "Didn't change ya, it ruined ya," as he sucked on the toothpick permanently housed in the corner of his mouth. "You won't never be the same," he added, "not none of you's."

He kept running his big mouth—as usual—until I wanted to ram that toothpick into the soft spot at the base of his throat and make him take back every word.

I hate to give that old codger credit, but turns out he was right. None of us *was* the same—not ever.

chapter two

I'M SURE YOU'VE HEARD PEOPLE say, "It'll be just like old times." Which is ridiculous—nothing can be like it *was.* They know that. Still, they say, "Come on over. It'll be just like old times." Maybe in the part of their brain that knows it *won't* be, they can't accept it, and their words come out of their mouth the way they live in their heart: a sweet memory, aching like a piece of candy that was always their favorite—and still is—only now it doesn't taste near as good as they remember. Memories are as strange as they are powerful. They can rest in the gentlest part of your heart, docile and dormant for years, meek and mild as a baby lamb. *And* they can pounce without warning, as ferocious as a lion denied food and freedom. Annie's a memory like that. My folks don't talk about it, and Rebecca and Clarissa won't admit to it, but that hardly means our wounds have been properly tended to. They're right below the surface, raw as fresh-skinned knees.

Annie died. Conversation regarding it ended soon after. We girls were very young. We had questions. It would have been much better and far healthier if we'd talked about it, placed Annie's three years with us in a memory box where our wounds and our sorrow would be safe, and when our hearts ached too much we could have opened that box and shared what was in it with each other. I would have shared my favorite: Annie clomping about in Pa's ancient four-buckle galoshes. She'd climb into those rubber boots—Pa wore a size thirteen, so they about covered her waist—buckle them up, and march around and around until she got so dizzy her eyes nearly spun off her face. Regaining her balance, she'd scramble to her feet for as many repeat performances as our stomachs or her begging would allow her. It never took much to keep her happy.

Once she got into the pantry and tore the labels off all the cans. Winter wasn't over. Even so, we'd already eaten all the vegetables Mama canned from the proceeds of her garden. We were down to eating the store-bought kind, the mason jars resting on the top shelf—sparkling clean and empty—waiting on next year's crop.

Annie scattered the labels she tore off the cans in every direction. The faded linoleum in the pantry was awash with color, pictures of peaches, tomatoes, green beans, beets, and fruit cocktail dressing the floor.

"What a mess," Mama said and proceeded to make a game of it.

We took turns selecting three cans, and when it was our turn, we'd give them a good shake to guess what was inside. Usually we were wrong. No matter—whatever it was, *that's* what we ate for supper. Pa wasn't amused.

"Brussels sprouts, corn, and peaches," he said. "Didn't we just have this last night?"

"That was the night before, hon,'" Mama answered. "Last night was okra, black-eyed peas, and cranberries." That was two of the better nights. One evening all three cans were the same. Beets, I think. "Well, lookie here," Mama exclaimed, her trademark grin displaying dough-boy dimples. "What's the odds of this happening?" Pretty good, I guess; it happened again a few days later.

"Well," she drawled, "they had a good special on beets. I reckon there's plenty more."

It'd of been nice to have used those stories like a salve, slathered the hurt with it. Surely, it would have been a *heap better thing to do*—as Mama was fond of saying—than to let our silences deny she was ever ours. Annie was woven into the very blanket of our life; pretty hard to find which threads were hers and yank them out.

"How come Mama and Daddy won't talk about Annie?" I asked my aunt Olivia that first Christmas after she was gone.

"It's too soon, Adie," she said. "Give it time." So I gave it plenty of time. Months stretched into years. Aunt Olivia took sick and died—some kind of heart ailment they never knew she had—and still, we didn't talk about Annie or what happened.

"It's all your fault," Rebecca would have pointed out. "How do you live with yourself, anyway?" As if I do. Rebecca kept running tallies on what was and what wasn't. She had all the answers and kept her words lined up like bullets to fire at you, if you were within range. There wasn't but three words I recall that never came out of her mouth, "I." and "don't" and "know." Rebecca didn't say those words for the obvious reasons. Whenever Clarissa and I came across something we thought might stump her, Rebecca'd say, "That's for me to know and you to find out!" And she'd flounce her red hair off her shoulders and march out of the room with her head tilted up like she was the Queen of Sheba and we were her servants. Used to irk me good. Mostly because her hair was so pretty and I liked the way it bounced when she twirled around. Mine was thin and stringy like Pa's and never did that that I know of. But it was hard for me to tell for sure. When I whirled about in the mirror, I could never get a good look at the back. I had a terrible fixation about it during my developing years when I was trying to figure out whether I was true ugly or just sorrowful plain. This book I read said to uncover your best feature and concentrate on that. I figured if my hair was my best one, I wouldn't have to stare in the mirror any longer to decide upon another, which was pretty much depressing me since none seemed apparent. Which brings back another thing about Rebecca that irked me—there wasn't one spot on her face that wasn't her best part. And she knew it, but how could she *not*? She had eyes. Still, she didn't have to act so stuck on herself because of it.

Rebecca was the smartest girl in her class, too—got all *A*s. She could have gone to a college. The counselor at school said she'd help her apply for a scholarship and started the paperwork. Before the ink was dry, Rebecca discovered she liked boys better than she liked books. She made other plans, which caused her a lot of grief. But you can't tell a girl who knows everything what to do. Turns out, she knew a lot more at a young age than we gave her credit for. Years later when she told me what she'd been hiding, it made my stomach forget where it lived.

"You should have told Mama and Daddy."

"He said if I did, the state would take us kids away."

"And you believed him." She nodded, and let more tears fall than I figured heaven had rain. I hugged her like I was the big sister and rocked her like she was a much younger one with her first broken heart.

"By the time I was old enough to figure out it was *him* they'd have taken, he was dead. Why tell and cause *more* grief?" Rebecca said and left to go back to work. But, all that sharing came later. Before that, mostly me and Rebecca wanted to stick knives in each other.

Anyway, Rebecca quit school her junior year and ran off with Riley Hooper. They started up a family quick as you can sneeze.

"Riley's a freight train loaded with promise," Rebecca boasted.

"Might could be," Uncle Burleigh said, "but he ain't never on the right track." Riley took off two years later with a caboose who'd been tagging along the whole time named Roxanne. Rebecca had one little boy and was fixing to have another when Riley left. She came back home for a while, and Mama took care of Riley Jr. while Rebecca worked and took some night classes to get her high school diploma. Daddy said, "You took the road to misery, girl."

"Oh, Charlie, hush! She took the scenic route, is all," Mama said, her green eyes—Pa said she stole 'em from a cat—flashing even greener as they pounced on him with a message he best be quiet. She liked spoiling Riley Jr. and tried to as best she could. We didn't mind. He was a sweet little guy, and we felt bad for him with his pa running off. A couple months later Rebecca moved out and nearly broke Mama's heart when she took little Riley with her. Rebecca had a new man in her life—Delbert Coffee—before the baby she was carrying from Riley Sr. was even due to be born.

Delbert was a locksmith and had his own business. Rebecca said she was really coming up in the world and ran around with her nose in the air. Mama said, "Well, la-dee-da! Sitting in the hen house don't make you a chicken."

Things didn't go well for Rebecca with Delbert like she counted on. She lost the baby a few weeks after they got married. Said she fell down the back porch steps carrying out the laundry to hang on the line. But the doctor caring for her told Mama she took a mean hit in the belly, one so bad he could see the bruise mark on the sac holding the baby. Mama suspected Delbert punched her in the stomach because he didn't want another kid around that wasn't his. He treated Riley Jr. real bad, called him a "dumb shit" and slapped him in the head when Rebecca wasn't around. Pa never found out and I was afraid to tell him. He'd have made sure Delbert didn't use his hands again for anything except pushing around his own wheelchair. Two months after losing the baby, Rebecca was pregnant again.

"Maybe it's for the best," Mama said. "Better chance he'll treat this one right, being as it's his." Rebecca had another baby boy and named him Clayton, after Delbert's pa who set him up with the locksmith business. Then a year later they had another and named him Girard, after no one in particular. Delbert strutted around like he'd invented baby-making. Mostly he was real jealous and never let Rebecca out of his sight. She was still as pretty as ever, and if you looked at her shape you would never guess that she'd had one baby, let alone three.

If you ask me, Delbert was one sick puppy. He had all these rules. When Rebecca took the car to visit Mama or to get groceries—whatever—he kept track of the mileage to see if it all added up. And he made her write down where she was every minute of the day. So that marriage didn't last either. When Pa asked, "What's the story this time?" Rebecca said, "I ran out of paper." Mama said, "It's complicated, hon, and I ain't got time to explain. I got cranberry-pepper jelly to get started if we're gonna have any extra money for Christmas. Don't none of you be bothering me, now."

Mama busied herself with her jams and jellies a lot, until life turned sour. Then she started making pickles and relish; anything that called for vinegar. We sure missed her jams, but her fruit pickles were a nice touch. They went especially well with pork. She'd save a jar or two and slap one down on the table every now and then.

So, Rebecca gave Delbert a divorce that Christmas, and he gave her twenty-five dollars a week and two nice brothers for Riley Jr.

"Those three little guys are worth all the trouble I been through to get 'em, so don't talk to me no more about them poor choices you think I made and how I ruined the best years of my life," she told Pa when he razzed her. Later, Rebecca got a bit wild. Pa said, "Fool girl. Runs after every man don't have a ring on and can't keep his pants on."

I guess Rebecca thought a man would make up for the hole in her that needed filling. Clarissa filled hers with food, and I filled mine with guilt. Years later, me and Clarissa talked about that—the empty spots in us that grew hungrier with time.

Rebecca said it was poppycock. "The empty holes is in your heads!" she said, which made me mad, since she butted right in on our conversation

"Who are you to talk?" I said. "You got yourself three boys by two different daddies, and you're not married anymore to either one of them. And according to Pa you're on the prowl for another." It was a mean thing to say. I told her later I was sorry, but careless words can do more damage than a hurricane, and no amount of apologizing is going to fix the damage. All you can do is level the land and start rebuilding.

Clarissa, on the other hand, could have filled in for St. Francis of Assisi, if ever he wanted a day off. She never said anything bad to anyone about anything. Maybe she should have. She let others do the talking. And while they talked she ate—and ate. Eventually she had so many pounds to lose to even get close to being a normal size that it's possible she kept eating because of that.

"At least I don't have any more holes that need filling, Adie," she told me. "Every single one's plumb full up with cakes, pies, and cookies!" She laughed when she said it, but any fool could see her face was lying.

"And if I get me a new spot feels empty, I'll just start in on the chips and dip," she added and bowled over like she'd told a really good joke. She had herself a giggle fit until tears poured down her face.

"Good golly," she said, "I'm laughing so hard I'm crying. You see that?" I saw a bit more than I cared to.

I probably should have helped Rebecca and Clarissa sort through their problems and find some answers. I loved them plenty, even Rebecca with her sassy ole mouth. And I'd taken my education, limited as it was, more serious than they had, so I might have had a bit more wisdom. Still, I was a mess. Mostly, I was afraid of turning into one of those people who get all fired up over fixing someone *else's* problems when they have the same ones, and a worse case of them at that. Mama said those kind are "more pesky than the Jehovah's Witnesses" that came calling at the door.

"At least them Jehovah's got good hearts. They're only trying to save your soul. Them others don't all have their rocks in a row. All they got is a bunch of opinions that make matters worse," she said. "Stay out of people's business."

It sounded like good advice. Not to say I didn't look for some answers. This one particular book I read on neurosis said to find the root of the sorrow from childhood and unravel the mystery from there—then took up two-hundred and seventy-three pages to say it, and not much else. It was a national bestseller. I wasted three dollars and ninety-five cents on that one, and so did plenty other folks. Somebody should have written a book about the people who bought it, read it, and made it a bestseller, and then printed their comments. Now *that* would have made an interesting book. It might have included better information on how to get to the root of one's sorrow, too, seeing as when you ask most folks their opinion on something, they're usually more than happy to oblige you. And a lot of them can't shut up and will give you their thoughts on something else while they're it. Especially women—Pa calls it double "indemlady."

"They discovered it in France," he said, explaining that it meant "in them ladies" and was a condition women were afflicted with after they got married.

"All them that has it don't have no shut-off valve in their brain, so they drip, drip, drip," Pa explained. "Drives a man to drink."

"Charlie, you telling that garbage to them girls again?" Mama yelled. She was ironing our school dresses but always kept an ear out. "I swear you are flat out gonna have them so messed up." She finished with Clarissa's and started in on one of mine, the purple plaid hand-me-down I hated. "Why just last week, I read this here article and it said—"

"What I tell you?" Pa interrupted. "Drip, drip, drip," and he winked.

I spent plenty of dollars on some other books before I realized the people writing them meant well but they weren't being too helpful. They talked about uncovering the root source, but they didn't give much instruction as to what to do once you did. I already knew our problem was not just losing Annie but the way we lost her, too. Where to go from there was a total mystery, so I gave up on helping Rebecca and Clarissa.

It came to me during catechism classes when I was studying to be confirmed in the Lutheran church. We went over the part about not pointing out the log in another person's eye if you have two in your own. Mama had switched us out of the Holiness Church when they informed her that makeup and movies were both serious sins.

"I can do without the movies," Mama said, "but why in heaven do I have to go without cosmetics?"

"They want you to scare hell out of everybody," Pa said. "Makes their jobs easier."

The Holiness ladies told Mama to concentrate on her spiritual body and to think of her earthly body as the temple of the Lord.

"Is that so?" Mama said.

"That's right, Sister Thacker," this Holiness woman said, who had her hair piled two feet on top of her head on account it had never been cut since the day she grew it, and Pa said she was older than rocks, so it was probably down to China and if she ever took it down the earth would tilt, so stay away from her and her kind or we would fall off the edge of the planet. How could we stay clear? Everywhere we looked, the place was plumb full up with women who had those same hair towers. Clarissa and I were terrified the whole time we were at that crazy church. Every time we walked through the door, we clung to each other like lint on a sweater.

"If we fall off the planet, Adie," Clarissa said, "we gonna do it together, okay?"

One of the women in the group showed Mama the exact page the scripture verse was on, about our bodies being a temple. Mama read it over and admitted it was all there, just as she said.

"I told you," this other Holiness woman said, who was three times the size of Mama. I wondered why she didn't stay clear of the sin that said not to eat too much.

"Well, this temple of mine looks a whole lot better with some paint slapped on it," Mama said. "And if you don't mind my saying so, yours would too."

"Well, I never—" the fat one said. Another butted in, "The Devil is working his evil deeds! Form a prayer circle, sisters! Hurry!"

The women surrounded Mama and one laid hands on her head and pressed down so hard her knuckles turned white. They started praying in tongues, supposedly so the Devil couldn't understand what they were saying. The first time I ever heard these folks do that, some of them were dancing with their arms raised up high. A few dropped to the floor and moaned while they twisted their bodies all around in a circle. Me and Clarissa started crying, and Rebecca told Mama somebody better call an ambulance.

"They're having some kind of fit, or maybe they been poisoned," she said.

Mama said to hush up. "This here's how they worship."

I told Pa when we got home that Mama had lost her mind. She'd joined us up with a church that accepted crazy folks who babbled and had fits, and the minister let them flop all over the room.

"Do we have to keep going, Pa?" Clarissa said.

"I think it's fun," Rebecca said.

"Hhmmff," Pa snorted, and went back to his paper.

A few weeks later Mama told the Holiness ladies, "All this praying in tongues is driving me batty. I grant you the Devil don't know what you're saying, but I don't know what you're saying neither." She grabbed Clarissa's hand—who grabbed hold of mine—and motioned with her head for Rebecca to follow.

"Nothing against you personal, mind you," Mama said. "Me and my girls are going on over to that Lutheran church down on South Street where they pray in English." True to her word, Mama took us over to Good Shepherd. It was the last time I saw the Holiness ladies. They were standing outside the front door of the white frame church. The paint was peeling and the latches were rusty. They looked so forlorn all lined up in a row with their hair towers and their long dresses that had the white crocheted collars, their lips pursed tight together like they'd each bitten off a piece of the same sour pickle. I thought about those scary Holiness ladies each time Mama got the bowls out to cut our hair. She was never any good at it. Pa agreed and said persons with hormones weren't safe to be around when they had sharp objects in their hands.

"That's why we menfolk that got any brains stay out of the kitchen when they're cooking," he said.

"What's hormones, Pa?" I asked.

"These particles floating around in women that stir up all kinds of trouble."

I asked Mama if that was true. She said Pa was exaggerating, as usual. It was all part of a woman's monthly pain.

"What's that?" I wanted to know. "And why's it called a monthly pain?"

"'Cause *mental illness* was already taken," Pa said and laughed.

Mama put her hands on her hips and gave him a look that said he best get out of her kitchen if he wanted to keep living. I was sure they were crazy and so fearful I'd catch whatever it was that drove them there that I hid in the bedroom.

Pa went down and had his hair cut at Fishburn's Barber Shop. Mama coaxed me back into the kitchen and cut mine.

"How many inches has it grown?"

"A good bit," she said. I sat still as possible—hoping my bangs would turn out even, for once—and studied on how long the Holiness ladies hair might have grown by then.

"All done," Mama exclaimed. I ran back to my room and looked in the mirror to see which one of the Stooges stared back. Then I kneeled down next to the bed and prayed that the Holiness ladies would repent and cut all their hair so the earth wouldn't tilt. When six haircuts went by and we didn't fall off the edge, I figured they had—or maybe they'd died.

I thanked God and told him it didn't matter which one.

chapter three

A WEEK AFTER WE LEFT the Holiness Church, Mama dragged out her nail polish and explained to Pa that the new church didn't have any rules against it. We older girls were doing the supper dishes. Annie was still with us. She was standing on a chair begging to help. Rebecca picked her up and plopped her on the floor, then fished a metal pot out of the rinse water and handed it to her to dry. She took to the task in earnest, her concentration stamped on her face like postage, the tip of her tongue protruding from the corner of her mouth, her pudgy fingers dragging the dishcloth haphazardly back and forth and up and down the curves of the battered old pan's surface.

"I done!" she beamed and held it up for one of us to retrieve. I handed her another. Annie looked like Sally in the Dick and Jane books they taught us to read from at school. I told my teacher, "I think they had her in mind. I'm pretty sure they did."

The teacher smiled and nodded agreeably, but all the kids laughed. My glee quickly dissolved into embarrassment.

I handed Annie the lids to the pots she'd already dried, thinking about how happy I was to have a little sister nearly identical to the one featured in our reading primer, determined to bring a picture to school and show the kids making fun of me that I was telling the truth. I never did, since none of the handful of black and white snapshots substantiated my theory.

Annie finished with her task and tossed aside the lids. I picked her up and danced her around the kitchen, her giggles filling the room. Clarrisa took over when I ran out of steam, and Rebecca stepped in when Clarissa did too. Annie was almost three and quite an armful. Back and forth we pranced about the room, having no way of knowing that in less than three weeks she wouldn't be with us anymore. She'd be gone forever, as in permanently—as in dead.

Mama prattled on; polish in hand, her fingertips pink as cherry popsicles.

"They got fewer sins over at Good Shepherd Lutheran," she announced. "They even play cards."

"Zat so," Pa said.

"You should come along."

"Forget it. I been to one of them Lutheran churches. They's too long-winded with their sermons."

"Well, the Catholics give a real short one. And you can drink and smoke. But you got to go to confession once a week," she said and waved her nails through the air. "Would you rather go there?"

Pa didn't answer. He turned the television on and popped open a can of beer.

"Well?" she said.

"Well what?" he said and sank into his favorite chair.

"Would you rather join the *Catholic* Church?" Mama asked.

Pa leaned over to change the TV channel. "I'd rather be hung from my thumbs and whacked on my pecker!"

Mama smacked him right on top of the head and ordered us out of the room, pronto.

Annie ran around the house jabbering, "Pecker, pecker," until Mama nearly stopped breathing.

"Charlie!" she said. "What in holy heaven am I gonna do when it pops out of her mouth in church? Huh?"

"She'd forget all about it," Pa said, "if you'd stop making such a big deal out of it." He was reading the paper and had the lampshade over his head twisted out of place so more light would shine on the pages.

"Well, she ain't so far," Mama snapped, and straightened up the shade.

"Then get her one them picture books got the birds in it and show her the kind taps on wood." Pa said. "Dad blame it, Ruby, how kin I read half in the dark?" He brushed her arm aside and put the shade back the way he liked it.

"You mean the woodpeckers?" Mama said.

"You know another kind does the same thing?" Pa shook his head sideways, gave the ceiling a quick glance, and stuck his nose back in the paper.

"That just might do it, hon,'" Mama said and patted his arm. She fussed over the lampshade a bit like she was trying to get it back to the exact position it was in before she moved it. Quick as a blink, Pa was back in her good graces.

"I'm gonna take *ever* one them ladies in the sewing circle a jar of my special ginger peach preserves, just in case," Mama said.

• • •

It wasn't but three weeks later that Annie died. That's when Mama took the Zippo back.

"Looks like you haven't been needing this to light your fire," she said, and they stopped talking to each other. Then Mama read a magazine article that said unresolved grief could lead to mental illness, and she decided to talk to Pa again, even if he didn't talk back.

"If he wants to go insane, that's his business," she said.

He wanted to go to the Red Rooster. And he did, every night after supper. Mama called it a dirty-foot beer joint. Pa asked her to come along.

"It's a dump. Has more drunks and loose women than it has stools," Mama said. "Why do you waste your time there, anyhow?"

"It takes my mind off things, Ruby," Pa said.

"Only thing that place takes is your money." Mama said. "No sense in me going and have it take more."

She never went with him. That was the good part. She didn't call him "hon" anymore, either. Funny how one little ole word can make such a difference in what goes on in a household. It was 1957. Three years later Mama got caught up in Kennedy fever.

• • •

Before the Kennedys made it to the White House, Mama didn't much care for politics or any of the men involved in it. According to her, Republicans were elephant butts and Democrats were donkey's asses.

"I don't care to be neither," she said and voted an independent ticket. That is until Jack Kennedy ran for president and Mama discovered Jackie.

"Finally," Mama said. "A man for the middle class"—which Pa insisted we weren't *part* of to begin with.

"What are we then, Einstein?" Mama asked.

"Upper poor," he said.

Mama got out her sewing machine and tried to copy just about everything Jackie wore. Pa said we didn't have money to be buying any fancy fabric with. That didn't stop Mama. She just bought the cheapest ones she could find, usually crazy cotton prints no one wanted, so they were on sale. Even so, Pa said we'd be in the poor house by the time the Kennedys left office.

Mama was especially crazy about the pillbox hats Jackie wore. "Not every woman can wear them, you know," she said. "Takes a certain bone structure." Whatever type that was, Mama figured she had it. Every one of the dresses she made had its own matching pillbox hat, but they didn't look much like Jackie's. Mama used Pa's baseball caps as a base. She cut the bills off and covered what was left in whatever fabric she was working on at the time. She used some stiff inter-facing material to make them a bit more square on top. Still, they were sorrowful to look on. Daddy knew when Mama was working on a new dress. Another one of his caps would disappear. He'd find the piece she cut off outside in the trash can.

"Doggone it, Ruby! You cut up my fish-hook one. Can't you leave one dang cap of mine be?"

"You can have this one back," she said and tossed it to him. "I can't get the smell out of it." Mama had sprayed it with Avon's Unforgettable for an entire week before she gave up and put it back the way she found it, minus the bill. Pa stuck his fishhooks back in it and wore it as usual, except by then it was a skullcap. Pa bought himself a big pair of aviator sunglasses to shade his eyes.

"You look like a Rabbi having an identity crisis," Mama said. "Throw that thing out."

"And you look like Jackie Kennedy having a nervous breakdown," Pa said. "So we's even."

Pa had a point. The cotton prints Mama used for her "Jackie" dresses would have made fine kitchen curtains. They were peppered with roosters or clocks or pots and pans. This pink one she loved had some kind of bath products speckled all over it—a mitt, dusting-powder boxes, and perfume bottles. Still, it was nice to see Mama happy again. And I'm especially grateful to Jackie Kennedy to this very day. After we buried Annie, Mama got very depressed and stayed depressed. Six years later, when she saw how Jackie carried the nation and stood tall for her children when the president was shot and killed, Mama tried to pattern herself after that memory. She carried on for us as best she could from then on. Even so, things were bad, especially since Pa took his refuge in booze.

Still, there were times I got away from what happened up on Cold Rock Mountain that last Sunday we had Annie with us. I'd go to sleep pretending it all turned out different. Annie didn't die. We came down the mountain the same as we went up, Louise and Red, Mama and Daddy, Clarissa, Rebecca, and Annie and me—a family like we were before. We'd say what a fine day it had been, Uncle Red and Pa bragging over who caught the most fish, Mama hugging Aunt Louise and telling her to come by in the morning for coffee. I'd wake in the morning believing it was real, that Annie was still with us. But the moment I'd *fully* open my eyes, my stomach would sink, remembering she wasn't.

Willa Mae said to be grateful for dreams. "Dreams is good," she said. "They lets you pretend till you no longer needs to."

Forgive me. I'm getting ahead of myself. Willa Mae and her words of comfort came much later. The fact of the matter is, we went up Cold Rock Mountain that beautiful spring Sunday, and we had Annie with us. And when we came down, we didn't. Who we were—and what we became—might well depend on which one of us you ask.

But I'm the only one who *saw* what happened. The others got told a story of what happened. There's a big difference.

chapter four

I FIND IT PECULIAR THAT one person's decision can affect another person's life even when they don't know each other from Adam's cat to begin with. Take Buck Jenkins's daddy. He came to Cold Rock looking for work and better pay in the carpet mills that sprung up all over Dalton. We had plenty of chicken processing plants, too, but Mr. Jenkins got a better opportunity at one of the mills. So when I was fifteen, Buck and his family moved here, and he turned perfectly normal girls into ones that drooled. They huddled in groups along the halls when he walked past and whispered they could live on his knee-quiver good looks and wide-shouldered body forever. Never need food again. Seemed rather silly, but they were older and popular, so I agreed with them. Mama said, "Only fools live on love, and they don't live long."

Course, I was crazy for Buck, too. I just never drooled over him, not at school anyway. Why bother? He wasn't about to notice me back, but I made up for it at home. I couldn't stop talking about him. Every other word that came out of my mouth had his name attached to it.

"Buck, Buck, Buck," Mama said. "You sound like a chicken."

"He's perfect for me, Mama."

"His kind chases everything that grows breasts," she said.

"I hope not," I said. "That's a big percentage of the population."

"He *thinks* he looks like Elvis," Rebecca said.

"He does!" I said. "He even has his hair."

"That's the only thing he has," Rebecca said. "That, and a high opinion of himself."

"You should see an eye doctor," I said. "You need your eyes examined."

"You should see a proctologist," she said. "You need your head examined!" she answered.

"Keep it up!" Mama said, "You ain't, neither one of you, gonna see daylight."

She had a hammer in her hand. She was cracking up kernels for some type of jam that called for brandy and planned on selling out of it at the fall festival that next week.

"All this racket. I can't hear myself count. No telling how many tablespoons of brandy I put in this prune conserve." She studied on it for a minute and then tossed in two more tablespoons.

"This better be right or they'll all wind up drunk on their ears."

Rebecca and I got out of there before she put us to work pitting prunes and sterilizing jars. Mama worked on her jam, and I worked on making myself look like Priscilla Presley, thinking I might get Buck's attention. I even bought two magazines that had some real pretty pictures of her in them. I showed Mama the one I liked best and asked if I could dye my hair black like Priscilla's. According to Rebecca, mine was mousy brunette, and that was when she was being kind. Otherwise it was baby-turd brown. Mama said, "You turn your hair that color, and I'll turn your other end a color to match." So it didn't work out. The store wouldn't give me my money back, either. I told the lady there I hadn't read any of the articles, just looked at the pictures, and folks do that right there in her store all the time to see if they want to buy them.

"And I got a store policy once they do," she said.

"And what is that?"

"Posted right there on the rack." I went over and stood on my tiptoes and read the card taped to the top shelf. *No loitering, no food, no drink, no refunds.*

"Well, thank you very much anyways," I said and hurried to get out of there before my cheeks turned red as Rudolph's nose. I hated that almost as much as I hated cabbage. It felt like a lit match was being held too close to my skin. It happened a lot. Other times, my face wasn't bad. I had black-brown eyes shaped like the moon, and thank goodness to gracious, Mama's turned-up nose. Pa's was the size of a hawk and near shaped like one, too. Not one of us girls got that nose. Mama said it was a miracle. Pa said she had nightmares every time she got pregnant. Mama said no wonder. "I was scared silly I'd have boy babies sprouting button noses and girl ones with beaks."

"Praise the Lord," Mama told us she shouted when each of us was born. "I ain't asking for nothing else so long as I live!"

I left the drugstore thinking up other ways I might get Buck's attention. Seeing as all the girls were after him, I only had to compete with fifty-nine others, if I didn't count Rebecca and Clarissa, which I didn't, since Rebecca wasn't interested; she had just met Riley, the one she later ran off with. And I didn't count Clarissa, because we had an honor pact that we wouldn't go for the same boy at the same time for as long as it took us to find one.

I couldn't come up with a way to get Buck to notice me, so I stopped trying and let the others chase after him. Not to say I stopped caring. I just watched and studied from the sidelines. You can learn a lot about a person doing that. When Buck groomed his hair, which was basically whenever he breathed, he'd do it with two quick snaps of his wrist, his lips pursed together and his chin jutting out a bit. Then he'd dangle his index fingers in his back pockets and saunter along, his knees flexed, his hips lagging behind like they were bones worthy of worship and would catch up with the rest of him once the girls took proper notice. Looked so silly. But you know, sometimes it even got to me.

Buck treated Jackson High like his own personal flower garden. That was irritating, but the girls didn't care. They just lined up, begging to be plucked. I never lined up, but I was hopeful, and eventually he got around to me. Rebecca said he just ran out of girls.

"You're the only one left he ain't gone steady with. You better watch it," she said. When he asked me if I wanted to wear his ring, I asked if he was asking for a joke.

"I'm asking for real," he said, and I said *yes* quicker than you can blink. Buck paid me so much attention and gave me so many compliments Mama said to be careful which ones I believed. My head was liable to swell up and I'd look like a freak. Overnight, everything changed for me. I was somebody. Even the girls at school took notice of me, which gave me a new appreciation of myself. It's sad to think it took a boy liking me to help me like myself, but that's how it was, so why lie? When I looked in the mirror, a different me looked back. My skin was pale and pink and smooth. Before, I'd thought it was flat and blank and pasty. Buck said my face was almost his favorite part.

"But I got two spots further down to consider," he joked. I smacked him in the arm for that. I was very self-conscious about my breasts. They didn't stop growing till they were the size of cantaloupes. The only bras the stores had that fit me were ones with four hooks in the back. They looked like armor. Once, this fat kid, Luke Bertram, snapped it. I thought a slingshot had slung me into a wall, and I turned around to see who fired it. I took to wearing undershirts over them after that, so no one could see the outline of those dumb looking brassieres through my blouses.

But it was heaven having Mama's creamy skin and dimpled smile. People at church said, "She could have spit you out *whole!*" True, I wasn't anywhere near as pretty as Rebecca or some of the girls in school, but I wasn't ugly anymore, either. I had a hard time understanding it at the time, since the year before, and the ones before that, I'd been pitiful. Mama said, "You were a little bud is all, Adie, and now you bloomed."

Buck spent all of his growing up years in Hog Gap, which sat on the top end of the Blue Ridge Mountains of north Georgia. Cold Rock was on the south end and not near as isolated. If they'd taken the time and money to build a road through Cold Rock Mountain, Daddy said the towns wouldn't be but thirty miles apart. But they didn't, and you had to drive clear around the mountain to get from one to the other, about a hundred miles.

Buck's daddy, Mr. Jenkins, took to going to the VFW dances every Saturday night. He never took Buck's mama with him, and he met this woman Norma, who served the beer there, and eventually run off with her. Buck said she was pretty much a looker.

"Daddy never could pass up one of them."

"I'm sorry," I said.

"Oh, he's been carrying on with women ever since I was old enough to notice they're different than men."

That should have given me fair warning that getting mixed up with a beau like Buck, who came from a pa who didn't put much stock in being loyal, would be a sure road to misery, but I didn't understand the connection at the time.

"This the first one he run off with," Buck said. "Crossed the line this time." Most of the people in town were busy exercising their tongues, something they did real regular. You'd think they enjoyed other folk's misery. I felt right bad for Buck's mama. But then I hadn't met her yet. When I did, truth be told, I wondered why his pa never left sooner. "She likes being a long-suffering woman," Buck said. "*Looong*-suffering. But I ain't gonna tell you all my pa put her through, so don't ask."

I nodded like I understood everything he was saying, and I certainly didn't know much of anything concerning the matter. Didn't even think about the fact that the sins of the father mostly plant their seeds in the hearts of the son.

"You know, whenever Pa dallied before, he usually come back the next day; if not then, at least a day or two later. Ma'd just wait it out, let him get whoever it was out of his system. She was used to it. This time he ain't come back. It's killing her."

"Maybe this Norma lady's the kind takes longer," I said.

"Takes longer for what?"

"For her to get out of your pa's system."

"Maybe so," Buck said.

But weeks went by and Buck's pa never showed up. His ma got tired of the long part on the suffering. She told Buck they should move on back to Hog Gap. That was about the time Buck took me home to meet her. It was right after he asked me to go steady and I said yes. He gave me his ring to wear, and I had two miles of yarn wrapped around it so it wouldn't slide off my finger. Buck picked me up and we drove out to where they lived on the edge of town. It was a tiny place, smaller than ours even, but there was only the three of them by then—Buck, his brother Austin, and his mama—so they made do. Austin was a couple years older than Buck. He near died right before they first come to Cold Rock. Talk was a man beat him in the head with a shovel, but for some reason, no one ever did anything about it.

"It's bad," Buck said. "Got hisself a baby's brain. Just don't stare at him though. Makes Ma mad."

"Oh, I'd never do that," I said.

"I told Ma I was bringing ya by."

"Think she'll like me okay?"

"Hard to tell. She ain't never liked nobody else I brought home." Buck had his arm around me and was driving one-handed.

"Maybe this isn't a good time for me to meet her," I said and sat up straight and turned toward him. "We should wait until Austin gets better."

"Adie," Buck said, "Austin ain't getting better." He glanced over at me. "Ever."

"Oh," I said. "I'm sorry. Still—"

"This as good a time as any."

"Maybe we should think on this a bit," I said. "She's only got you, now."

Buck pulled into a driveway riddled with potholes, where a brand new baby blue Thunderbird sat, looking right peculiar next to a run-down house.

"Too late. We're here," Buck said.

Verna Jenkins was standing on the cement stoop waiting on us. She was tall and large-boned like Buck, and I saw right off he had her nose. He had her eyes, too. Only Buck's were large and brown as a Black Angus bull. Verna's were the same color, but they were small and beady. Looked like they'd fit better on one of them pit bull dogs. I got a bad shiver just looking at her.

She shook my hand when Buck introduced us. It got lost in hers and she clamped down hard. I wanted to rub my knuckles when she finally let go, but I thought better of it. She looked like the type that might take offense.

"This is Adie," Buck said.

Verna wiped her liver-spotted hands on her apron, which struck me as something she maybe should have done before we shook hands, seeing as now I had something sticky on mine. Then she put her hands on her hips and looked me over good with her lips pinched together tight. She didn't say anything. So I said, "How do, Miz Jenkins. Please to meet you." She nodded.

"I brought you a jar of jam." I held it out to her. "It's real good. Mama sold every one of them at the festival last year except for this one. Has some brandy in it. Hope you don't mind. Daddy said it all gets cooked down so it won't make you drunk or nothing." I was so nervous I couldn't get my mouth to shut up. Verna took hold of the jar, turned it over, and read Mama's hand-printed label.

"Prune Conserve," she said. "What's it for, constipation?"

"Oh no, ma'am," I said. "It's for toast." Verna tossed her head back and laughed.

"Told you she was something, Ma," Buck said. I guess she liked me okay. She didn't say anything to make me think otherwise, just opened the screen door and motioned me on in. "I got to feed Austin," she said. "Have a seat." She pointed to a chrome kitchen chair with gray plastic upholstery that had seen better years. She sat down at the table next to a full-grown man who resembled Buck. He was tied to the chair with a jump rope.

"Time to eat, Austin. Open up; I ain't got all day," she said and spooned in a tablespoon of puréed yellow food that looked to be squash, but could have been sweet potatoes. Austin gagged, and the glob she'd pushed in fell out on his stubbly chin. It was real sorrowful. He was wearing a giant bib made from a cotton terry towel. Verna was hand-feeding him like an infant, and the poor fella needed a shave. She scooped up the mush he'd spit out and shoved it back in.

"Eat, Austin," she said. He swallowed hard and that lumpy glob of yellow goop disappeared. He spit it out a second time, twisted his mouth wide open, and rubbed his eyes with his fists. I watched him cry like a baby that had lost his bottle.

"Stop that now!" she said and took the corner of the huge bib tucked around his neck and wiped his mouth.

Austin pulled away and shoved the bowl of food off the edge of the table. I caught it before it hit the floor but most of it landed in my lap. I scooped it up best I could and put it back in the bowl. It was cold.

"Here." Verna handed me a dishcloth. "Wipe yerself off. There's soap and water in the sink bowl." Austin was crying and banging the table with one fist and chewing on his other.

"He might-would eat this better, ma'am," I said, "if it were heat up a bit, don't you think?"

Verna gave me a look instead of an answer, and I'm sure, not her best one. Any chance I had of endearing myself to her went to the dogs along with the puréed supper she'd tried to feed Austin. She grabbed the bowl out of my hands and plopped it on the floor. One of her feet sent it sliding over to the hounds. They liked it fine.

"How old're you, girl?" Verna asked me.

"Seventeen," I said. "Well, almost."

"So, yer sixteen?"

"Yes, ma'am."

"Too young for my boy. He's near a man. What's your daddy letting you see a grown man for? Ain't you been brought up right?"

"Oh yes, ma'am. I've been brought up fine," I said. "How old's Buck anyway?" I already knew he was seventeen. At least that's what he told me.

"Eighteen come July." It was March.

"Well, he don't act it," I said. "My pa might not have noticed."

"Hhmff!" she said and got herself a bottle of ginger ale from their icebox. I waited, hoping she might offer me one. Guess they were out, because she didn't.

"Why don't you two gals get acquainted," Buck said. "I got me some things to take care of."

"Tie Austin in his swing out back 'fore you go," Verna said.

Buck guided Austin outside. He waddled like a toddler who'd just learned to walk. Buck held his hand and coaxed him along. He was so tender with him my eyes smarted.

"We're gonna go swing, Austin," he said. "Come on. Gonna go swing!" Austin was all smiles. Some noises come up from his throat I couldn't make sense of. Not really words, not even baby ones, just grunts and grumbles. Gibberish. Fancy a beating doing that to a perfectly good brain.

"Come 'ere," Verna said and motioned to me. I got up from the chair and stood still as night changing into day. Verna turned me around and studied my parts like they were pieces of fabric that might make a good quilt, if they were cut up and put together right. Buck came back in from the yard.

"He's good for an hour at least," he said. "Sure loves that dang swing. It ain't even moving. Just drags his feet in the dirt and grins, like it's getting ready to." Buck shook his head sideways. Verna still had hold of my arm.

"I think my ma's expecting me home about now," I said.

"She is, or she isn't. Which is it?" Verna asked.

"She is, ma'am," I said.

"Then you don't need to think it. Say it."

"Yes, ma'am," I said.

"We just got here," Buck said. "Yer ma didn't say nothing about you having to come right home."

My ears turned red. Verna let go of my arm and I sat down on the chrome chair once again.

"Here," Verna handed me a wet rag from the sink. "Wipe that crap off the table. You hanging around, might as well make yerself useful."

Buck took off, for *where* I had no idea, and left me there the rest of the day. When I got home I curled up on my bed and stuffed my face into my pillow. I didn't want Rebecca to hear me crying and make some smart-aleck comment. Buck was the only boyfriend I'd had. No sense in her ruining it for me. Buck was having no trouble doing that on his own. I told myself things would get better. I just had to do a bit of adjusting, is all.

Buck taught me a lot. Stuff I'd been wondering about and should have asked Ma about, but didn't. Then he got himself all stirred up one night and didn't pause long enough for me to have a say so. *Bang!* I didn't need to wonder anymore about what I'd been wondering.

Buck had a 1953 Chevy in pretty good shape that had these soft brown corduroy seats. It happened one night while we were parked out in the pasture behind his house. It was over before I could spit. Nothing much to it, really; I had more fun on the Octopus ride at the fair, even though I have never to this very day told Buck that. But he acted like he'd gone to heaven on a Harley the way he carried on. And he yelled out some God-awful things that make my cheeks red to this day just thinking on it. I wanted to tell someone about it. Rebecca seemed rightly the one, her having been married and being a mama to boot. She and Riley Jr. were still with us at the time while she worked and went to night school. I wanted to ask her if she thought I'd go to that special spot outside hell that Pa said girls go "if they do" before they were married. But every time I tried to get a conversation going, Rebecca would meander onto something else.

"I sure hope I'm not going to hell," I told Buck.

"You going to hell, it ain't on account of this," he said.

"What if I get in a bad way—"

"Shoot," Buck said. "You're darn near still a virgin."

"Well, Miz Avery in health class said sperm can swim right up a girl's leg."

"What?"

"She did. I promise you she did," I said.

"That's hogwash," Buck said.

"You sure?"

"Pretty positive," Buck said and nodded.

But Buck was wrong. Sperms *could* swim; at least his could. If I was near still a virgin, like he said, I was a pregnant one, and that was a fact.

Pa said he was going to put him in the ground. Mama said not until he marries her, you're not. My folks were more upset than I'd ever seen them. Said I shamed them good.

"Can't stay here no more," Pa said. "You and Buck best git on back to where he come from."

Mama said, "Probably best. Everybody will be talking about you, Adie." Then she said it's one thing not having any respect for myself or for them, but how could I just throw away my education?

"Rebecca quit school too!" I said.

"She waited till after she was married to do what you been up to," Pa said. I wanted to tell him that wasn't quite true. She'd been up to it, alright. She just never got pregnant till after they were married, is all. Instead, I told them I was sorry; I didn't mean to shame them. I wanted another chance.

"I'll never do it again," I said.

"Adie, this ain't something you can take back!" Mama said. "You're a grown-up now."

"But I haven't had near enough time to learn half of what I need to be a real one!"

"Too late, now," Mama said. "You take a drink, you gotta swallow." Supper was over. Pa got up to head over to the Red Rooster.

"We was counting on you, Adie," he said before he left.

I went upstairs and sat on my bed and cried, knowing my dreams would die on the windowsill with me not there to blow life into them. I wanted so badly to keep them, to give back those few minutes in the back seat of Buck's car. In thirty seconds I was a grown-up, and I didn't even know I was, till now. I looked in the mirror to see if it showed. The same face looked back. I started packing my things. Clarissa came in and helped fold what little I had.

"I'm gonna miss you," she said.

"I miss you already," I answered, and carried my bag downstairs to wait for Buck. Pa was still gone, but Mama came over and gave me a short hug. Her eyes were puffy and her nose was red.

"You do good, now, Adie," she said. "Be a good wife and . . . and—" She patted my arm, took a tissue out of her apron pocket, wiped at her nose, and went into the kitchen. And that was that. I learned a lot about regrets that day.

Buck was late showing up. I left my suitcase on the front porch and went over and sat down on a small patch of grass under the magnolia tree to wait on him. Mama peeked out the window, one hand inching back the curtain. She let it fall back into place when she saw that I could see her. Buck was coming, wasn't he? I had nowhere to go if he didn't. I started getting more than a little bit nervous. Not able to sit still any longer, I walked to the side of the house and stood below the window I'd watched the trains out of each night. Mama took pride in her housework. The panes were spotless. They winked when the last of the sunlight hit the glass and bounced off their panels. It was eerie. I was no longer on the inside, and the windows watched me. My plans were trapped up there. They were right there on the sill where I left them. I blinked, and I shouldn't have. They slipped over the edge and fell to the ground. They once had a strong voice. They said, "You have a bright future. You'll make a difference. You're going places."

They lied. I got as far as the courthouse on Second and Main.

chapter five

VERNA DROVE US OVER TO the courthouse on Saturday in her blue Thunderbird with the top rolled down. Buck wanted it up so his hair wouldn't blow. I wanted the same so we wouldn't look like a parade. Verna wanted it otherwise.

"It's two against one, Ma," Buck said.

"It's me against *I don't give a holy hoot,*" Verna said. She liked how she looked flying down the road in that long, sleek, expensive vehicle. I asked Buck where she got the money for it, and he changed the subject. When I asked him again, he said, "You must not of heard me the last time you asked that same question."

"You didn't say nothing."

"Then you heard me good, didn't you?"

Verna *was* a sight in that car, a pretty one. She was tall, with real good bone structure. Part Cherokee Indian on her mother's side, Irish on her pa's. She had hair black as midnight and a shapely smile with large even teeth. But when she snapped her jawbone closed in front of your face, it'd scare the meanness right out of you.

Verna studied on the meaness and got all *A*s. She was critical of everything and everybody, including herself, but Buck knew how to humor her. She picked us apart the night before we got married then started in on herself. She said her arms were getting flabby, her face was starting to sag, and her stomach was turning to mush.

"Ain't one good part *left* of me, is there?" she said and turned to Buck.

"Well," he said, "there ain't nothing wrong with your eyes." It was the second time I heard her laugh. It was a beautiful sound and a powerful sight; so many twinkles left in her eyes, but just enough blindness for her not to notice.

The courthouse was older than Moses, but it had new benches out front and a clock on the tower that still worked and all kinds of azaleas and dogwoods and Bradford pear trees planted on the lawn. Verna brought along her camera and one roll of black and white film. We planned on sitting on one of the benches for a picture, but workmen were painting them green when we got there.

The wedding ceremony was over quicker than you can swallow, so I'm not sure you could even call it one. The judge opened his Bible as soon as we got into his chambers and said to Buck, "You got the ring?" Buck nodded.

"Repeat after me," and we did. He promised me what I promised him, except the words the judge gave me to say included *obey* and I took note of the fact that Buck's didn't. We each "plighted our troths" one to the other. Not knowing for sure what it meant, I wanted to ask before agreeing, but the stern look on his face told me not to. He said, "I now pronounce you man and wife. That'll be five dollars," and it was over.

"Ain't I supposed to kiss her?" Buck said.

"Suit yourself," the judge said. "No extra charge."

Verna handed us the papers the judge's clerk had prepared, and we signed our names where it said to. It wasn't exactly what I had in mind for a wedding, but the judge's chambers were nice. There were flowers in a vase on the table next to the wall, which I thought was a special touch. And Verna bought me a new dress to wear. It was pale yellow. It wasn't really a wedding-type dress, so it didn't have a veil. I saw this little hat with a net that matched it pretty good, but of course any extra money Buck and I had was needed for more important things, so I wore my brown headband instead. When we got there, Buck took the white carnation Verna had pinned on his sport coat that morning and tucked it in my hair. My headband held it in place. I got a quick glimpse of myself in the mirror outside the judge's chambers, and for a moment I felt like a bride. It was just like Buck to do something special from out of the blue. He could be such a jerk, but then he'd surprise me and I'd forget that he was. He was especially well-practiced at doing just that whenever I was mad at him over something he knew I had every right to be.

When we left, I thanked the clerk for the flowers. "It was real nice of y'all," I said.

"No need to thank me," she answered. "His Honor has 'em delivered every morning along with the coffee and donuts."

We had lunch at the Crowe's Nest Cafeteria and Verna paid. I looked around to see if maybe Mama and Pa would turn up. Seeing as everyone was talking about us, I figured they'd be gabbing on the fact we'd gotten married and were over here having our wedding brunch. Rebecca and Clarissa came. That was special. It would have been extra-nice to have a sit-down-and-serve-me lunch, but "fools that follow get what they find," is what Mama said.

"Mama's hiding out," Rebecca said. "Thinks folks in this dumb town are talking about her. That she ain't a good mother. You know, look what happened to Annie. Now you." I nodded.

"But Pa told her not to worry on it," Clarissa said. "Don't forget that, Rebecca." My heart lifted.

"Huh!" Rebecca said. "What he said was, 'Don't worry on it. Look what a mess God made with Adam.'" Clarissa motioned for Rebecca to hush, but Verna and Buck thought it was right funny.

"She sent these, Adie," Clarissa said and handed me two jars wrapped in scented paper. Mama's familiar scrawl was on the labels: *Old-Fashioned Grape Jelly* and *Peach Jam*.

"She got the names on them switched around by accident, but she said you'd have to be blind, dumb, or both not to know which is which," Clarissa said.

"It's our first wedding gift," I said. "Look, Buck. Isn't that nice of my mama?" He gave a quick nod and went back to wolfing down his second helping of country fried steak, mashed potatoes, fried okra, collard greens, black-eyed peas, and cornbread.

"I'll write her a thank-you soon as we're settled," I said and handed the package to Verna. Then I got to blubbering. Imagine that? Jam and jelly jars making a body weep.

"You okay?" Rebecca said and handed me a paper napkin. I dabbed at my eyes and nodded.

"You're the prettiest bride I have ever seen in this place, Adie," Clarissa said.

"I'm probably the *only* one you've ever seen in this place," I said, the tears forgotten.

"Still—" she said, "you are." Buck had his arm around me and was smiling at everyone that came in. I squeezed Clarissa's hand.

"Thanks for coming," I said. "It means everything to me," and it did. "You too, Rebecca." I felt really good right about then. Who said my life had to be over? I had as many days ahead of me as I had before. It was up to me to make them good ones. I just needed to keep my attitude on the part of the cherry that wasn't the pit.

"Adie and I are walking home," Buck said. We were staying with Verna and Austin and moving with them to Hog Gap in a handful of months.

"Show this town we got nothing to be ashamed of," he said and steered me towards the entrance. He let go of my arm and turned back.

"Hand me that sack, Ma." Verna held up a brown paper grocery bag.

"What's that?"

"It's a surprise. Don't be so nosy," he answered. I turned toward the door. An elderly couple was on their way in.

"Meet Mrs. Buck Jenkins," Buck said and gently placed me in their path. It was Mr. and Mrs. Findley. They were older than Egypt, not known for being friendly, and had faces molded in stone that said so. They looked up at me, their eyes blank as unused paper.

"How long you two been married?" Buck said and held the door full open. Mr. Findley silently guided his wife through the door. He turned and looked at Buck.

"Sixty-one years, come June fifteenth," he said.

"Sixty-two," Miz Findley corrected, "and it's the eighteenth! How many times I tell you, June eighteenth?"

Buck plucked the lone wedding flower out of my headband.

"Well, Happy Early Anniversary!" he said and offered her the carnation. She stood still as a statue, but one small shaky hand inched out of her pocket and accepted the offering. She gave Buck a smile wide as Texas.

"We been married two hours," Buck said and beamed.

"God help you," Mr. Findley said.

"It's God *be with you*," Miz Findley corrected and yanked on his arm.

Mr. Findley winked at Buck and shook his hand. "Good luck, son," he said, and we were out the door. Buck opened the paper sack and dropped a string of tin cans on the ground. He grabbed my hand and took off running. I went flying along, trying to keep up.

"Just married! Just married!" he yelled. The cans clanged on the sidewalk behind us. The Findleys stood at the front window of the Crowe's Nest, along with Clarissa, Rebecca, and Verna, and waved. The cook ran out.

"Stop!" she shouted, and ran toward us, tossing handfuls of rice. Buck turned around with me in hand and beamed. We watched as the others flew out the door and hurried to join her. They each grabbed a handful of rice from the bag in her hand. Buck pinned my neck carefully in the crook of his arm. He leaned down and kissed me. I felt the rice kernels raining down on our heads. Cheers echoed up and down the street. Buck looked up and grinned. A small crowd had gathered.

"This is just the beginning, puddin'," he said. "Just you wait." He tugged on my arm and we took off running again. The cans followed.

"Just hitched!" Buck bellowed.

"Bye!" people called out after us, the elderly Findleys among them.

"Good luck!"

"Congratulations!"

"Have fun!" Clarissa said, waving wildly. We clanged onward, the tin cans banging on the pavement. Folks waved from their cars, honking their horns. Children followed, their ice cream cones dripping a milky path behind us. More cars gathered. Soon a caravan of cars was lined up beside us!

"Toot-Toot-Toot!"

"They're just married!" Mr. Findley yelled to some folks coming out of the drugstore.

"Hey, y'all!" Buck nodded and beamed. "Thanks for coming! Thank you very much." He squeezed me tighter around the waist with one hand and waved back with the other.

Attitude was no longer a word. It was everything. We rounded the corner and the wedding party broke up.

Buck was still grinning from Texas to Tucson. "Don't you worry," he said. "You're gonna love Hog Gap."

"You think?"

Buck stopped in front of the hardware store.

"Heck yes." He used the palms of his hands to slick back his hair. He had a habit of doing that. It was shoe-polish black. But it surely didn't need any help staying in place. It was slicked back permanently with Vitalis. Buck dumped half a bottle on it each morning.

"Sure thing, puddin'," Buck insisted, "You'll love Hog Gap."

"I don't know. I've never been anywhere but Cold Rock," I insisted, while he fixated on his reflection in the grimy old window at Mitchell's Tool & Hardware. Then he reached for my hand.

"C'mon," he said and jaywalked us across Main Street. There was a traffic light and a crosswalk at the corner, but Buck ignored them. He didn't have much use for rules.

I ran behind him—my hand hidden in his—girl-grin happy for the first time in weeks. Just think; we were married! He'd be mine forever.

"Wait till you see Hog Gap. You'll know what I'm talking about," Buck assured me. I asked him what was so special about it.

"For starters, it's got just what a body needs. And it ain't got these dang asphalt roads burn your feet to hell. Everything's dirt and gravel. Way it's supposed to be. Some parts are still pretty much all wilderness. Got more pigs than people. Got deer, cougar, bears even. Shoot, it's got critters in them woods up there ain't nobody seen before."

Hog Gap didn't sound too good to me, but the way I felt about Buck right then, he could have said we were headed to Cow Pie Valley and I would have thought we were moving to north heaven. I did wonder if Hog Gap had plenty of girls who'd swoon over him, or if he'd have to get over it now that we were married and had a baby coming.

"How long you figure we'll have to live with your mama?"

"You got a problem with that?"

"No," I lied, "but I read where married folks have a better chance at being happy if they're off by themselves," I said.

"Probably so," he said. "We'll stay for the time it takes me to get us a place. How's that?"

We ended up staying just about the entire time I was waiting on the baby, most of it in Cold Rock. Then, finally, we made the move to Hog Gap, and I spent the last month there still living with Verna.

Buck didn't keep a job long enough to get us any money, and he gave most of what he made each week to Verna for groceries. Then when we would get a bit put aside, he'd just up and quit his job. While he was looking for another, the money we'd saved had to go for groceries. Around and around it went.

But Verna always had plenty of money. She drove around in that fancy, blue T-bird and shopped for pretty clothes left and right. I asked Buck if she had herself an inheritance or something and he said, "It ain't none your business where she gets her money," so I stopped pestering him about it. But it was mighty strange, seeing as she didn't work at a job but was always cashing these checks that came in a pretty white envelope with gold lettering.

Buck worked for just about everyone in Hog Gap that had a job to offer. He was running out of employers when we got what I thought was the break I'd been praying for. But then, Mama always said, "Careful what you wish for and mighty careful what you pray for." I wasn't thinking about that when Buck came home and told me Norman and Evelyn Fletcher, who owned the Five, Dime & Penny—about the only store in town had anything worth buying—thought Buck had "potential." They had no sons of their own and were planning on training him to help Mr. Fletcher manage the store, and their only daughter Imelda Jane was going to help. I'm pretty sure Imelda Jane was what Mama was speaking about when she warned me about praying for what I wanted instead of what we needed.

"I start next week!" Buck said. "This is a real opportunity, Adie. You realize that?" he said, rubbing the palms of his hands together. "I'll probably have to work nights, weekends, but this is the big time."

Mornings, nights, afternoons, weekends—if that's what it took for us to have a place of our own, I was agreeable. But the store closed at six during the week, and it wasn't open on Sundays, so some of the hours Buck turned up gone concerned me. I started wondering why he had to work *those* hours, too, but I didn't want to trouble him over the first real job with potential he'd had. Plus, I was getting real close to having our baby and wasn't thinking much about anything else but the poor condition I was in. My back felt like a vise had hold of it, my feet were puffed up like inner tubes, and my belly stuck out like a watermelon too ripe for its vine.

We went to church that last Sunday before the baby was due. Imelda Jane was there with her folks. She made Rebecca look like the old maid in the deck of cards. Her family's about the only ones in town who had any money other than the mayor and the doctor maybe. She came up to Buck after the service wearing the prettiest clothes I'd ever seen and looped her arm through his, like it belonged there. I wasn't sure what to do.

"This is Adie." Buck jerked his head at me.

She nodded and said, "Excuse us. We have some important business that can't wait." She walked him on over to the chinaberry trees at the side of the church building. They talked with their heads together. Verna Jenkins acted like it was the most normal thing under heaven, a husband just sashaying off with his boss's daughter, arm in arm—in front of God, the pastor, the church folks and his wife—without so much as a howdy-do.

I got a strange feeling in my heart watching Buck with Imelda Jane. First, it hurt sorry. Then, it hurt mad. It was a fit of jealousy is what it was, one so bad I couldn't control myself. I marched right over to the chinaberry trees, yanked Imelda Jane's arm off of Buck's, and replaced it with mine. Then I twisted off the only white gloves I owned, which had a little hole in the finger of one of them, and said to Miss Imelda-dressed-to-the-T's-ain't-I-something-Jane, "You see this ring?"

"Beg your pardon?" she said in a soft sugary drawl. She tossed her head to one side and fluffed the back of her long hair.

"You see this ring?" I repeated. "With a diamond in it?" My voice had a drawl too, but it came out sounding like a hoot owl maybe been raised in the south.

"You mean that sweet little ole yellow band with a sequin in the center?"

"This is *not* a sequin," I said. "It's a *genu-wine* diamond!"

"Really?" she said and smiled at Buck like they had a secret.

"And we got a certificate that says we can trade it up for a bigger size anytime we want, so long as we pay extra!" I was powerful mad and didn't much care if she knew it. "Well, you see it or not?"

"What *is* your point?" she said. "We are discussing business matters here."

"Then I guess you best discuss them matters during regular business hours. This here is Sunday church day and my husband's coming home with me." I took Buck's arm and gave it a tug. He stood there grinning like he'd heard a good joke, and there was nothing funny about it, a totally pregnant ready-to-burst wife and a snot-nosed storekeeper's daughter fixing to catfight over him.

And that was just the beginning. Had I known where it was headed, I'd have gone back to Cold Rock, begged Pa to take me in, and waited out front with my belly till he did. Instead, I reminded myself what Mama said about marriage.

"It's a lifelong puzzle. You just keep working on it till it fits."

That sounded reasonable. The problem was mine had one piece too many to ever be one that would.

chapter six

SOMETIMES LIVING WITH BUCK WAS like living with a crazy person. He would say the strangest things. Like when I asked if he was sweet on Imelda Jane. He said, "Nope. Cross my heart and pass the whiskey."

What was that supposed to mean, that he was telling me the truth for once, so we best celebrate? And then I asked him where he'd been all night long. And he said, "Out learning stuff."

"Like what?"

"Like I don't deserve you."

"Buck Jenkins, you don't need to be going anywhere for *that*! Last night I figured that very same thing out just waiting on you in this kitchen."

I learned something else, waiting on Buck: There ain't a whole lot of things can hurt you worse than a man you love being with another, when he's only supposed to be with you. I was pretty sure Buck had been with Imelda Jane and planned on being so again. But, I was set to have the baby any day and was still trying to find us a place of our own. I decided to think about it later when I had more time to figure out what I could do to change it. That's when I ran into Murphy

Spencer. He owned most of the land around Hog Gap. Buck said Murphy's pa left it to him when he died.

I was at the corner grocery store with a short list Verna gave me and was telling Miz Bailey, this kind, elderly woman who runs the place, that I was hoping to find a spot just for Buck and me and the baby.

"You had any luck?" she said.

"Not so far, and my time's running short so it doesn't look good." Miz Bailey's watery eyes lit up.

"Murphy!" she called to a tall fellow up at the front of the store. "Murphy Spencer! C'mere and meet Adie Jenkins." He tossed a fifty-pound bag of dog food over his shoulder like it was a sack of air and came back to where we were standing.

"Willa Mae's cottage still standing?" Miz Bailey asked.

"Sitting the same as she left it."

"This is Adie Jenkins," Miz. Bailey said. "Married Verna's boy."

"How do," Murphy said. He tipped his head and touched the bill of his cap lightly.

"They need a place of their own," Miz Bailey explained.

"How soon you be needing it?" He looked at me, his eyes big as lakes.

"Yesterday," Miz Bailey snapped. "That ain't a giant turnip she's toting around."

"It's not in any condition to move into," Murphy told her and set the dog food down next to the counter.

"You got a problem with them moving in, fixing it up?"

"Well," Murphy ran his fingers, long as rulers, across his chin. It was clean-shaven, had a cleft, and looked like it could take a good punch and not move out of place.

"How much will it be?" I asked.

"Oh, I could probably pay you—" he removed his cap and scratched his head, "say, twenty-five dollars a week."

"Aren't we supposed to pay you?"

"Can't charge you with all the work you'll be doing to get it in shape," he said.

"Can't work around the clock," I said. "We need to pay for the time we're not working and just living. How much is that?"

"Only has two rooms, not counting a bath. Plumbing's not working. You'll need to fix that. Roof leaks." Murphy looked up at the ceiling tiles in the store. "Guess ten dollars a week ought to cover the living part."

"I'll take it!" I yelled, startling the baby. It jumped, and mostly that week and the one before, it hadn't moved around much.

"I mean, *we'll* take it," I said and patted my stomach. "Me and Buck and the baby. We'll take it. Just like it is!"

"Well, come on, then," he said. "I'll show you where it's at. Remember now, it ain't much. But I reckon with a bit of work, it'll do."

I followed Murphy out to his truck. He tossed the dog food into the truck bed, where a black Lab was running circles at the mere sight of him. Murphy reached over and scratched his ears and patted his backside.

"This here's Worry," Murphy said. "Say hello to your new neighbor, boy."

"You named your dog Worry?"

"Yep."

"What'd you do that for?"

"Suits him," Murphy said. "It's about all he does when he ain't with me. Don't you, boy?" Murphy rubbed Worry's shiny coat. He panted and wagged his tail.

"Does he bite?"

"Only those try to hurt me," Murphy said. "All the others he licks to death."

"He's got a mighty long tongue to do it with," I said. Murphy let out a chuckle. I started to climb into the truck.

"Here, let me help you on up there," he said. I held tight to the grocery sack while he did. Murphy climbed behind the wheel and drove down Fat Possum Road. It was gravel. He followed it for a half a mile then made a sharp left turn onto a dirt road. While we bounced over the ruts, he pointed out landmarks, who lived where and what roads led to Civil War battles that'd been fought. I sat transfixed.

There was something about Murphy. Something rare and special that spread through the truck like sunshine. His smile lingered, his words dangled when he spoke, and his movements—strong and lazy at the same time—fit his body like comfortable old clothes. I listened and watched out the window as we wound through the woods to a clearing where a small cabin with a lopsided front porch sat resting on large stones. Murphy helped me down from the truck. He was ceiling tall and a bit too thin. And about the only ones that wouldn't notice his head had never caught up to his ears were those needing glasses and didn't have them. I suspect some folks may have found him a bit strange looking, but I liked how his parts came together, especially his eyes. They were hazel lakes large enough to swim in. When he grinned he looked a bit like Jimmy Stewart, and when he laughed his mouth opened so wide you could see every tooth. I decided he was handsome. Not in ways that make women swoon, but fine-looking in other ways that counted. He talked about the people that lived around Cold Rock, the good, the bad, and why we needed both. He pointed to the ones who needed help and why each of us should help them.

"When you do that," he said, "you end up giving more to yourself than you ever give to them."

He had the best-looking heart I ever glanced on. He was a bachelor, he said, when I asked. "Not the marrying kind," he added, when I wondered out loud, why was that?

What a shame. He'd be a fine husband, the kind a girl would be proud to take home to her family. That's the way I'd wanted it to be that first time Buck came over, seeing as he was the first boy that ever paid any attention to me.

"What do you think?" I'd asked Mama after Buck left that day.

"I think he could charm the pants off you," she said.

"Just make sure he don't," Pa said.

I never took it serious. Of course, by then I was crazy about Buck, so even if I had, it might not have made much of a difference. Buck's the kind of guy an inexperienced girl will take one look at and say, "He can eat crackers in my bed anytime." At least until he does and they figure different. Not to say he doesn't have his charming side. Buck can toss you a smile that makes your knees give way. My folks didn't see it like that. They weren't happy when he came around and didn't bother hiding it. When Buck started calling on a regular basis, Pa never even bothered to get up from his chair. And Mama would just yell out, "He's here again, Adie!" Then she'd turn to Buck and say, "You better make it quick. I got plenty chores around here for her to do."

Now someone like Murphy—if I had taken *him* home—it would have been an entirely different story altogether. I can just picture Mama flitting about the house. "Hon, it's Murphy Spencer! Don't keep him waiting, now." She'd crinkle up her face a bit and pat his arm. "I'll just go get her. Won't be a minute." And she'd call up the stairs, "Sweet thing? You ready, sugar?" when nobody in the house called me sugar or sweet thing since I lost my baby fat and the dimples in my butt.

• • •

Maybe it's for the best my folks sent me away. I missed them, but I wouldn't have to hear Mama harping on what a good catch I let get away by settling on the first nibble that took my bait. She just didn't realize Buck would be a fine catch, once he grew up. Besides, it wasn't a fair comparison. Murphy was a full-grown man. He was probably twenty-five years old! So Buck still had time. There was plenty of years left. And I was willing to work real hard at being a good wife while he finished growing up.

This cabin Murphy said wasn't anything special was as good a place as any to start. And it would be special enough to me. It'd be a place of our own.

"There's a privy out back you can use for starters," Murphy said. "Plumbing's in, but it's not connected to the septic tank. I can help with that. Bring some pipe. Tie it in."

"It'll be fine," I said, and I meant it. I'd spent months taking orders from Verna. During the first few weeks after we got to Hog Gap, I got up every morning thinking on what I could do to make her happy, to get her to like me better. After nothing worked and she was still cross as an old toad, I mostly went around counting up the abandoned wells on the property, hoping she'd fall in one. That got me feeling guilty, so I went back to trying to please her. I'd do her and Austin's laundry, along with Buck's and mine. She really liked the way I did laundry, and told me so. That was nice. But eventually her criticism about everything else would wear me down again. She said I didn't have a lick of sense so many times, I started to believe her. And the closer I got to having the baby the more tired I was from doing the long list of chores she gave me each day. I was willing to pee in a shed and poop in a privy to put an end to it, if that's what it took. It'd be like being on vacation.

"Real fine," I said.

"Okay then," Murphy said. "When you moving in?"

"The day Miz Bailey said."

"What day was that?" Murphy asked, and scratched at his forehead, dislodging his cap.

"Yesterday," I said. "This ain't a giant turnip I'm toting around," I mimicked Miz Bailey and we laughed.

"Well, you're surely not in any condition to be moving your stuff."

"What stuff?" I said. "It's just Buck and me. That's it. Some clothes, but I can carry them in one basket. And I got some baby things stored up, didies and blankets."

"There's a bit of furniture in there. You're welcome to it."

"There is?" I climbed the steps up to the porch and peeked in the soot-stained window. He followed.

"There's Willa Mae's old dresser, a bed frame and mattress, some quilts." Murphy said.

"There's a table and four kitchen chairs!" I said. "Three that match."

"That's right, table, chairs. Forgot about them," he said. "I got an extra sofa I'm not using stored at my place. Could let you have it. No sense going to waste."

"That'd be nice. Guess we'd have everything we need to get started."

"There's no dishes or pots and pans I remember."

"I don't cook," I said.

He laughed. "What you gonna eat?"

"Guess I best get a few dishes and a couple of pots and learn how to cook," I said. "We got some money put up."

"Willa Mae's a fine cook. Built her a new place back of mine." He flagged his thumb toward the right side of the cabin. "From what I toted over, she's got more pots and pans than a body could use in one lifetime. Save that money you got put by for the baby. I'm sure she can spare a few."

"Who's Willa Mae?"

"She's my mammy," Murphy said.

"You mean she's your mama?"

He shook his head and his bangs swung free of his forehead. "No, I mean she's my mammy," he said. "She raised me. Didn't have a ma."

"What happened to her?"

"She . . . she . . . ," Murphy looked down at Worry. "I had Willa Mae," he said and shook his head. "She'll be by to check you out. She's nosier than you," he said with a grin.

"Oh," I said and felt my cheeks flush. "This always been her place, then—"

"Hers and her mama's before that."

"Golly, how old is this thing?" I looked at the worn-out cabin wondering if it might fall down on our heads some night.

"Been here *awhile*. This land's been in my family for over a hundred years, Adie. My pa built this place for Willa Mae's family after the Freedom come." Murphy said and looked at his watch.

"The Freedom?"

"For the slaves," he said. "You *do* know about the slaves, Mr. Lincoln, and what happened in Dixie, don't you?"

"Oh, sure," I said. "Miz Lou taught us history at Jackson High in Cold Rock. Mostly she talked on Mr. President Lincoln getting shot. That was her favorite part. And she said the Yankees stirred up trouble for the South didn't need stirring at all. 'Course I know the North fought the South to set the black folks free. I just never heard it said like that." A patch of clouds inched over the trees shading the cabin. Murphy glanced up.

"Like what?" Murphy said.

"Like what you said. 'When the Freedom come.'" The clouds inched apart. The sun reached through the cracks in the foliage, splashing the ground with fingers of light. Worry chased them about like they were squirrels and he was going to catch one.

"No matter. Folks ain't familiar with a lot of things around here. The ones that are don't want to talk on it. Reckon a good bit of it's in that book Willa Mae totes round." Murphy headed for his truck. Worry gave up on the dancing sun shadows and ran alongside him.

"You ready, boy?" Murphy dropped the tailgate and the dog leaped in. Then he spotted some squirrels at the edge of the woods; real ones this time. They were frozen in place, busy chomping on nuts. The dog nearly went crazy trying to jump out of the truck to get to them. The squirrels were gone in a heartbeat.

"What's in it?"

"Nothing at the moment, just the dog."

"No, I mean that book Willa Mae totes around."

"It ain't my business to say," Murphy said. "Better ask her."

"Oh—" I said and felt my cheeks getting warm again.

"She might read you some." Murphy pushed in on the tailgate and it snapped in place.

"Tell her I said so." He motioned to me with his head. "We best be going."

"Oh, I'll walk on back to the store," I said. "It's not far."

"It's no trouble," he said.

"I just want to tidy up a bit, get acquainted with our new home, you know, make a list of what we might need—"

"Is that okay? You being in, well, in that, ah, condition—"

"Walking is the best exercise women having babies can do. The doctor in Cold Rock told me some even keep walking the whole time they're in labor. Speeds it up, I think," I said.

"In that case, don't be walking around too much till you get home." I nodded, when I should have been listening. Murphy got behind the wheel and turned the truck around. He leaned out the window.

"You're *real* sure?" I nodded again.

"Okay," he said, and he waved. I waved back and Worry barked. I watched him drive off until the oversized tires stirred up a mushroom cloud of dirt that swallowed them whole.

I started cleaning up the cabin as best I could. I gathered wood and boiled water in an old metal bucket left out on the back stoop. Then I scrubbed the old plank floors with some borax powder I found under the sink and dusted cobwebs with a big stick I found in the yard and tied with rags. Had a burst of energy I couldn't understand, seeing as I'd been so wore out just days before. I had a fairly long walk home and figured I best get going, but I was excited about our own place so I kept thinking, "just a little bit longer," "I'll just finish this," "I'll just do that." The kitchen started to look like a home. Soon as I had the baby, I was going to write Mama and get her recipe for sweet cherry jam.

"Best housewarming there is," she said. "You cook yourself up some sweet cherry jam, let it bubble up good, and you'll smell heaven in your kitchen for weeks."

I stayed on working and dreaming, not knowing the danger I was in. Most likely Verna was having herself one big hissy fit, seeing as I hadn't come straight back with her things. At the moment I didn't much care. For once, I was using my time for something I wanted. I told myself I'd worry about the price I'd pay later.

That was foolhardy. It cost me a lot more than I counted on.

chapter seven

IT DIDN'T TAKE ME LONG to realize I'd hurt my back stretching to get the last of the cobwebs. Then, out of nowhere a fierce spasm grabbed hold of me from behind and nearly knocked me to the floor. It quickly moved around to my front and grabbed hold of my tummy and wouldn't let go.

"Ooooohhhh," I moaned, and wrapped my arms around my swollen belly. It was hard as stone. The pain got worse.

"Sweet Lord, help me!" I gasped. "I hurt something awful." My stomach lurched. I was gonna be sick. I leaned over the sink and held on. The room was starting to spin. Parts of my breakfast, bits of ham, and pieces of the biscuit I'd eaten hours earlier were mysteriously reappearing and marching up my throat. I swallowed hard and managed to make them return to where they'd been. The pain in my body eased. Relieved, I gathered up the bag with Verna's store-bought things and started for the door. It was a tad less than a mile back to Verna's place. Maybe I could work out whatever muscles I'd hurt while I made my way there. I took two steps and what do you know? I ruined the nice clean floor planks I worked so hard on. The water bag the doctor said would break near my time came swooshing out. It poured down so fast and hard I thought the baby might come along with it. I grabbed hold of myself, bent over best I could, and took a look. The only thing I could see was the sticky mess on the floor, and my belly still swollen, big as ever. I had to hurry and get on home. I might be having the baby real soon. I made it out onto the porch, took hold of the one railing still standing, and started down the steps. A vise grabbed hold of my belly and clamped onto my insides. Pain shot upward, then downward, then wrapped itself around me like a piercing hot flame. I couldn't remember anything ever hurting so bad. Not even when Papa took the strap to me one summer when I sassed him and said I wasn't gonna help Mama do chores any more because she played favorites and always sided with Rebecca. Not even when my arm got caught in the washer wringer the year I was ten and nearly got mangled before Mama rammed a piece of wood between the rollers and wrenched it free. This hurt worse than both those times put together.

I lay down and curled up on the stoop, waiting for the pain to stop for good so I could get up and go home. Instead, it rushed over my body like a giant hungry wave. Then it was gone. I got back on my feet and inched down the steps, thinking if I just didn't jar myself too much I could make it back to Verna's. Nobody knew where I was— just that nice Murphy Spencer, and there wasn't any reason for him to come back. Why did I tell him I'd be fine anyway?

I made my way down the winding dirt driveway and got as far as the gravel road that led back to town.

"That's my place up there a piece, just over the ridge," Murphy had said that morning and pointed to where the road broke off to the left. I glanced up the steep incline. I could make out the tip of a chimney. It had to be Murphy's. I turned and started up the embankment. It was closer than Verna's. I'd have to go there. I started climbing the steep hill. It was peppered with rocks. I used them to grab hold of, leaning over my belly to reach them. I clutched at the rocks ever so carefully, inching my way farther and farther up the hill. *One more step, one more step, one more step, one more step.* I was going to make it. Then my foot hit a clump of loose grass and slipped out from under me. I lurched forward trying to catch myself but the weight of my body flung me backwards. I tumbled down the hill. The rocks that had helped me make my way up now pummeled me on the way down. I careened down the hill like a runaway wheelbarrow.

"Hellllllllllp! Hellllllllllllp!" I screamed and braced myself for more rocks. None came. My ears were ringing, but I was no longer moving. I'd made it to the bottom. My clothes were all wet. I was ice cold and started to shiver. I rolled onto my back and stared up at the sky. It was near black as night! Rain poured from the clouds. I'd been so caught up with being pummeled by rocks I hadn't noticed. Maybe this is what happened to those who had babies and weren't married long enough to have them the proper, respectable way.

"Oh, Lord," I said, "if you're gonna take me, please do it now before I suffer any longer. I'm sorry for my sins, I am, I am . . ." The wind picked up and got right nasty. It slapped the rain hard against my face. Like a blow from a strong hand, it knocked me to my senses. I had to get back to the cabin. There was an old mattress and bed frame. If I was gonna die in agony, at least I could do it on a soft mattress. I took the winding path back to the cabin. It had turned into a river of mud. I sunk inward with each step. My shoes made a sucking sound as I fought to pull each foot free from the muck. It took too much of my strength. I'd have to walk through the brush to get back to the cabin. I didn't have enough strength in my legs to tote me *and* my belly through the thick slop the path had turned into. The sides of the path were heavy with kudzu vines and dead tree branches knocked down from storms that had passed through before. They tore at my face and arms, poking here and jabbing there, breaking the skin when I pushed forward too fast.

I slowed down. There was no telling how long it took to make it back to the cabin, but I had three more of those bad waves of pain along the way. I dropped down in the bushes until they passed. I prayed for mercy. When it didn't come, I prayed for death, and when that didn't arrive, I prayed I had a guardian angel who would come and help me. Finally, the cabin was before me, but it didn't look real. An angel *was* waiting—a very strange one, too. She had on a long flowing skirt, purple and yellow and red, with a shawl that didn't match draping her body.

Her hair was wispy and gray and flowed past her shoulders. She looked well fed and her skin was a nice shade of honey, but it had more lines than the Shakespeare play teacher made us read.

"Glory be the Lord and Savior!" she said. "Who be scratching on you like that, child?" She came down off the steps and grabbed hold of me.

"Murphy told me you is having a baby. Sweet mercy from the good Jesus! He don't say you is *this* ready!" She was a strange angel indeed. She knew Murphy! She came to my side and had me up the steps in no time.

"I prayed the Lord would send you," I said. "What took you so long?" Lightning flashed across the sky, stretching its fingers over our heads like spokes on an umbrella.

"Goodness to Jesus, child, I comes by to say, hey, see's you be needing something." Thunder pounded out the rest of her words.

"Lord of all the glory!" She took hold of my arm. "Gits in the house! That lightning gwine gits us for sure we stays on this porch." The lightning snapped again. It reached out to us but settled for the branches on the oak tree rooted in the yard instead. "Mercy," she said. She took hold of my arm and dragged me through the doorway.

"Murphy said you gone move in here. Might could need some things. So I comes over. Nobody be here. And I say, 'Ole Willa Mae just have to come back.' The storm catch me and I got to wait. Good thing, too, cause here you is."

"Ohhh, you're. . . . Willa–" A pain dove straight for my belly, this time not bothering to come via my backside. Stabbed me like a railroad spike. "Aaaaaarrrrrrrggggggghhhhhhh," I screamed. "Help me!

Pleeeeeeeeease, help me, these pains been coming since before the storm."

"Mercy, child," Willa Mae said. "Let's git you in the bed. Don't have no sheets on it, but I got some in that trunk." She pointed to the old wooden chest at the end of the bed.

"Can't go nowhere in this storm child, till it pass. This be real bad one. You see that?" More thunder and lightning cracked all about the cabin. Snatches of light streaked through the smudged windows and flashed about the room. Willa Mae settled me onto the mattress and started stripping me of my clothes.

"We got to gits you out of these wet things, honey. Catch yourself and that baby what you got in your belly a death from the cold."

"Wait! Waaaaaaaait! Just till this pain passes."

"Takes a deep breath," she said. "Now blows out your mouth like this, 'wheeeeew, wheeeeew, wheeeeew,' like you gone whistle but no whistle come out. Do's that."

I did like she said best I could. "Wheeew . . . wheeeew . . . wheeeew . . . wheeeew . . ."

"Keeps doing that," Willa Mae said.

"Wheeeew . . . wheeeew . . . wheeew," I kept at it, not believing it would make the pain lessen but finding it did.

"I knows that better. Ole Willa Mae got a bag of tricks help you, child. You rests a bit. Rests . . . rests . . . rests," she crooned and wrapped me in the soft faded linens she pulled from the trunk.

"Willa Mae gone take care of you, child. You and that li'l baby gone be fine." She plopped a big comforter around me and tucked in the sides. She used the same bucket I'd used earlier to heat up the water to scrub down the plank floor. She boiled more water and tore strips of linen from one of the sheets she pulled from the trunk.

"Things be fine. Sweet Lord gone helps us." Her way of saying the words made me believe they were true. Maybe I *wouldn't* die.

Then the pains started in again and the storm grew meaner along with them. I got scared again. I knew Buck would be home by now.

He and Verna would be wondering what had happened to me. Maybe they'd go get Mama and have her help look for me. She'd come; she'd be worried, wondering where me and the baby were, and then when they found me, she'd be with them! She'd make everything better. She'd fix soup and toast with warm apple butter.

"My mama . . . tell Buck . . . please . . . they'll be wondering where I—" I gasped.

"Hush, now," Willa Mae said. "Saves all your strength. You be having this baby soon. Storm gone be over, too. Then I gets word to Murphy, and then Murphy takes care of everything."

"But—"

"Sssssssshhhh," Willa Mae said. "Baby be here soon, poor chile."

She might have been right about a lot of things—storms and Jesus and blowing air out your mouth like a whistle—but she was wrong about that.

Having the baby didn't turn out the way it was supposed to at all.

chapter eight

PEOPLE WRITE ENTIRE BOOKS ON "natural" childbirth, when having a baby is like trying to blow a grapefruit out your nose. Does that sound natural?

When the pains started in again, I thought about what Verna'd been saying to me—and anyone who'd listen—for months. She said I didn't have a lick of sense. It made me so mad my face turned purple. But I guess she was right. If I'd *had* a lick of sense, I wouldn't have gotten myself in trouble and ended up in Hog Gap on a stormy night wracked with pain. I'd be home with Mama picking strawberries and making jam.

I tried to picture how sweet the baby would be, sweeter than Mama's pecan pie. But things got rougher, and all that came to mind was the sorrowful fact I'd rather have bamboo shoots rammed under my fingernails then go through any more labor.

Willa Mae tried to make the best of it. But the storm didn't cooperate. It got worse as the hours wore on just like my pains. She checked out the window, then checked on me, checked out the window, checked on me. Back and forth, till she wore herself out and made me dizzy in the process. Finally, she dragged a chair in from the kitchen and sat down next to me to rest. She found an old windup clock that still kept time and placed it on another chair as a makeshift nightstand.

"I hate that clock," I said. "It chews on every second like a cow with its cud."

"We needs it, child," Willa Mae said. "Keeps track on the pains." I watched her lemon-yellow arms waddle in the air while she tucked in the sheets. Hours limped along.

"That clock ain't working!" I said.

"I'm gone get you thinking 'bouts something else," she said and dabbed at my forehead with a cloth she rinsed out in the basin beside me. Her hands were thick, warm honey, pink in the center, soothing and gentle.

"Murphy said you might read to me from a book you carry around."

"Murphy say that?"

I nodded.

"Best not makes no liar out of that fine man," she said, and her eyes snapped open. They were large round circles that rested on her face like shiny black pools surrounded by snow. "You keeps doing that breathing. I gits it from my satchel." Willa Mae shuffled out of the room and came back with a cracked brown leather binder tucked under one arm. It was held together with an old black shoelace. She laid it at the end of the bed.

"This be it," she said and lit the kerosene lamp.

"Murphy shuts the power down when I moves, but this works good. Some things is like that. Still works even when they's old." Willa Mae fumbled with the match, and a soft glow lit up the corner of the room. Another pain erupted below my belly. It quickly wrapped itself around my spine and surged upwards.

"Uuuuuuuuuuuuuhhh," I gasped and sucked in a deep breath, releasing the air through my mouth. I turned and rolled to my side.

"Wheew. Wheew. Wheew . . ." I panted, just like she'd taught me.

"Keeps doing that," Willa Mae said. She rubbed my lower back while the pain swallowed it whole. "You doin' real good." I clung to her words like sap on a tree and welcomed the strokes from her broad hands. It was all I had to ease the pain. Once it passed, Willa Mae lowered herself onto the chair. Her vast bottom spilled over both sides. She placed the journal carefully on her lap, opened the cover, and ran her fingertips lightly over the pages. They were peppered with watermarks, fat, dimpled, inviting pages with uneven edges the color of whiskey. A faint musty odor drifted into the room. I settled under the covers and breathed in the scent, curious about what was inside, praying that whatever it was would help keep my mind off the pain. Willa Mae tucked her glasses carefully around each ear.

"These from Murphy," she said, "He gits me new pairs by and by as I needs 'em. They looks real good on me, too."

I nodded that they did and took another deep breath. Willa Mae stroked the binder resting in her lap and began to whisper the words spread out on the page. My eyes were heavy and my body ached, but the soft mattress underneath me was heaven. I closed my eyes and concentrated on the sound of Willa Mae's voice as the story drifted toward me. The words from the past inched forward, and the present slid backwards. I let the cabin rise up and carry me with it as the birthing continued.

What a battle. The pain beat me down. It bruised me bad. It wounded a soft, tender spot inside that used to be me. I cried out when I rode the worst of it, but Willa Mae's murmur—soothing and steady— never let up. Her velvet words carried me past the hurt. They tossed me gently into the current of another girl's life. I bobbed up and down on the swells. When the next wave clamped hold of my belly, I slipped under that current and mercifully got lost somewhere beneath it.

• • •

Them nice white folks what builds this cabin for me say writes down how you 'members it. How your chilluns be sold and tells about when the freedom come and that mean ole Massah has to set you free. Writes it all down, lessen you forgets. I won't forget, not none of it, I say. I still sees my little chillun's faces and wonder they still be out there somewheres, but how I gone know if they's looking back? I be ninety best I know. They growed up and old theyselves by now, but the white folks keeps at me. "Land sakes, I gwine writes it down!" I say. This how it go.

I running longside the wagon and the speculator men got my babies. They got Thomas, he three, but he thinks he older. They got James and LuLu, too. That wagon near full up when it get here and still they stuffs more poor niggers in it. This fine-looking big colored woman, with a face round as the moon and real shiny, got hold of LuLu. She be patting LuLu's back and moving up and down, while she do's, but that kind Negro woman ain't got what that chile need. LuLu still take the milk be in my breast. She been fussing the whole time they takes her, now she howling. I got my hand on the wagon and when she keeps doing that fussing, my milk comes in again. I runs real fast and stay with that wagon, and I reach out to that woman got LuLu, thinking maybe she hands her back to me and I can hides her somewhere without Massah be knowing bouts it. And then, James see me and he start crying and reaching for me to takes him. He hardly much bigger than LuLu.

"Mammie!" he say in the sweetest voice what the Lord gives him.

"Gits me, Mammie," he say, and whilst he doing that, Thomas be waving and smiling. He think he going somewhere and be coming back soon. He keeps up that waving all the while that wagon bumping long this road got more holes than Massah's old socks. I still running and doing my best to keeps up.

James, now he waving, too, but James not smiling like Thomas be doing. He got good sense, James do. That little boy got a sadness to him like he knows what things be bout. He knows when that wagon comes, the folks get in never comes back. Mostly, Thomas forget that, cause he is hit in the head with the cracker when Massah whips some poor nigger won't wuk harder and Thomas get in the way when that bullwhip snap back. Near kill him, it do, and he got a scar in the front of his head got a ridge big as a snake. Mostly now his black hair, what be real kinky, hides it good.

The wagon going faster now, and I be having trouble keeping ups with it. And that speculator man what drive them mules, have it go even faster. Use the bullwhip on 'em, same kind they beats us folks with. My legs is young and strong and I can't let that wagon goes so easy, and I keeps running after it. But they's a hole in the ground that grabs my foot and down I goes. My foot stuck bad in that hole and when I twist to get it out, this pain shoots up like a hot poker be branding it. I yanks it free, but that wagon mostly be gone when I goes limping after it even though I wants to run. I's still waving, but my chilluns is getting smaller and fore long I can't see none my babies sweet faces what got them pretty brown eyes, no more. And my eyes works good, too. I ain't but seventeen, best I know.

'Magine them babies own daddy sell'em like that, like they's no more than a sack of good eating taters. Law say he can. He be the Massah. Ain't nothing I can do's bout it, and dat's a truth.

The speculator mens take all three them babies be mine and Massah's. And they takes one more thing. Just reach their big hairy white arms down, what got them wiry muscles, and takes my heart, the whole thing. Maybe not, maybe it climb in that wagon all by itself. Ima tell you, everything pretty much be gone after that.

Two year later that Freedom come and I goes looking for them babies. I do's that nigh on fifteen year, but I ain't never seen 'em agin. And dat's a truth.

That be Marse Major Stowers I makes those chilluns with, but he weren't the master I be born to. That be Massah Jordan. I was the third girl of my Mammy. There was seven of us chilluns counting four boy ones was my brothers. They was all born before me and I never knew none them and never seen none them neither. Massah Jordan buy Mammy from her old Massah and she be having the baby in her belly be me when he buyed her. Massah Jordan be a good Massah and he say he not one to buy a woman to take from her chillun be's left behind, but Mammy's old Massah say he be selling her and what baby she got in her belly anyway, so he might as well takes her as another.

Mammy was a house servant done all the cooking and we was royalty and dat's a truth. When I's born, Mistress Jordan sure nuf love me, she do. And Massah and Missy keeps loving us like we be's their own. Missy gives us pickaninnies pennies on Saturday for to buy stuff with. Throw'd them shiny monies right off the big front porch for us to cotch. We chilluns push and shove to get them shiny monies and I always gets me some, even though I be mostly the smallest. 'Cepting one time I not get me any of that shiny money, but Missy seed it and say, "Stand back, children. This is for Tempe." And she lean over the rail of that big front porch house was a castle for sure and drop two of them pennies clean into my hand and I cotched them quick 'fore the other chilluns rush at me. Missy say, "Harold, Ollie," they be's some the other little Negro chillun what live on Massah's place, "You got yours. Let Tempe be, or I'll whup you now." And Missy sashay her full skirts 'round in a circle and flounce off into that big house wherefore Mammy be cooking her something good to eat that morning for her breakfast, 'cause Mammy was a fine cook for sure she was.

I be too young in those days to be's a working Negro child on that plantation. That long time before the big war come between the gray and the blue soldiers. We chilluns spent our days just playing and having 'bout the best chilehood chilluns can have. We hitch us rides to and from the fields when we's able and sometimes we gather all the rotten fruit lay on the ground in the orchards and throwed it at each other. And we chase the ganders 'bout and we make plenty games up fore to play, too. The Negro man Old George, couldn't do no regular wuk no more, care for us in the day while all the mammies be at wuk. He be pretty good to us, 'lessen we get out of hand. When we does that, he say Raw Head and Bloody Bones come to gits us in the night and land sakes we be good after that. Massah Jordan tell Old George to feeds us chillun all we wants so we grow big and strong and can do the wuk some day. Old George breaks up the cornbread and puts it in the big trough what he made for us to eats from and he pour the buttermilk over that bread. Then we eats it with the dipping spoon he gives us to eats with. We'uns stands in line like we little piglets and eats till our bellies full. We's acts like little pigs, too, pushing and shoving so to keep our place. Some chilluns don't use no spoon and 'fore long the corn bread and the buttermilk turn near red as the clay be on there hands. At nights we gits our dinner like that, too, but the vegetables go in with the cornbread and the milk and the pot-licker, and some meats, too, whatever kinds they got for us, that's what they puts in. It be pretty good that way. Old George make it up and we gits all we want so that be good, too. Mostly, it sure be heaven in them early days for me. Later when things git bad when Mammy be gone I thinks back on them days and sure miss them forever and dat's a truth. That was long before the Freedom come, 'cause when it come Mammy be no longer where I could ever find her and I never did know if she seen it or made use of it. Missy be gone by then, too, so I lost both the women I loved the best in the whole world and they was good to me. Yes, they was.

Massah and Missy had six chilluns of their own and they was the best friends I had. Four be girls and two be boys. The girls be Hannah, Ellen, Louise, and Caroline. The boys, one he be the baby, they was Luke and William. How I love that fat baby William what had the yeller curls and blue eyes. I help Mammy kere for him and totes him for Missy when she let me.

"Sit still, Tempe, and hold him tight. He's a handful," Missy say.

"Oh, I hold him tighter to me than a squirrel hang on that tree," I tells my Missy and points yonder to the tree with one hand and near dropped that baby on his head with the other! But she cotched him, 'cause Missy stay real close when I hold that fat baby William what was a handful. And a good thing, too. I git me a whupping for sure I drop that baby. Missy be 'bout the finest lady in that land, for sure, but my mistress not one for nonsense or dropping no babies on their heads, 'specially one be her baby William what she neared died birthing and scared Mammy to death thinking she would them three days that baby what's supposed to come out and didn't, then finally did.

I loves my Missy and my Mammy to this day. Hard to think which one I loves more. And they loves me too, wherever they is. They never lays a hand to me, 'cepting once and then I deserves it for sure. I et all the pies Mammy baked for the wedding guests come to stay for Missy's sister what married that fine soldier be in the gray army, 'cepting there wan't no fighting gwine on at the time I know of.

"What you got all over your clothes?" my Mammy say.

"Nothing," I say, and looks down and sees my tackling shirt all we colored chilluns be wearing covered in the blackberries and the strawberries what dripped down from the pies I et.

"You be in Mistress Molly's berry patch?" Mammy say.

"No'm," I tells her and dat's a truth. I be by the back window where them pies be cooling and eat'em with my fingers soon's they cool and then hardly, 'cause my fingers was burnt some, they was.

"Best not be in Missy's berries," Mammy say.

"Oh no'm," I tell Mammy, and run off to the window again and finish with the pies I am eating, 'til my belly near bust. Come for a time later my belly swelled up from them pies and I be in the terrible pains and rolling on the ground and hollering like the ladies does what have the babies. Missy hear me moaning and runs out to me and Mammy comes too.

"Tempe," Mistress says, "What's wrong, child?" She sure be worried, 'cause she loves me, that Missy do.

"I et the pies," I say. "They's poisoned!"

"What?" Missy say.

"Mammy, what fore you poison them pies?" I ask Mammy. Mistress look at Mammy like she be waiting for her to explains a good answer. Mammy say, "Them pies be the best in Georgia. I bakes 'em for Sissy's big wedding party. Ain't no poison in the pies!" Mammy cross her arms and put out her chin. "Uhm, uhm, uhm," she say.

"Oh my, Tempe," Missy say, "Did you eat Mammy's pies?"

"I did. I et the pies," I say. "They's poisoned and I saves Sissy and I saves all da others what might eat them pies from dying."

"Uhm, uhm, uhm!" Mammy say, and shake her head. When I gets done being sick from them pies, Missy give me a whupping, but not too hard, 'cause she love me, that Missy do. And Massah Jordan he loves us all and was the finest master in the land for sure and we go on like that for pretty good many years. When Miz Caroline, their oldest girl child, is near a woman, Massah get the fever, might be that scarlet one he got, might not, no one else gets that kind fever he got I know of. And Massah die. Lordy, how we carry on. They let all the Negroes be his march right through the big parlor where they got him laid up all nice on the satin kivers. We chilluns mostly thinks on him like he our pappy and for me I figure he was for sure my pappy. My skin be light yeller and Mammy's be dark, and my nose don't spread far on my face like most them others.

"Massah Jordan be my pappy," I say to the other chilluns and soon it gets to my Mammy what I be saying and land sakes did she lay on me good.

"Who say Massah Jordan be your pappy?" Mammy say.

"I say, Mammy. My skin be yeller and my nose not wide."

"That don't make for him be your pappy," Mammy say, and she whups me. So dat be another time I gits whupped. I near forgot dat one.

"Don't be telling them made up stories in your head again," Mammy say.

"Who fore be my pappy? He be a white pappy?"

"Lordy, Lordy," Mammy say and goes inside to cooks the food in the big house. After Massah die a black lady wuk a'side my Mammy tells me I got three white maybe pappies and nobody know which one be him, not even Mammy.

"Your Mammy's old Massah, who Massah Jordan buys her from, has three sons weren't but near boys, and when the mistress be gone

one day they ties your Mammy on the floor and what they done, they does all day," she say. "Mammy tells her mistress when she come home 'cause Mammy a sight and Mistress beat them boys, but she send Mammy away when she learns a baby be come from it. That baby be you."

"What be their names," I say.

"Who names?"

"Names of them maybe pappies."

"Land sakes, chile, I don't knows the name be that Massah! How'm I gwine know the names of them sons be his?" she say. "What you needs to knows that fore?"

"I needs know who my pappy be," I say.

"That not how it wuks," she say. "Where your head?"

So I don't gets to know who be my pappy, but I pretty for sure knows he be's white.

chapter nine

"Where your mercy, Lord?" Willa Mae said as she checked on the storm again. Nothing had changed, except we were out of kerosene for the lamp and the cabin was dark. At three in the morning, Willa Mae said I needed help.

"The pains not doing right," she whispered. "I got to gits Murphy. The storm be settled some, maybe." A bolt of lightning lit up the sky outside the window.

"Maybe not," she said as she patted my arm gently, her face as pained as my body. "But I gots to go, 'gardless."

"Don't leave me! Pleeeeease, don't leave me!" I cried. "The pain's worse!" Knives were carving up my insides. Bricks were smashing into my back. I thought I might just split down the middle, and Willa Mae needed to be here for that. I figured I'd die, and I surely didn't want to do it alone.

"Please, please, please—"

"I can't count them babies I delivered, Miz Adie," Willa Mae said. "They's so many. We gots to git you to that birthing place in Mountain City. Your little baby be in trouble, child. We needs help!"

I writhed against the blankets as another pain grabbed hold of me.

"Pulls on the sheet-ropes!" Willa Mae said. She placed the loops of the makeshift ropes around my hands. Hours earlier she'd braided strips of sheets, making two long ropes. She tied them to the springs, one under each side of the mattress. Then she pulled them back up to me, one for each hand, with a loop knotted in place to hold onto. When the pains got bad, I pulled on the sheet-ropes with all my might. I pulled hard. I yanked the ropes like *they* were the pain and I had it; it didn't have me. I pulled and yanked and hollered till the pains eased and I could rest my head on the pillow again and wait for the next one. Willa Mae wrapped herself up in her shawl and stole away into what was left of the storm. I clutched the clock. When the lightning lit up the room, I could make out the time.

At four a.m., I heard a truck pull up and the door to the cabin open. Footsteps poured into the kitchen, some heavier than others. I was too weak to look up and see who they belonged to. Their voices overlapped one another, Murphy's, Willa Mae's, Miz Bailey's, and a man's voice I wasn't familiar with.

"Adie," Willa Mae said, "we's here. I gots Murphy. And them fine Bailey folks be here too. You gwine be *fine* now." Murphy and Mr. Bailey hoisted me and the wet pile of sheets that surrounded me into the back of the truck bed and placed me on the quilts Miz Bailey laid in place. They helped Willa Mae climb up next and waited until she was settled in beside me. Murphy climbed behind the wheel, where the Baileys sat waiting, and headed down the side of the road. He drove through the kudzu and vines, knocking holes in the foliage and leaving more twisted and broken branches hanging by the wayside. I guess storms hadn't knocked all them scratchy vines down after all, but trucks traveling along the sides of the mud road after rainstorms had made them impossible to drive on.

"Willa Mae," I screamed. "I'm hurting so bad!'

"Poor child," she said and stroked my forehead. "Keeps doing that breathing." She wrapped her arm around my shoulder and pulled the blankets around us as best she could to keep some of the rain out.

"I'm gwine keeps telling you more that story. I knows it by heart." she said. "You hangs on!" The truck lurched hard to the right and thumped onto the gravel road.

"We gwine make it—" Willa Mae crooned.

• • •

Time be moving long and soon Miz Caroline be old enough to marry and Massah Major Stowers come to calling. 'Fore long they's a wedding and she be Miz Caroline Stowers, then. Missy send Mammy and me to be with her and her new husband, that Major Stowers. His name be John and his hair be mostly red, but it got some gray spots in it, too. Folks say all them Negro chillun what got the red hair on his plantation be his. Major Stowers lots older than Miz Caroline, but is powerful rich and has more darkies than anybody. Major Stowers scared me good and he was for sure mean and dat's a truth, but he always act nice in front of the other white folks. But he whups all the Negroes and tells the overseer to do it, too, so they stays scared and not run off. He says we is to call him Massah Major. The first thing Massah Major do when he brings home a new slave he buys is whup him good in fronts of all the others.

"Put the fear a God in him," he say. And sure enough, it do. I know my mistress never want fore us to go. I know because I hear her crying some nights before we ever leaves. I be sleeping at the foot of her and Massah Jordan's bed. In the cold months I get whatever Missy need in the night so her feet stays warm. I brings the chamber pot and wipes it clean. And I stoke the fire and keeps it burning through the night, too. In the summer I don't got to do that but I still brings the chamber pot if'n mistress need it in the night. And I fans her in the hot weather with the turkey feathers. And I keeps the flies off her too, 'cause there weren't no screens on the windows to keeps them off my Missy. But I be sure not to stomp my feets to keep them flies away. I do that, it wake Massah Jordan up. He be sleeping in the bed with Mistress before he got that fever and goes to sleeps in the ground. He be a good Massah, all the time he sleeps in the bed, but none too happy I wakes him in the night. I use the feather fan and keep the flies away all the whiles I cools her. But that night I hears her crying, Massah already be in that ground with the big stone on his head what gots his name writ on it.

"Why you crying Mistress," I say to Missy that night. "You be missing Massah?"

"Master and Miz Caroline and now you and Mammy," she say.

"Why you send me and Mammy, you be missing us?" I say. She don't say no answer to me, but I thinks it 'cause she love Miz Caroline and wants Miz Caroline to be happy, cause Miz Caroline loves us, too. Mistress was the finest lady in the land. I tells you that and dat's a truth.

Now Massah Major Stowers fancied Miz Caroline and gives her 'bout everything she ask for. Even so, I'm not sure she feels 'bout him like that. She had this pretty beau run off with a girl what was her friend. Mammy say that's the one she wants and just settle for Massah Major 'cause he rich and she show her friend the good life she got herself now. If that be true, then that friend what stole Miz Caroline's beau be the cause of what happen next to all of us.

Miz Caroline marry Massah Major, and we goes along with her. Only Massah Major Stowers not take to Mammy's cooking. He gots his own cook, he tell Miz Caroline. The other Negroes tells us he even gots some chilluns with that cook. Soons after we gets there, Massah Major takes me and Mammy to Ellis and Livingston Auction Depot in that city in Georgia what be called Columbus, before we even staying on that plantation 'fore but a few months. He does it when Miz Caroline be visiting old Mistress. He do. Dat mean ole Massah say, "Git yore black asses in the wagon." And Mammy take my hand and we gits in the wagon like he say.

It's not too far to this Columbus place in Georgia. When Miz Caroline come back she asks the overseer where Major and Mammy and me is and he tells her 'cause she say she dismiss him if he don't. Miz Caroline tell him to drive her to that depot and be quick, too. But we was there way before that, and they's already gots Mammy stripped to be bid on and they's looking her over good. The speculator man what done the bidding oiled her skin. He run his hands with that oil all over her body and my Mammy be ashamed and tries to cover up her body have no clothes on it. Our real Massah Jordan never do that. But all that oil make Mammy glisten and she sure be pretty with all that oil on her and plenty men bids for Mammy. Higher and higher they bid for her. One man winned her off the block. That man what buys my Mammy pays a thousand them dollars be green for Mammy. And that's more den most pays, 'cepting for the big Negro bucks and they pays even two of them thousand green dollars for the ones be strong and can do all the wuk.

They was fixing to put me up next and they takes my clothes off to show my skin be good and my bones be strong. I calls for that Massah who buyed my Mammy to buys me too.

"Missah Massah," I yells to him. "Looks what a shiny strong body I gots. And I's wuks good, too!" He never looks back. Mammy's mouth moves for me to be a good chile and do what my Massah asks whoever my Massah ends up to be. And that man what buys Mammy puts her in this wagon he got hitched to the mules and he drives away.

"Mammy, Mammy!" I cries. Soon that wagon just a tiny spot before my eyes and 'fore long it not even that. It be gone. 'Bout that time here come Miz Caroline and the overseer man in the buggy coming up the road on the other side of that platform they got us on. Miz Caroline weeps when she find out Mammy gone and she asks Massah Major to please for him to let me come home with her. She be having a baby, she say, and needs me to help her. Major excited fore to hear about the baby. We ain't none of us heared about no baby before from Miz Caroline. He say whatever his darling wants his darling gets and that's how I comes to put my clothes back on and gets to goes home with Miz Caroline and Miz Caroline say Mammy be gone for good so best forgets about it. She do. She say dat. And dat's a truth.

• • •

They took me to the hospital in Mountain City. The sign out front said Carolwood County Hospital, but it was just a big house sitting on top of a steep embankment. It had a view of the Blue Ridge Mountains that was postcard pretty. Murphy said it was built by one of the richest families around these parts as a summer retreat. They called it Carolwood after their only daughter. Miss Carol left it to the county when she died. Willa Mae said the doctor who ran the hospital was a descendent of Miss Carol's and lived in a home built behind the original house with a passageway connecting the two. I can't remember his name because I was screaming too loud, but he said my baby was coming out backwards and that was the reason I was having so much trouble.

"Take her into delivery," he yelled, and the nurse and the orderly that came out to the truck to get me did just that.

That doctor was a magician. He pressed around on my stomach for a time and said, "There; baby's turned. Won't be long, now." At the time, those were the sweetest words I'd ever heard for my entire life.

"Good thing you had Willa Mae Satterfield with you, young lady," he said. "Best granny midwife we ever had. Been delivering babies in these mountains before I was born."

"And I delivers you when you born," Willa Mae said. "Don't forgets that." She edged close to the side of the table next to me.

"Wouldn't be here if you hadn't," the doctor said. The nurse placed each of my feet in the metal stirrups and belted them in place. She strung a sheet across my tummy. Willa Mae flexed my knees and pressed them gently wide apart.

"Brings your chin down your chest, child." she said. "And hunch your back and keeps it round as you can. Grabs hold your legs." She placed my fingers behind my knees.

"That's good! You do's that real good, child," she whispered. Willa Mae's face inched close to mine. Her hands were cool as well water, and her crooning was a balm laid on my suffering like a magic salve.

"Now hold tight and when you feels likes you gots to push, do it hard as you can. I'm gwine count to ten. Keeps pushing whole time I'm counting. This be over soon."

"Ohhhhhhhh, it hurts baaaaaaaaad," I said but tried my best to cooperate.

"Poor baby. Mercy Lord!" Willa Mae said, and her eyes rose to the ceiling. "Where your mercy?" I hung on to the backs of my knees and pushed like Willa Mae said to all the while she counted.

"That's real good," she said.

"Breathe deep through your mouth," the nurse said. "And stop fighting it. You're making it harder on yourself!"

"Leave this poor child be," Willa Mae said. She stared at the nurse, her eyes black and angry. "She be doing best she can!" The next pain reached up between my legs and sliced like a razor. My belly pushed down hard against it without any help from me. I was too weak to help it along. Willa Mae wrapped her arms about my shoulders.

"Just leans on me," she said, "and we just push hard as we can." The doctor was on a little stool at the end of the table.

"One more good push, young lady," he said.

"We doing it," Willa Mae said. I pressed against her, grabbed my knees, let out a scream to scare Geronimo, and pushed with all my might.

"Here's the head," the doctor said. "Hold it! Don't push! Pant! Pant!"

"Wheeeeeeew. Wheeeeeew. Wheeeeeew," I blew out my mouth.

"Here's the shoulder," the doctor said.

"Am I having the baby?" I yelled. "Am I?"

"Child, your baby be here!" Willa Mae said. "You gots a fine baby girl."

I pulled myself up on my elbows. The doctor and the nurse had the baby down between my legs, which were still strapped to the metal stirrups. I leaned forward far as I could to get a peek. They used a little rubber bulb and sucked at her nose. She let out a puny cry. Her skin was drenched in some kind of sticky flour, but beneath it, her skin was gray-blue. The doctor whisked her away.

"Oh, let me see her!"

"She's having trouble breathing," the nurse said. "You can see her later, if she makes it." She pressed hard on my belly with her fist.

"Aaaaaaaaaaaaaahhhhhhh," I sure wasn't expecting that, and it hurt bad.

"What'd you do that for?" I said. "I just had a baby from there!"

"We got to get the afterbirth out." She kneaded my belly like she was punching down bread dough. "Don't give me any trouble now," she said crossly, and Willa Mae was no longer there to comfort me. She'd gone to get Verna and Buck.

"I want to see the baby," I said.

"Don't get your hopes up. That way, you won't be disappointed," she said and wheeled me to a little room down the hall and gave me some orange juice. Thankfully, she left me alone for a spell. When she came back, she said the baby weighed just over five pounds and her lungs weren't fully developed.

"Be better you don't see her," she said. "She probably won't make it." I started to cry.

"Sometimes it's for the best," she said and rolled down the headboard and turned off the light.

"You've got plenty of years to have babies when you're older and can handle it." She showed me the call button and left me be. When the shift changed, I snuck out of the room and found the nursery where they kept the babies, but my baby wasn't there! I started to panic and wandered down another corridor. I found her there. She was in a little room all by herself. She was the sweetest thing, like one of Mama's little pickled cherries! Her skin was no longer blue; it was a soft pink, but it was still a bit wrinkled. They had her in a special bed with round holes cut through the sides. I reached through one of the openings. Her fingers magically curled around mine.

"Mama's here, baby. Don't be scared," I whispered. "It won't ever be for the best if you don't stay with us, no matter what that nasty old nurse says." The baby's eyes were closed, but she stretched her little legs and arms all the while I talked to her.

"If she comes in tomorrow, just don't listen to her, okay?"

"Listen to who?" Another nurse was at the door to the nursery. "You're not supposed to be in here. The incubator units are off limits," she said.

"I just wanted to see my baby. Make sure she's all right," I said.

"You need to get back in your bed. We'll let you know if her condition changes."

"Grace," I said.

"I beg your pardon?"

"Her name. It's Grace," I said. "Grace Annie."

"Go on back to your room. We'll let you know if Grace Annie—"

"Just Grace," I said. "The Annie part's silent."

"All right . . . just Grace," she said. "I'll put that right here on this little placard over her bed. Okay?" I leaned around to see the card she pointed to. It was white and had a pink angel etched on the front that was holding a banner with a long blank line.

"Now, off your feet and back to your bed." She pointed to a room down the hall. It wasn't even the right one.

I stood my ground and stared at Grace through her see-through bed. I didn't want to leave her. I shouldn't have to. She'd been with me all these months. She needed me now more than ever. Didn't these hospital folks know that? Didn't they realize a mama should sit next to her little baby at a time like this? Stay by her side and hum every lullaby she ever learned? And if that baby lived, she'd remember deep down in her baby soul that her mama loved her right from the start. And if she died, she'd know her mama never *ever* wanted her to, and knowing that might be enough to help her hang on, so she wouldn't.

I didn't budge. The nurse cocked her head sideways and slowly folded her arms across her chest. She twisted her lips out of shape, lowered her chin, and fired her eyes at me like darts. I narrowed mine, pursed my lips, and returned the same, but I could feel the tears coming. I swallowed hard and took a deep breath.

"I'm a grown-up," I said. "So I'll be back," I added and marched to my room. I made it as far as the edge of the bed they'd assigned me before I broke down. I knew what was best for my baby! These people—all that schooling—and they didn't know anything! Grace needed me as much as she needed that incubator. And I needed all the prayers I could muster. I dropped to my knees.

Pleasegodpleasegodpleasegodpleasegod . . .

chapter ten

THE FOLKS AT THE HOSPITAL were wrong about Grace; her lungs were fine. But they scared me bad. I was a nervous wreck the whole time I stayed in Carolwood. Buck came by with Verna, soon as Willa Mae let them know what had happened.

"You give us a terrible fright, Adie," Verna said. "What's the matter with you, anyway?"

"I'm real sorry—"

"I went down to the grocers myself when you didn't come home. Elmer was working the cash register. Said he hadn't seen you, but Miz Bailey was the one to ask since he just got there. By then, she was on her way to visit her sister in Chattanooga and—"

"Did you see the baby?" I burst out. I thought if I heard that whiny voice one second longer I was gonna kill her.

"They got her in that contraption," Verna said. "Couldn't see too good."

"We looked through the glass," Buck said. "Why they got her in that thing anyway?"

"She's a bit small, is all. The doctor thinks her lungs need help—"

"We ain't lost a Jenkins baby since—" Buck said.

"Be just like you to start something," Verna said, glaring at me. I swallowed a hurtful lump in my throat and looked up at Buck.

"Ma, you got no business talking to her like that—"

"It's the truth," Verna said.

"You forgit you lost a ba—" Verna's face went white again, and she grabbed hold of the edge of my bed. Buck took her by the arm and set her down in the chair next to it.

"I'm sorry, Ma," he said. "I got a big mouth. But ever since Pa took off you been meaner than a dog with rabies, and you . . . you . . . well . . you ain't gonna take it out on Adie." I think I loved Buck more at that moment than God loved *us*. Buck patted Verna's shoulder.

"You heard Willa Mae. She ain't seen a harder birthing since she delivered them twins ol' lady Markus had herself." Buck swung his arm around my shoulder and plumped up my pillow.

"You been through enough, puddin'," he said. "Ain't no one gonna pick on you. That right, Ma?"

Verna gave a slight nod. She wrapped her arms around her waist and rocked back and forth. Her cheeks were flushed. She was having trouble keeping her lips steady. She sat quietly, her face blank, her eyes glassy. She rubbed her oversized knuckles and continued to rock herself in the straight back chair. Whatever it was Buck had started to say, the mere mention of it had turned Verna to jelly. Maybe she couldn't help it she was sour as vinegar. Mama said some folks were fine so long as the sailing was good, but give 'em a storm and they sunk like a sack of bones weighed down with concrete.

"You can't direct the wind, Adie," she said. "But you can always adjust your sails." Maybe Verna didn't know as much about sailing as Mama did, and she was lost on a sea of sorrow.

"Miz Jenkins, you are gonna *love* this baby," I said. "She is so sweet. Just think. You're a gramma now!" I smiled at her. She didn't smile back. She did something better. She stopped rocking and got out of the chair. She leaned over and smoothed the sheets and blankets around me and patted them into place. One of the nurses, the only nice one I'd met, peeked in the door and told them they had to leave.

"She needs her rest." She was right. I was pretty tired. Verna and Buck headed for the door.

"We'll be back, tonight, Adie," Verna said. She grabbed her hand-bag to leave.

"Buck?" I said. He looked up, but didn't say anything. Verna walked out into the hallway.

"Willa Mae said no one could find you . . . to tell you . . . about the baby . . . she said no one knew where you went—" Buck looked down at his boots. "Where were you, anyway?"

"I was . . . ahh . . . ahh—"

"And Mr. Fletcher told Willa Mae you and Imelda Jane never come back to work the store after lunch—"

"We had some . . . some supplies to pick up . . . is all . . . he . . . he probably forgot." Buck's eyes were looking at everything but me.

"We got a baby now, Buck."

"I know that."

"Did you tell Imelda Jane?"

"I ain't said nothing yet, but I'm going over to get her . . . I mean her and me's doing inventory tonight so . . ." Buck was chewing on his lower lip. He reached out his hand and touched my cheek.

"I gotta go—"

"Buck," I whispered his name like a prayer. "You got a whole lot of responsibilities to pay attention to now."

"I'm doing the best I can, Adie." He twisted his lips and scrunched his brows together like he didn't know what else he could say. When I blinked at my tears he was gone.

• • •

Me and Grace got to leave the hospital that next week and went home to our new cabin. Murphy and Buck had it all ready. The septic tank was connected, and the rotten boards on the front porch and the broken handrails had been replaced. Mama and Clarissa drove over from Cold Rock, and Rebecca came along and brought her boys. They scoured and cleaned the cabin and scrubbed all the windows. When they finished that, they cooked up enough food to last until Christmas. They brought along so many packages for me and Grace I thought it was.

Riley Jr., Clayton, and Girard, Rebecca's boys, fought over who could hold Grace next. They took too many turns. Mama got nervous and put a stop to it.

"You want to play pass the potato, I'll heat one up for y'all in the oven," she said. "Now, go on outside and sweep that yard up."

Pa was at work, so he didn't come, but then I don't know if he would have made the trip even if he could have. He hadn't answered any of my letters that I'd written special just to him, and I hadn't seen him since that day eight months ago when he told me to leave. But Mama was mostly back to being her old self. Leave it to a new baby to heal old wounds.

"I bought you some lemon curd, Adie!" Mama announced. How I loved lemon curd. She remembered! Mama only made it on special occasions since it was troublesome to make and didn't keep long.

"Eat it up quick."

"Don't worry about that. It'll be gone by tomorrow." I gave her a hug. "Pass this on to Pa, okay?"

"I'll try, but his head's thick as concrete," she said. "If he jumped in the river, he'd be a goner."

I put Grace to bed when they left and climbed in myself. She'd gained a pound and a half already and was crying and carrying on when she was hungry and wet, just like a regular-size baby. But since she was so small for her age, I had to feed her every two to three hours. It was pretty much wearing me out. It wasn't a problem in the daytime, but I was afraid I wouldn't hear her in the night and she'd starve to death by morning. But her cries woke me just like Willa Mae said they would. I sat straight up in bed the first night the moment I heard her. It was sticky and hot. The bed linens, the only ones we had us so far, were twisted and pulled loose at the bottom. I reached around to fix them as best I could in the darkness. My side was damp with sour milk and sweat. Buck's was empty and dry. My hands found his pillow. I leaned in and sniffed the hollow where his head should have been and inhaled what was left of him for the night. I loved Buck's smell. There was something about his body odors. Even when he didn't smell sweet, his scent made my knees quiver and my heart jump. Grace let out a tiny wail. My breasts, both of them, turned on like twin faucets. Milk came dribbling down the front of my night-shirt. I unbuttoned it and tried to recall which one I fed her from last. Willa Mae said to take turns with them. They were swollen and plenty sore. And I had big knots under my arms. They started form-ing before I even left the hospital.

"Oh honey, you're engorged," the nurse I liked said. "It'll settle back down once your body figures out how much milk you'll be need-ing to keep your baby happy."

"How's it do that?" I asked.

"Nature takes care of it," she said. "It's all based on how much your baby eats. Takes a while, is all."

"How long is that?"

"Is what?"

"A *while*?"

"In your case, I'm not sure. I ain't had no seventeen-year-old mama nursing a little baby before," she said. "In the meantime, just make sure you alternate which breast you put her on. And put some warm packs under your arms."

"Willa Mae already told me that," I said. "But I'm having trouble keeping track."

"Here." She handed me an oversized safety pin. "Put this pin on your nightie on the side you feed her from. Then when you finish, transfer it to the other side and that's the one you use next time." I was sitting in an upright position in the hospital bed that made itself into an "S" shape if you wanted it to. Grace was laid out on a pillow cross my tummy. I took the pin from the nurse and hooked it to my nightshirt above where Grace was feeding.

"You need to get yourself one of them good nursing brassieres with extra support," she said.

"Oh, I will, soon as we get some extra money," I told her. Which meant by the time Grace was ready for grade school I'd get one, the ways things were going. For all the hours Buck spent at Fletcher's store, his pay sure was small. Now that we had our own place, there was lots of extras to pay on I hadn't thought about, like electricity and water. We needed to get a telephone, too, what with the baby.

I found the breast with the pin. Good thing it was there to remind me. I was still feeding Grace around the clock, and it had me plenty confused.

She fussed again. I switched on the one small light we had in the room. Grace's mouth, shaped like a sweet, little heart, rooted around till she found skin and she started to suck. But it was her little fist that she'd stumbled upon. She wrinkled her face up and let out a good cry when it didn't bring what she needed and wanted.

"Here, baby," I said and picked her up. She smelled of Johnson's baby oil and talcum powder. She curled her arms and legs into a ball, like she was still tucked inside me. I loved seeing her do that, like she was telling me she favored that soft warm spot she came from, where I grew her and kept her safe. Her head, still covered in dark fuzz, was shaped nice like Buck's. She rested in the crook of my arm, her lips smacking and searching. I loved watching her do that, too.

"Sweet baby, sweet baby," I crooned singsong to her and helped her latch onto the nipple. She clamped down hard and sucked like her life depended on it. When I realized it did, I laughed out loud, relieved by the fact that her will to survive was God-given and fierce and she knew it and took it serious. Ten days old our baby girl was, and she knew all that.

I rocked Grace and nursed her, looking at the bare walls of the shabby room that held us, knowing what was important was in my arms. It didn't much matter what wasn't on the walls. Of course, what wasn't in the bed did. The thought of Buck curled up asleep next to Imelda Jane somewhere made me gasp. I drank in the air, my mouth open wide, swallowing hard like Grace. Traces of Buck, still hanging about, rammed themselves like a fist down my throat. He'd sneak back in the morning, thinking I was none the wiser. And I'd let him. I'd have to; I loved him. Besides, Grace and I didn't have any other place to go to, even if I didn't.

Come dawn, I heard his boots creaking across the floorboards. Grace was stirring again for a feeding, but I pretended not to hear till he was in bed making snoring sounds, which was a pretty dumb thing for him to do, because he didn't snore to begin with. Buck had plenty of bad habits, but that wasn't one of them. He rolled over and let out a snort. I would have laughed, it was so silly, but my body still hurt from the birthing cuts where my stitches hadn't healed, my breasts were filling up tight again with milk, and now my heart ached, too. I crept out of bed, pretending like I was trying not to wake him. By then Grace was howling.

"Dang, she's got herself a pair of lungs!" Buck sat up and called out. "How'm I supposed to sleep 'round here?" He pulled the covers back over his head and burrowed under them.

You might could try staying in your own bed at night, for starters.

chapter eleven

"GRACE ANNIE JENKINS, I BAPTIZE thee in the name of the Father and the Son and the Holy Spirit. Amen." Pastor Gibson Crawford poured the water over Grace's head. She wrinkled her brow and drew her legs up in a ball under the christening dress Verna made her, but she never did cry. Verna decided after the service that Grace was to be called *Grace Annie*. "It's more fitting, Adie," she said, giving me a stern look. "You call her *Grace* and folks will think she's a Yankee."

There was a potluck social after the service. I brought along a jar of Mama's chunky homemade catsup. Folks in Calhoun couldn't get enough of it. They always bought every jar she made each year, but she saved me one.

The church social today wasn't in honor of the baptism or anything. It'd been planned all along as a welcoming for Reverend Gibson.

"Y'all can call me Pastor Gib," he said. He'd been transferred over from this church in Decatur. We all got in line to meet him and his family before we set about to eat.

"This is my wife, Edwina, and my daughter Margaret Mary," Pastor Gib said when each of us inched our way to the front. I liked Margaret Mary right off. She was older than me, but I couldn't tell by how much. She had the eyes of a woman but a real lean figure like a tomboy. When she walked you had to run to keep up. She pranced like a new colt, her brown hair shiny and sleek. It was near-perfect, tied up in a ponytail. Margaret Mary's eyes were the same color brown as mine, but I noticed hers sparkled when she laughed. She got a plate of food from the table and came over and sat next to me under the oak tree. I had Grace Annie with me, of course. I didn't go anywhere without her. She was sound asleep, tucked in a basket propped in Buck's old wagon. I rested next to her on a blanket I got from the Army-Navy Store and leaned against the oak tree. Its trunk was as wide as a trailer.

"You mind if I set with you?" she said.

"Be right nice," I said and smoothed a spot on the blanket for her. The day was near perfect, the sun full out, but not burning hot. The lilacs and azaleas were in full of bloom.

"Yelling for us to take notice," Margaret Mary said as we admired them.

"You glad to be here?" I said.

"It doesn't pay to like a place too much," she said. "We move around a lot."

"I didn't know preachers moved around," I said. "My mama dragged us from church to church trying to find one that suited her."

"Sounds like my pa," she said. "Where you from?"

"Cold Rock."

"We've never been there, but pretty much every place else," she said. "Pa always manages to mess up—! There I go. Hanging out the dirty laundry. Mama would have my hide."

I smiled and just pretended I didn't hear correct.

"You got a sweet baby," she said. "You must be real proud of her."

"She's real good," I said. "Mostly she just sleeps and eats."

"She's so tiny," she said. "How old is she?"

"Three weeks tomorrow. She was real small to begin with. And they thought her lungs weren't developed good, but they were wrong. She weighs six pounds now," I said, proudly.

Margaret Mary smiled. "Can I hold her?"

"Sure." I reached in the wagon and picked Grace Annie up out of her basket and placed her in Margaret Mary's arms. She rocked her gently then settled her back against the tree and rested there with her.

"Which one's your husband?"

"That's him over there," I said, pointing to the food tables where Buck was filling up his plate. Imelda Jane came up behind him and grabbed a biscuit off of it. He reached for it back, and she run off laughing, her black hair flouncing in the wind. Margaret Mary's eyes watched her movements before they looked back at mine. We carried on a conversation, even though our lips never moved. I cleared my throat and looked away, hoping one of us would say something.

"Who's that tall fella fetching the stick at the dog?" she said.

"Oh, that's Murphy," I said. "Murphy Spencer." I watched her watch him. I knew a look like that—the same kind I gave Buck first time I seen him.

"You want to meet him?"

"Do pigs still stink?" she said.

"Well, come on then," I said and took the baby from her arms. Grace Annie stretched her arms and legs but never did wake up. We walked on over towards Murphy.

"Murphy!" I called out. He was about to toss a stick back to Worry and spun around in our direction. The stick went flying at us instead of Worry. Margaret Mary caught it in midair and brought it back to him.

"That's quite a catch, ma'am," Murphy said.

"I've played my share of church softball," she said. "I'm a pretty good outfielder, matter of fact."

"This is Margaret Mary, Pastor Gib's daughter, Murphy," I said. Murphy reached over and shook her hand.

"Pleased to meet you. I didn't hurt you, did I?" he said.

"Not yet," Margaret Mary said. She drew the words slowly out of her mouth and stared Murphy in the eyes the whole time she spoke them. She glanced away for a second, and when she looked back she smiled at him with her mouth closed and her head lowered, but she kept her eyes held up toward his. Murphy flushed. She grinned. She had real pretty teeth. I wondered if Murphy noticed she had such pretty teeth. Margaret Mary turned and tossed the stick to Worry. The dog caught it before it hit the ground and fetched it back to Murphy. Murphy tossed it back to Margaret Mary. She took hold of the stick.

"Here, boy," she called out. Grace Annie started to fuss. She was hungry. I took her back to the car to nurse her then went back to the blanket I'd spread out under the tree and put her back in her basket.

I watched Murphy and Margaret Mary run circles with Worry. They looked right fine together. She was a lucky girl having a daddy come to Hog Gap to preach. I looked around to see what happened to Buck. He wasn't anywhere in sight. Neither was Imelda Jane for that matter. It was just me and the church women, who were busy ogling Grace. Later I noticed Murphy and Margaret Mary walk off toward the creek. After that, I didn't see hide nor hair of either one of them till it was time to head home. Buck came sauntering out of the woods by himself. Two minutes later Imelda Jane came through the same spot and headed off in the other direction toward her folks.

"Adie," Margaret Mary called out. "Wait up," she said and came over to our car. Buck put the wagon in the trunk. I got in the front seat with Grace Annie on my lap.

"Murphy says you live right next to his place. Thought I might come by to see you."

"That'd be right nice. I don't get much company. Only Willa Mae." We drove off. I asked Buck where he was all day.

"Just walking along the river bank," he said.

"Same river bank Imelda Jane went walking on?"

"It's a free river bank, Adie," he answered as he hit the accelerator.

Willa Mae was waiting on us when we got home. She took Grace Annie from my arms and tucked her into her cradle. I told Buck he best fix his own supper; I wasn't feeling well. Actually, I was thinking about the time this woman from Macon poisoned all her husbands, wondering why I'd had such a hard time understanding how a body could do something like that. It made perfect sense to me now. I asked Willa Mae if she'd read to me.

"Help soothe my nerves," I said. "I'm so mad at Buck, I just wanna put a pillow over his head till he croaks."

"Poor chile," Willa Mae crooned and took out Tempe's journal.

•   •   •

Miz Caroline don't have no baby be growing like she say she do and Massah Major be pretty mad 'bouts dat, and sends me out to the cabins instead of living in the big house with the house servants like I always done my tire life. I begs Miz Caroline to lets me stay in the big house, but she say be glad Massah not be selling me to the speculator man what coming soon and she see what she can do later cause he still crazy mad over there be no baby coming.

The cabins where they puts me, they was shotgun houses and they has three rooms built one in front of the other just like the barrel on the shotgun and dat's why they calls them dat. The chilluns is put in the back part to sleep and the ones be grown or nearly so, in the front one. In the middle was a big fireplace what was built from stone where the cooking be done. This be called the kitchen part. It don't have no floor, just dirt, but we sweep it like it do, when we told to. The beds be strung from the walls. They is hung from poles hooked into the walls and they's planks laid cross them poles. And we has ticking mattresses filled with the corn shucks. It don't make for no good mattress and dat's a truth. But that's where we sleeps. I meets a color gal be older than me. She be Liza. Her skin be yeller, too, like me. We work the fields every day 'til Saturday noon and then we rest a bit. Liza's Mammy be Massah's cook and she say Massah be her real daddy, but he not treat her no different.

That next year Miz Caroline have herself a baby for truth. A boy chile, Henry. And Massah Major carry that chile all around the cabins and makes us call him young Massah. 'Magine that. He a baby and Massah Major say, "He is your Massah now, too, and y'all calls him that. 'Hear?" I never do gets to go back to being a house Negro. Liza say that's too bad.

"Massah comes out here at night and lie down with all the colored gals is in the front room," she say.

"Oh, I's in the back room," I tells her.

"You won't be fore long," she say. "When he see's you be's a woman, he gwine move you to the front where we all is."

"I ain't no womans," I say.

"You best tell your body parts," she say, "They's pretending to be's and they's doing good at it."

That puts a fright on me and I tells Liza I be's sure not to cause no troubles and works hard to looks like I not be's a woman. "I ties deze lumps on my chest down good with some deze rags," I say.

"That not works for long," Liza say. "Dem lumps gonna grows to be mountains and Massah be watching. He tries all the color gals, sooner den later. He sleeps with me and I be's his own blood."

"That ol' Massah Major, what be your pappy, sleeps with you, Liza?" I say.

"Plenty times. My baby Martin be his. That's why he slow in the head. Too much blood from the same vein, Mammy say."

"When I moves to the front room to sleep, I best run and hide," I say. "I don't want no baby be slow in the head!"

"Where you hide?" Liza say. "He find you sure. Beat you good and sleep with you, he want." I be maybe not yet thirteen, but close to it. Massah Major like the older girls was shaped like women. After he sleeps with them pretty colored gals, then he marries 'em to the man he want for each one to marry. He match them up to make good, strong chillun. Massah Major tells Liza to go with Calvin fore to be married. No preacher come though. They just step backward over the broom they puts crosswise in the doorway, and Massah say, "You're married. Be sure and make your Massah lots of children." And the peoples he marry do, too. They do's whatever Massah say, 'cause they be's scared of him.

'Cepting for one gal, her name be Nicey, she say she not marry Big Jake when Massah tell her to jump backward over the broom. Massah tell her three times to jump over that broom and Nicey say, "I ain't jump the broom with that Big Jake. His face be's ugly!" Massah Major pull the dress Nicey be wearing clean off her back. Then he puts her in a buck to whup her. This be how he do that. He makes fore her to squat and then he takes a cowhide strap and ties her hands together in front of her knees and when he do's that her elbows be stuck out. He use this other cowhide strap and ties her ankles together real tight. Then he slide the handle of the broom he told Nicey to jumps backward over. He slides that broom in front of her elbows and in back of her knees, so now she be hobbled over like a chicken in a barnyard. Nicey flopping all about trying to get away from Massah. She know a bad whupping be coming when you put in a buck. This is the way the whipping be done. He makes for us to watch good or we be next. First Massah beat Nicey's back with a cat-o-nine tails what bring the blisters. The cat-o-nine tails be strips of leather wound around a stick. The strips is braided past the handle and the ends all be tied in knots. And they spreads all out when Massah snaps it. This be the "cracker" and that's what splits the skin and makes fore the blisters. Some calls it a bull-whip. When Massah gots all the blisters he be's happy with, then he breaks them blisters with a leather strap. Then he pours the salt on all them cuts, and somes them cuts slit clear to the bone, they is. When he do that, Nicey wiggle just like a worm on the ground, she do. Nicey got no place to run to, hobbled there like a chicken, all trussed up. Massah beat on her while she beg him to stop, and he keep pouring that salt on.

"Pray, Massah," she say. "Mercy, Massah." Massah say for us to keep watch this. He catch our eyes closed he say, we next. When Nicey too weak to ask for mercy no more, Massah cuts her loose, but she don't move. We goes to help her, but Massah say, "Let her be! And let this be a lesson to y'all. When I say jump the broom, you jump the broom!"

"Yes, Massah," we yells to him. Nicey jump the broom with Big Jake next time Massah tell her to and later she laughs on it, 'cause Jake be a good man to her and she like him fine and they have many strong babies. He just don't look like he be fine, 'cause Big Jake face be real ugly. But after they jump the broom she see his heart and it look good and he be real fine to her and Nicey mostly be real happy, and don't take no more whuppings from Massah. She say, "Yes, Massah," when he tells her, "Do this. Do that." And she do.

When Miz Caroline find out Massah Major be whupping on the Negroes she raise a big fuss with the Massah. We'un's in the cabins can hear her, even. Mostly after that, Massah Major treats the folks better. One of the house gals goes with Miz Caroline to visit the plantation be Massah Major's brother. The story go, the woman Massah's brother be married to has all the house servants wearing clothes made from hemp, be real scratchy. Miz Caroline at dinner tells the man be her brother-in-law he should be ashamed of himself putting his Negroes in such rags. His face be red and the next day he tells his wife she is to get the cloth won't bruise the skin and be quick. She do's dat and spend time sewing the dresses while Miz Caroline be there to help. But she never like Miz Caroline much no more. She tells her husband not to 'vite them again. But he do anyway. Miz Caroline say she not going, but she always send that same house gal along with Massah Major and she asks her questions when they comes back, to be sure the Negroes there is not wearing the scratchy cloth no more.

And Miz Caroline tells Massah Major be sures to make good matches for us to marry so we be happy and have good many babies. I sure be glad about that, 'cause come the end of that year, Massah Major say for me to jump the broom. Massah have one the Negro mens with him, and he say, "This buck will be your husband by week's end." He do. Dat's what Massah Major say. I be's thirteen best I know.

• • •

Margaret Mary came by every few days to visit. She'd stay just long enough to be polite and then head next door to see Murphy.

"Come back soon," I told her, "and don't rush off!" But she always did. Even so, I looked forward to seeing her. I hadn't had a good friend since my time in high school back in Cold Rock, and with Buck being gone so much I got a bit lonely. And, of course, I missed Mama something awful. Missed Pa now and then, too, even though he was mostly real hard to get along with and had been ever since Annie died and he started to drink too much. I wrote Mama every week. Sent her a picture of the baby that Verna took.

I was grateful I had Willa Mae. She came by every day, and a good thing, too. I learned more about babies from her than you could read in a book. She taught me how to care for the umbilical spot on Grace that used to be hooked onto me. I took little cotton tips dipped in baby oil and loosened up the edges each time I changed her diaper, and soon it fell off, just like she said it would. I had a lot of questions for her. Some had nothing to do with babies and were just the nosy kind. Things I wanted to know about her. But she didn't talk about herself, so I jumped in and asked.

"You got any children, Willa Mae?"

"Had me chilluns, once," she said.

"Well—"

"Dey's gone," she said.

"Where'd they go?"

"Ta' glory,"

"You mean—"

"Dey's only one kind a' glory, chile," she said.

"My sister Annie . . . died," I said. "She . . . she was . . . three years old. She drowned in Cold Rock River."

Willa Mae jerked to attention so fast I thought her head might snap off her neck.

"A sorrowful thing when the little ones dies," she said, her eyes full of tears and distant as the top of Cold Rock Mountain.

"I was there . . . when she died . . . and . . . and . . . my pa . . . he . . . he—" I stopped myelf. Willa Mae dabbed at her eyes. They were vacant, liked nobody lived there anymore.

"Willa Mae? You okay?"

She waddled over to the window, Grace Annie tucked in her arms, and settled into the rocker. "I be's fine. Just needs me a little dis fresh air."

There were holes in the screen. The only things coming in were the flies. I reached for the swatter in case one got too close to Grace.

"Were your children . . . little . . . like Annie?" I knew I shouldn't be so nosy, but it was a problem for me not to be. Mama said it was a major character defect and I best work on it. Maybe I would, starting tomorrow. Right now it was just getting interesting.

"Dey was babies," Willa Mae whispered.

"Ohhhh—" I said. "I'm sorry. How'd . . . how'd they . . . die?" I asked softly, looking at Grace curled up fast asleep in Willa Mae's lap. She stroked the baby's forehead like her fingers were feathers.

"Dey drowns in dat same river. I don't likes to thinks on it." She placed Grace in her cradle.

"I'm sorry—I—I don't much like to think on . . . Annie . . . neither," I said, seeing the pain in her eyes and regretting the fact my prying put it there.

Willa Mae sat back down and stared out the window. Her face glistened with tears. I picked up one of Grace's clean didies and patted her face like it would break if I rubbed too hard.

"Sweet chile," she whispered and pulled the cloth from my hands. I took the journal out of her satchel and placed it in her lap, pointing to the spot where she left off. I curled up on the floor and leaned my head against the side of her lap. She smelled of Ivory soap and baby powder and lavender. Listening to her read was better than going to the picture show. Her voice was soft and smooth as Mama's prized linens.

• • •

Massah Major be pretty good matchmaker, 'cause who do you think he tell me to jump the broom with? Grady Stowers. He be's the best one to jump the broom with and that's a truth. All the black folks I ever knowed always take their Massah's name for their surname. That why Grady be Grady Stowers, after hiz Massah. And I be Tempe Jordan after my old Massah.

Grady be 'bout six feet tall with a nice face I likes more than I likes mine, even though peoples tell me I am the prettiest yeller gal in these parts and long ago my old missy, Mistress Jordan, say I could fool some folks I be white. But I'm not, she say, and don't ever do that. It makes for all kinds of trouble, she say.

Most the time Grady be real happy, even though ain't much to be happy 'bout. When people ask, "Why you always be happy, Grady?" he say, " 'Cause I's thinking 'bout the time I will be." Grady say some day we's all be free as the white folks. He say his mama saw it in a dream was a revelation. Grady pretty much believed it, but nobody much else did.

When Massah say it's time for us to jump the brooms, Miz Caroline makes for us a special wedding up on the front porch. She decorates that porch with flowers just like a garden, and Massah mix the shine for us to drink. Land sakes Grady drinks too much that stuff. When it comes time for us to jump backwards over the broom, that be no problem for me, but Grady trips over his feet. His toes longer than the pickles we makes and puts in the big barrels. He near breaks his neck. Miz Caroline say, "You're in trouble now, Grady Stowers. I declare. Mark my words. You're in trouble for sure." Miz Caroline tell that because the story goes whoever jumps the broom first be the boss of the marriage. And Massah say, "Grady, fore long you be afraid to open your mouth Tempe not say to." Massah laughs and has hisself a good time and drinks plenty more that shine, too.

There be three stories I always likes to tell about Grady. The fust is when we'uns that live in our cabin don't get enough to eat. Grady takes to fishing when Massah Major tells him to and catches plenty fish for Massah. But for every fish he catches he saves the next one for us and we cooks them fishes up at night when it be real late. Cooks them right over the outside fire but we gots to burn rags to cover the smell.

And Grady hides potatoes from the field in the woods and later gets them when Massah sure asleep and we puts them in the ash to bakes. There's no better eating food on God's earth than potatoes cooked in the ash and dat's a truth. When Massah catch Grady hiding the potatoes in the woods he beats him and when he finds the fish Grady not give him when he gives him the others he chains him to the cabin outside at night till the fishing not be so good no more. Soons as Massah thinks Grady be learning his lesson he stop doing that, Massah do. But Grady go right back to hiding the fish and taking the potatoes for to put in the ash. And that be after he got plenty scars on his back from the cracker on that bullwhip, too.

Grady say, "So long as he don't beat me dead we will haves us fish to cook and plenty potatoes in the ash." And many nights Grady steals one Massah Majors chickens for we gals to cook the next morning whilst we do's our chores and gits ready to go to the field. Massah Major gives us a bit of chicken when he pass out the other meat and the beans and flour and taters and such, but it neber be near enough for all the hard work we do. Guess he thinks it is, but it ain't. So Grady be out to git as many them chickens he kin. He steal so many them chickens when they sees his black face coming they runs for the hen house!

The second story is 'bout the patterollers what patrols in the night looking for the Negroes have no pass to be off the plantations. They whips them when they finds them and puts the dogs on 'em, too. The dogs kin eat the skin from the bones and they does. They is the hungriest dogs I ever knowed of. One woman belonged to Marse Hawkins, the next plantation over. She runned away when Marse Hawkins's wife takes her baby what looked like Marse Hawkins and gives it to the speculators for to sell. The patterollers cotched up to her that night she run off and they sets the dogs on her and they eats the breasts right off her where her milk be still coming in.

The story about Grady and the patterollers go like this: One Negro man belong to Massah Major, he be fancying a gal belong to Marse Hawkins, that same Massah that owns the colored gal what got her breasts eat off. When the corn husking go on in the fall he see her all during that time 'cause the plantations git together and gets the wuk done faster. But when it over, he be missing that gal and he asks Massah Major for a pass for to go see her and Massah Major say they be plenty colored gals for to pick from on his plantation and tells him no he can't have the pass. So this man be unhappy and goes to see the pretty gal he be missing on Marse Hawkins plantations plenty times anyway and he not have a pass for to do that with. One night when he be gone and the time is right for him to be back we hear the dogs what be 'cross the fence, not fifty feet away. The moon is high and we see the dogs closing in on him. His name be Samuel and he growed up on Massah Major plantation with Grady. Could be brothers, might not be though. Neither one knows who their daddy be. Grady see that the dogs soon to be on Samuel and he be running too long to have much strength left. Grady jumps himself over that fence and takes a club and beats at them dogs till Samuel get over the fence and back to the cabin. Grady makes it back, too, before the patterollers cotched up to the dogs. Grady be bleeding and be bit up pretty bad from the dogs, but the dogs not be in too good shape neither and they be whining to their masters, the patterollers, when they catch up to them. But the patterollers beats the dogs worse for not cotching who they send them after.

The last story I likes best about Grady is when he plays a tricks on Massah Major. When the corn shucking time comes it last mostly for many days, and Massah Major gives the pickers plenty likker late in the night after the food be et and the music be played. Massah Major drinks plenty shine too, and goes to sleep sitting in his chair got the armrests by the fire watching the shuckers. Grady ties Massahs laces together in the shoes Massah be wearing. For a time comes when the shucking be mostly done for that night and Massah wakes up and he be fixing to go back to the big house and when he try do that he fall on his face almost in that fire. Grady rush over to the fire and save Massah from falling on the flames and Massah say, "You saved me boy. You saved old Massah." And Grady say, "Yes'm Massah, I saves you. I do. I saves you good!" Land sakes we laughs on that when Massah go off to bed. He never do wonder how his shoes tied like that. Guess he thinks he so taken with the likker he do that hisself. So Massah don't git Grady dat time. But den later Grady gits in powerful trouble and Massah git him good.

Lordy, Lordy, ain't nobody never forgets what ol' Massah do to Grady. I don't likes to thinks on it. Hurts real bad in my heart when I members it. All deze years later it still hurt my heart like it be's happening yesterday.

chapter twelve

I SPENT MONTHS WORRYING ABOUT Buck off dallying with Imelda Jane and feeling sorry for myself because of it. Mama always said if you're going to sit and stew, stew something you can eat while you're at it. I took out her recipe and made up a batch of stewed tomatoes. They didn't turn out too good. I added too much salt and not enough sugar. And I didn't know how to use the pressure cooker. They exploded and made a real mess. While I cleaned it up, I got to thinking that having a husband who didn't keep his boots where they belonged was hardly a bother compared to Tempe's troubles. Besides, there were more important matters to concern myself with than Buck's choices—like our future, for instance. I made a plan. I was going to be the best wife and mother possible. Maybe my example would coax Buck to follow suit. However, some not-so-blessed events got in the way. To begin with, it didn't appear that Buck had any regard for the future. He mostly lived for the moment at hand. And he was happy flying by the seat of someone else's pants, Imelda Jane's to be exact. I soon realized if he wasn't going to work hard to better our lives, then it was, plain as pie, up to me. But what could I do?

I thought about it for days with no answer in sight. It started to depress me. Mama said it couldn't be post-partum from having Grace Annie. She was six months old. I told her it was post-*partner* from having Buck.

I went outside to tackle the garbage that was scattered out behind the cabin. Buck promised me he'd see to it, but he hadn't. What a mess. Soggy, empty spools of toilet paper—swollen twice their normal size—rested on the ground alongside broken beer bottles, worn-out tires, a handful of rusty coat hangers, and cords of twine. Cereal and detergent boxes with nothing inside but slugs and mouse droppings were scattered close by. I raked the entire mess into one heap, counting on Murphy to help me haul it off to the dump. Standing back to admire my hard work, I realized the three old sheds out there looked to be in pretty good shape. They were much too big to be outhouses, but by the smell you wouldn't have known it. They were each about fifty feet long and a good twelve feet wide, all lined up in a row. The boards were weathered gray, but the wood didn't budge when I kicked at it and the roofs were intact. That's when it hit me, the answer to my problems.

Willa Mae was inside taking care of Grace Annie while I tended to the yard. There wasn't a cloud in sight. I cupped my hand over my eyes and watched the sun peeking through the trees. My idea was perfect! I ran in to get Willa Mae.

"Are those old sheds chicken coops?"

"They's chicken houses," she said. "Chicken coops is little crates you carries the broilers to market in. Folks always mix dat up."

"Good enough," I said. I was jumping up and down, bouncing around the kitchen like a human pogo stick. "Did you raise any chickens when you lived here?"

"Land sakes, no," she said. "Das too much work for an ol' wore down body likes mine. My mammy chicken farmed here when she was starting out and I helped. And I gots my fill of it, sure enough."

"Those coops have about everything a body needs to be a chicken farmer," I said.

"Takes lots more, chile. All dat's dere is the houses," she said.

"One to start the chicks in. Nother to raise the broilers go to market. Third to grow the pullets."

"Pullets?"

"Dey's the ones lays the eggs."

"A body could make a good living growing chickens," I said.

"Lot a' work and worry," Willa Mae said. "Gots to fix da feed, clean da coops. Gots to keep da ground 'round dem clean, too. And dey's all kinds disease chickens kin git if you don't keeps everything clean, and somes git sick even whens you do."

"Chicken diseases?" I said.

"Das right. Gasping Disease, Fowl Pox, Chicken Typhoid, Bumble Foot, and dey's Newcastle Disease, too. Hens git that, they stops laying eggs."

"But they have medicine for those diseases, right?"

"Somes. What you got gwine on in dat head?" Willa Mae said. "You be hearing what I saying?"

Of course not—my head was already busy chicken farming. It was perfect. I could provide well for us until Buck got his head straight. Besides, I wasn't afraid of hard work. And I wasn't going to let some old chicken diseases scare me, neither. That decision, I am sorry to say, led to my losing Grace Annie. The chain of events that followed seemed innocent enough on their own, but when lined up in a certain order, it was like a tornado blew in and rearranged the landscape and everything around it. Having no idea trouble was headed right at me, I bounded out the door.

"Watch Grace Annie for me, will you please?" I called over my shoulder. "I'm gonna go see Murphy."

"And you gots to have chickens to start da flock with. And where dey's gwine come from?" Willa yelled, and plopped her hands on her hips. "Uhm! Uhm! Uhm!"

I turned around and walked backwards, telling her not to worry. I had everything covered. She was mumbling away. "What you be thinking up next?"

I didn't answer. I turned and headed up the hill to Murphy's.

"Chicken farming . . . half-pint chile . . . no sense . . . nohow . . ." Willa Mae was still standing on the porch muttering.

I should have listened to her. It would have saved me from more grief than a mama can bear.

• • •

I spotted Murphy loading wood into his pickup when I made it to the top of the ridge leading to his cabin. His was four times the size of mine and Buck's, and it had a wraparound porch with rockers that stretched forever.

"Murphy!" I called to him.

The sky was still as blue and clear as Cold Rock River. My decisions would pay off. The world was a beautiful place, and I was well situated in it. Worry tore off from the far side of the house and near knocked me down licking my face off.

"How you be, Adie?" Murphy said. "Worry! Git!" Worry dropped his paws off my chest and plopped onto the ground. He pranced in a circle around me, his tail wagging to beat all Dixie, his tongue lolling in the air. I rubbed his ears and patted his backside.

"Good boy," I said. "You remember me."

"He's like an elephant," Murphy said. "He doesn't forget nothing, good or bad."

"Murphy, I've decided I'm gonna be a chicken farmer like you," I said and marched up to the truck and leaned on the wheel well. "So, I need you to learn me how to raise chickens."

"You what?"

"Those coops—I mean those chicken houses—behind the cabin are just sitting there going to waste."

"So just like that, you figure you're gonna chicken farm?" Murphy scratched his head.

"Yep," I said. "Made up my mind. You gonna help me or not? I ain't got all day. I got a baby at home, ya know."

"That's the thing, Adie. Takes a bit of time, chicken farming. There's a whole lot you got to be privy to. It ain't something you learn in a day." Murphy tossed the last piece of wood into the truck bed. He took off his work gloves and slapped them against his coveralls.

"For starters, I figure you can give me just the basics," I said.

"The basics?"

"Like what they eat and when do I pick the eggs," I said. "And which ones go in which house. I want to get started right away."

"You're serious about this, are you?" he said matter-of-factly.

"I am, and I'm a good learner, too," I said. "And I'm not afraid of hard work."

"Well that's good, 'cause you have no idea," he said. "You thought about where you're gonna get your starter crop?"

"My starter crop?"

"There's five ways to start a flock, Adie. There's day-old chicks, half-grown pullets, ready-to-lay pullets, hatching eggs, and breeding stock."

"Well, which ones you got plenty of?" I said. "That's the way I best start. And I'll be needing to pay you back once I get them growing good."

"You don't ask for much, do you?" Murphy said, grinning.

"Willa Mae told me you had hundreds of chickens, more chickens than anybody round these parts."

"That I do," he said. "Reckon if you're serious I can help you get started."

"What I do first?"

"I guess we best take a look at them houses and see what you'll be needing to get 'em in shape." Murphy jumped in the truck. "Climb in." He pushed the passenger door open. "I'll drop you off. I got to deliver this load of wood and then I'll be back. You can sweep them chicken sheds out while I'm gone. Make sure you get the ceilings and the walls swept down good, too."

"Ceilings, walls, and floors, whatever," I said.

"Then I'll show you how to scrape any droppings stuck to the boards. You'll need lye to scrub the floors, the dropping boards, the roosts, and the walls with." Murphy looked over at me. My eyes were opening a bit wider.

"Told you it was work, girl," he said. "You changing your mind?" I shook my head.

"You'll be needing a sprayer and some Creolin to disinfect the interior and some crankcase oil for lice and mites. You got any carbolineum?" he asked.

"Carbo who?" I said. He laughed.

"Just playing with your head. I'll get what you need and add it to the bill—which is growing by the minute."

"And I'll be paying every penny of it back, too. Every single cent. That's a promise."

"Why Adie Jenkins, I believe you will."

"Yes sir. You absolutely have my word on it."

"Then I guess we be partners, partner." Murphy stuck his arm out and shook my hand.

"Partners," I said as I pumped his hand back. "Why are you doing all this anyway, Murphy?"

"Ain't you heard?" he said and looked over at me and winked. "I'm a right nice guy." For a second I thought I saw something else in his eyes. If I did, it was gone in a flash. Maybe I imagined it.

"What about that husband of yours?" Murphy said. "He in agreement with your decision?"

"He will be when I start showing him it makes money." Which reminded me, I had to get home. Buck wanted me there when he got off work whether he actually came home afterwards or not.

"I gotta go." I turned and ran back down the hill my heart nearly bursting. When I got to the bottom I hugged myself. *Adie girl, you got yourself a plan! You can do this! You can!*

But once we got the chicken houses ready, I wasn't so sure. I found out exactly how much I knew about chicken farming, which was absolutely nothing. Murphy set out to educate me. He brought over two hundred chicks in different sizes in separate crates!

"There's many kinds of chickens, Adie," he said. "And they're grouped according to class, breed, variety, and strain. Understand?" I nodded as if I did.

"The *class* is mainly the place where they come from. The *breed* is how they're similar, say, in shape, things like that. The *variety* is based on their color or their plumage or even their comb." I puckered my lips and twisted my brow, trying my best to follow along.

"The comb," Murphy pointed to the top of his head, "the part sticks up on top their heads. And the *strain* is what comes about over the years when you breed the chickens."

"Well, it's all a bit confusing."

"Adie," Murphy said, "the first three terms have to do with characteristics—size, shape, and color. Now, strain has to do with *quality*, what makes them distinctive."

"Why don't you just tell me the parts I need to know; like what do I feed them and which ones sleep in which coop?" I said.

"I'll get to that," he said. "Now, what I brought you are pullets—they're the egg breeders. These others are the cockerels, thems the ones you'll sell at market. You paying attention, Adie?" I nodded.

"Now, we'll separate the pullets in about six weeks and put the majority of them in the laying house. We'll keep about fifty good pullets in the growing house for the next batch of chicks. The pullets are Leghorns. They're the best egg layers. They're pretty much considered the smallest of the breeds."

"Uh-huh," I said.

"Single Comb Leghorns," he said.

"There you go again," I said. "Can't you just tell me what to feed 'em, when to pick the eggs they lay, and be done with it for now?"

"Now Adie, you got to know the basics," he said. "We're talking purebred chickens here. No mongrels amongst them. Pay attention, now, and have a little patience. Soon this is gonna all make sense."

"Purebred chickens," I said. "I never heard of that."

"Well they grow faster and they lay more eggs than mongrels."

"So these aren't mongrels?" I said.

"Nosireeeeee," he said. "Purebred."

"Well they look a bit puny, don't you think?" I said. "Not that I ain't grateful, mind you."

"These are *half-grown* pullets, Adie," he said. "Give 'em time. They'll reach maturity at six months. Come fall, they'll be ready to begin laying. You'll get top dollar for your eggs in the colder months."

"What do I give them to eat?" I said.

"I'll show you how to mix the mash. Milk, corn, and green feed will do, so long as they get plenty outside time in the sun."

"Maybe I best write all this down," I said, not privy to the fact that with all this learning, destiny was setting me up for sorrow.

"Don't worry. I'll go over all of it again. I got to tell you what to watch out for too, so they'll stay healthy. Nothing worse than sick chickens. Wipe your stock out in no time."

"I think this is enough chicken learning for today," I said.

"In a minute," Murphy said. "Now these here in *these* crates are New Hampshires, the cockerels, these are the broilers you'll take to market. You'll have plenty for yourself, too. This way you can grow into your business." Murphy unloaded the crates and put them in their proper shed. Made for quite a stink.

"No one said chicken farming smelled good," he said. "That's the down side." More likely he meant "down wind," because when it blew, just right, whooooooeeeeeeee those chickens could make a smell. But the Leghorns were mighty good egg layers, and soon I had a passel of customers lined up at their doors when I came around each week with cartons of fresh eggs. I bought an old wagon with wood slats built around each side and toted everything in it, including

Grace Annie. Tucked her in a basket that fit down in the front part by the handle and away we went. Soon the cockerels grew into big, plump broilers. I sold them at about ten weeks old, then culled the pullets a week or two later, getting rid of those that wouldn't be good laying hens. I got where I could tell which ones were and which weren't without asking Murphy. Then I set aside about fifty good ones to start the next batch of chicks and put the others in the laying house. Hot dang! I was a chicken farmer.

You'd think Buck would have been right impressed. But the only thing he said was, "First it's baby shit. Now it's chicken shit," and shook his head. Maybe the smell of money would change his mind, once I got things really going good. I rolled up my sleeves and got to work.

Basically, that's a good description of how the events that led to my sorrow got started.

chapter thirteen

Buck quit coming home for supper, but I could hardly blame him. I couldn't cook.

"Willa Mae," I said. "Murphy told me you are the best cook in Hog Gap."

"Murphy say dat?" she said.

"Yes'm," I said.

"Guess dat's be truth. Dat fine man don't never lies."

"Well, we got something in common," I said. "I'm the best at being the worst."

Willa Mae shook her head. "Murphy be da worst."

"Buck won't even come home to supper anymore. Says I'm trying to poison him."

"Is you?" Willa Mae said and grinned. Her smile was still pretty, even though she had plenty spaces where her teeth once were.

"Lord knows I got reason to," I said, shaking my head. "Think you could help me learn to cook so the food's edible?"

"Land sakes, chile," Willa Mae said, "A gal what learns herself to chicken farm kin do's about whatever she puts her mind to do's."

"Maybe Buck will come home then," I said.

"Least for supper," Willa Mae said.

"My mama says one way to keep a man faithful is to keep his belly full."

"Cooking be good," Willa Mae said.

"What should we start with? I got some fixings for meatloaf and some ketchup," I said.

"Meatloaf?" Willa Mae said. "How 'bout we start with one dem chickens?"

"Wouldn't do to be eating up my livelihood," I said.

"You gots plenty chickens. Good chicken farmer needs to know how to dress a chicken right. Dere's tricks to gitting dem feathers off," Willa Mae said. "We can scald pick 'em, dry pick 'em, or wax pluck 'em."

"If it's all that trouble," I said, "how about we start with that meatloaf and ketchup—"

"We gwine start with one dem chickens. Den you decide how you want to pluck dat chicken."

When Willa Mae strutted through the chicken range, the chickens seemed to know what was coming. They squawked and flapped and scattered in all directions. Even so, Willa Mae had herself a plump bird drawn up by the feet in no time. She brought him over to the porch and promptly wrung his neck. Then she stuck it and hung a weight on the lower part of the beak.

"Once it bleed out we kin scald pick it," Willa Mae said. "Dry picking, dat's too much work and has to be done right when it's stuck or da feathers set and dey won't loosen." I swallowed hard.

"You okay, chile? You don't looks good to me," she said.

"I don't think I've ever seen a chicken killed right before my eyes," I said.

"Heavens 'ta glory!" Willa Mae said. "You be a chicken farmer now. You best git over it."

"Oh, I will," I said, then promptly dropped on the ground in a heap. When I came to I was laid out on the bed and that chicken was laid out on the counter fixing to lose its feathers. Willa Mae had a cold cloth to my head and was edged up on the bed next to me.

"Dere, chile. You be better now?"

"I think so," I said. "What happened?"

"You got weak in da knees and soft in da heart when I bled dat chicken. 'Member dat?"

"Oh, Willa Mae," I said. "I don't think I'll ever be up for doing that. Raising chickens is one thing. Killing them's another."

"Takes time," Willa Mae said. "Jist like most things."

The rest of the afternoon I took chicken cooking lessons; prepared a right nice dinner, too. Buck never made it home, so I made that same dinner the following night.

"I made you supper, Buck," I said. "You coming in to eat?" He gave me a look like he'd been shot in the back. "It's not like before," I said. "I learned to cook yesterday." Buck scratched his head.

"Yesterday?"

"Yup."

"You darned near poisoned me last time I ate what you fixed," he said.

"Well, now I learned how."

"Ain't nobody learns to cook in one day."

"I did. Willa Mae says I'm a natural at putting ingredients together." I popped open the oven door. A smell took hold of the room and wouldn't let go.

"You should stay home and eat with me tonight," I said. "You won't be sorry." Buck inched through the doorway and took a deep breath.

"I made us a chicken." I said. "Wrung its neck, just for you." I scrunched my lips together remembering that poor chicken's terrified eyes. Good golly. What a woman will do for a man. I killed one of my own chickens. Twisted his neck like Willa Mae showed me. It wasn't near as easy as she made it out to be, either. I jerked and twisted and screeched louder than that poor chicken, but I got the job done. The others flapped around the yard, squawking like they might be next.

"Buck, buck, buck," they cackled.

"You got that right," I said. "Buck, Buck, Buck. He's the reason for all this." I looked down at the chicken whose neck I'd stretched limp.

"Your pain's over, little fella," I said. "You just rest yourself now." I took him over to the chopping block I fixed up in the shed, took his head off, and laid it to one side. I stuck him and bled him out, and then I plucked every feather he ever grew, patting him down as I went. Next, I cut off his feet, removed all the parts that weren't edible, and took him back to the house to wash and stuff. I used an herb and breadcrumb mixture moistened with a fresh egg I got from the hen house, whipped it up with a bit of milk. I rubbed that plucked chicken's nubby skin with butter paste mixed with sage and sprinkled him good with salt and pepper. As he baked he turned a golden brown. The juices sizzled and popped as they collected in the bottom of the roasting pan. Those drippings would make a fine gravy, and it was going to be an even finer meal. The proof was sitting in the kitchen chair. Buck inched himself closer to the table and picked up his fork as I heaped his plate full of chicken, mashed potatoes, gravy, butter beans, coleslaw, and cornbread.

Imelda Jane may have a few things she figured Buck was in want of, but once he tasted my chicken, there was no telling what could happen to his heart. I'm sure many a good man has been turned around by a woman's fine cooking.

"A man got more'n one kind a' hunger in his belly," Willa Mae said that afternoon before Buck got home.

"If that's the case," I told her, "I might as well start with the one keeps him alive and go from there." Grace Annie smiled when I said it like she was listening and learning, already. And it looked to be working. Buck had cleaned his plate.

"Might try a bit more of that chicken, Adie," he said. "Seeing as you went to all this trouble." I served him up a second helping of everything. He ate every bite, and for once he even settled in for the night. Took off his boots and loosened his belt. And here I hadn't even brought out the pie I'd made using a jar of Mama's peach pie filling she'd brought me on her last visit.

Imelda Jane, you think you can steal my husband? You best think again! I'll fight you with every chicken in my hen house. With those thoughts firmly in place, I cleared the dishes while Buck stretched out on the sofa and rested his dinner. My plan was working. The thing is, Imelda Jane was working on one of her own.

chapter fourteen

FROM THE KITCHEN WINDOW I watched Willa Mae trudge up the driveway toting a satchel stuffed full with what looked like everything she owned. And I said to no one but myself, since Grace Annie was asleep, "What in a pickle barrel is Willa Mae doing?" I left the pots soaking, dried my hands, and ran out to ask her. I never got a word out of my mouth. No sooner had the door swung shut behind me when she called out.

"I'm gwine to dat Savannah place down on da ocean." She dropped the satchel next to the stoop and sat on the bottom step.

"Oooooh," she said. "Loss my wind, chile, toting all dis."

"You should have come and got me. I'd have helped you," I said.

"Gonna see dat pretty water. Promised me I would for I head 'ta glory. Ain't getting no younger."

"You're going off by yourself?" That didn't seem like a good idea.

"Dat I am. Got a cottage all set on the beach at dat Tybee Island spot. Gonna watch the sun come up on dat pretty water and plant my feet in the sand dey got there, too." Murphy's truck pulled up on the dirt driveway. Worry jumped out of the truck bed and bounded over to the porch.

"You all set?" Murphy called out.

"Jis' waiting on you's," Willa Mae said. She pointed to her bag. Murphy placed it in the truck.

"Hold on," Willa Mae said. "Almost forgot dis." She opened the satchel and pulled out Tempe's journal.

"You keeps dis for me, honey," she said and handed it to me.

"But Murphy said you ain't never let this book out of your sight," I said.

"Till now dat be's true. I know it be safe by you, chile." She placed in it my arms. "You kin reads more from it, you wants—"

"Where'd you get this journal, Willa Mae?"

"Bes' I remember it be tucked in my cradle, and I totes it round eber since," she said.

It wasn't enough to satisfy my curiosity, and I pestered her a bit more, but that's all she'd tell me.

"Things in life be important, you needs find out for yourself. Dat way you won'ts never forgets'em. And dis be something best nobody never forgets."

"Won't be the same you don't read it to me."

"Well you kin waits. Dats for you to decide. I gots to be gwine, now." She gave me a hug.

"How long you planning on staying?" I said.

"Ain't decided dat yet. I'll send word and da address if you like when I gits it." Murphy helped her into the truck.

"I'll miss you," I called out. "Me and Grace Annie both."

"Give dat sweet baby a kiss and a hug," she said. "I be's back!" Murphy loaded her stuff into the truck and they were off. I was happy for Willa Mae if she wanted to stay by the ocean a spell, but I hated seeing her leave. She was part of each day. Not counting Grace Annie, the best part. What was I gonna do without her? I was going to get myself in serious trouble, that's what. This is where that chain of events I mentioned to you earlier picked up a good deal of momentum.

There was always plenty of work to do what with chickens and the laundry I took in, along with caring for Buck and Grace Annie. Even so, I was working on a good life for us, and once Buck grew up a bit, I figured we'd pretty much have it made.

During the weeks before Willa Mae left for Savannah, I built up a heap of confidence in my chicken farming abilities. I'd made a lot of good decisions, and the profits showed it. But I made a bad one, too. I forgot to tell Murphy about the leak in the roof of the breeder coop.

I set out to fix it myself that day he took Willa Mae to Savannah. I put Grace Annie down for her nap and gathered up the tools and pieces of wood I needed and hoisted them up the ladder. Climbing up and getting situated on the corner of the coop where the boards had rotted away wasn't any problem. My plan was to be finished long before Grace Annie woke from her nap, hungry and in need of a change. That's not how it worked out. I'm not sure just what happened or where I went wrong with how I went about fixing the part of the roof that needing fixing. All I know is my foot went through a section that didn't have a hole in it when I stepped on it, and it had a good size one once I did.

That hole swallowed my leg clear up to my hip and my foot was twisted and caught up in the crossboards. Something sharp sliced though my overhauls and cut into my leg. I knew I was bleeding. It's not that I could feel it; strange as it sounds I think I could smell it, a metallic odor that floated upward and made me dizzy. I yanked at my leg to free it, but it wouldn't budge. My boot was stuck in the crevice where the corner boards of the roof joined together. The more I struggled the weaker I got. I might have lost touch with time for a spell. The next thing I knew, Grace Annie was hollering to be picked up, and it seemed I'd just put her down. The sound of her cries told me she'd been at it for awhile. There was hoarseness to her wails I'd never heard before. It near broke my heart. I wasn't one to let her cry whenever she started in.

The sun had been high, near overhead when I'd climbed up the ladder. Now it had slipped almost to the horizon. My leg buried in the coop was numb, and the one plopped beneath me on the roof wasn't too much better. Again I struggled to free myself and failed.

"Help!!!" I yelled. "Please! Help!!" Maybe Murphy would hear me, though it wasn't likely. He was probably still on his way back from Savannah.

The wind picked up. It was blowing strong, drowning out everything. I could barely make out Grace Annie's cries, and she wasn't but thirty feet away. There was no telling when Murphy would get back. It could be hours. And even then, there'd be no reason to come over here. I was in trouble, and my poor baby along with me.

I struggled and yelled the entire afternoon to no avail, whatsoever. When the sun set, eventually the wind died down. I screamed even louder. No answer came. I drifted in and out of a strange kind of sleep. The next time I became aware of my predicament, it was dark. Grace Annie wasn't crying any longer. Not even the pathetic little wails I'd last heard her make. Her being so quiet worried me to a panic.

"Grace Annie!" I yelled to her. "Grace Annie! Can you hear Mama? Wake up and cry!" Nothing. She didn't respond. No one responded. Only the sound of my own voice, hysterical and sobbing into that black night, came to greet me. And then, it was over.

I heard Murphy's truck pull up in front of the cabin. Worry bolted from the bed of the pick-up and made a dash for the chicken coop.

"Adie?" Murphy yelled out.

"Up here," I called back weakly. "Up here—" Worry stood below me barking. Murphy ran towards the coop.

"Adie, what in thunder—"

"Go see about Grace Annie," I said. "Please go see about her first, Murphy," I said. "I ain't heard her cry for hours!"

"I will in a minute, Adie," he said. "I got to see how bad you're hurt first. You bleeding?"

"I don't know. I can't feel a thing in my leg," I said. Murphy climbed up and punched the roof with his bare hands, cutting chunks of skin from his knuckles.

"Jeez, Adie," he said. He attempted to free my foot from the crevice and inched my leg out of the hole.

"Aaaaaaaahhhhhh," I screamed.

"Hang on," he said. "Your ankle's broke. This gonna hurt some." I near passed out when he freed my foot from the crevice and inched my leg out of the enlarged hole he'd made with his bare hands. He plopped me over his shoulder like I was a sack of baby onions and backed down the ladder. Then he carried me in his arms like a man does his bride and placed me on the front seat of the truck. Worry followed along whining and begging to get close.

"Get Grace Annie . . . she's in her crib." Murphy took his shirt off. There was a ragged cut on my leg just above the knee that traveled clear to my groin. Murphy folded his shirt in half and wrapped it tight around my leg, then made a run for the cabin. He came out with Grace in his arms.

"Uuuuuuuuhh!" I gasped when he handed her to me. Her body was limp and her eyes were closed.

"Grace Annie! Oh, Grace Annie!" I said. "I'll never forgive myself! Never!" I grabbed her and clutched her to my chest. She let out a howl to wake Dixie's dead. Poor thing had just cried herself out and fell sound asleep. I started laughing hysterically but quickly ended up crying right along with her. I looked over at Murphy. His face was more serious than I'd ever seen it; his hands tight on the wheel. He glanced at us every few seconds, then placed his eyes back on the road.

"You okay, Adie?" he kept saying. "You okay?" I was checking on Grace Annie and then glancing on him, tears running down my face. And all the while I was thinking, *Wouldn't it be wonderful if Buck were like Murphy? A man who took care of me? Who pounded holes in roofs with his bare hands? Who said sweet things to me like, 'You okay, Adie? You okay?' and said it with a look of concern so sincere it left marks on my heart. Wouldn't that be something?*

More likely, it'd be a miracle.

chapter fifteen

M Y ANKLE WAS BROKE IN two spots, and it took more than a
hundred stitches to sew up the cut on my leg. Even so, Doc Taylor
at Carolwood County Hospital where Murphy took me said I
could go home in a couple of days. Verna came and got Grace
Annie. She wasn't hurt, just hungry and wet, with a bad case of
diaper rash that she'd never had before. Just the same, this woman
came in and started asking questions like she was being neglected
on a regular basis.

"My name is Evelyn Mackey," she said. "I'm with Hicks County
Family and Children Services. I need to ask you some questions."

She had a brown wooden clipboard with a stack of papers
attached and a face like a pickled beet.

"What for?" I asked.

"There appears to be some concern over the care and treatment
of your child."

"There must be some mistake about that, ma'am." I said. "She
gets the best of care. Of that I can assure you."

"That's what I'm here to determine. According to my records—"

"What record is that?" I asked. She turned over the top page on her clipboard and pursed her lips tight, cleared her throat, and give me a look like I was irritating her.

"This report we received—"

"Report? What report?"

"Miss Jenkins, I'm afraid—"

"It's Mrs. Jenkins—"

"I beg your pardon?"

"It's Mrs. Jenkins. I'm married, proper-like and everything,"

"Mrs. Jenkins, as I was saying," she said and flipped the top page on her clipboard back into place. "I'm not at liberty to divulge our sources."

"Well, just tell me what this report is about, then," I said. "Can you at least do that?" I said and pursed my lips together. My ankle was throbbing under the cast, and the stitches running up my leg were burning something awful. I was miserable and in need of another shot for the pain, and this woman was starting to get on my nerves.

"I am here, young lady, to determine the best placement for the care and treatment of one Grace Annie Jenkins, age . . ." she flipped through the top pages on her clipboard again, "seven months."

"Placement? What are you talking about? Her place is with me!"

"There has been a report of neglect . . . indications child has been left unattended for a matter of hours . . . said child left to lie in her own excrement—" Ms. Mackey was reading from her chart.

"Excrement? What are you talking about?"

"The child has a severe diaper rash infection, her vocal cords are inflamed and—"

"Miss Mackey," I said. "I had an accident. I was stuck on the chicken coop. I didn't deliberately leave my baby—"

"So, you are *not* disputing the facts presented that you left the child unattended?" Miss Mackey was scribbling notes on her chart without letting me explain.

"I went out to fix the hole in the roof of the chicken coop, and I was coming back in after I finished and then I—"

"Thank you, Mrs. Jenkins. That will be all for now," she said.

"Miss Mackey," I called out as she was leaving the room. "What'd you write down on that clipboard? Don't I get a copy of that thing?"

I heard her heels clicking all the way down the hall. By the time I got out of the bed, got to the crutches the nurse left for me in case I had to use the bathroom, and made my way to the door, she was gone. Later when Doc Taylor came to check on me, I told him about what she said.

"Just a formality, Adie," he said. "Family Service always pokes around when we have a child that needs attention."

"She said she was here to do a placement or something on Grace Annie," I said.

"Now don't you be worrying yourself on that," he said. "She's just doing her job. She'll fill out the paperwork, pick up a copy of my examination, and that will be the end of it, okay?"

"Are you sure?"

"Sure as I can be," he said.

"But she said they had some kind of report about neglect!" I said. "What about that?"

"Don't know anything about that," he said. "You must have misunderstood her. You just rest, now. I'm going to let you go home in the morning."

He was good on his word, too. I had to sign papers in the morning saying I'd make payments on the hospital bill, and then I was released. Murphy came to get us since Mr. Fletcher had Buck working double shifts during inventory.

"I sure want to thank you for what you did for Grace and me," I told Murphy.

"You'll have to thank Worry for that," he said. "He was jumpier than a flea on a hot skillet that night. Kept whining and pawing at the door. I finally went outside to take a look around. Noticed there weren't any lights on at your place. Seemed kind of strange, so I come over to check on you."

"It was our good fortune you did, Murphy," I said. "And I won't ever forget it."

"Told you I was a right nice fella," he said.

"Guess Margaret Mary's figured that out, too," I said. "Willa Mae said you been seeing her right regular," I teased him.

"She did now, huh?" he said.

"Yup. You two a couple now or what?"

Murphy shrugged his shoulders. "She's a real fine person, Adie. But I think she's counting on too much from me, if you know what I mean."

"You mean, you still don't fancy yourself settling down, having a family," I said.

"Reckon not," he said.

"Why not? Seems like the natural order of things."

"Can't," he said.

"Can't or won't?"

"Can't," he said. "One I want's taken." And he winked. I thought I saw that funny little spark in his eyes again, and then it was gone.

I went home and hobbled around best I could. Murphy came over each morning at the crack of dawn and took care of my chickens, which irritated Buck to no end.

"You're more than welcome to do it," I told him. He rolled over and put the covers back over his head.

I had time to curl up with Tempe's journal. Now that Grace was all right and I was gonna be fine, it was kinda nice being an invalid. I got to stay in bed and read.

• • •

Grady and me don't have no babies right off and Massah tell Grady, "You must not like that near white filly I jumped you with," he say. "Best git to it, boy." Grady not say nothing to him 'cause black mens been taught to keeps their head down. And Massah say, "Maybe I best help you out." Up to then things be working out real fine and mostly

Grady and me, we be's real happy. And I sure love that Grady, I do, and I knowed he loved me, too, and dat's a truth. Only was once or maybe two times we ever fussed at the other, so we was well suited. Then Miz Caroline died in the childbirth having a third baby for Massah Major and the baby, it died too. But Massah Major has the two little boy chilluns to takes kere of they's already got fore she die, and Massah he fetch a yeller gal from the cabins to kere for them. Right off Massah marry agin and bring a new mistress home to the plantation. Lordy, Lordy them times was hard. This colored gal what Massah brought up to help new mistress kere for the chilluns was a pretty yeller gal what have dat long black hair hung down her back. Her skin be light and her features look more white than black, they do. New mistress, her name be Madeline Bonner and she be too old for to have children and we in the cabins think Massah want it that way so he not lose another wife and have to git another to raise his two boys. Mistress Bonner studied on the meanness worser than anybody I ever knowed. Anybody she gits her hands to she be mean to, 'cluding them little boys be Massah's. And they growed up to be mean because of it I thinks, too. Massah Major never seen her be mean, but we'uns did lots a' times. Fust thing Mistress Bonner do when she gits to the big house is chops that pretty yeller gal's hair off to the scalp, that gal Massah brought to the house to kere for his little boys. Massah pretty much like that pretty gal. 'Member Massah Major gots the red hair, and he has red-haired chilluns wid that gal. They be's kept down in the cabins with us while they's mama help Mistress Bonner kere for Massah Major's chilluns. He be sore fit unhappy when he see her pretty hair gone. If he said anything to Mistress, we never knowed about it. Mostly he turned out to be skeered of her as much as we was, and stayed clear of her. And Massah, he took to coming down to the cabins agin at night to sleep with the colored gals he fancied there, and when Miss Caroline be living he mostly stopped doing that.

That be about the time things get stirred up that the war what free us be coming. But it be hard for us to know what was gwine on. Ain't the one of us could read good 'nuf to know what was in them papers was on the table in the big house, but talk was the Yankees be coming and land sakes all the white folks round dese parts say them Yankees was coming to skin us alive. I never could figure on why them Yankees would do that if they be wanting to free us. Even so we be skeered, 'cause lots a' things white men do's make no sense and dat's a truth. Grady and one the other mens hide by the window to the big house and try to hear what Massah Major say about them papers when he talks to Mistress. Mostly Grady say it be a long time yet, that the southern mens and the northern ones be still talking and fussing up in that Washinton place. One day I be's in the big house to help with the spring cleaning that year and Mistress Bonner has some lady friends over to drink the tea and eat the cakes the cook makes and Mistress be pouring that tea from the silver pot and I hears Mistress say, "Whatever will happen to us if those dreadful Yankees free all our slaves?— Sugar?" And one the lady friends, Miz Ivy Cole, say, "Yes, two lumps, please," and then she say "Why should we worry on that? Our boys can leave after breakfast, whup those Yankees, and be home for dinner, I declare." That's what she say, and she dabs at her mouth with the silk linen put by her place for her to use. And Mistress Bonner say, "Well, all this talk of war is giving me fits. If you are wrong, Ivy, and the Yankees free the Negroes, good Lord, who will do all the work?" And that other lady what eats the cakes and drinks the tea, she be Miz Lillie Singleton from town, she say, "Madeline, if the war comes and the Yankees win, you best not worry on who'll do the work. You best concern yourself on which darkie will murder you in your bed. You haven't treated them very well, my dear." She do; she say that, and Mistress Bonner's face turn white and it real white already.

A few months after Massah marries Mistress Bonner, he comes to the part of the cabin where Grady and I be sleeping all this time and tells Grady to go outside and sleep near the dogs. Then Massah climb in the bed be Grady's and mine! Lordy, what that man do's under them kivers! And what he habs me do! But I do's like he say 'cause he twists my arm behind my back and pulls it to my neck till it pops and he say he pull it clean from the socket if'n I don't. And it feel like he already pull it from dat socket. I still be's hardly pass thirteen year old, I thinks, and then I habs the baby be Thomas after Massah do's that, and then I habs James when he keeps doing that, and I habs LuLu, too. Me and Grady, we pretend they's ours, but they sure nuf looks like Massah. I 'members it 'cause I can't forgets what ol' Massah do's to me. And after LuLu be's born Massah keeps coming out to the cabin and when he do he tell Grady, "Git!" And one night Massah tells him dat, they's a full moon. And Grady goes out by the dogs like he done all the times before, only this time he comes back in. He gots a club in his hand be thicker than that one he beat them dogs with. That be the bloodiest night I ever sees. Lordy, Lordy—only one them mens be's alive come morning.

· · ·

Someone was knocking at my door. I tucked the journal aside and hobbled over to see who it was. Couldn't be Willa Mae; she was still at Tybee Island.

"Be right there!" I called, and hobbled over on my crutches. I spotted Margaret Mary through the screen door. She had on a yellow cotton sundress. It looked like the one I'd seen in the display down at Mary Ellen's Fashions, the one I told Buck I'd sure like to have, and he said, "And I'd like to have a rich uncle."

"Come on in." I motioned to Margaret Mary and pushed the door open with one hand and leaned on one crutch with the other. "The chicken smell will stick to that pretty new dress you stand there too long."

She grinned and smoothed the front of her dress.

"You look wonderful, Margaret Mary," I said, realizing I wasn't dressed proper for entertaining guests. I had on a pair of baggy pants and one of Buck's shirts.

Margaret Mary stood proud, tall as me plus a foot. She'd gained some weight—filled out in what Mama would say were all the right places.

"Here," she said, handing me a basket of fruit. "This is for you."

"That's right nice of you, Margaret Mary," I said. "Me and Buck love fruit. Least I do."

"I'm real sorry about your accident. Murphy told me all about it," she said. "You doing okay out here by yourself?"

"Making do, best I can," I said. "We ain't got nothing fancy though, just getting started," I said, embarrassed nothing good was baked even to help mask the air drifting in from the chicken range. "Smell is from the chicken coops," I explained. "Finds its way in here sometimes."

"Gotta have chickens," she said. "Lord made them, too." I motioned to a spot for us in the kitchen around the table. "Don't sit too close to the window. If the wind shifts, the hen house odor's like to knock you over," I said. She took the chair on the far side of the table.

"You want to see Grace Annie?" I asked. "She's growing like a little cornstalk."

"Yes, please," she said, and we went and peeked in on her in the only other room there was to our place, not counting the toilet spot, which now thankfully worked in case she had to use it. Margaret Mary patted the blanket I'd tucked around Grace real gentle like. The baby didn't stir from her sleep. Her breathing was soft and even. I noticed a bit of milk resting at the edge of her mouth. Margaret Mary picked up the clean didie tucked at the bottom of her bassinet and dabbed at it. She'd make a fine mama to some lucky baby, no doubt. All of a sudden the thought of who she might be making them with cut hard into my belly and took me by surprise. My face got red.

"You alright?" she said.

"I'm fine," I stammered, knowing full well I wasn't. I'd surely fry in hell for the thoughts going through my mind. Murphy's eyes, his ears, his lips, his hair that stuck up in the middle, even his smell, grabbed me with a force so strong I thought surely he was in the room, ready to carry me off—send me to heights I'd never been to before—and here his maybe bride-to-be was sitting down for coffee, not knowing I was consumed with hunger for her man. I never realized parts of me had been thinking on Murphy like that till then.

Buck had once tried to explain to me about a fire in the blood that built up and made him take leave of his senses. Now, it made sense. It *was* a fire in the blood. And if it was the kind one couldn't stop, like Buck said he run into, we were all in big trouble. Everywhere my thoughts glanced, Murphy swirled around them.

"Adie?" Murphy touched my shoulder, and I nearly swooned into the door frame.

"Here, you best come sit down," he said before I realized it wasn't Murphy at all. It was Margaret Mary. The spell had passed. I took a deep breath, hoping I was safe. Instead, a powerful fear of what I just discovered welled up in my belly and churned my stomach. I made my way to the toilet and tossed up the perfectly good grits and toast I'd had for breakfast.

"You okay in there?" Margaret Mary called out. "Adie?"

"Be right there," I said weakly. I wiped my face in the mirror and checked to see if it'd changed. I couldn't see any difference to speak of, which was amazing, seeing as what had changed inside. I dabbed at my mouth with a cold rag and rinsed the sour taste out of it with a bit of peroxide.

Wherever those feelings came from, put 'em back! You hear? I stared at the reflecton in the mirror, hardly knowing her. *You already got a husband. You got a baby! What's wrong with you anyhow? You got no right! You want to rot in hell?*

I opened the door and made my way to the kitchen table that wasn't but a handful of feet away. Still, it was a bit slow going with my crutches.

"You sick?" Margaret Mary said.

"I'm okay," I lied.

"Not having yourself another little bundle are you?"

"Good heavens, no!" I said and sat down at the table.

Margaret Mary licked her lips and cleared her throat. She smiled and shook her head. Her ponytail danced behind her like a prized mare. She sat up straight, took a deep breath, and let it all out—like she was getting ready to make a speech but forgot what she was supposed to say. I watched as she took another big gulp of air, wondering what her problem was.

"Murphy and me are getting married Saturday—we'll be neighbors—I thought I better tell you—what do you think of that?" she blurted with out stopping.

"Aaaahhhh . . . well . . . it's . . . how'd this happen? I mean, y'all make a right nice couple. I just didn't know—"

"Guess it'll surprise a lot of folks, happening so soon." I sat there too shocked to say anything and wobbled my head up and down like a Kewpie doll.

"It's not really a bride time of the year for a wedding, but—"

"Good a time as any—" I said, not happy for them like I should be and mad at myself for not being.

"Truth be known, it should have been a lot sooner," she said. "People will be counting on their fingers in a few months. Mama's having herself a hissy fit," Margaret Mary said. I turned around to get the coffee pot so she couldn't see my face.

"You mean you and Murphy are . . . having . . . a ba—"

"That's it in a handbag," she quipped. "I've been too scared to tell anyone. I haven't had my monthly in going on three months!"

"You want some of this coffee? It's near fresh," I said, pouring her a cup whether she wanted one or not, my hand shaking so bad it looked like it had the palsy. Margaret Mary touched my arm to steady it.

"I come here to let you know it's no secret to me I'm not his first choice," she said.

"Reckon?" I said, and I finished filling her cup, acting like I had no idea who she might be talking on.

"Cream?"

"I'm no fool, Adie" she said. I turned and fished in the cabinet drawer for spoons.

"They don't match good, but they're clean," I said and passed one to her. I didn't look her in the face, thinking hers might be glued to mine.

"Sugar?" I turned around to fetch it off the counter.

"You hear what I'm saying, Adie Jenkins?" she said, her voice so loud it startled me.

"Doing my darndest not to," I said and put the sugar on the table. I put two helpings into my coffee and stirred, took a big swallow, and tossed my best smile in her direction. She had the kindest brown eyes. Funny, Murphy said hers were almost like mine. Imagine that? "Her hair is, too," he said. "Same color."

"There's never been anything between Murphy and me, Margaret Mary. And that's a fact," I said.

"Oh, I know that. And it's not like he came right out and said something in particular even," she said. "It's just . . . well . . . it's the look he gets when he speaks on you, you know?"

I looked at her, but barely breathed.

"So Murphy asked you to marry him when you told him?" I asked.

"It wasn't like he had much choice," she said.

"Well, a man needs to own up—"

"Listen, Adie," Margaret Mary said. "I need to tell you something. I . . . I want us to be good friends and—"

"Course we will be," I answered, chewing on my bottom lip like it was an afternoon snack. "We can help each other out, both having little ones and—"

"It wasn't Murphy, Adie. It was me. I'm the one . . . I'm the—" Margaret Mary twisted the hankie in her hands. "Fact is, I . . . I threw myself at him. Caught him in a weak moment. What do you think of me now? You still want to be my friend?"

"I . . . I—"

"I probably shouldn't marry a man don't love me back."

"Murphy will always do right by you," I said.

"Right," she said.

"Who can say what love is anyway?" I said. "It ain't what we read in books, I can tell you that."

"I should marry him then, even though he doesn't—?" she said.

"Be a fool not to."

"Don't want to be a fool," she said.

"Surely not," I said. "Look where it got *me*."

The wind shifted and sent us a good whiff of the chickens. "See what I mean?" I said.

We laughed, and while we did, more chicken smell floated into the room. We laughed again. Two more whiffs and we couldn't stop. We held our bellies and howled. The more we laughed, the funnier it got. Strips of girl giggles pealed out of our mouths and drifted out the same window the chicken odors floated in through. Tears welled in our eyes and poured down our cheeks. Still we laughed, laughed like we hadn't had a good one in a very long time, like it might be even longer before we ever did again. The chicken smells kept coming— real or imagined, they poured into the room. My sides ached. Guess hers did, too. I rubbed at mine and she grabbed hold of hers, still we couldn't stop howling. The screen door squeaked open and Buck walked in. What a fright we gave him. There we sat, two girl hyenas laughing and crying, rocking our bellies, holding our sides, bound forever by coffee and babies and men and chicken shit.

chapter sixteen

THE WEDDING TOOK PLACE ON Saturday at the courthouse. As the months rolled on, Murphy seemed right keen on being a daddy. So now I had a happy young married couple next door. I made up a batch of Mama's cherry brandy and transferred it into a fancy empty liquor bottle Miz Jenkins let me have and gave it to them as a housewarming present. Margaret Mary invited me in and showed me around. Murphy's cabin was fit for royalty. He'd built it himself. From the size of it, surely he must have planned on marrying and having a family someday, even if he did tell me when I met him he wasn't the marrying kind. I pushed away the daydreams I'd been having about him and concentrated on the choice I made in Buck. I figured we had as good a chance as any at having a good life. The days quickly turned into months. It wouldn't be long before Grace Annie was a year old. I could hardly believe it. But I had to admit, things were going real well for me and Buck for once.

Then Grace Annie took a bad fall off the dressing table a few weeks after Murphy's wedding when I was changing her diaper. The changing table had a plastic belt to hold her in place, and I looped it round her waist and went in the kitchen to fetch a clean didie. I'd just pulled them from the clothesline and hadn't had a chance to fold them yet. They were still in the basket by the back door. I wasn't gone for maybe half a minute when I heard a loud thump. I raced back to Grace Annie, my heart climbing right out of my chest. She was on the floor. She'd hit her forehead on the right side. A nasty goose-egg was already forming and she was screaming bloody beets. I grabbed her without any diaper on and raced over to Murphy's. He drove us to town. Margaret Mary came, too. The four of us were scrunched together on the front seat of the truck, with Grace laid across me and Margaret Mary's lap.

The doctor at the emergency room said her eyes were clear and there wasn't any blood coming out of her ears. She didn't seem tired or sleepy and wasn't crying any longer, so he felt she'd be fine, but I'd have to leave her overnight for observation just to be sure. They took X-rays of her entire body and said for me to come back in the morning.

"Don't worry, Adie," Margaret Mary said. "Kids are tough little creatures."

"I can't believe I left her on that dressing table," I said. "I thought she was safe. I—"

"Shhhhhhhh," Margaret Mary said. "Accidents happen, sugar—"

We went back to the hospital early the next morning. This man in a brown suit asked me to step into his office. He had a sign on his desk said Emmitt Carlsbad, Hospital Administrator. I thought maybe he was worried on how I planned on paying the bill, since we already owed them money for when I birthed her and for the time my leg went through the roof of the chicken house.

"I'm back to my chicken farming," I said. "I'm pretty much all better."

"I beg your pardon?"

"I'm chicken farming again, and the money I get the end of the month, well, I can pay—"

"Miz Jenkins—"

"It's Mrs. Jenkins," I said. "I'm married, all proper and every-thing."

"*Mrs.* Jenkins, I'm not here to discuss payment. County is taking care of the charges on this—"

"County?" I said. "Why are they doing that? We're not beggars," I said. "At the end of the month I can pay—"

"Mrs. Jenkins, County is taking your baby into protective custody pending a full investigation concerning her injuries." He gave me a piece of long white paper, a Writ of something or other. It had words on it like parts of it came from the Bible. It said, "*Pray the court* this and *Mercy of the court* that."

"I don't understand," I said. "It was an accident. She fell—"

"If that's the case, then you have nothing to worry about. You'll be notified by the court when a preliminary hearing date is scheduled," he said. "I'm afraid that's all the information I have. Normally, Miss Mackey would be here to address all of this. You came by too early. She's due at nine o'clock."

"My baby. Can I see her?"

"She was transferred over to county juvenile care last evening. Surely you were informed—"

"But the doctor said they were keeping her overnight for observa-tion—"

"Perhaps it was *this morning* when they took her. Really, Mrs. Jenkins, I am a very busy man. You'll have to talk with County for the specifics. Now if you'll excuse me," he said and opened the door and motioned me out.

My knees shook so bad I could hardly walk down the steps and out the door to Murphy and Margaret Mary. Murphy was leaning against the truck. Margaret Mary was sitting sideways on the front seat, with the door open.

"They took Grace Annie!" I said.

"Who took her?" Margaret Mary jumped down and rushed up to me. She placed her arm around my shoulder.

"County took her. They think it wasn't an accident!"

"We'll see about that," Murphy said. "Come on, get in the truck, ladies. We're going over there right now; straighten this mess out."

But it wasn't that easy. Miss Mackey said we had to wait for the hearing.

"Can I see her in the mean time?" I said. "She's never been away from me."

"I'm afraid that's not in the child's best interest," Miss Mackey said. "She's been placed in a private home environment, and we want to give her time to adjust without getting confused."

"But—"

"You'll have to wait for the hearing."

"I need to call my husband!" I said, wondering if she'd let me use her phone.

"You'll be notified by mail."

"But . . . can I least call my—"

"Good day, Miz Jenkins," she said.

I had to hold the front of my chest walking back to the truck. It felt like it'd been caught in the hinges of the door Miz Mackey had slammed shut in my face.

I got notice of the hearing. It wasn't for four more weeks. I fed the chickens and tended to my egg customers. Each morning I woke up and pounded my head. Wake up! Wake up! You're having a nightmare. But it's hard telling a nightmare to wake up when you're already awake to begin with.

Margaret Mary came by to keep me company. Her belly was growing fast. Murphy set about making baby furniture; all hand-carved pieces; the most beautiful shapes of wood I'd ever seen. Me and Margaret Mary spent some of the afternoons after I finished my chicken chores snapping pole beans and baking pies for the church bazaar. There was such a large crop of beans we decided to pickle them and sell them at the fair, along with the pies. Kept us busy. Even so, I got lonely for Willa Mae.

At night I took Tempe's journal out of the trunk and moved my hands over the pages, thinking that might bring her closer. Before long, the words drifted off the page and into my head, carrying me back to a time of busted dreams and crumbled lives, to a place that had shackled freedom. Tempe's story pained me, but it let me see through her eyes what I couldn't bear to see through mine. That life could be meaner than we counted on. That we best be brave and persevere if we expected to have a fighting chance. Tempe took up a permanent spot in my heart. She climbed into the air I breathed and whispered to me in the wind at night. On days I was the saddest, I looked for signs of her everywhere. Once I thought I spotted her outline in the dew on the grass. Another time I was sure her tears rained down when the storm clouds burst. I rocked the journal in my arms like a baby on the nights Buck was out. When I grew tired of that, I curled up under the covers, my eyes perched at the edge of the pages, the words before me hills and valleys I could get lost in.

• • •

They digs a hole and throwed his body down in that hole and kivers it up with dirt and that be all there was to it. Weren't no talking gwine on. I kin still hear that dirt when it hit the body. "Womp . . . womp . . ." it go and soon they's nothing left of Grady I kin see, not even the bloody shirt was all stuck to his back. Massah Major say, "Any a' you niggers ever lays a hand on me I'll put you in a hole just like this one, only I'll leaves you alive 'fore I do." Massah Major say be sure I watch what happen good and then he say he takes kere of me later.

"Git," he say. And I gits, but mostly I be in some kind of powerful peculiar state. Nothing be's seeming like it's real to me. Grady dead and put in that black hole and the worser part be in the morning when I wakes up. The wagon with the speculator men show up and Massah Major sells my chilluns and puts them on that wagon and that's when I be running alongside the oxen what pull that wagon to see's my chillun one las' time.

When I was a younger girl I ask my old Massah's chillun to teach me to read some and write my name and they say, "It's against the law we do that." And dat older boy be Luke say, "No law says we can't read to you." And I sits next to Luke and has him reads to me and I say, "That what them words say there?" And Luke, who be reading say, "Yes it does. I am the best reader in the school. I am the smartest in the school, too."

"Where it say 'once upon one time'?" I say, and he point to the words and I say this one say 'once' and this one say 'time'? and he say yep it do and it take a long time but I learn to read pretty good that way and if he so smart why he never cotch on be a good question. And dat's a truth.

When my chilluns is born I puts my 'nitials on the bottom sides of their butts with a hot stick. The babies cries when I does it, and it breaks my heart mostly, but what kin I do? If they's ever sold I kin maybe find them and knows they be's mine. When they's going off in the wagon I am happy I do's it, even though the babies cries hard when I burns them like that when they's small. Yes'm I burns a big letter T on der butts to shows they be's mine, Tempe's, but they squirms lots and the scar it makes looks like it be a cross, it do.

I don't like to think on what happened when Grady come back in the cabin with the two-by-four that night he died, but it sits in my head and won't go away. Grady be's real quiet when he come back in the cabin dat night and I not eben know he be's there. It real dark in dat cabin. Massah Major have me underneath him in the bed be hooked to the wall doing what he do and Grady stumbles over the stool sits by the door. Massah Major jumps off the bed buck naked and sees Grady in the doorway and the moon is shining in the cabin, and he can see the board in his hand and Massah Major takes the poker from the fireplace and he runs it clean through Grady 'fore Grady knows it even there. I hear Grady groan like he be already dead when that poker stic his belly and he drop down to the floor.

"Massah Major!" I's screaming. "Don't kills him! Oh please, Massah!" But Massah Major picks up that board Grady drop when his belly git stuck with the fire poker and Massah beats Grady's head with that board 'til they's a big hole in it. The chilluns from the back room is up and crying and the grown folks is out of their beds and standing round looking at what Massah done. I am on my knees begging Massah Major not to kills Grady.

"Oh Massah, mercy, Massah," I say, but Massah is pounding at what be left of Grady. He mostly dead already, I think. And then I looks down and I know's he dead, 'cause I see's in that moonlight that Grady's 'tire head, dat pretty head what habs the face I love—da whole thing—be gone.

chapter seventeen

Ma's just trying to look out for you, Adie," Buck said on the way over to her place.

"Well, she's picked a sorrowful way to do it. What right has she got telling county I ain't a good mama?"

"Adie, I don't think that's what she had in mind. It's just—"

"If you're gonna defend her I ain't listening!" I put my hands over my ears.

When we got there, Verna was sitting at the kitchen table, sipping her coffee like nothing had changed. Meanwhile I was falling apart.

"What makes you think you have all the answers?" I asked the moment I got one foot in the door. Verna glanced up and heaved a sigh. Grace Annie was sitting on the kitchen floor playing with a wooden spoon. I reached down and picked her up and slammed the spoon down on Verna's table.

"You got a husband run off," I said, Grace Annie on my hip. "You ain't done too good with Buck. And Austin, I know he's back to being a baby, but you don't even let him enjoy being one. Seeing as he don't know any different, can't you at least let him do that?" Verna didn't bother to answer. She got up out of her chair and just poured herself another cup of coffee. I wanted to pull her hair out.

"You try to control everything and everybody, and you judge people. You do and you know it! And it's not your job. Just how do you think Grace Annie is going to benefit by that? Huh?"

She sat like a rock roosting on a mountain.

"I know I made some mistakes and I should of been more careful, but didn't you ever do anything wrong when you were learning?" I said, wondering if she'd even admit it if she had. I turned to Buck.

"And how come you ain't standing up for me? We're supposed to be a family. Stick together. What's a matter with you? This is our baby I'm talking about! You just gonna let them take her away from us?"

"Adie, what's the problem with letting Ma take care of her for a while?" Buck said.

"It ain't just a while. It's for an entire month. And County placed her here without even telling us."

"I knew where she was," Buck said.

"It would have been nice for you to have told me, don't you think?"

"I figured you'd just have yourself a hissy fit, like you're doing now," he said.

Verna finally opened her mouth and joined in. "Adie, you best accept the fact she's staying with me, at least until the hearing. If County says yer fit, you'll get her back. If they don't, you best, well, you best hope they let me adopt her," Verna said. "That way you'll get to see her."

"Adopt her?" I said.

"Just what do you think a placement is?" Verna said.

"She's not an orphan! They can't just put her out for adoption—"

"They can do anything the law says they can."

"And where did they get this idea I might not be fit to have her anyway? What'd you tell them?"

"Nothing they didn't already know. You spend too much time tending chickens to do right by her, and they saw for theirselves what happened."

"That was an accident, her falling, and you know it!"

"And what about that time you climbed around on them chicken coops all hours of the night—"

"It wasn't night. It was her nap time, and I was fixing to be done in half an hour—"

"Well you weren't, and it was a stupid thing to do. Leaving that baby alone in the house. You ain't got a lick a' sense."

"Well, I made me a mistake is all. And anyway, that was ages ago!"

"What's done is done," Verna said. "I think you and Buck best go on home now. I got to give Grace Annie her bath and get her in bed." Verna took the baby from me and headed toward the bathroom. Grace Annie let out a howl.

"It's okay, honey," I said. "Mama will be back." Verna handed Grace Annie her favorite rubber duck. "We're gonna have a nice bath, honey," she crooned, taking her by the hand. Grace Annie grinned.

"Murphy says I can get a lawyer and have him in the courtroom with me the day of the hearing," I called after her.

"Maybe you best do that," Verna said. "You might could use one." She turned around and looked me square in the eyes. Mine were having a hard time looking back. They were filled with too many tears to contain themselves. They went the only direction they could.

"C'mon Adie," Buck said. "Let's go." He put his arm around me. "We can talk about this later when things cool down, okay?"

I went home thinking maybe this could bring us together. Make a real husband out of him—one of the worst things turning out to be the best things, like Mama was always talking about. But the truth is after that things got even worse. Buck sided with his ma. I took in more laundry and saved every penny I could to get a lawyer. Verna let me come over two times a week and spend an hour with Grace Annie. But she didn't let me take her out of the yard. And I didn't get enough money put together for the retainer that every one of them lawyers I called said they'd have to have before they'd come to court with me, so I ended up going alone. Willa Mae still wasn't back from Tybee Island, and by the sound of her letters, she planned on staying a while. Something about an interesting gentleman friend she'd met. I didn't know what to do. I was sure Murphy would give me the money if I asked, but I owed him so much already and I didn't want to be leaning on Margaret Mary's man. He was her husband. He shouldn't be coming to my rescue all the time like he was mine. But I should of asked him, because it didn't go well in court for me the day of the hearing. Verna had a lawyer with her. And she never said anything about her getting one! Why did she need a lawyer? I was the one they were trying to take the baby from. I found out soon enough. They were petitioning the court. When I got to sit in the witness chair and give a statement I was real surprised to see my sister Rebecca in the courtroom. I'd sent her a letter weeks ago asking her to come visit again and to bring Clarissa. That was before all this business with Grace Annie. I hadn't heard back from her. There she was, just when I needed her.

The petition Verna's attorney made to the court was a request for a contingency to give more time before the judge had to make a decision. The judge agreed and said for everyone to be back in six months and cracked his gravel.

"Court adjourned," he said.

Six months! Annie would be a year old by then. Didn't that judge realize how much time I was losing with my baby girl that I could never get back? I made my way to the back of the room. Rebecca rushed up to me.

"How'd you know to be here? I said.

"Didn't," she said.

"Then how come—?"

"Pa's had himself a heart attack."

"Ooooh, noooo—"

"He's got pneumonia and his kidneys is failing," Rebecca said. "Ma says you best come right away, if you wanna see him."

"Is he gonna die?" I started shaking. I wasn't sure I could take any more bad news.

"He's had a heart attack," Rebecca said. "It looks bad, Adie. His liver's probably shot, too."

I got dizzy and lost my balance. Rebecca reached out to steady me. "Now, don't go getting weak in the knees on me!" she exclaimed. "I need you to keep yourself together, you hear?" I nodded. "I'm having a hard enough time as it is what with Ma and the kids and—"

"Pa's just got to see Grace Annie!" I wailed. "She's Annie's namesake. Just wait here a minute. I gotta talk to Buck's mama."

"Make it snappy," Rebecca said. "We got a long drive."

I went over to where Verna was huddled with Evelyn Mackey and told her about my pa.

"That's a shame," Verna said. "You go on and head back to Cold Rock. Buck's old enough to fend for himself."

"But Verna," I said, "I've got to take Grace with me. She's Annie's namesake. Pa's never even seen—"

"You ain't taking Grace Annie," Verna answered. "Didn't you hear the judge?"

"Just so Pa can see her!" I said. "Please!"

"The baby ain't going nowhere," she snapped.

Miz Mackey stood there looking pleased Verna was standing her ground.

"You can come with us," I said. "That'd be fine."

"Adie," she said. "Grace Annie and me can't go prancing 'round the countryside. We got schedules to keep. And who'd take Austin anyhow?"

"We'll take him, too—"

"Sorry about yer pa," Verna said. "But yer wasting yer time. Like I said, Grace Annie ain't going nowhere. And the only place I'm going is home."

"Come on, Adie," Rebecca said. "We gotta go."

"But—"

"Miz Jenkins' right," Rebecca said. "You're wasting your time." Verna nodded, looking pleased Rebecca was agreeing with her. "You can't turn hearts with them got none to begin with," Rebecca deadpanned to Verna, catching her off guard.

"Hhmmm!" Verna huffed and marched out the courtroom door.

Miss Mackey crossed her arms and gave Rebecca a look like she was white trash and not fit to be in the courtroom.

"Bunch of pickled prunes," Rebecca said and took my arm and steered me toward the door. Evelyn Mackey glared at us as we brushed past her.

"You work hard being ugly or were you born that way?" Rebecca said.

"Well, I never—"

"You have now," Rebecca called out loudly.

Murphy and Margaret Mary were outside waiting for us, with the truck double-parked at the curb.

"Don't you worry about a thing," Murphy yelled.

He got out of the truck, told Worry to stay, then dashed around to the other side to help Margaret Mary. She was eight months pregnant, but Murphy took hold of her waist and lifted her gently to the ground like she was lighter than air.

Rebecca honked her horn and motioned for me to hurry up.

"I'm coming! Just a minute."

Margaret Mary smoothed the front of her dress and waddled over and hugged me.

"Just go be with your pa, okay?" she said, patting her tummy. It was about to pop the buttons off her dress."

"But what about Grace—?" I wailed.

"Don't worry about that, Adie. We ain't gonna stand by and let that woman keep Grace," Murphy said and slammed the door to the truck shut. "We'll get Henry Durham on it soon as you get back. He's the best lawyer around these parts, Adie. Don't you worry!"

"Well, I don't have near enough money saved up—"

"I'll just have to add it to the chicken bill, now won't I?" Murphy said. "Speaking on chickens, we'll look after yours while you're gone."

"Oh Murphy, I can't ask y'all to do that, what with the baby coming—"

"Sure you can," he said. "I got my money invested in them. You ain't paid it all back, remember?" he quipped and put his arm around my shoulder. Margaret Mary put hers around me too and grabbed hold of Murphy's elbow.

I was sandwiched between two of the best folks God ever created. It made me blubber even more. Rebecca laid on the horn again.

Murphy pulled a handkerchief out of his back pocket. "Dry them eyes," Murphy said and handed it to me. It was freshly ironed and smelled of after shave.

"What have I ever done to have such good friends?" I said, wiping my tears.

"That's the thing about friendship," Murphy said. "It don't need to be earned. It's a paycheck waiting, just for showing up."

Rebecca started honking non-stop. I threw up my arms and ran over to her car.

"Now, please don't be having the baby while I'm gone," I called out.

"No chance of that," Murphy yelled. "Doc says we got at least another month."

Rebecca tooted the horn and tore out of the parking lot with me half-hanging out of the front passenger door. "I ain't got all day," she said and hit the gas pedal.

It was the same car she had when I left Cold Rock, an old brown Ford with the fenders nearly rusted off. It wasn't known to run all that good.

"Don't worry," Rebecca said. "I got a new man in my life. He's a mechanic. Things don't work out, least I got a new engine in this thing." Rebecca slammed the car into third gear and hit the gas pedal.

She turned the corner on two wheels and headed down Hog Mountain Road. I nearly fell out the door.

Rebecca's first husband, Riley Hooper, had taught her to drive before he took off with that girl Roxanne, so she never learned right. Riley drove like a stock car driver determined to win. I think that was why most of Rebecca's engines fell out. She drove just like him. She hadn't improved at all since I last rode with her, but maybe her choice in men had.

"He's a mechanic for real?" I asked.

"Can strip a car, shuffle the parts, and put 'em back like new," she said.

"Well, that's good," I said. "That last one wasn't very talented."

"That one didn't make no money to speak of," she said, "but he had another talent that made up for it." Rebecca turned to me and grinned. Talk like that made me feel uncomfortable. Buck had that same talent. And if practice makes perfect, like Mama always said, then he was pretty near perfect. Trouble is, he didn't do all of his practicing at home.

"Why didn't Clarissa come with you?"

"She's with the kids," Rebecca said. "Wait till you see her. She's lost fifty pounds."

"She has?"

"Joined Weight Watchers."

"I'm real glad. I was worried on her."

"You worry on everything, don't you?" Rebecca said.

"Try not to, but—"

"No sense in it," Rebecca said. "Life's a card game, Adie. Just play the hand you're dealt. Lose one hand, there's another one being dealt."

"Willa Mae says, 'Life's a kettle. Put in what you got.'"

"Who's Willa Mae?"

"She's a friend of mine. She has this journal she gave me to keep for her," I said. "It's written by this girl, Tempe, who was a slave a hundred years ago—"

"This Tempe girl worry on things, too?" Rebecca said.

"I don't know," I said. "Best I can tell she just opens her heart and lets what's in it come out."

"That don't sound like one worrying on things. Maybe you can learn something from her."

Rebecca opened up a sack on the seat cushion next to her and took out a sandwich.

"Help yourself," she said. "Egg salad."

I reached in the bag. Rebecca stepped on the gas pedal again. "Let's see if this new engine's any good."

The old Ford flew down the road, the tires spraying chunks of gravel like a popcorn popper gone mad, while the car careened from side to side. Somehow, we managed to get to the fork in the road that led to the cabin with all of our body parts intact.

"Slow down and take that dirt road there, off to the left," I said, pointing. Rebecca swerved the car onto the dirt, but she never slowed down. Rebecca was a reckless driver, but at least she was skilled at being one. We made it to the cabin.

I packed my green satchel with some of my things, tucked Tempe's journal into a worn pillowcase, placed it on top, and we set out.

I didn't see any evidence Buck had made it home from work and wondered if he was off somewhere with Imelda Jane. It wasn't a good idea leaving him here to fend for himself.

"What're you thinking about?" Rebecca asked, and started the car. "You got a mighty peculiar look on your face."

I tossed my bag into the backseat. "Nothing." Actually, I was thinking it was a sorrowful thing to be married to a man that needed babysitting. Especially now; I'd missed my monthly and my breasts were sore. That's how it started with Grace Annie. I knew Buck wouldn't be too happy if I was pregnant, seeing as we were still having money problems. Mama would say, "If you are, you are. Stop worrying on it, Adie. At least you don't get morning sickness like I did each and every time." Which was true; at least it had been with Grace Annie.

We drove in silence. No sense in telling Rebecca. She'd blab it to everyone. Right now she was busy anyway, checking the rearview mirror every few miles.

"What you looking at?" I asked.

"Making sure no one's following us."

"Who'd be following *us*?"

"The law," she said and sped ahead.

Hog Gap and Cold Rock still had the mountain between them with no road cutting through. The only way to get from one spot to the other was to take the two-lane highway that ran around it. In the distance, Cold Rock Mountain rested like a fat king on his throne. The sides sparkled like jewels as the sun bounced off chunks of granite embedded along the edges.

When I was growing up, that mountain took the breath right out of me. For sure it was the most beautiful place in the world, until Annie died there. I looked up at that big fat king of a mountain, its belly a crystal lake that had no bottom.

Why'd you swallow Annie? She was good to you. Don't you remember? She fed you flowers.

chapter eighteen

AFTER ANNIE DIED, PA STARTED drinking. It was no wonder he was bad sick with liver and heart problems. My own chest wasn't feeling too good either. Heart attacks and heartaches, it was hard to tell which was paining me more.

"You ever think back on when we were kids?" I asked Rebecca.

"No," she said.

"You don't ever pick out a favorite time and go over it in your mind?"

"Try not to," she said. "What good would it do?"

"I don't know if it does any good," I said. "But I like to do it. Makes me happy. We did have some good times, didn't we?" Rebecca gripped the wheel tight but didn't say anything.

"Like that New Year's when Mama and Pa had that party." I said. "Remember?"

"You mean the night Louise was sashaying around Pa, hanging all over him?"

"I think everyone was doing a bit of that."

"You didn't take a good look," she said.

"I watched everybody good as you," I said.

"You didn't read between the lines," Rebecca said.

I knew what she was getting at. I hadn't understood it at the time, but something happened later where it all made sense. Then the pieces fit together like a picture puzzle, one I put out of my mind so I wouldn't have to believe it really happened. That particular New Year's night was the only time Mama and Pa ever had a real type party with lots of folks over. We girls were supposed to be in bed. Rebecca and I peeked around the corner from the sleeping porch. Wasn't long before Clarissa joined us. Pa was dancing with Aunt Louise. She had on a shiny red dress. It was too tight, and her butt wiggled back and forth all the while she danced to the music.

"Lou, you got a face put Jayne Mansfield to shame and a body would too," Pa said. Me and Clarissa covered our mouths and giggled. The record player was going full blast. The floor boards hummed and tickled our bare toes. We laughed harder.

"Sssssssssh . . . be quiet," Rebecca said.

"Can't no one can hear anything above all this racket," I said.

Conway Twitty was singing "It's Only Make Believe," Daddy's favorite. Mine too. Mama was serving steaming hot bowls of vegetable soup, spiced apple rings, and fruit compote. She said the combination brought good luck. I'm not so sure. Or maybe she forgot an ingredient in one of the recipes. It turned out to be a very bad year.

Close to midnight, she started passing around glasses of Mogen David wine.

"Everybody! Git a glass, now," she said.

Arms, attached to bodies dancing about the room, reached around the others trying to grab one as Mama walked by. They were jelly jars Mama saved once we got the last lick from the bottom. Real pretty jars.

"Charlie," Mama said. "Git a glass, honey. The New Year will be here and gone."

Everybody was laughing and hugging on one another. Mama turned the record player off and switched the radio on and dialed up the volume. The announcer was counting down the numbers to the New Year. *"Happy New Year, folks!"*

A singer crooned "Should Auld Acquaintance Be Forgot." Everybody clicked their jelly glasses together and downed the wine Mama'd passed out. Then the kissing started. Pa was kissing Louise like the men in the movies do.

"Louise, let go of my man, you hussy!" Mama said, but she laughed when she said it and Louise did, too.

"And Charlie, stop hanging on her like some moonsick boy not dry behind the ears. Red and me's liable to think something's going on." Mama looked over her shoulder.

"Red? Where are you?" she said. "Git over here and make your wife behave herself."

Red was dancing with Ruth Mosley and didn't hear her. Pa pinched hold of Mama's backside and squeezed her behind. Mama brushed his hand away.

"Stop that, Charlie," she said. "And behave yourself." Pa let go of Louise and put his arm around Mama's shoulder and pulled her close to him. He tugged her head backwards and smacked her on the lips. Pa's other hand was cupping Louise's butt. Louise didn't bother pushing his hand aside like Mama did when he patted hers. Mama took note.

"Cut it out, you dirty old man," she said and swatted his hand off Louise's butt. They all laughed.

"Louise, honey, trust me," Mama said. "It ain't no big thing." Aunt Louise laughed.

"Well, if it ain't no big thing, then I guess it ain't no big thing!" Louise said and winked at Pa.

"Happy New Year, everbody!" Pa yelled.

His voice sounded funny like his tongue wasn't working right. Mama grabbed hold of him and gave him another smack on the lips.

"Happy New Year, hon,'" she said.

"This gonna be the best one yet, Ruby," Pa said. He drank another swallow of wine. Mama caught sight of us girls.

"Girls, git back in bed," she said. "This party's for grownups. You'll have your turn soon enough."

"Ah, let'em have a toast, Ruby," Pa said. "Bring this year in right. C'mere, girls."

We gathered around Pa—Rebecca, Clarissa, and me. Annie was sound asleep in her crib the last time we checked. Mama turned the record player back on full blast. Annie padded out in her jammies that had the bunny feet, rubbing her eyes. I picked her up and bounced her about the room.

"It's New Year's, Annie!" I said. "We're having a party and Pa said we can come."

Pa stuck a paper horn in Annie's mouth. She blew into it and giggled when a curly paper tongue whipped out under her nose. Mama said she was the sweetest baby this side of heaven. She was right about that. But Pa was wrong about the new year being the best one ever. It turned out to be the worst year.

"I've been having nightmares about Annie again," I said to Rebecca as she drove. She had the window rolled down and her arm hanging out like a truckdriver. She nodded, but didn't say anything.

"You blame me, don't you?"

"I used to. Shoot, you were just a kid," Rebecca said. "Pa had no business taking off and leaving you at the lake with Annie."

"He said to stay on the path. We went off to the lake on our own."

"He had no business leaving you two by yourselves, period. That nonsense about him seeing bear cubs and going off to see if the mother bear was nearby—"

"I saw them," I said.

"Bear cubs?" she said.

I shook my head.

"Pa and Aunt Louise," I said. "They were . . . on this blanket . . . I saw them and they were—"

I fidgeted with my hands in my lap, wishing I hadn't said anything, but not able to stop myself. I took a deep breath. "I saw them good as I'm seeing you."

chapter nineteen

Rᴇʙᴇᴄᴄᴀ ᴄʜᴇᴡᴇᴅ ᴏɴ ᴛʜᴇ ɪɴsɪᴅᴇ of her mouth. She did that when something bothered her bad. She'd been doing it since she was a kid. It drove Mama nuts. She said it made the inside of her mouth look like tomato chutney and she'd get herself a cancer if she didn't stop it.

"They were laying in the grass . . . on top of that blanket . . . they had their clothes off."

"Shut up!" Rebecca said. "I don't want to hear it." But now that I'd finally opened my mouth it ran like a faucet.

"This is a fine time to be bringing all this up," she said. "You trying to get back at Pa?"

"No!"

"You making all this up?"

"It's the truth, Rebecca."

Rebecca pulled the car over to the side of the road and slammed on the brakes.

"I went to get some more flowers for Annie. She was throwing them in the lake and watching them float."

"So you just wandered off with her next to a lake?"

"I told her not to go in the water . . . to stay on the bank."

"She was a baby . . . what were you thinking?"

"That's just it. I wasn't thinking. I just . . . I was coming right back . . . just gonna bring her some more of them pretty flowers that had the red parts in the center . . . she liked them best. Then I heard something . . . these peculiar noises. I peeked through the long grass and I saw them. I scrunched down and I watched. I knew it was wrong to spy on them, and I knew what they were doing wasn't right. But it was like I was nailed to the ground. I don't know how long I stayed. When I got back to Annie, she was . . . gone.

"I called out to her, 'Annie! Where are you, sugar?' I kept calling her name. I ran down the bank to the edge of the water, to see if she was dipping her feet. That's where I found her, in the water. She was floating on her tummy—right below the surface. I could see the backs of her legs and the curls on her neck. Remember how her hair always got real curly when it got wet?" Rebecca had her hands wrapped tight around the wheel. She sat stone-faced, staring out the windshield.

"I got a big stick off the bank and tried to reach her, pull her back to me.

"'Annie!' I said. 'Kick your legs, Annie! Flap your arms, honey!' I couldn't reach her with that stick. And none of us knew how to swim, you know that. I ran and got Pa. He was stepping into his pants, and Aunt Louise was fixing to put her bra on. She was slipping her arms through the straps and her breasts were dangling. I remember thinking she had really big breasts. And I noticed they had pretty pink nipples that stuck right out. Isn't that just the craziest thing to remember?"

I looked over at Rebecca, waiting for her to say something. She laid her head on the wheel, her hands still wrapped around it so tight her knuckles were white. When she looked up, she glared at me, her eyes darting back and forth from one side of my face to the other.

"Pa yelled at me, 'I told you to stay put with Annie! What you doing coming over here?"

"'Pa!' I said. 'Annie's . . . Annie's—'"

"I don't want to hear no more," Rebecca said. "She's dead. Let it alone!"

"I've been keeping it inside me all these years, Rebecca. I need to talk about it."

"You never told Mama?"

"Never."

"Well, it ain't no time to bring it up now."

"I know, it's just—"

"Just what?"

"It's like it can't rest . . . can't rest unless I get it all out."

"Louise wasn't really our aunt, you know," Rebecca said.

"I know, but she was like family . . . her and Uncle Red."

"He wasn't our uncle, neither," Rebecca said. She pulled the car back on the road and drove like the devil was after us.

"And she didn't die the way Mama said she did."

"What you mean?" I said.

"I mean she didn't die in no car crash." Rebecca slowed the car around a curve in the road.

"How'd she die then?"

"Red strangled her before he drove the car off the cliff," Rebecca said.

"But it was an accident. The paper said so."

"The paper said no such thing. Mama just read to us what she wanted us to hear. Made up the words as she went along."

"Why?" I said.

"Ask Mama. It ain't my place to say," Rebecca said. "But I will tell you this, little sis. It's all finally making sense to me. And I ain't blaming you no more for what happened to Annie. I blame myself," she said. "If I'd of told Pa what Red been doing to me all them years, he and Louise would have been long gone. And Pa wouldn't of been off with Louise doing, you know—" Rebecca took out a hankie and wiped her nose. "And Annie'd still be with us," she whispered.

"You can't be sure of that, Rebecca," I told her, and patted her arm. "If you'd of told, they would have put Red away. But Louise might of stayed on and tried to make up for what Red done, and her and Pa might have ended up like I found'em anyway."

Rebecca drove on without talking. I laid my head back against the seat cushion and tried not to think of anything, but the closer we got to Cold Rock, the more the memories came rushing at me.

After that summer when Annie drowned, Pa never drank Mogen David wine again. He started in on what Mama called the "hard stuff." He went to work every morning. He came home to eat supper every night. He set the whiskey bottle on the table next to his place. Mama dished the food onto his plate and clanged the pots and pans around, but she didn't ask him how his day went and she always used to do that.

Once, I said, "Pa needs you, Mama. He's hurting bad over Annie, maybe worse than any of us."

"He ain't hurting worse than me, Adie Thacker," Mama said. "I was her mama. I carried her. Ain't nobody hurting worse than me, for God's sake, and I don't ever want to hear that crap come out of yore mouth again!" She grabbed my arm and gave it a shake.

"You hear me, Adie girl?" Mama yanked hard on my arm.

"I hear, Mama, I hear!" I said. "You're hurting my arm."

"I'll hurt more'n yore arm, I hear that kinda talk again. Your Pa's got Jack Daniel to keep him company. What have I got?"

"You got us, Mama!" I said, but she didn't hear me. After Annie died, she grew cotton plugs where her ears used to be.

I wanted to tell her she had her friend Bernice Mosley. She came calling all the time, asking about her. Red and Louise moved away right after the funeral, so Mama didn't have them. We got word later they were dead, and we girls all cried. Mama laid the paper out on the kitchen table. The top line said "Rudolph 'Red' Pearce and Louise Allen Pearce found dead at scene off Pine Cliff Rd."

chapter twenty

IT WAS NEARLY DARK WHEN we got to the hospital. Rebecca pulled up to the front entrance and stopped the car.

"Pa's on the third floor," she said. "I'm going home to check on the kids."

I got out of the car.

"Here, take your bag," she said. "You'll be staying with Mama. God knows there's not a lick a room at my place."

She drove off. I toted the green satchel inside and asked the lady at the check-in desk where the elevator was.

"Who you here to see, hon'?" she said.

"My pa," I said. "He's had a heart attack."

"I'm sorry, darlin'. What's his name?"

"Charlie Thacker."

"Let's see . . . we have a Charles H. Thack—"

"That's him," I said.

"He's in room three-twelve, sugar," she said. "Take the elevator at the end of the hall and turn right when you get off, first door on your left."

Mama was sitting on a chair outside the room. She had on a flowered house dress with her old brown sweater wrapped around her shoulders. And she had on penny loafers and white socks. Mama always wore rolled down white socks with her loafers even though it wasn't in style anymore. She stopped dressing like Jackie after the president got shot and killed and Jackie married Onassis. I remember the nation being upset about it, but Mama said she couldn't blame her none. Still, she didn't like the way she dressed after that.

"Pants that don't even reach her ankles, striped T-shirts, and a scarf tied around her head like a field hand," Mama said. "What kinda fashion statement is that?"

"She's got a different lifestyle now, Mama," I said.

"Maybe so, but it ain't worth getting my sewing machine out for." She was still her bubbly self when she said it. But that was ages ago.

Now, she looked wore out. Her hair was limp and her skin was pale. For a second I wanted to go over and slap her silly. Ask her why she'd been so mean to us all those years when we needed her. The next instant I wanted to hug her and tell her everything was going to be all right. Times were hard on her, too. She was hurting inside, maybe doing the best she could. Back and forth, resentment and forgiveness battled inside me like punch-drunk boxers staggering about until the next round.

"Mama?"

"Why Adie—" Mama got up and put her arms out to me.

"Oh, Mama," I said, glad the soft feelings inside me were winning the fight. There was so much I wanted to tell her, but all I could do was cry. She took a hankie out of her bag and wiped my tears like she did when I was very little and I'd hurt myself. I squeezed my eyes tight. My knees were skinned and my elbows were split. Of course they weren't, but for a moment it was as if they were. The feel of Mama's arms, the sound of her voice, her smell, something from Avon—Unforgettable, I think—it all came back.

"Mama, I'm so worried about you," I said.

"Don't be crying for me," she said. "Any burden I got, I pretty much deserve."

"Don't say that, Mama."

"It's true. I didn't do right by you girls . . . all those years—"

"But you tried Mama, didn't you?

"I hope I did. I hope—" Mama's voice cracked.

"Don't look back, Mama. Willa Mae says, 'Happiness comes in the front door. You go 'round back, you might not hear it knocking.'"

"Who's Willa Mae?"

"She's an old friend of mine; I mean, she's this older person who's a new friend. She's real special. She took care of me and Grace Annie when I got hurt."

"I shoulda been there for you. I been meaning to come. I got the pictures." Mama opened her bag again and took out the envelope I'd sent her.

"See? I keep 'em with me. I showed yore Pa, but he got all that medicine in him," she said. "How's Grace Annie?" Mama looked at the pictures in her hands. "I think she looks like yer Aunt Orlene, specially on this one here." Mama pointed to one with Grace Annie trying to put a rattle in her mouth.

"They took her . . . Mama . . . they said—"

"Took her where?"

"She fell off her dressing table and County took her right from the hospital. They thought I wasn't a good mama. Now Verna's got her and—"

"The hospital . . . she okay?"

"I think so. The doctors said they couldn't find where it hurt her, and they watched her good. But now Verna's got her, and she wouldn't even let me bring her with me, so Pa—"

"Verna Jenkins?"

"Uh huh. I think she's on their side. She said I best get a lawyer when I told her I had that right."

"Oh Adie, I'm gonna come back with you—"

"Will you, Mama?" I said. "Will you come and tell them I am *too* a good mama?"

"Soon's we take care of yer Pa—" Mama brushed the strands of hair out of my eyes.

"Is Pa gonna get well?"

"They don't think so, honey—"

"But I haven't had a chance to . . . to . . . why does he hate me so?"

"He doesn't hate—"

"When Annie . . . when she died . . . it was . . . it was an accident . . . I didn't mean to leave her," I blubbered.

"Adie . . . he hates himself. There's a difference."

"But he blames me for what happened that day. I know he does—"

"He blames himself. That's why he can't face you. He can't face himself."

"But it was an accident—"

"Was it?" Mama said. "Some the things went on up there didn't have to be wenting on up there—"

I looked at Mama. I held my breath and waited.

"Your Pa's got loose lips when he drinks—"

"What do you mean?" I said, knowing full well what and hoping it would be and praying for it to be. I wanted it out in the open where we could smack it around and break it into tiny pieces, bits small enough for me to swallow. I wanted the knot in my throat and the boulder in my chest to leave me be.

"Let's just say there's some things . . . some things you don't know about that day . . . things better left unsaid—"

"No!"

"No what?"

"I want them said. I know about it, Mama!" I blurted out.

"But how do you—?" Mama's words hung in the air as she sucked in her breath, her brow wrinkled up in thought. In an instant, the lines on her forehead disappeared as her face muscles relaxed. She'd discovered the answer to her own question before she'd even exhaled.

"You were *there*—" she breathed out softly.

"I was," I said. "And I saw them," I whispered.

"Oh, Adie," Mama reached for me. Her green eyes opened wide and froze in their sockets. She put her arms around me. "You were seven years old. Why didn't you tell me?"

"I couldn't, Mama," I said. "Losing Annie broke your heart. I didn't want to break it worse. I wanted it to heal."

"Well, it all came out anyway—"

"Pa told you what happened?"

She nodded.

"When?"

"A long time ago," she said, tears welling up in her eyes.

"Did you forgive him?"

"Eventually," she said.

"Then why didn't things get better between—"

"My forgiving him wasn't the problem, Adie," she said and tucked loose strands of hair behind my ear. "He wasn't able to forgive himself."

"Why didn't he tell me, Mama?"

"It wasn't something you tell a child."

Mama stared at me and cleared her throat, then swallowed hard. "You been carrying that secret around all these years . . . well, no more," she said. "You ain't done nothing wrong."

I hugged her so tight I could feel her rib bones. She tucked her hand under my chin and brought it up level with hers.

"But I did do wrong! I left Annie," I said. "I went off to get her some more flowers and, oh Mama, I shouldn't of done that. That's what's been killing me all these years. Not what Pa did, what I did!"

"Hush," Mama said. "You were little yourself. Had no business being left alone on that mountain with Annie . . . you hear me?"

I nodded, but I couldn't get the bad feelings out of my heart. They'd clung to my insides so long, it was like they were part of me.

"I should of gone with you girls, but no, I was worried that my cranberry-orange relish was gonna melt before we could set down to eat all the food I toted up there," she said. "Weren't none of it your fault, Adie. And it's a sorry shame you been thinking all these years it was. Now, dry your eyes and go say good-bye to your Pa." Mama smoothed my cheeks and patted my clothes in place like I was still a child in need of attention.

"What should I say? Should I . . . tell him—?"

"Tell him what's in your heart, Adie," she said and turned me toward the door to Pa's room. "And tell him to listen—that way he'll hear better."

chapter twenty-one

IT WAS A RELIEF TO know that Mama was coming with me when I went back to Hog Gap. I wanted her to teach me how to be strong. For certain I wanted to tell her I was probably pregnant again, and what in heaven was I going to do? I wanted to curl up in her lap and let her fight my battles until I could face them alone. If that didn't work, I just wanted to lean on her. That alone would make everything feel better.

Pa never woke up, so I didn't get to ask him to forgive me for leaving Annie alone up on the mountain. Mama had his body sent over to William Crawford Funeral Home until she could decide what to do. The neighbors came by and brought the usual assortment of food. Mama sat them down and served them her pears soaked in wine.

"Takes the edge off," she said.

We girls gathered in the back bedroom while they clustered around Mama like grapes on a vine.

It was the first time in quite a few years we'd spent any time together just being sisters.

"He's with Annie now," Clarissa said.

"What difference does it make? He's dead," Rebecca said

"He was our pa, Rebecca," I said. "Don't you hurt for him a'tall?"

"Maybe," she said.

"Why can't you show it?" I said. Rebecca stood there acting real tough, but tears welled up in her eyes.

"Why can't any of us show it? Why can't we finally say the things we've kept inside us?" I said. "I'm tired of pretending everything's all right when it's not."

Clarissa started crying. I put my arm around her and what d'you know? Rebecca put her arms around the both of us. We cried for a while, hugging and patting each other, stopping now and then to catch our breath or pass around the tissues. Then we'd start in again, three sisters finally giving one another comfort while we shared our sorrow. I think we cried over what we should have cried over years ago. For the hurts and regrets we never got out when Annie drowned. For keeping our thoughts on how it must have been for her those last few minutes locked inside us. Picturing her calling out and struggling all alone in that deep water with no one there to help her. Crying for Pa and what he missed with us and us with him. For Mama and the years she spent alone when Pa hid in the bottle. Mostly, I think we cried for each other, for the times we could have shared our pain and didn't. I cried pretty hard over the fact we were finally doing that now. When we finished, it got real quiet. Mama tapped on the door.

"Girls? Someone here to see you," she said. She opened the door a crack. "It's Delva and Marie, here to pay their respects."

Rebecca opened the door and motioned for her friends to come in. Mama went back to the ones gathered in the front room.

"This is Adie," Rebecca said. "She's the pregnant one Pa run off I told you about."

"Rebecca!"

"Well, it's the truth," she said. "This is Delva."

Rebecca pointed to a tall thin young woman with red hair and buck teeth.

"How do," she said.

"And the one's got the teeth don't stick out is Marie," Rebecca added. Marie smiled. Her teeth were near perfect. But poor Delva; hers were too large to fit into her mouth. And leave it to Rebecca to point it out, when it didn't need pointing out at all.

"You girls know Clarissa," she said.

The girls nodded and both said how sorry they were and so on, and they'd lost their pa, too, and ain't it terrible.

"Oh, it ain't so bad," Rebecca said. "He weren't that great of a guy."

"Rebecca!" I said.

"She's just saying that 'cause we're all cried out," Clarissa said.

"Oh what the heck! Let's get happy!" Rebecca said, and she started the "remember whens," and I gotta tell you, it was pretty funny.

"Listen to this," she turned to Delva and Marie. "When Burt Hollis and his family first moved in down the road apiece. . . . Oh that's right, you never met any of 'em; they moved away before you got here."

"Rebecca," Clarissa said, "tell the story!"

"I'm getting there," she said. "Well anyway, they moved into the old Harris place just down the road," Rebecca waved her hand in the air and pointed out the window. "And one of his kids started a fire and burned most the house down. Well Pa's home, and he sees the smoke and he hightails it down the road cause he knew some family had moved in. Hadn't met 'em yet, or anything."

"Get to the good part," Clarissa said.

"Well, Pa," Rebecca says, "he gets there, and this woman and about five little kids is near hysterical, jumping up and down, screaming and crying and carrying on, and this one little guy tells Pa that Pete's inside. He's screaming, 'Pete's in there! Pete's in there!' And Pa don't know Pete from Adam's cat. Hell, he don't know none of them, and the woman is rocking this baby in her arms, ten, eleven months old, and the baby is screaming louder than the kid yelling about Pete.

Now Pa can't get a straight answer out of this woman, so he goes flying into the house to get little Pete, and by this time flames is just shooting out the windows everywhere, and—"

Rebecca is bent over laughing when she gets to this part, and Delva and Marie look at each other like she's taking leave of her senses.

"What in high heaven is so funny about that?" Delva says.

"'Cause Pete's a . . ." Clarissa butts in, "Pete's . . . Pa near kills himself running into that house . . . and . . . Pete's a—" Clarissa is laughing too hard to continue, and so am I.

"Pete's a turtle!" Rebecca blurts out.

Delva and Marie still don't quite get the humor in all of it. Come to think of it, it wasn't funny at the time, but years later we thought it was, even Pa. He used to tell it best.

"I made it out with that dang turtle, too," he said. "If I was gonna meet my maker in that blasted fire, I sure as hell was gonna have something to show for it. And what'd you know? The dadblame thing bit me!" Pa said.

"Once he got in there, how did he figure out Pete was a turtle?" Marie asked.

"Said he looked in every bedroom; there weren't but three," Rebecca said. "And the last one he come to had a crayon sign that said ANYONE LETS PETE OUTA HIS BOX DIES!"

We all bowled over. Delva and Marie finally got it and joined in.

"Tell 'em about when Pa toted Mama's purse home from the church picnic," Clarissa said.

"Oh God," Rebecca said. "He near got arrested." Rebecca loved telling that story, too. We got drenched in a storm that came out of nowhere. Mama asked Pa to get her purse off the table while we kids ran with the food and blankets and lawn chairs back to the car. Later that night, Mama went to get money for the milk man coming in the morning. It wasn't even her purse.

"Hon, you took Emma Weeks's purse!" Mama said. Her wallet and driver license was inside.

"Well, I'll be damned," Pa said. "That old bat, she'll think I done it on purpose."

"Now, Charlie, why're you saying a thing like that?" Mama said. "She's a good Christian woman, goes to church every Sunday. You go Christmas and Easter, and then we got to drag you."

"That's right," Pa said. "You forget what she said to me the last time?" Mama looked at Pa but didn't answer.

"'What you been waiting on, Charlie—six strong men to carry you in?'" Pa mimicked. "Mean-spirited woman, I'm telling you," Pa said.

Miz Weeks did call the law on him, but they got it all cleared up. And Mama got her purse back. It was still sitting out in the rain on the picnic table.

Thinking back on those times made me sorrier than ever that I didn't get a chance at the hospital to try and make things right between me and Pa. I figured maybe I could talk to him at the gravesite in case the part of the dead that lived on could hear. But Mama had him cremated.

"It don't cost near as much as a regular burial," she said. "Besides, I want to put him in Cold Rock River, so he can sort of be with Annie."

"Trying to rub his body in it?" Rebecca said.

"Course not," Mama said. "It's just . . . well, his heart never left that spot where Annie took her last breaths. I figure what's left of him best join up with where his heart's been all these years."

We climbed the mountain together, Mama, Clarissa, Rebecca, and me. We gathered in a circle at the edge of the lake, near the spot where they found Annie. Mama said a prayer she made up.

"Glory be. Alleluia. Amen," she said when she finished. She motioned us girls to put the magnolia leaves in the water we'd toted up the mountain so she could scatter Pa's ashes on top of them. Mama brought them up in her favorite pail, the one she planted geraniums in each spring and put out on the front stoop. The funeral parlor wanted too much money for this urn they recommended.

"This is our deluxe model," the funeral director said. "It's made of solid copper with inlaid tiles imported from Italy."

"Well, I don't mind spending good money on something special," Mama said.

"This is one you'll treasure," he said. "I'll see to it that the dearly departed's ashes are placed in it—"

"Hold on a minute," Mama said. "We're not keeping him."

"I beg your pardon?"

"We're gonna scatter him in a special spot we got picked out," Mama said. "Just put the dearly departed in a plain container to go."

That funeral man put the fancy urn away. He brought out a plain white cardboard box and handed it to Mama like it would contaminate his hands if he held it too long.

So there we were, all gathered around, fixing to send Pa to his final resting spot at he bottom of the lake. Mama tipped the bucket and tossed the ashes as far across the surface as she could. The wind caught hold of them and carried a good many of them off. We pretended not to notice that parts of Pa were floating over our heads. We stared at what was left of him floating in the water.

"Charlie, honey," she said, "We're all here, all your girls, even Annie. Well, she's here in our hearts. Rest yourself good, now. And stop blaming yourself for what happened up here. I know you didn't mean it, hon. It's past time we put it behind us. God knows we've suffered enough over it. Besides, the good Lord promised a safe landing, not a calm passage. And all things considered, life usually works out the way He intends for it to, so maybe He wanted Annie up there with him all along. If that's the case, and you hadn't cooperated the day she left us, He would of just found another way. You was a pretty good husband and father up till then. It's a shame you weren't worth much after, but I forgive you and I think the girls do, too. That right, girls?" Mama said.

"Uh-huh," Clarissa said, and I nodded. Rebecca looked at Mama with her lips pinched tight together.

"Maybe not Rebecca," Mama said. "She still don't look none too happy—"

"Don't be telling him that!" Rebecca said.

"You forgive him or what?" Mama said.

"I reckon," Rebecca said and sighed.

"That's good," Mama said and put her arm around her shoulder. "Let's not take any bad, sorrowful feelings down the mountain. Let's leave 'em all up here, okay?" We nodded.

"Well, that's it, hon," Mama said. "We're going now." She headed toward the path down the side of the mountain that didn't slope quite so steep, and we followed.

"Mama, did you mean all that stuff about Pa cooperating with God and Him maybe wanting Annie up there all along?" I said.

"Sounds like hogwash to me," Rebecca said.

"Why are you being so nasty?" Clarissa said.

"Did you mean it, Mama?" I asked again.

"You know, girls," Mama cut in, "sometimes the worst thing turns out to be the best thing. And sometimes the worst thing *stays* being the worst thing. But no sense telling your Pa that when he just got thrown in the lake."

chapter twenty-two

"WHAT YOU GOT THERE?" CLARISSA said, eyeing the journal laid out on the bed. I was perched at the edge drying my hair with a towel. The old fan on the dresser whirred away, sending too much cool air toward my wet head. I moved to the far side of the room away from the blades.

"It's Willa Mae's journal," I said. A few more rubs and my hair was nearly dry. I hung the towel on the metal hook on the back of the door, wondering what it would be like to have hair like Rebecca's, hair so thick she said when she washed it, it wasn't even dry by morning. "She's off to the ocean. She gave it to me to for safe keeping."

"Who?"

"The lady who gave me the journal—Willa Mae," I said. "She took a vacation." I took my robe off and put my pajamas on. My skin smelled like Mama's lavender soap I'd used for my bath.

"Mama mentioned her. What's it about?" Clarissa asked, but didn't wait for an answer. She disappeared into the closet to get out of her clothes and change into her night ones. The closet was about the size of a bathtub tipped on its side. I heard her knocking and bustling about. She opened the door and climbed out from under a rack of clothes, wearing a pink flowered nightie that hung to the floor.

"I made this out of bed sheets," she said. "Can you tell?" I was about to tell her I couldn't.

"What'd you say this is about?" she said and flipped back the bed covers.

"A slave girl born a hundred years ago; it's her diary."

"Oh, let me read some!" she said and climbed up on the bed.

"Maybe I better get permission before I let you do that," I said. "Nothing against you, Clarissa, but Murphy said—"

"Murphy? Who's he?"

"He's . . . well, Willa Mae was his . . . oh, bother, you need to come for a visit," I said. "It's too late to explain," I said and climbed under the covers. "I've been wanting you to do that, anyway. You should see Grace Annie."

Clarissa's face brightened. "Soon as I get some time off." She plumped her pillow and adjusted the blankets to suit her. Even with the weight she'd lost, there wasn't much left of the double bed for me once she claimed her share.

"Best not stay up too late," she said. "Mama wants y'all to get an early start come morning." She pulled the lamp chain on her side of the bed and that part of the room went dark.

"I won't." I lay on my stomach near the edge of the bed and opened the journal, quickly finding my page marker. "This light gonna bother you?"

Clarissa didn't answer. She'd already nodded off. I huddled under the covers. The words on the soft yellow pages carried me back to a time when the color of a person's skin—not the presense of a soul—determined who was human and who was not.

• • •

Massah Major don't waste none the years the colored gals kin be having babies. He be building his stock up like he do his animals. That next week after Grady be gone, Massah come to me and says I's to jump the broom with Johnson. Why he pick for me to be wid him I don't know. Johnson was the driver Negro, that be the boss over the other slaves what works the field picking the cotton. We is to pick a hunnert fifty pounds a' that cotton ever day or we gits a whooping for sure and dat's a truth.

Why Johnson gits to be the driver Negro, I don't knows about that neither. But the folks in the cabin say he could pick two hunnert pounds cotton and be the bes' worker and that why he be's the boss Negro. I not sure that be's the truth. He work that good, knowing Massah Major, he still be doing the work. Could be he boss 'cause he big as the wagon come git the cotton we puts in the oak baskets. That wagon be waiting fer us to pour in the cotton what we picked and when it be full the oxen pull that wagon to the horse-power gin. They gits it ready for the worker gals what do the carding and the spinning at night when the field work be done.

The others pretty much look up to Johnson, him being the boss-man, and Johnson love strutting in front all the colored folks, he sure do. Could be why I neber like him good. Johnson is long over six feet tall and got a strong black body kin whip two field hands at once, if'n they don't picks the cotton good when he tell 'em to. Mostly he not real mean, jist go by the rules Massah give him and we alls do like he say so nobody much git whipped. And Johnson's mama teach him to treat the colored gals good and he do. Das why I don't knows why I not happy to be jumpin' the broom wid him. Could be Grady be my man still, even when he be dead. But I jumps the broom with Johnson and he struts 'round good for all to see, 'cause member they all thinks I am da prettiest yeller gal what Massah Major got. And after dat, the Massah tells us to take to the bed and gives us dat little cabin be only one room and used for six, seven days after each couple be married. In dat cabin I tells Johnson I am not gwine in the bed with him and that be final, so not to be pestering me. Now I know Johnson kin beat me and make me do like he say, but I know he not about to do that. All the colored folks would see he got to beat me so's to lie down with him. No man be the strutting kind wants for that, so Johnson he begs and begs for me to come to the bed. Near morning he gives up and goes to sleep. He say, "Tells you what, Tempe. I not make you lies wid me so longs you don't tell nobody." That be a good deal and I agrees. 'Course no babies never come from our jumping the broom and Massah Major be watching but it never happen. Come a year later he tells Johnson I'm not married to him no more and marries me to Clyde, what belonged to Marse Hawkins. Clyde come on Saturday nights to be with me and then he goes back on Sunday. Johnson never struts so good no more, not even when he bossing in the fields. But Clyde and me not hab no babies neither and we should 'cause I lies in the bed wid him many nights. He a good man like Grady and after all that time I's lonely so I lies with Clyde and it be pretty good, doing dat, too. But no babies come even though I lies wid him many months. Massah gits the doctor to see me and the doctor says, "She got the spasm's." Whatever dat was, guess it keeps me from habing the babies. Johnson he be real glad when he see no babies be coming. And Massah Major not pester me agin 'bout having the babies once the doctor say I gots the spasms.

That give me time to think on how I am to git my little chilluns back be mine. I heard dey was maybe in Atlanta. But sometime after that a black gal Massah buys say she see her Massah in Alabama buy three little chilluns from the speculator man come over from Georgia, so I think maybe that could be dem and they's in 'nother state by now. And Nicey say, "Dey's might could be in Lousiana or eben Virginia. No telling where dey is. Dat speculator man, he goes here, dere, eberwhere."

"That be right?" I say.

"Das real right," she say.

And dis sassy color gal say, "You ain't never gonna see dem chillun's agin. Bes' jist gits dem out yore head."

The years is going by, sure 'nuf, while I am dere on Massah Major's place. Den in April 1861, the war dey say is coming for the longest time show up. It start when the grey soldiers from the south fire on Fort Sumter. Johnson tells us that be's in dat South Carolina place and I thinks maybe my chillun is there and hopes they's not git killed when the soldiers shoot at dem Yankees and dem ol' Yankees shoots back. Later, the war is going on ever'where and all the white mens is signing up to fight, even the young boys is. And Marse Hawkins, he send Clyde to go fight in his son Lawrence's place when he got a notice he got to come fight. Dey say he kin do that. So Clyde go off to that war to fight. Dey goes to Virginia and long time later we hears dat General Jackson be called Stonewall is shot by one his own men up dere and he dies come eight, nine day after dat.

Things was mostly going crazy. Some the Negroes don't wait for the war to free them. They run off to the Union lines and escapes. One dem comes back. He say the Union soldiers put him to the fighting and he skeered he be killed dead for sure, and weren't no sense being free if he's dead. Some the Negro mens that run off to fight has womens and chilluns back on da plantation. And their Massahs be angry 'bout dem running off and he sells dere families and don't keep the family wid each other when he sells them. And somes the others that stay, dey is beating worse than befo', so it not be good if a black man run off to fight in dat war and he got a family.

Massah Major not treat me no better and no worse for Clyde be fighting in dat war, 'cause he know Marse Hawkins send him to fight in Lawrence spot and Massah Major say he do the same he got a son fighting age. 'Course he got plenty sons, but they is black and he not gwine count them. That war go on lot longer than the southern folks think it will and three years go by, least. We hear thousands of mens is kilt on both sides. No word come 'bout Clyde and I thinking he maybe be's dead and dat make me have a bad ache in my body. He a pretty good husband, and I sure be's missing him and hopes he not dead and kin come back to me, and we kin goes looking for my chilluns, 'cause Clyde tell me once he do's dat wid me. "We find dem chilluns is yore'n, Tempe, when da freedom come." He do. He say dat and dat's a truth.

chapter twenty-three

"WAKE UP! REBECCA'S MAKING BREAKFAST," Clarissa said and pulled the pillow out from under my head. "Mama went to get the spare tire fixed and says to be ready when she gets back. How can you sleep with all this racket going on anyway, Adie?"

Rebecca's boys had the cartoons on the TV turned up so loud, I wondered that very same thing.

"I guess I stayed up too late reading," I said. I pulled a pair of red pedal pushers out of the duffel bag and slipped my arms into the white blouse I'd packed for the ride home.

"You best git in here, Adie," Rebecca yelled. "There won't be nothing left."

When I got to the kitchen, food had taken over the table. Biscuits, sausage and gravy, grits, scrambled eggs, bacon, fried potatoes, toast, applesauce, hotcakes, maple syrup, whipped butter, spoon bread, double thick slices of French toast, apple butter, Mama's blueberry marmalade, and tomato-basil jam. Orange juice was in a glass pitcher on the sideboard, and hot steaming coffee was in a pot on the stove.

"Goodness to heaven. Who's gonna eat all this?" I said. I no sooner said it when Riley Jr., Clayton, and Girard started grabbing the bowls and fighting over the platters.

"Clayton's taking all the gravy agin, Ma!" Riley Jr. yelled.

"Am not," Clayton said

"Liar!" Riley shot back. "Yer worser'n yer pa! He was a big liar, too!"

"Well yer pa was a skunk's butt!" Clayton said.

"Hush up the both of yous," Rebecca said. "Neither one of you got a pa to brag on."

"Is Riley's pa a skunk's butt, Mama?" Girard said.

"No, honey, he's a horse's derriere," Rebecca said. "Now eat!" She turned to me and pointed to the food.

"Adie, git yourself a plate. I swear you're skin and bones, girl," Rebecca said. "Don't you cook there in Hog Gap or what?"

"Not like this," I said. "You could feed the whole town, I reckon, with this spread."

"Well, Delva and Marie's coming," she said. "And Mama'll be back soon. Ronnie went with her."

"Ronnie?" I said.

"Ya, Ronnie," Rebecca said. "My mechanic fellow . . . guy that keeps my engine tuned." She winked.

Delva and Marie knocked twice, then opened the screen door and walked right in.

"Morning y'all," Delva called out.

"Move over, you little hogs," Marie said and oinked at the boys. They giggled and snorted back at her.

"Don't encourage them, Marie," Rebecca said.

Marie covered her mouth and snorted behind her hand again. The boys followed suit.

"Marie!" Rebecca yelled.

"Okay, okay!" she said to Rebecca, then turned to the boys. "Be good pigs, now, and don't oink at the table."

Rebecca handed us girls plates, and we proceeded to pass around the platters.

"You boys finished?" Rebecca said.

"Uh-huh," Girard said.

"Excuse me?"

"Yes ma'am," he added. Rebecca eyeballed Riley and Clayton.

"Yes ma'am," each said.

"Well then, go on outside and let us grown bodies eat in peace." The boys went flying toward the back door.

"And rest your bellies 'fore you run wild in that yard, hear me?" Rebecca called after them.

The food was delicious, and the conversation a welcome relief from my troubles. If I *was* pregnant, morning sickness obviously wasn't going to be a problem. I had second helpings and no trouble keeping it down. Rebecca put away the leftovers and plopped back down on a kitchen chair.

"I cooked," she said. "You gals kin wash and dry." She tossed the dishrag to me. "The towels are in that top drawer," she motioned to Delva and Marie. "Don't be shy." I filled up the sink with hot sudsy water and started washing the plates.

"We had a bit of excitement at our place this weekend," Marie said.

"You ought not be running your mouth, Marie," Delva said. "Ma will box your ears in, girl, she finds out."

"How's she gonna find out?" Marie asked and popped her eyes open wide and stretched her neck in her direction. Delva shrugged her shoulders and gave her a suit-yourself-it's-your-funeral look.

"We got this girl cousin," Marie continued. "She come to town with her ma yesterday to spend the Easter weekend with us, our ma and her ma's sisters. Well, seems she got herself in the family way again," Marie said.

"Again?" Clarissa said. "How many times she done it?"

"Once before, when she was fifteen. And her pa went after the fellow what did it. He weren't but a kid. Damn near beat him to death with a shovel before somebody stopped him."

"This supposed to be a funny story?" Rebecca said.

"Sounds awful," Clarissa said. "What happened to the kid who got beat in the head?"

"I was getting to that," Marie said. She finished drying a glass, tossed me the dish towel, and continued the story.

"They take him to the hospital, and our uncle, he pays the bill, and then gives his ma a bunch a' money to shush up—say it was an accident—and not call the law on him. Then he sends our cousin off to Atlanta to this unwed mother's home and tells everybody she's off at some fancy girl's school, Woodruff Academy, I think. The funny thing is," Marie said, "guess who the daddy is *this* time?"

"Who?" Clarissa says.

"Guess," Marie said. Clarissa shrugged her shoulders. I finished drying the glasses and started in on the plates.

"Come on, guess," Marie said.

"Same boy who done it last time," Rebecca said.

"Nope," Marie said, and grinned. "His younger brother!"

"That other kid weren't never right in the head after that beating our uncle give him," Delva said.

"That's why he give his mama all that money," Marie said.

"Mama says he's *still* giving her money," Delva piped in. "Bought her a fancy car, too."

"That's a terrible story," I said, realizing there was something very familiar about it.

"And that ain't the half of it," Marie continued.

"Last night our cousin said she ain't going away this time, that she's keeping this baby. Says she loves the daddy, and she's got it all planned out, they're gonna get married. When she said that, our aunt dragged her around the house by her hair. About pulled every bit of it out by the roots, she did. Real pretty hair she got herself, too. "

"Golly," Clarissa said. "Then what happened?"

"We got up this morning, and Ma is having a major breakdown. She'd rather be struck by lightning than git a long distance phone bill, and our cousin's on the phone to her pa in Hog Gap and she won't get off the line! She's crying, carrying on, telling him all about the baby and who the daddy is and how much she loves him and they can't git married for the time being 'cause he already is. And our aunt is having a heart attack when she hears our cousin on the phone, because the reason she come to us in the first place is she weren't never gonna tell our uncle. Said this time he'd likely beat the one that did it to death."

"Hog Gap?" I said. "Did you say Hog Gap?"

"Surely did."

"Hog Gap, Georgia?"

"That very place," Marie said.

"They own a store over there," Delva said.

"They got a bunch a' money," Marie added.

"Adie lives in Hog Gap now!" Clarissa piped in.

"Well, I'll be," Marie said.

"Maybe you know her," Delva said and turned to me. "Her name's Imelda Jane. Imelda Jane Fletcher."

The plate I was drying popped out of my hand and crashed to the floor.

chapter twenty-four

LET ME TELL YOU SOMETHING Mama did after Annie died. She brought this man home for supper.

"This here's Larry. His uncle owns the new filling station," she said and handed Pa the mashed potatoes.

We ate our dinner like usual, stealing glances at Pa to see if we could get a read on what he was thinking.

"Good money in the filling station, iz there?" Pa said.

"Think I'll have me a bit more of them taters," Larry answered and nodded. It was the weirdest thing. We girls kept waiting for something to happen.

"You got anymore of them taters?" Larry said, and Mama nodded and got up to get them.

"Charlie, you want some more? Git Charlie here another helping while yer at it, Ruby," Larry said.

And Mama did. But her face looked like it come out of the deep freeze—except for the vein on the side of her head. It was dancing with itself. She told us girls to gather up the dishes and get cracking. If she was trying to make some kind of statement by bringing this fellow Larry home, we never did figure out what it was.

Pa and Larry sat down and played checkers. Then they went on over to the tavern. Mama didn't say *hey, yoo-hoo, hee-haw,* or *toodle-do.* She wiped her hands on her apron, stood by the front door, and shot them a look that could drop a turkey if it'd been a gun. Then she turned on Art Linkletter.

"Don't be bothering me, girls," she said. "I got a headache could kill a herd of elephants."

I don't recall anything else happening that night. I do know Mama never brought any more men home for dinner. I figured there was some kind of powerful statement she was trying to make but never did figure out what it was or if the message got across. I told myself someday when I grew up I'd ask her. Now here we were, headed back to Hog Gap. It'd be a good time, but it no longer seemed important to me.

"You're awful quiet," Mama said.

We were about halfway there. It was taking us a while since Mama always drove the minimum speed posted, and this time wasn't any different. It felt like ninety degrees in the car and climbing. I was sticky as a hot cross bun and warm as one just pulled from the oven. Mama had the radio on to WYME, the country station. Patsy Cline was singing "Sweet Dreams," one of her favorites. She waited till it finished playing, then turned the radio down while I leaned my head out the window to catch the breeze. The air slapped my skin, thick as syrup and heavy as a quilt.

"I said, you're—"

"Did you ever forgive Aunt Louise?" I said and pulled my head back in. I fanned myself with a church bulletin from Calvary Baptist I spotted on the floor mat. Mama pinched her lips together, took in a deep breath, then let the air slide slowly out her mouth.

"I did," she said. "Course, I never got a chance to tell her." She dabbed at the sweat slipping down from her forehead with the back of her arm. I offered her the makeshift fan. She shook her head and kept driving.

"Took me a long time. Ya know?" she said and looked over at me. I nodded.

"Yah," I said.

"Yah," Mama bobbed her head in time with mine. "Long time I worked on trying to forgive her," she said. A small smile crossed her lips. "Know what I found out?"

"What?" I asked.

"Forgiving your enemies ain't nothing. The hard part's forgiving your friends." I thought on that a minute.

"Forgiving husbands ain't so easy, neither," I said. Her eyebrows shot up.

"What are—"

"You forgave Pa. How'd you manage that?"

"Seeing as he was punishing himself—"

"I'm having a real hard time with Buck—" I said. "He . . . he . . . he's seeing this girl Imelda Jane."

"Don't he know forbidden fruit creates a terrible jam?" Mama said.

"Speaking of jams," I said, "there's a good chance he's gotten himself into one."

"How so?"

"This girl's folks own the store where he works." I traced the scar on my leg with my finger. It was still bright pink, and I could make out the pin holes where the stitches had been. A raggedy line, it ran from the side of my knee clear up to my groin.

"Looks like Frankenstein's daughter," I said.

"What's he see in *her*?"

"Not her," I said. "My leg . . . it's a mess." Mama glanced over at me. "Oh honey, it'll fade."

"She's real pretty, beautiful even," I said.

"You know, I wanted to come see you at the hospital when you wrote what happened, but your Daddy got real sick right about then and—"

"It's okay, Mama," I said. "But what am I gonna do about Buck? He says he can't help himself. Says he didn't have a good example growing up—"

"A man good at making excuses ain't much good for nothing else," Mama said. "He got that girl in trouble?"

"He might of—" I said. "Oh, Mama! Everything is so messed up. Grace Annie is with Verna. Buck's off making a new family. I never gotta chance to tell Pa—" I started blubbering. "And what's worse, I think I'm pregnant!"

"Good Lord!" Mama said. "Well, don't cry—"

"I can't help it!" I said, and my chest heaved "I knew about Buck . . . I mean, I think I knew, but I didn't do anything. I thought maybe it would just go away."

"Like every lovesick woman that lived—"

"Mama—"

"Adie. Stop beating on yourself. Don't you know love makes fools of everyone?" I shook my head.

"Now, you listen to me, hear? We might not call the shots, but let me tell you something, we set the rules." Mama fumbled with her handbag but kept one hand on the wheel. She handed me her hankie.

"Stop sniffling and wipe your nose," she said. "And make up your mind what them rules is gonna be."

"Rules?"

"That's right," Mama said, "house rules. A body can't walk on you, Adie, unless you let 'em. You draw the line. And when you do, you tell Buck his toes cross that mark, he's out. Then you concentrate on getting Grace Annie back where she belongs. You march in that courtroom and tell them if they got a problem with your skills as a mama, you'd be happy to take some learning classes and when can you start. They know that baby belongs with her mama. You just got to stand up for yourself, Adie," she said. "Now you listen to me like you never listened before. Comes a time in every life when you know things is never gonna be the same. Something happens that might be out of your control, even. But when it happens, *what* you do defines who you are, what you stand for. From that, you get your direction, your focus. Without it, you're just a rowboat without a paddle. Only place you can go is where the current takes you." Mama pulled the car over to the side of the road. She leaned over and cupped her hand under my chin.

"Hear me good," she said. "That current never took me to any of the places I shoulda been," she said. "Adie girl, you gotta do what I didn't. Decide where you're going and how you plan to get there. You sit back and others are gonna make them choices for you."

What she said gave me the shivers. I'd stayed up half the night lost in Willa Mae's journal, and Tempe had said near the same thing. Maybe she was reaching out, trying to tell me something. And maybe she was using her words and mama's words to do it.

• • •

Dat ol' war keeps gwine on and comes a time when the Yankees makes it into Georgia. They steals everything they kin and Massah Major has us to digs a big hole and puts everything in it, even somes the cows and pigs, Massah Major has his grey uniform on from the time he was in the army when he be's a young man. He wears that uniform and sits on the porch when the grey soldiers comes by. Den one day, two Yankees come and sees Massah on the porch in that grey uniform and Massah runs into the big house. The Yankee mens run up the steps and go in after him. We hears the shooting going on inside and we thinks deys killed Massah Major. We don't think dat be so bad, but we is skeered dey is coming to gits us next, 'cause Mistress Bonner say when the war start the Yankees is coming to kills us for sure.

"Them Yankees will see all of you dead," she said, "They don't want any slaves, so they going to kill all you slaves so they're ain't any." She do, she say that and we mostly believes her, 'cause the Yankee mens is stealing all the animals and burning all the crops and taking all the food and we-uns is mostly starving by then.

When the door to the big house be opened, we is peeking 'round from the cabins to see if da soldiers be coming for us. One of the Yankee soldiers, the big tall one, comes out on the porch and we gitting ready to run for sure. Den I sees he be a Yankee soldier look jis' like Massah Major and I looks agin and it is Massah Major! He is wearing one dere uniforms and gots one der guns in his hand. It be the rifled musket fires the minié ball. Massah Major tells somes the Negro mens to come into the house and carry out the Yankee soldiers. And when they do that, one dem soldiers clothes is missing. He be shot right in the forehead. The other one is shot in his chest. Dey both dead, but their eyes is open. The Negro mens bury them in the woods.

After that, Massah Major mostly don't sit on the porch. He sit by the window in the big house and when he see who coming up the road he put the uniform on what match the one they be wearing.

The fighting goes on for real long time, and talk is the Yankees be winning. Mistress Bonner start acting real nice to us, so I think that talk be's the truth. Soon the Yankees is close by. We hear the cannons firing and somes say they is burning Atlanta. We kin see the red sky in da distance, too, so it might could be dey is burning dat pretty city. Mistress Bonner be 'bout fit to be tied, she so skeered. All the black folks say we's gonna be free, and I am thinking on what I's gwine do when they frees us. I knows I gwine looks for my chilluns, but they's plenty places they might could be. When the big Yankee general what name be Sherman burns down Atlanta, I knows I got to decide where I's gwine go and how I's gwine git there, 'cause once dat freedom come I gots to decide t'ings for myself. Can't let Massah or Mistress or no others decide dem t'ings for me, no more. Dat way I knows I really be free, 'cause free folks, dey decide for theyselves about things. And dat's a truth.

• • •

"Adie, you listenin' to me?" Mama said.

"Yes, ma'am," I said. Finally, we were almost there. The sign ahead said Hog Gap, Population: 833.

"Sometimes you gotta fight hard for what you want," Mama said.

"That way, even if you don't get it, at least you know you tried. And if what you tried don't work, then you gotta try something else. You get the picture I'm painting?"

"Uh-huh," I said.

"Well, pick up a brush and paint over any clouds got the silver lining. When you're going to war, you don't need any fairy tales or rose-colored glasses coloring your judgment. You need to see things exactly the way they are. You got to know where you're coming from to know where you're going to—"

"I get it, Mama," I said. "I get it."

"And you got to plan ahead. You think it was raining when Noah built that ark?"

On and on Mama went, just like she did when we were little. Only now it made sense. She'd gotten so smart since then.

chapter twenty-five

MAMA MADE ONE OF MY favorites—chicken curry and noodles—for supper. It was very special having her make it just for me, and I picked a chicken and wrung its neck for the occasion.

"Adie girl," she said, "you do that like you know what you're doing."

"Mama, I *do*!" I said and realized she was as proud of me as I was.

We did the dishes and I made up a bed for her on the sofa. She wouldn't take the bedroom when I offered it. Said Buck and me needed the privacy more now than ever.

"I'm pretty tired, Adie," she said. "I'm gonna turn in, but go on about your business. Light won't bother me."

"Don't you want to wait up and see Buck?" I said.

"I think you best wait up and give him a copy of them rules. 'Night," she said.

Lights flashed through the window as Buck's car pulled up in front of the cabin. His boots hit the front step two seconds later.

"Go on," Mama said. "Meet him at the door. Don't back down now." I bit my lower lip and nodded. By the time I made it to the door handle and pulled, Buck had hold of the other side and pushed. The door knocked me in the head.

"Ooouch!"

"What you doing jumping up on me like that?" Buck said. I rubbed the spot on my forehead and felt a small lump taking shape.

"You might could ask if I'm okay," I said. "I know it wasn't intentional, but the door smacked me in the head. Think you could pretend you care at least?"

"Sorry," he said. "I had a long day. All I wanna do is eat and go to bed. What'd you cook me?" He laid his lunch pail on the kitchen table and noticed Mama curled up on the sofa.

"You didn't tell me your ma was coming back with you," Buck said. "Howdy Miz Thacker."

"Buck," Mama said, with a nod. "I'll just go in the bedroom for a bit. Let you two have some time alone."

"No need for that," Buck said.

"Actually, there is," I said. "I got something I need for you to hear."

"What's going on?"

"I think you best sit down, Buck." I pulled a kitchen chair out and turned it in his direction and looked him straight in the eye.

"We got to talk about the new baby," I said. Mama went in the bedroom.

"New baby?" he said. "Good God, don't tell me you're pregnant again." Buck buried his head in his hands and groaned.

"I . . . I . . . the new baby . . . you and Imelda Jane are having," I stammered, not ready to tell him quite yet.

Buck opened his mouth. Nothing came out but air. He lowered himself into the chair.

"When'd you find out?"

"I think just now," I said. "I mean, I heard this silly story, see . . . but I was hoping that's all it was. Isn't that just the funniest thing?"

"It probably ain't mine, Adie. Talk is she's been sleeping with—"

"Buck," I said, "Don't ruin the truth by stretching it."

"God, Adie," he said. "How the devil did I get us into this—"

"You give the devil a ride, he's gonna wanna drive," I answered. "And—for the record—it's your mess. Not mine." I put my hands on my hips.

"Don't act so high and mighty," he said. "What'd you know anyway?"

"I know one thing, Buck," I said. "Just because you treat me like dirt don't mean I am." I marched over to the door and opened it wide.

"And I know the difference between a doorway and a doormat. You came into my life and there's nothing keeping you from walking out of it. But you are *not* gonna wipe your feet on me anymore while you make up your mind whether you're coming or going. And until you decide, you are *going*!" I shouted.

Mama came out of the bedroom when she heard me screaming.

"Adie girl," she said. "You okay, honey?"

"Fine, Mama," I said. "But Buck's got to be going, don't you, darling?" I said in my sweetest voice. Buck stormed out. He slammed the door so hard I jumped. A second later he came back in.

"Forgot my dad-blame lunch pail." He looked like someone had drained the air out of him. His chest wasn't puffed out near as much, and his chin wasn't stuck out as far as usual, neither. He marched out the door again, but I noticed he closed it the way one is supposed to.

"Adie, you did real fine," Mama said. "Now stick by your guns."

"I best not do *that*, Mama," I said. "I might shoot him."

chapter twenty-six

SOMETHING WOKE ME IN THE night. I bolted straight up and peered into the darkness. The trees outside the bedroom window were making scary shapes on the wall, and the branches were tapping on the pane, or were they? Was something out there?

I heard the floorboards creak. My heart pounded clear up my throat and into my head. There were voices whispering in the next room! I grabbed hold of my chest to keep my heart from beating so loud, afraid whoever they were, surely they'd find me. The bedroom door was shut, but it had no lock. Light came creeping under the frame and I spotted something shadowy moving towards the bottom. I sucked in my breath. There wasn't a bat or a broom or anything even resembling a stick to defend myself with. I tiptoed to the closet to get a hanger. Maybe I could make a poker. *Oh, God, I near forgot. Mama was out there!* The door swung open.

"Uuuuuuuuuuuuuuuuuhhhhhh." I sucked in deep breath.

The door burst open. "Adie?"

"Jeepers creepers, Mama, you give me a scare!"

"Honey, put that hanger down 'fore you hurt yerself," she said.

"Pastor Gib from your church is . . . what you got that hanger bent all out of shape for anyway?" she said.

"Pastor Gib is here?" I said. I laid the hanger down on the bed. "Mama, I near killed you with this thing! Sneaking up on me—" Mama waved her hand like it was nothing.

"He tried to call, but he says your phone ain't working. Put your robe on, honey," she said. "Did you know your phone ain't working'?"

"Why are you whispering, Mama?" I said. "There's no one here but us."

"Good question," she said. "Habit I guess, middle of the night and all—"

"Pastor Gib?" I came out of the bedroom tying the front of my robe together. He was standing in the kitchen area with the door wide open.

"Is everything all right?"

"Margaret Mary's at the hospital," he said. "Murphy sent me over to ask if you'd please come."

"Sure I will," I said. "Did she have the baby?" Pastor Gib nodded.

"A little boy," he said, then started to cry and headed toward the door.

"Pastor Gib?"

"I got to get home. I haven't told her mama yet . . . she'll be worried—"

"Pastor Gib," I said. "What's wrong? Can't you tell me what's wrong? Margaret Mary's doing fine, right?"

He got in his car, turned it around in the front yard—which was okay seeing as it was all dirt and mostly for the chickens to run around in and get their sun each day—and drove off.

"Mama, you've got to drive me to the hospital," I said when I got back in the house. "Something's wrong. I just know it."

"Honey, you really ought to git yer phone fixed—"

"Mama, there's nothing wrong with the phone. I didn't pay the bill last month is all. I was saving every penny hoping to get a lawyer," I said. "I gotta get dressed. What time is it anyway?"

Mama walked over and looked at the little clock on the stove.

"Oh, that clock don't work," I said. " There's one on my night table."

Mama headed toward the bedroom. "What's it matter what time it is?" she said. "It's the middle of the night."

"I don't know . . . I'm going crazy . . . something's wrong—" I said. "We gotta hurry, Mama. Get dressed! Hurry!"

"Let's just get there in one piece, okay?" she said and went to fetch her clothes. I waited for her on the porch, pacing like a lion in too small a cage.

"Mama? You ready? Mama?"

"I'm comin'," she said. "Hold on . . . where's my handbag?"

"Mama—"

"Never mind . . . I found it!" She called out. Down the porch steps she came, clutching her purse and dangling her keys. "Let's go." I jumped in the car.

"Please let this old junker start," I said.

"Hush up. You'll jinx it." She turned the key and the engine sputtered.

"Oh, Mama!" I said.

"Hold on, just hold on." She turned the key again. More sputters, then nothing. "Third time's a charm," Mama said. "Keep the faith!" She flipped the key. More sputters, but this time it took hold.

"See?" She laid on the gas pedal and revved up the engine.

Relieved, I leaned back in the seat and closed my eyes. Mama drove slowly down the dirt road, turned onto the gravel part, and headed in the direction I pointed her in.

"If we hurry, we can be there in forty-five minutes," I said.

"I don't see good at night," she said. "We'll git there when we git there. Settle down. You ain't gonna do this Murphy fella and his wife a bit of good if you don't. Who is this couple anyway?"

"Oh Mama," I said. "They're the best friends a body could want. They're . . . just wonderful . . they're . . ." I sat in the front seat of Mama's old Pontiac as it bumped along that gravel road and told her all about Murphy and Margaret Mary and Worry and the baby. I told her about chicken coops and chicken farming and the furniture Murphy carved and about the baby clothes me and Margaret Mary made. I told her of the pies we baked for the fair that didn't win a prize and the blue ribbon we got for our watermelon pickles that did, of the times we shared and the ones we still planned on, and I cried remembering it all.

We made it to the hospital in under an hour. Mama took hold of my arm, led me through the front door, and headed toward the information desk.

"This is where I had Grace Annie," I said. "This is where I came when I got hurt on the roof. This is where we took Grace Annie when she fell off . . . this is where that doctor said—"

"Shhhhhhhhh." Mama said. "It's gonna be okay. Now take a deep breath and stay calm." My heart was racing. Bad news hung in the air like bad breath. Murphy wouldn't send for me in the middle of the night unless he . . . he . . . I couldn't even finish the thought.

Mama was at the front desk, whispering to a lady that had blonde frizzy hair. She wore glasses with purple and blue rhinestones and double-dangly bauble earrings that jiggled when her jaw moved. Her mouth was covered in orange lipstick. I didn't know orange could be so orange. An assortment of little animal pins were attached to one side of her smock. A zebra, a turtle, an elephant, and some kind of bug, or maybe it was a bee. I stared at them, hoping they'd distract me.

"He's in the visitor's lounge at the end of the hall," Mama said. "Come on." She took hold of my arm and we ran-walked down the corridor. She stopped when she got to the door that said, Family Visitor's Lounge and smoothed her hair. Then she smoothed mine like we were gong to see the principal and wanted me to make a good impression. She tapped once, then opened the door. I closed my eyes, afraid to let them see what would be inside.

"Adie—" It was Murphy. He whispered my name so softly I thought maybe I'd imagined it. He stood at the doorway, his arms loose at his side, his face shadowed with beard growth, his clothing wrinkled, his shoulders shaking.

"This is my mama—" I said.

Murphy nodded, his face filled with anguish. I leaned in against him and he wrapped himself around me. His head dropped to my shoulder. His mouth brushed my ear.

"She . . . just started bleeding and it wouldn't stop . . . she had the baby and then . . . she . . . she . . they said there was no way of stopping it . . ."

"The baby?"

"He's . . . okay—"

I felt his tears leaking into the collar of my blouse. Mama tiptoed out and shut the door.

"I did love her, Adie," Murphy whispered. "You believe me, don't you?"

"Yes," I said softly, hugging him tighter.

"Not like you . . . not like you, but I did . . . I . . . I—" he said.

"Shhhhhhhhhhhh," I said. "I know . . . I know." I rested my head in the hollow of his neck. I felt his breath against my cheek. "Oh Murphy, I loved her too."

We clung to each other, our tears flowing out of us like a never-ending river of sorrow.

chapter twenty-seven

MURPHY'S SUFFERING WAS WRITTEN all over his body, from the way he jerked his head back and forth when the townfolks came calling to the way his feet shuffled when he walked out of a room in the middle of their sentences. Murphy cared for Margaret Mary; he told me so. But knowing him, that wasn't enough. She'd given him a son, a whole new generation, and caring was important, but he should of loved her more, when he just loved her sort of. That was stamped all over his heart, guilt striking him like a sledgehammer.

My own life wasn't working out too well, either. At the doctor's office the nurse said, "Your rabbit died."

When she saw the look on my face, she put down the clipboard. "Not what you wanted to hear, huh?"

I shook my head sadly, "When am I due?"

"Better ask the doctor," she said, picking up the clipboard, "but I'd say in about eight months."

Buck came by to get some things that afternoon. He was full of surprises, that one.

"I joined the Marines," he said. "Leaving in the morning for boot camp."

"What about Imelda Jane and the baby?" I said. "And what about me and Grace Annie? I planned to have her back here real soon, you know." Buck was dumping his tee shirts and socks into a dirty green duffel bag.

"I stay around here, her Pa is likely to kill me." Buck said. "That wouldn't do you and Grace Annie any good. Least now I can send you some money. Least I'll be alive," he said and hoisted the duffel bag over his shoulder.

"In case you're interested," he said, "I would have never left you for her."

"Is that so!" I said, more a statement of anger than a question. "Then why did you bother getting involved with her in the first place?"

"Adie, women like her are magnets for men like me," Buck said. "Strutting around, waving everything they got like it's better than money . . . when the truth is . . . is . . . Adie, don't you know you're what men want in their hearts?"

I looked at him and didn't answer, but I felt the words slide over my temper and begin massaging my anger.

"She's only what men use," he said. He balanced the bag over his shoulder with one hand and headed for the door.

"You ain't gonna have no more trouble with Mama or County over the baby," he said. "I straightened that all out this morning—"

"But . . . how'd you do that—?"

"Let's just say there's some stuff Ma and Imelda's pa would rather no one knew about. He knows everybody in town and has most of the money that floats around the place to boot. So it wasn't real hard once I explained what the deal was." Buck shifted the duffel bag from one shoulder to the other.

"See? I ain't all bad, darlin'," he said with a grin. "I'd give ya a kiss, but you'd probably smack me."

I stood there too shocked to say anything. I was getting Grace Annie back!

"I'm gonna send you money, soon as they pay me and every month after, too," he said. "I signed up for that Vietnam place. Most are ending up there anyway. The pay's better, too. Besides, I reckon I'm gonna need to be a hero for you to ever let me come back home," he said and tried to laugh but it come out more like a huff.

"Serious, Adie," he said. He dropped the duffel bag on the porch and reached for me. "I'm gonna make you and Grace Annie proud of me. She's gonna grow up knowing her old man did his part in that war over there. She is. I swear. I'm gonna be a real man when I git back, too, Adie," he said. "But I need you to wait on me and write to me. Can you do that?"

I couldn't answer. There was a knot in my throat. I swallowed hard trying to get rid of it. I bit my lip and shook my head sideways. No good. The tears started in. The next thing I knew, my arms were around Buck's neck.

"Honey, listen," he said. "I don't expect you to forgive me for all I put you through, just like that." He snapped his fingers. "I just want another chance is all, okay?" I nodded. "I want to prove to you I can change. Can I have me another chance?" he said.

I nodded again. He kissed me good, patted my hair down over my ears, then picked up the bag.

"I gotta go," he said. "I'll be at Ma's. I told her you'd come by for Grace Annie in the morning. Give her one more night with her grandbaby. That okay?"

"Uh-huh," I said. I followed him down the steps. He tossed his duffel bag through the open back window and climbed into the car.

"Adie?" he called out, and turned over the engine. "Why you doing this?"

I pursed my lips together and tilted my head to the side, not sure what he meant.

"You know. Giving me another chance," he said.

It was a very good question. And I had a very good answer.

"Well, it ain't because you deserve it," I blurted out.

"Why you giving me one, then? Can't be just my good looks."

"Because I'm . . . I'm pre . . . I'm pre—" I looked down at my tiny belly and stumbled over the word, wondering if I should tell him the rabbit died.

"Well, I'm pre . . . pretty sure that's what being married's all about, Buck," I said. "Taking chances."

He grinned. "Whooooooeeeeeeeee!" he yelled and spun the car around, stirring up a cloud of dust as big as Texas. I fanned my arms to no avail. The thick mass danced about in the humid air before slowly descending on everything beneath it, including me. I brushed at my clothes, managing to rub the moist particles of dust into the fabric instead of onto the ground.

What's next, Lord? You take away my pa and give me back my baby. You take away Margaret Mary and give me back my husband. Maybe I best not ask what's next. But, whatever it is, pleeeeease, pleeeeease don't let it be twins!

• • •

In the morning I took the wagon and went over to Verna's to get Grace Annie. She was walking! Trying to pull herself up on the furniture. Verna was watching every move. Her eyes were swollen and her face was puffed up.

"Losing all my babies," she said and blew her nose.

"That's not true, Miz Jenkins," I said. "Buck's coming back, Austin ain't going anywhere, and you can come over to visit Grace Annie and me as often as you want. You can babysit, too," I said. "In case I get a hankering to climb up on some old chicken shed." I laughed and what do you know, she smiled. Goodness to heaven. God had a way of taking so much and giving back even more. Grace Annie was coming home. Verna was actually smiling at me. Maybe she'd find out she liked me, that she was happy Buck had married me. And maybe Vietnam *would* make a man out of him. If a war could do it, this would be the one. The papers showed every day how bad it was.

Look magazine had pictures to break your heart and haunt your soul. The soldiers in the photographs looked like boys, except for their eyes. They were full grown.

Grace Annie toddled over to me and held up her arms.

"Well, aren't you a big girl!" I exclaimed, picking her up. I danced her about the room. "We're going home!" I crooned. "You wanna go home?"

She grinned, then she smacked her lips and planted a sloppy kiss on mine.

"Oh, a nice big kiss for mama," I said and blew air bubbles into her neck. She giggled out loud. A tooth was making its way to the surface—her first molar. It had to be a sign; a beautiful reminder that even important things, necessary things, can have small beginnings. But with time and care, they can grow, grow so strong that nothing can ruin them. A tooth, it was a good sign. Even a fire won't burn up a tooth. We tried to do that once in a science class experiment and it didn't work. The teacher burned one in the sink. We piled on paper and twigs, and then he splashed it with lighter fluid. The entire heap burned to ashes, except for the tooth. It was still there—charred black—but still there, waiting to be brushed good as new. You know, some things, no matter what, just can't ever be destroyed.

chapter twenty-eight

MURPHY NAMED THE BABY SAMUEL Spencer Murphy after his pa.

"They called him Smokie," Murphy said. "Far back as I remember."

"Did he smoke a lot?"

"Hams. Best this side of the mountain. Story was you could smell him coming from here to west Texas." He placed his finger against the baby's palm, and he grabbed hold tight. Murphy sported the first real smile I'd seen in days.

"Guess we'll call this little fella Sam. What do you think, Adie?"

I picked up the baby and tucked him in my arms. He curled into a little ball. He weighed five pounds. He had Murphy's strong chin and the same eyes the size of lakes, only smaller ones, is all. His hair was light brown fuzz, the color of Mary Margaret's, but there wasn't much of it.

"He didn't get her hair," Murphy said. "Her hair was real pretty. Like yours, Adie," he said. "Been nice he got her hair."

"Oh, this'll all fall out," I said. "It's baby down. Then he'll grow a fine head of hair his mama'd be proud of." I carried Sam out to the truck while Murphy paid the hospital bill.

"Hey, little Sam," I said. He was wide awake and searching for the sound of my voice, like he could see it if he tried hard enough.

"It's a fine name, Murphy," I said. "Margaret Mary'd be right pleased." Murphy drove us back to the cabin. I held Sam tight when we hit the potholes. He fit in my arms like he belonged there, safe and snug, not aware he had a mama he'd never see, never know. A sadness grabbed hold of me, one mixed with shame. Why was I here with her baby? I had one of my own. And her man? I had one of them, too, at least one that was showing promise of becoming one.

Still, me and Murphy had an easy way of speaking to each other, sometimes with words, other times with looks, maybe a nod, or a grin. It was a friendship the likes of which I'd never had before. There was love involved, sure, but it was the kind that has no beginning. The kind birthed in a circle, so there's never an end.

Murphy was headed to Tybee Island to get Willa Mae. Guess her gentleman friend would have to wait. I asked Murphy to drop me off at the doctor's. "I'm having some female troubles," I said. "Miz Jenkins will bring me home."

"Nothing serious, is it?" he asked, his voice full of concern. He opened the passenger door and helped me into the truck.

"Surely not," I said, glad he hadn't guessed what the real nature of the visit was. I didn't want him to know that I was most likely having another baby when he'd just lost Margaret Mary having his.

"Think you could help Margaret Mary's folks finish making the funeral arrangements while I'm gone?"

"Of course I can," I said. I was more than agreeable to helping out in any way I could; anything to make them feel a bit better. We were all in a sorrowful state, but they'd lost their only child, so naturally it was worse on them. Having lost Grace—for the time being at least—gave me a taste of how painful that could be. "What did you tell Willa Mae?" I asked.

"Just said, 'the baby's here and we need you.' No reason to give her a fright," he said. "She's got a bad ticker." Murphy tapped on his chest.

"She does?" I said, chewing on my lower lip.

"You didn't know?"

I shook my head. "Only thing *I* know about her heart is how big it is."

"That's just it," Murphy said. "It's too big."

I looked at him, my mouth twisted like a question mark.

"Enlarged," he added.

"For sure?"

"What the doc says." He paused and got real quiet. "Funny thing about hearts, they can cause all sorts of problems." His eyes, those pretty lakes he watched the world through, grabbed mine. "Nothing worse than a big ol' aching heart, Adie."

I got lost in Murphy's eyes when he said that, knowing I was sure to drown in those lakes if I wasn't careful.

"Especially one that's got no cure," he said.

I snapped my eyes shut. His were trying to tell me something it would be better for me if mine didn't hear.

I handed Murphy the sack lunch I'd packed for him to take on the drive down to Tybee. "It's egg salad," I told him. "Don't let it sit too long or it might give you a bellyache."

He took the bag and motioned for Worry to get in the truck. "What am I gonna do, Adie?" he said. "What in God's good heaven am I gonna—"

"Sometimes all a body can do, Murphy, is breathe in and breathe out," I said. "How about you just do that for the time being?"

He nodded sadly and drove off. I watched till he was out of sight.

He called Margaret Mary's folks Wednesday morning to say that he and Willa Mae were in Savannah and on their way back. I finished the arrangements for Margaret Mary's funeral. Mama stayed on and baked enough pecan pies to stock a bakery.

"Can't never have enough pecan pie when sorrow comes calling," she said. "Folks need something sweet to swallow when times is hurtful." Between the two of us, we had everything in place by the time Murphy and Willa Mae got back. The weather was so nice it was irritating. Strange, how the best kind will show up for the saddest of times. The dogwoods and azaleas were in bloom. The poplars, elms, maples, and chinaberry trees were different shades of green and full. Not much moisture hung in the air, so our lungs breathed good for a change. About lulled me into thinking we'd recover. Such perfect weather for a swim in the creek, a picnic in the woods, maybe a hike up the mountain, a wedding—anything except a funeral. But Margaret Mary was laid out fit for heaven, wasn't anything going to change that. So, a funeral it was.

I put Grace Annie and Sam to bed and sat down to watch television. We had two stations to choose from. *The Danny Thomas Show* was on. It was a good one to watch. Any problems they had were solved in half an hour, and there were good laughs while they fixed them. *The Dick Van Dyke Show* was next. Rob and Laura Petrie's troubles were over in thirty minutes, too. Later the news came on. The weatherman said no rain was in sight. Maybe it was better sending Margaret Mary off on a day so pretty you couldn't doubt God or His talents. Gray-black rainy days were sad enough. Why add the memory of burying someone you loved into the mix?

Mama stayed on with me and Grace Annie and baby Sam. Clarissa came with her, and did they spoil those babies! It did give me a lot of time to myself since they wouldn't let me get near the one of them. While I waited on Murphy and Willa Mae, I got out Tempe's journal. Getting lost in Tempe's life was a good way to get my mind off mine. I heard Sam let out a wail. The little guy had powerful good lungs. He sucked the formula down every three hours like he'd never have another go at it.

"Mama?" I said, a bit too loud.

"I got him," Mama said. "Stay put."

"It's my turn!" Clarissa shot back.

"You fix Grace Annie's supper and give her a bath," Mama said.

"But Mama!" Clarissa said.

"You kin take the night feedings. I need my beauty sleep," Mama said. "And Adie's been sickly."

I still hadn't told her why. Hadn't told anyone. I kept hoping it wasn't true even though all the evidence pointed to the fact it was.

"I want her to get some rest," Mama added.

I poured myself a tall glass of lemonade and went out on the back porch Murphy had built onto the cabin last month while Margaret Mary and I baked the pies for the fair. Oh Margaret Mary—one month you're here and the next one, you're not.

You left us too soon . . . you should be here with Sam . . . you should . . . be here with Murphy.

I looked out at the azaleas Buck had planted and let my eyes get lost in their dark pink blooms. The journal rested in my lap. Sifting through the pages I'd grown attached to, I quickly found the marker I'd placed in its folds and started to read, not knowing it would be quite a spell before I was able to do so again. There was more trouble aimed at us. It would hit its mark before I ever got back to reading the journal.

• • •

We was working in the fields. The year be 1865 bes' I remember. The conch shell blows and Johnson yells for all us to drop our hoes and go to the big house. "Massah got sumpin' he gwine say!" When we gits to the porch, Massah is standing on the steps.

"Y'all listen good. The damn Yankees has freed your black asses," he says. Jis' like dat! Thas what ol' Massah say.

"You're as free as me, but that don't make you white and it don't make you equal. Any you want to stay and work I'll give you five bushels of corn and six gallons of molasses and a side a' meat when the crops come in. You'll get your eats and your clothes while you work for me." Das what he say.

"You can work, you can leave, you can starve. Don't make no difference to me. I'm not responsible for the one of you no more."

Mistress on the porch with Massah and she jis' stares down at us. Then Massah say, "But ain't the one of you to leave till the man comes with the writ that says you're free to go."

Soon the soldiers come and the little chilluns run under the beds and hide and the Yankee soldiers bend down under the beds and pokes in their faces and says to come out from under there. "You are free. You are free!" Weren't none them chilluns understood what it meant. "All yous are free," they says.

When they's gone, Massah reminds for us to stay 'til it be announced with the paper writ we kin go, so we stay on and work 'til this man come with a paper from the Pres'dent Lincoln lives in the North and he says we's free and not to work no more if we don't git paid. Soon, the man what got that paper tells us we be free, be gone. Mistress come and speaks to us. I still hears her all these years later like she jis say it.

"Ain't nobody gonna take care of you anymore. Lord have mercy on you!" she say. "What're you gonna eat? Not one of you has money for clothes. Those you got on will rot off your back in six months. You leave, you will starve on the streets or die in the poorhouse," she say. "Take your pick." Somes is plenty skeered and stays on, but I not be's one of 'em. I's free and I's going.

Once we wuz free, the law say the slaves wuz married by jumping the brooms all gots to be married agin. Somes 'cide not to be and jis quit. They say they's free and they is staying that way! Clyde neber come back from the war. Weeks go by so I figure he be killed. I wouldn'ta quit Clyde. He be's a good husband and I would marries him over, so long as he say it be fine we go look for them chilluns be mine. Likely he would, seeing we never had no chilluns of our own. Somes of the other black mens who went off to fight in that war for the south made it home, but Clyde not be with any of them, so I left that plantation and never looked back on it. I start walking and the roads was full of black people making their way to where they thought freedom be waiting, lak they was sposed to pick it up somewhere and take it wid'em. Everybody say, "Where you be going?" Some says, "I don't know. I's following yous." Another say, "Maybe dat Carolina place what got da cool breeze in da ebe'ning." And I say, "Mebbe I goes dere along wid you." But ol' mistress be wrong about us left to starve and have nothing to eat.

All along them roads the white farmers stops us and say, "How you like to come works for me? I gives you a piece a ground and what you grows you give me half. The rest be yours." And one say, "I got two piece of the same size ground for you. Come work for me, you got two shares." Land sakes! They's fighting over us! I took work with one farmer through Christmas 'til the crop be lay and din't go to that Carolina place. He paid good wages, too. Said I was one the bes' workers he seen and he say for me to stay on. I tells him I am headed to da places to find my chilluns. I shows him the map I keeped had all the places marked down.

"You come back when you want to," he say. His place be near Macon, not far from Atlanta where I be heading next. I went back many a time and work for him to gets money to keep looking for Thomas and LuLu and James. I went to all them places be on that map I keeps wid me, and I goes back and keeps going back to them places. Each time I goes, I can't find da chilluns. The hard part be thinking on where they was. The other hard part be figuring how old they was and what they might could look like. When I sees plenty chillun might could be mine I'm looking at dese little ones and I think they kinda look like theys maybe mine. Then I realize, no, mine's much bigger now, but my mind plays tricks and I sees my little chilluns in my head like dey looks to me when da speculator men takes 'em way, all dem years before. I never did get me a good picture in my head what they might could look like now. Twenty years go by maybe. I think by then I 'bout thirty-five years old and I be's so tired of looking, 'cause it break my heart neber finding dem babies be mine.

Once agin I goes back to the Macon place and work for the white farmer be so kind to me. He be John Evans and he got a good wife called Mary Katherine. When I am there that las' time I meets Tom Barber who be raised on Marse Barber's plantation near Savannah. Marse Barber is the meanest Massah there eber was, Tom say, and he run off many a time and got the scars clear down his back to show for it. The scars have ridges so deep his back be like a tree and them scars be dat tree's thick ol' branches. Tom Barber is working five acres for John Evans and needs help with the crop and ask me to joins in. They's good white folks and work right long side us when the crop grow too big for us to handle. Still they gives Tom half, and they pays me out of their half. Tom be tall and real light skinned and he sure be's handsome. I be's thinking he gots a white pappy, and he say probably he do, but he ain't never know his mammy or pappy, so hows he gwine know? He's sold 'fore he's old enough to remember, he say.

Tom be's younger than me, but he say I looks real fine for a woman and how a body gwine tell. And if a body see's dat I be's older, he say he wouldn't kere none, 'gardless. The years go by and Tom say, "Hows 'bout we's git married?" And I say, "We kin do's dat." So we gits married in this church was built in Macon for all the Negroes want to be Methodists. Then I be's a Methodist and we haves a wedding and I be's Mrs. Tom Barber and pretty much happy for a time, till Tom gits to liking the corn likker. That corn likker never do him no good. That stuff mostly make a man crazy. And dat's a truth.

chapter twenty-nine

MURPHY HAD A HEADSTONE CARVED with drawings of dogwoods set right in the marble.

Margaret Mary Murphy
June 20, 1940 ~ May 11, 1966
Wife, Daughter, Mother, Friend

She was laid to rest at the far end of Grove Hill Cemetery. Her head rested inches from a big old chinaberry tree that'd lived there far longer than any of the bodies gathered around it. How they dug a spot so close to the roots of that magnificent tower of wood is a mystery since I wasn't there to watch. But the fact they were able to gave me comfort in the days that followed. I pictured the roots of that great-great-granddaddy tree cradling Margaret Mary like outstretched arms reaching deep under the red Georgia clay, hugging her, rocking her, protecting her from whatever else scurried under that clay and the black earth beneath it. The sun rose high and burned hot the day of the burial, but it rained near steady the thirty days that followed. Then the flowers came out—petunias, honeysuckle, Queen Anne's lace, roses. The azaleas blossomed, the variegated privet ballooned, the Leyland cypresses soared, and the hostas mushroomed. Margaret Mary was dead, but the earth and the flowers didn't care and the sun didn't notice.

"Willa Mae," I wailed. "What ever are we gonna do without Margaret Mary?"

"We gwine do right by this li'l baby to begins with," she said. "Dying is the other half of living. The day we's born we heads towards glory. And good thing we got dat glory, too, or dat sadness jist 'bout kills us," she said when we gathered after the ceremony. "You be's glad you haves a friend you can miss so good. Not everybody haves that."

Pastor Gib's home was full of folks milling about, tasting the food, hugging and clasping hands, shaking heads. Miz Crawford sat white-faced on the maroon chair next to the sofa, her arms crossed tight across her chest, her hands clasped firm against her arms, garden hands, long fingers brown from tending her vegetables, yanking its yield. Heads leaned down and whispered words I couldn't make out. She nodded at some, ignored others, but never spoke that I could tell. The dining room table was packed with food. Fried chicken, coleslaw, three-bean salad, collard greens, honey ham roast, sweet potatoes, biscuits, corn fritters, snap beans, thick sliced tomatoes, and mustard potato salad. On the table in the kitchen were pies: key-lime, coconut cream, southern pecan, apple, peach, and cherry. Willa Mae brought her soufflé pie, and Mama wanted to know what was in it and how to make it.

"This here's not one them secret family recipes, is it?" Mama asked.

"Da only secret is why it takes so long to bakes it. Dat recipe I gots don't tells why," Willa Mae said.

Next to the pies, cakes lined the cabinets: German chocolate, Boston cream, lemon, angel food, and caramel cream, along with an assortment of fudge brownies. Children darted in and out through the screen door leading to the kitchen, their voices floating into the living room. They snatched at the tables, tugging at pieces of cake and slices of pie, the crumbs quickly gathering at their feet and following their shoes out the door. Miz Hadaway, who'd appointed herself in charge of the youngens, bustled around, wiping up bits of frosting and pieces of crust and crumbs fallen off the table, keeping pace with the small bodies that ran out onto the back porch.

Mama had Grace Annie on her lap. She'd given her a cookie with bits of chocolate in it. Most of the chocolate was all down the front of her dress, the only real good one she had that still fit her. She'd outgrown everything.

"Adie, come take dis precious boy chile," Willa Mae said. "I'm plumb wore down." Willa Mae clutched at her chest with one arm and held baby Sam tight with the other. Her face was distorted and white as cotton. I ran to her side and took Sam, all the while screaming for Murphy.

"Help!" I yelled. He was at my side in a Dixie second. He gathered Willa Mae in his arms and carried her over to the sofa like she didn't weigh more than a small sack of onions. The women seated on it scrambled out of the way.

"Call an ambulance!" Murphy yelled. He loosened the collar of her dress, yanking it completely away from her neck.

"You can call dem, but I ain't going to dat hospital place," Willa Mae said. "Dey can give me more dem pills I gits from the doctor. I clean run's out. Das all I needs."

The ambulance arrived within ten minutes, and three men in white bustled around checking her life signs. I watched one of them squeeze the black rubber bulb, then slowly unscrew the silver knob hooked to one side. "One-eighty over one hundred," he said.

"Respiration one hundred," another one said. "Pulse sixty-two."

"Ma'am, we need to get you over to the hospital. Let the doctor check you," the first one said. He motioned to the others to bring in the cart.

"Guess dat be okay," Willa Mae said. "But den I be coming right home."

Sam stirred in my arms. I looked down at him while the men lifted Willa Mae and placed her on the stretcher.

Sweet baby—life's a teeter-totter, little fella. Up, down, up, down. And when it stops, it's all over. Guess there ain't much a body can do but enjoy the ride.

• • •

The sorrow that was still heading our way didn't have anything to do with Willa Mae having heart pains. In fact, the doctor let her come home in two days. He said the traveling and the funeral was too stressful, but she'd be fine, just needed plenty of rest. Murphy and me went to fetch her.

Murphy put an old mattress out in the truck bed. I used some of the linens I found stuffed in the bottom of Willa Mae's trunk I still kept at the foot of the bed. I tucked the sheets around the lumpy mattress best I could and put a nice quilt down for her, too. Two orderlies helped us lift her up into the truck and off we went, Grace Annie on the seat between Murphy and me, Sam in my arms. Grace Annie stood up, spun around, and grabbed hold of the back of the seat cushion. She placed her forehead against the window glass and pressed her tongue against the pane like it needed to be tasted.

"Weemie," she said and pointed to Willa Mae. Her face lit up in a grin.

"Yes, punkin,'" I said. "Willa Mae's all better. She's coming home." Grace Annie turned and tasted the pane again.

"No, no, Grace," I said and tugged at her arm gently. "Dirty, ucky, ucky," I said and made a face. She laughed. "Ucky, ucky," she mimicked. Sam lay sleeping in my lap, his little head nesting in the curve of my arm.

"Weemie, Weemie," Grace Annie chanted, not taking her eyes from the window and all the while bouncing up and down on the seat.

"Bah, bah," she said and waved at Willa Mae, her baby voice soft and sweet. *Buck, you are flat out missing so much.* Grace Annie took hold of Murphy's arm, grasping his shirt with her fingers. Murphy kept his hands firmly on the wheel as the pick-up lumbered down the gravel road. Even so, he turned his head and gave her a smile.

"You having a good time, sugar?" he said.

"Da-dee," she chirped, still clinging to his shirt, but now just using one of her hands. She patted the top of his shoulder with the other. "Da-dee," she repeated.

Goodness! Sam clung to me like I was his mama, and Grace Annie took to Murphy like he was her daddy. Truth be told, we *were* like a family, took most of our meals together even. And Murphy was just about everything a gal could hope for. He was becoming his happy self again, accepting Margaret Mary's death as part of God's mysterious plan. When he looked on me, I no longer had to wonder whether I saw something shining in his eyes. It was more than obvious. Eyes can talk if you let them. I tried hard not to let mine talk back, but my heart did. I kept thinking what it'd be like be with Murphy, *really* be with Murphy. What a mixed-up mess. Buck best hurry and get home pronto. Mama said lonely hearts and lonely bodies had two cousins they hung out with: Double and Trouble. Thank goodness I got a letter from Buck to remind me.

It was postmarked Fort Monmouth, New Jersey. We'd never been apart—unless you count the times he didn't come home at night—so it was the first one I ever got from him. He did send me a card once for Valentine's Day. It was real pretty, but he forgot to sign it. The letter was written in dark black ink on plain paper. I saw right off he couldn't spell very well, maybe one reason he wasn't partial to writing letters.

Buck got sent to Fort Monmouth after he finished boot camp at Fort Benning. He was taking some kind of signal training for communicating in war times. I tore open the envelope. It was packed so tight with paper he'd taped it shut to hold it together. He near wrote me a book.

Deer Adie,

I ain't much good at this hear letter writing, but I got a lot I want to tell you, so I'll do my best. I never really liked myself before I met you, even though I strutted around like I was God's present to women. But I knew you would save me the first time I seen you, You were different from the other girls. Had this look about you. Kind of girl don't think she's real pretty, doesn't thro her body around, stands back like you'll ask someone else to dance but you can tell she wishes it was her. You were like that. I find that real attractive in a girl. Adie, girls been throwing them-selves at me my whole life since I was ten. It started the day Ella Sims come across first base with plenty time to spare, since Oscar "slowpoke" Adams couldn't pick up the ball she hit and here he was in mid-field and the ball run through his legs even. He turned around backwards to chase it. When he got it, he can't throw a ball neither, Ella coulda had herself a home run. It was fourth grade recess and the guys and the girls played softball together. When Ella got to first base she threw herself on the spot our teacher marked off for it to be and then instead of heading for second, third and home, she flung herself into my arms like the speed of her trip to first base had made her too dizzy to stand. "Buck Jenkins, kiss me and you kin strike me out!" she said, then puckered her lips and laid one on me. Her lips were the size of a pig's butt and that was the smallest part on her. I spit when she took her lips off mine and the whole school laughed. "I'm putting a pox on you, Buck Jenkins," she yelled. "A pox! Hear me?" From then on, Adie I been having trouble with women. She come from the devil, that Ella Sims, and I ain't ever shaked loose a' her. It's like I ain't got much time 'fore I end up where she come from and I got to live it all, do it all, see it all. Know what I mean? You ever had a pox laid on you?

Boot camp was really something. They rousted us out of bed by 5 o'clock for a ten mile hike in full gear ever morning. It was hotter'n a overheated hissing radiator and some the guys didn't do real good. This guy from Mississippi had some kinda break-down from the sergeant yelling at him so much. They put him in the hospital ward for brain cases, but I think he's getting out. I mean out of the marine corp, not just the hospital. I don't mind it too bad, the yelling and stuff. I see what they're doing is breaking us down and building us back up the way we need to be if we're gonna be in war and expect to be alive once its over. It's given me time to do some thinking on how I got built the first time around. I'm thinking maybe some the things you don't know about me might could help you see why I'm not what I coulda been.

I never told you what happened in Hog Gap long before my folks moved on over to Cold Rock. I'm not talking about Austin. I'll tell you about that later. Well, before Austin ever got his head beat in we had us a little brother. Born pretty late to my folks and it was one heck of a surprise. They sure did dote on that little guy. We all did. They named him John Andrew after each of their pas, who's both dead (that's why you ain't never seen 'em). When Andy—that's what we called him—was two years old Pa backed his truck over him right in our front yard one morning. He wasn't even supposed to be out of the house. Austin and me took turns watching him on days Ma did the washing out on the back stoop. It was Austin's turn and he went back to bed and took Andy with him. But Andy musta got up and went outside. Our yard was so full of potholes Pa didn't even know he run over him. He drove on to work like usual. Ma finished hanging all the clothes on the line out back and come in the house when she fin-ished. She found Austin in bed in the back bedroom. I slept in the attic was made up for me and never heard a thing. Ma thought Andy was in bed with Austin since this blue blanket he dragged around with him was mixed in with the covers. It was summer and we slept in sometimes if our chores was caught up from the night before. Later Ma yelled for us to get our butts out of bed and she went out to sweep the front porch. She noticed what looked like a pair of Andy's p.j's laying in the front yard and went to fetch 'em, figuring they blew off the clothesline. They were Andy's pajama's alright, but he was in them. His skull was crushed. You could see the tire marks on his face where the truck ran over him. I ain't never fergot Ma carrying him in the house and putting him on the table. Parts of his brains was stuck to her apron. And Ma says, Buck, git me some that antiseptic out of the medicine cabinet and some them bandages left from when yer pa hurt his hand. Me and Austin was staring at what was left of Andy like we weren't believing what we're seeing. Know? And she says, Go on now, I got to fix Andy up. Our baby's hurt hisself.

Eventually, she come out of it and I ain't never heard no one scream so loud, not before, not since, not even from the hogs at bleeding time. Adie, we was different people after that. Pa blamed Ma. Ma blamed Pa, who blamed Austin. It was a vicious circle of finger pointing. Don't think the word accident *ever got thought about, let alone spoke on. It was like it had to be some-body's fault in order for them to even try to live with it. I remem-ber thinking, why is that? Can't something just happen by chance? Isn't that what an accident is? Or do you gotta blame yoreself or somebody else ever time something bad comes about? Ma said accidents do happen, on occasion, but rarely. And she said this weren't no accident. It was negligence and when you got negligence, you got a body should be held accountable for it. Look-ing on it that way I wondered how far up that accountability went. Not wanting to get smacked in the head, I didn't ask, just wondered.*

Ma was probably reliving her share of that responsibility thing when you had that accident with Grace Annie. She ain't mean to the bone, Adie. She's just hardened up a good bit around all her edges. It comes from her getting hurt so bad and not tak-ing to it good. She firmed up to survive it, I think. She weren't planning on keeping Grace Annie for good. She probably was thinking she was protecting you from yourself the way she wished somebody would of done her. If she hadn't of left Andy in Austin's care without following up, he might not a got run over. I think the parts about you she don't like is the same ones she don't take to in herself. After Andy died, Ma and Pa pretty much made Austin's life miserable after that. I did my best to be a good brother to him, but that alone ain't enough. Later on, Austin fell head over heals in love with this girl. She got pregnant and he wanted to marry her and get the heck out of Hog Gap. He come to me pretty excited, seeing as he had a job all set in Hamilton up the road a piece. Bought a ring, plain gold band, and was going over to give it to her. He never made it back in one piece. The girl's pa beat his head in with a two-by-four. Near killed him. Brain damage was so bad Pa said it was a shame it hadn't. But I think it hurt him bad knowing he hadn't made things right with Austin before it happened. There was a tenderness in him after that I hadn't seen before. Ma was in a pretty bad way by then. She'd lost her baby Andy and now Austin had turned into one. He was eighteen years old.

Adie, the man who broke Austin's skull was Mr. Fletcher. That's why he give me the job when I come back. He's been giving Ma a bunch a money each month since he near killed Austin and he bought her that T-bird, too. I'm sure by now you've figured since it was Mr. Fletcher beat him, that the girl Austin was crazy in love with and was having a baby with was Imelda Jane. And yore right. I shoulda told you long ago. And for damn sure I shoulda never got involved with her myself. Can't rightly say why I did. 'Cept she's a big tease and I was a fool. Or maybe I wanted to prove that Austin was the fool, that Imelda Jane weren't no good to start with and he wouldn'ta never been happy with her no how, so what'd it matter his life was ruined over it anyhow? It woulda been ruined either way. Know what I mean?

After that beating, Imelda Jane didn't do much to make me think any different. Matter of factly, she did stuff no respectful girl would think of doing. Once she had three of us over to her place when her folks was out of town. She didn't even make them other two guys leave the room while they waited their turn with her. I ain't proud of that, Adie. It just goes to show how low people can go when they don't have no respect for themselves. I ain't just talking about her. I hope you can work on forgiving me. I'm working hard on that part myself.

This sergeant drilled stuff in us I should of had drilled in me long ago. He's a veteran from the Korean War and has stories to tell you wouldn't believe. During part of that war it got so cold and they weren't dressed for it and they near froze to death. He said he found out then the human body can endure a lot more than most people think it can, given the opportunity. He drove us pretty hard during the day, but taught us about duty and honor and country. I think he's probably a hero from that Korean War, even though he never said he was or nothing. For sure I admire him and want to be as much like him as I can be by the time I'm ready to leave for Viet Nam. (He said most of us is going there and the fact I signed up for it makes pretty much for sure I am.) I think this war might do for me what nothing else so far been able to. The future will tell. I just hope it ain't too late to be the kind a man I want to be for you, Adie, and the kind of daddy I want to be for Grace Annie. When I look back at all the running round I did with other women, all I see is a fool. And when I look at you I see how beautiful you are, inside and out. And I see our children in your eyes, Adie. Not just the one we already got. I'm talking bout the ones we might could have yet that ain't even been thought of. I pray to God I ain't took away their chance of that happening and snuffed the life out of them 'fore they even have one. I might could forgive myself for a lot of things, but that ain't one of them.

Think you could send me a picture of you and Grace Annie? Two would be good. One for my wallet and one for over my bunk. It would be a big comfort to me. I'm really missing you, Adie. I never knew how much you meant to me till you ain't near me no more. One of the stupidist mistakes a man can make is taking somebody for granted. Another is being so blind I didn't notice that the man was me. Notice I said, was.

> *Luv, yer husband forever if you'll have me,*
>
> *Buck*

P.S. Please write back soon's you can. And watch out for Murphy, Adie. That man's got some kind of special designs on you. Now, I know you might find that hard to believe what with you being kind of plain and all. I don't mean nothing bad by saying that, but you know, you ain't exactly the kind of woman men gets the hots for, if you know what I mean. And that's all Murphy's got on his mind. I've seen his kind before. I'm speaking from my heart, Adie. I ain't no fool. I seen the attention he been paying you. I had a talk with him before I left. Told him to leave you alone or there'd be trouble. He said the trouble is we both love the same women. And I told that smart aleck the trouble is only one of us got her. You know what he said? Which one? See what I'm talking about? So watch him good.

chapter thirty

I DON'T THINK PEOPLE WORRY much about losing an arm or a leg. Probably don't even think about it, except maybe for those fighting in wars. Most folks just go about their business, me included, expecting their body parts to always be there. I mean, it's not like you get up in the morning and say, "I best be careful today, I could lose my arm!"—or, you know, a leg. But that's what happened.

After Margaret Mary's funeral, things had been going quite well, considering. I was busy caring for Sam and Grace and the chickens. Murphy was finishing the extra room he added onto the cabin for the new baby coming. I had to stop denying it when I could no longer hide the fact I was pregnant. Keeping it a secret turned out to be a bad decision. With Buck gone and Murphy part of my daily routine the folks in town were having a field day ragging on who was the father. Verna was having one hissy fit even though I assured her that Buck was absolutely the father and there was positively no chance whatsoever anybody else was. Even so, she insisted on talking to the doctor to see how far along I was.

"What for?" Murphy asked.

"Guess she wants to make sure Buck was still even around."

Regardless of the gossip and trouble with Verna, Murphy and I fell into a good routine. Sam stayed with me and Grace, and Murphy came by each day and stayed until nightfall. Willa Mae did, too, to help out with the kids. We tended the vegetable garden and had enough beans to feed the whole town. Mama always made three-bean salad with any extras left over from canning, but the recipe called for some canned beans—wax and the big flat Italian ones—to add to the garden fresh ones, and I didn't have any on hand. I was big as a barrel and didn't much feel like going and getting any.

Me and Murphy worked the chicken business together, mine and his, while Willa Mae tended to the babies. We took dips in the creek when the work was done and short walks at night when the babies were bedded down. It was on one of them walks that things got a bit out of hand.

I had a lot of feelings stored up for Murphy, and they all came rushing out. We weren't just being stalked by trouble; we were waving our arms and calling its name. I'm not saying we had relations like a husband and wife. But we surveyed the land and came close to tilling the field. I tried to ease my guilt by reminding myself that Buck had gone ahead and planted the crop with Imelda Jane, and they had a harvest that'd soon be here to prove it. So what could be so wrong? But, deep down, I knew it wasn't a good idea to measure my conduct based on how he measured his. Mama always said we determine what our deeds are and then our deeds determine who we are. But then Mama said a bad apple spoils its companions. Maybe Buck was a bad apple and it was too late. Maybe I was spoiled.

"I need to get my life back on track, Murphy," I said.

"You need to see a lawyer and get a divorce, Adie," Murphy said and brushed the hair out of my eyes.

"Murphy, I can't hardly do that. Buck's fighting a war." Murphy traced the curve of my cheekbone with his fingertips, which sent a shiver down my backside.

"In fact, we can't be going off like this anymore," I said. "It's not right."

"What's not right is Buck leaving you pregnant, Imelda Jane in the same condition, and then hightailing it off to fight a war that don't need fighting," Murphy said and pulled me to him.

"We're a family, Adie. I'll do right by you and the kids. And I'll treat this new one like my own. That's a promise."

I told him it couldn't ever be, but as summer passed on, he wooed me and wore me down. It wasn't hard, seeing as I'd grown up a lot in the last year and knew I loved him like I'd never loved Buck. Mama told me grown-up love was knowing *all* the right buttons and never pushing them. I finally understood. I couldn't imagine hurting Murphy in places where he was tender.

"All the women in my life have left me, Adie," he said. "My mama run off, Margaret Mary's gone. Stay with me, Adie. Marry me. Say you will." He kissed me with such a hunger I got lost. Before I knew it, I said yes.

"I will, I will," is what I said. And I meant it. It was all decided. Murphy and I would get married and be a family. Buck would have to make a new life for himself when he returned. He could stay in the cabin. Grace and me and the new baby were moving in with Sam and Murphy as soon as it was official. I got busy packing. The baby was due in a month, and I wanted everything ready. I sorted through baby clothes and tended to my chickens. I cooked and cleaned and kept myself busy. I fretted over what I'd tell Mama and how I'd face Verna now that I'd made my decision. Truth be told, I was scared. I told Murphy, "My mama says there's consequences when you make selfish choices." He didn't say a word, just stroked my hair and kissed the top of my head.

To keep my fears in check, I kept myself too busy to worry during the day and too tired to bother at night. I thought of Murphy and our new life. It was laid out like dinner.

Before we could pull up a chair and dig in, an official letter from the government arrived. The news inside changed everything.

chapter thirty-one

THERE'D BEEN AN ACCIDENT. A soldier in front of Buck dropped a grenade while they were running during some kind of maneuvers. The recruit was new at war and had straightened out the pins on all of his grenades ahead of time, maybe thinking that would make it easier to pull them out in case of attack. The letter explained it made them live grenades. One fell from this young soldier's pack. Buck was behind him. As he ran forward, it exploded beneath him. He was alive, but he was hurt real bad. He was coming home. But one of his arms and one of his legs wouldn't be with him.

"He's at this Walter Reed Hospital somewhere in Washington. Once they teach him to do for himself as much as they can, he's coming home."

Murphy nodded. "We'll help him every way we can, Adie," he said. "See that he gets settled and has what he needs—"

"I can't leave him now," I said. "Murphy, he's only got one arm and one leg."

"If that's what it takes, I'll give an arm and a leg, too."

"Don't make jokes, Murphy. Everything's a mess. How am I gonna take care of two kids and Buck?"

"You're going to marry me and let me take care of everybody, that's what," Murphy said.

"And what about Buck?"

"Him, too."

"Oh, Murphy. I married him for better or worse. If it was something good that happened to him, I could walk away, but I can't leave him when he's down. I just can't."

"You worried what people will think?"

"It's what I'll think of myself."

I turned and went back into the cabin. I needed to feed Grace and Sam. It was lunchtime. The temperature had dropped, and I pulled my sweater tighter around me to ward off the October gust of wind swirling around me. I was close to eight months pregnant. In no time there'd be another little one counting on me. Talk in town was Imelda Jane had her baby. Folks said she was confident Buck was coming home to her and a hero to boot. Had her Pa convinced she'd be a proper married lady before too long and all the talk would die down. I wondered how Imelda Jane would feel about having Buck back in her life once she found out he was missing two main body parts.

I wondered, but I didn't sit and worry on it. I had chickens to get to market and coops to get ready for a new brooder batch, and the garden was full of vegetables that needed canning. Mama was coming to stay for a week to help me. She brought Clarissa and we got busy with the tomatoes. They were big, red, and juicy. There was no way we could eat all of them before they spoiled, so Mama designed a plan of action.

"First, we'll make spaghetti sauce. If there's any left, we'll make barbecue sauce and then chili sauce, in that order," she announced.

It was good to be together and extra nice having her help out with the babies. Even so, I didn't have much time left in the day to read Tempe's journal. I snatched a few minutes here and a few others there whenever I could. Life didn't seem near as bad when I compared mine to hers.

Course I had no way of knowing tragedy had *another* arrow aimed right at me.

• • •

After I marries Tom Barber we keeps sharecropping for John Evans and his wife 'Lizabeth. They treats us real good and don't never cheats us on the work we do's. And did we raise a big crop! They gives us our fare share when the crops come in. We had us some chickens and plants a garden to grows the vegetables we eats. At nights we goes to the candy pullings and to the corn shuckings, too. Only dis time we goes to the shuckings to shuck what be ours. Then, ten year after dat, when I be's 'bout fifty-years-old, I figures, me and Tom has a baby! People say it be a miracle and some the others be calling me Sarah from da lady in the Bible so old and hab that baby Isaac. Guess da spasms jis' up and lebes me. We has a girl baby and has skin like light honey. She be our heart, and dat's a truth, so dat's what we calls her for short. We do see she be's a bit slow at learning things, but is a real sweet chile for sure, even so. But, we don't gits no more babies and we sure do's all dat stuff what makes 'em, too, so our baby girl keeps us real happy and everything pretty much perfect, 'cepting Tom Barber still be drinking that corn likker and gits in trouble with the law now and again. John Evans goes to the sheriff and gits him out and says what a good worker he is. Can't hardly do's without him, he say.

They say dat corn likker kin gives you a disease that gits worse as the years go on. I think that be's what happens to Tom Barber. He gits worse and worse from that stuff. And he gits in all kind fights. Land sakes he comes home sum nights and hiz body all beat up like he be's some big ol' ally cat. He be's crazed from that likker.

He don't lay no hand on me. Nothing like that. Jis pass out on the floor if'n he don't makes it to the bed, but mostly he makes it to the bed. Stinks real bad sometimes and one night he be smelling so bad I gives him a bath while he be snoring aways! Dat's how I finds out something terrible. I don't wants it to be true, but the more I checks the more I knows it is. It was the end of the world for me and dat's a truth, 'cause what it is I find be's something no woman should ever habs happen to her and dat's a worser truth.

chapter thirty-two

WILLA MAE GOT HER STRENGTH back and spent her days helping me with Sam and Grace Annie. We were washing Grace
Annie's baby clothes, lining them up for the new one coming,
when we got a real surprise. Miz Fletcher's car pulled up in the
driveway and Imelda Jane got out. She had her baby in her arms.
She nodded to her ma and Miz Fletcher drove off. *What in the
world was going on?*

"Willa Mae!" I yelled. "Imelda Jane is outside with her baby."

"Bless deze pecks-a-pickled-peppers," she said, wiping her hands
on her apron. We were fixing to start canning what we'd plucked
from the garden.

I was too stunned to move. My mouth dropped open like some
wide-mouthed bass. Willa Mae opened the door and asked her to
come in. Then she went over and stoked the fire up good in the fireplace. It was December and freezing outside.

"Comes over here and gits you and dat baby warm."

I stood with my mouth open when what I wanted was to ask
Imelda Jane what she was doing coming by. I couldn't seem to get
enough wind in my lungs to form the words. And I looked a fright. I

hadn't been sleeping well at all. I was a week beyond my due date and bigger than a truck.

"You want to see me and Buck's baby?" she blurted out.

Oh, that will about make my week, I thought.

"He's a boy. I named him after Buck. This is Buck Jr."

"That's not Buck's real name," I said. She handed me the baby. He was Buck's all right. Had the same little cleft in his chin and big round brown eyes. He cooed when I snuggled him in my arms.

"He's a real nice baby, Imelda Jane," I said and handed him back to her.

"I heard you were having another one," she said, nodding at my belly.

"Let me takes that little baby and you two's can talk better," Willa Mae said. "And where yore manners, Adie? Haves your guest sit down."

Willa Mae took the baby and turned to Grace Annie. "You comes 'long, too. Come here and see this here little baby."

Grace Annie ran as fast as her little legs could toward Willa Mae.

"Me wan' hole baby," Grace Annie chortled. "Me, me, me," she chattered, her arms reaching up while Sam crawled after them.

"I'm sorry, Imelda Jane," I said and motioned to the sofa. "Please have a seat. Did you come all the way out here just to show me the baby?" I asked, not knowing what else to say.

"Well, that," she said and folded her hands in her lap and smiled sweetly. "And to tell you I've . . . well, me and Buck been writing each other, and he'll be moving in with me and Buck Jr. when he gets home. Daddy's gonna have a big parade for him and everything."

"Is that what Buck said?"

"Oh, Buck doesn't know about the parade, yet—"

"I mean did Buck tell you he was, he was moving in—"

"Well, we haven't worked out all of the details yet, but now he's got a son to think of—"

"He's got a lot more than that to consider."

"Well, certainly, we are *not* going to leave you and your babies high and dry. We'll make provisions. My daddy will—"

"You don't know, do you?"

"Know what?"

"When's the last time Buck wrote to you?"

"Ahh . . . let's see, it was . . . Are you trying to tell me you are conniving behind my back to keep him and . . . 'cause if you *are*, let me tell you a thing or two right now—" Imelda Jane bolted straight up and clenched her fists together.

"Imelda Jane, if he's what you want, I am not going to stand in your way. I can assure you of that!" She sat down. "Are you prepared to marry Buck for better or for worse?"

"I surely am," she drawled and nodded her head decidedly.

"Well that's good, because the worst has happened. I'm sorry to be the one to tell you, but—" I went over to the cabinet and took out the letter the government had sent.

"Buck's had an accident. He . . . he . . . here—" I handed her the letter.

She stood up once again, shook her hair off her shoulders, pointed her chin firmly in place, cocked her head to one side, and started to read.

I started toward her. "I think you best sit down—"

It was too late. She was obviously a champion reader. She got to line three and collapsed before I could get to her.

"Willa Mae!" I screamed. "Come help me. Imelda Jane's out cold!" All three babies started to wail. Willa Mae nearly tore the bedroom door off its hinges.

"Glory to da sweet Jesus!" She said. "Did you kills her?"

chapter thirty-three

IT WOULD HAVE BEEN REAL nice to find out Imelda Jane wanted Buck even with the misfortune that had befallen him. That wasn't the case, but I could hardly blame her for deciding she wasn't near as much in love with him as she'd reckoned. She went off to Atlanta to a finishing school and then on to a junior college just for girls, and the baby was put up for adoption, poor little tyke. So now Buck had a baby son he'd never see.

While I waited for him to come home, I worked hard to stay plenty busy, hoping I wouldn't have any time left to think about the condition he was coming home in. I helped Willa Mae make muffins with all the strawberries she gathered. They were too good. I ate most of them as fast as they cooled from the oven.

The folks at Walter Reed hospital said Buck was doing as well as could be expected and they'd keep me informed of his progress. They gave him an honorable discharge and full disability, which came to three hundred and seventy-four dollars a month—hardly enough for a family of soon to be four. Thankfully, the chicken business was a good supplement to it. From Buck's letters I could tell he was having a hard time of it. In addition to experiencing a great deal of depression, he was experiencing all sorts of infections in his intestinal tract, and the doctors couldn't seem to get it under control. He had raging fevers, and one day the hospital notified me that I should be prepared to come up there at a moment's notice, that it was real serious. Some sort of a staph infection they thought he might have picked up during the surgery had got in his bloodstream. But there was no way I could travel no matter how bad it got. Willa Mae was baking her special strawberry muffins that I loved. Sam and Grace Annie were playing nearby with some blocks laid out on the floor. And Murphy, determined not to give up his plans for us marrying, came by every day and mooned around before taking Sam home for the night.

I remembered what he'd said about taking care of us, including Buck.

"It doesn't look good," I said. "He's real serious sick. They want me to go up there if it gets any worse—"

"The only place you're going is the hospital."

"I know—" I rubbed my stomach. I was probably already in labor. My back had started paining me that morning.

"If need be, I'll go," Murphy said.

I nodded.

"What if he don't recover, Adie?"

"Oh, Murphy, don't say that. That could bring Buck bad luck. Don't even think on it, okay?" I said. "That'd be the worst thing that could happen." Then I remembered what Mama always said: *Sometimes the worst thing turns out to be the best thing.* I didn't want to think about that. Poor Buck. The pain in my back was getting stronger and moving around to the front. Now I knew it was time. That's exactly how it started with Grace.

I went inside and packed a little suitcase and phoned the doctor. He said to come to the hospital when the pains were five minutes apart. I asked Willa Mae to look after Sam and Grace Annie and the chickens. I lay down on the bed and pored over Tempe's journal while I waited. It could be a while.

• • •

You members when I branded my chilluns when dey was jis' little babies? You members, don't you? I puts a big "T" for Tempe on dey butts, means they be's mine? And it scarred all over like a big blister burn? Members dat? And dem marks heals good and dey's look like crosses. Sure you members. Dat be 'portant for you to members for whats I gwine tell you next.

That night Tom comes home with all dat corn likker in him and him smelling so bads I gibs him a good bath right while he in the bed. I takes all his clothes off and warms dat water good and wash his 'tire body down. He is sprawled on dat bed on his belly and I yanks his pants off and pulls his shirt right up over his head. The candles on the wooden table by the bed gibs me plenty light to see by and I notice when I wash down his backside dat he gots dat same kind mark on his butt I puts on my babies. I looks closer and shore enough it be jis' likes it. My heart 'bout jumps from my chest and I shoves him over so he be's laying on his back and I yanks on his hair to gets a good look at his forehead and see if it got dat scar Thomas gits when he a boy 'cause he is hit with the cracker from the bullwhip. Members? Well, Tom got too much hair for me to tell, so's I get the razor he use each morning to shaves his face and I shaves his hair on the front side of his forehead. Tom is full up with dat corn likker and neber moves. I shaves dat part of his head and dere is the big knot of a scar from the cracker. I knows then what I done! I has married my own son Thomas and has a baby with him eben, and my heart is sick at da thought and so is my stomach. And I goes outside and gits on my knees and throws up everything be in dat stomach. Den I stays der on my knees and da sorrow resting in my heart near kills me, it do. And dat's a truth.

chapter thirty-four

MY LABOR PAINS GREW FARTHER apart and finally stopped altogether. I was fixing to have a ten-month pregnancy. Mama said, "I
heard of it happening."

"That'd be just my luck," I told her.

The good news was Buck's infections were finally under control
and the hospital discharged him. They flew him back to Georgia, and
he took a bus from the base.

I felt right guilty for thinking them thoughts about the worst
things maybe being the best things, and I asked God to keep my heart
in the right spot and my mind in the right place. It was hard to do.
Willa Mae said, "Life not easy. But what don't kills you gits you
another chance to tries again, so don't be's worried."

It was a bit confusing. There were too many questions and not
near enough answers. I figured the best thing for me to do was love
people as much as I could, understand them if they'd let me, honor
my promises, don't tell lies, and pay attention to the road in front of
me. 'Course I realized just when I thought I knew where I was going,
the road was likely to fork. But maybe if I charted a good course I'd
recognize the best path to take when it did.

Buck learned to fend for himself pretty well. They fit him with a metal leg that strapped onto his stump, which made him pretty happy at first; gave him a good bit of hope. Soon they had a metal arm for him with a hook on one end. He did real good with that, but his stump just flat-out refused to toughen up. The skin constantly split open and chafed badly each time Buck put his weight on it. It got so raw it was just too painful to even try and use the metal leg. When he'd wait and let it heal and try again, he'd get the same result. Then infection set in. It was a neverending battle. Buck got real depressed and lost his excitement over getting the arm they'd promised him.

"You won't be putting your body weight on the arm," I said. "It's likely to work real well for you."

"Great," he said. "Then I can have my choice which arm to use to switch TV channels with while I sit around here doing nothing." His depression got worse, so they gave him these pills to take, but he said they weren't helping him and gave up on them. I had to give him credit. Buck never turned to drinking, but his sadness dragged him around like a worn-out mop.

Grace Annie was running all over the place. I was mixing up a batch of these snowball cookies I got out of the Christmas issue of *Family Circle* magazine. The doctor said it was important for me to stay on my feet and coax my body back into labor. I put a batch in the oven and looked up to check on Grace Annie. She waddled over and grabbed hold of Buck's pant leg that had no leg in it and gave it a good yank.

"Buck, can you keep an eye on her?"

Buck reached down with his good arm, pushed the stump of his other arm against her and hoisted her up. Grace Annie gave him a wide-mouthed grin, her mouthful of teeth lined up like flower buds. Buck pulled her toward him and laughed out loud. Grace Annie pushed her hands together, clapping wildly, and promptly lurched out of his grasp. I lunged to snap her up, and dumped the cookie dough all over Buck in the process. Maybe I shouldn't have moved so fast;

Buck might've kept ahold of her. Or she may have simply toppled into the sofa cushions next to him. It was too late to wonder, plus it's a mother's instincts not to take chances. Buck's face soured.

"I can't even hold my own kid." He brushed the wet dough off his shirt and onto the sofa, snatched his crutches, shuffled to the bedroom, and slammed the door. Grace Annie started to cry.

"It's okay, sugar," I said. "Daddy's not mad at you. Daddy doesn't feel good. It's okay." I gave her some crackers and she settled down.

"Shame we don't have any crackers big enough for Daddy," I said and offered her another.

"More!" she said and reached for the box.

Murphy was still determined that he and I should carry on with our plans, that Buck could stay on and live in our cabin and Grace Annie and I and the new baby, when it arrived, would move to his place. He was building some ramps to our cabin to accommodate Buck's wheelchair. Buck told him to forget it and go back where he come from. Actually, he told him, "Get the hell outta here. I don't need for you to be doing nothing for me."

"I'm doing this for Adie," Murphy told him. "Since she's so bound and determined to take care of you, I'm going to make sure it ain't too much for her. You *have* noticed her condition, I take it?"

Buck never answered. Just went off to the chicken coops. He spent a lot of time out there, hours in fact. I never could figure that out. It sure wasn't because he liked chickens.

"Murphy, please don't say things to Buck about me having to take care of him, okay? He's having a real rough time."

"Adie, Buck's not my concern. You are."

"He's my husband, Murphy. It's not right you coming around. It's like, well, Buck, he—"

"Adie, I'm not going anywhere. Don't you see that staying with Buck is not doing either of you any good?"

I tried my best to explain to him that waiting wasn't going to change things. But nothing I said seemed to get through to him.

Then I thought maybe a letter would. Grace Annie was asleep. I waited till Buck was too, then I sat down to write it. I ripped up more paper than I could spare, not quite sure what to say. Finally, I just wrote the words down exactly the way they were sitting in my head.

Dear Murphy,

I know before we got word about Buck being hurt I told you I'd marry you. But his getting hurt changed everything. It made me realize how far I meandered from my vows when I got caught up in my feelings for you. I had no business doing that. I have this fear that what happened to Buck happened because I dishonored my vows by saying I'd divorce him and marry you. Like maybe it was the only way for me to be jolted back to where my place in life is. I have terrible guilt about that. And, if the good Lord is doing this to get my attention and I don't respond, think about poor Buck. He could end up looking like Humpty Dumpty!

Murphy, I've just got to do all I can to make his life one worth living. He's real broken up right now. He even thinks that this baby I'm carrying is yours! He does. I have told him on the blood of Jesus, that's not the case, but I don't think he believes me. Your coming around is only making it worse on all of us. Not to say that I don't appreciate all you're doing for us. I do, but you have got to understand that I can't leave Buck. You don't think much of him and for some good reasons, but I know him better than anyone and there's goodness in him, too. People don't see it. I sometimes have trouble seeing it. But I know it's there.

I love you with all my heart, but I still have love in there for Buck, too. Sounds strange, I know, but maybe you don't have to stop loving one person to start loving another. I wish that we could be together like we planned, get married and be a family with Sam and Grace Annie and the new baby, but I got to stop thinking on it. It hurts too much. Let's face it. The sad truth is I'm gonna grow old taking care of Buck. But I want my children to grow up knowing that the promises we make are meant to be kept.

My mama says love has many faces. The one I'll have with Buck will never be the one I'd have with you. I will miss that all my life, but how can we destroy Buck's life and then expect to build a happy one of our own?

I wish I could do what I truly want to do, but I can't. It would never work between us. I'd be full up with guilt. What kind of life would that be for you? Murphy, you and me, we met too late. Even so, I'll love you longer than always.

Adie

chapter thirty-five

BUCK AND I HAD A baby boy the following week. Turns out the doctor had miscalculated my due date and I wasn't late at all. The labor was as easy as Grace Annie's was hard. I hadn't counted on that, but what a relief. He weighed just over nine pounds and still I had no trouble delivering him. He was the cutest baby—looked just like Buck. What a blessing that was. I loosened the blanket and held the tiny bundle up for Buck to see. His mouth dropped open and his eyes lost their blank stare. He gawked and I watched while he discovered what I'd known all along. The muscles in his face, normally pinched tight as the bands on a bow, relaxed their grip and the corners of his mouth quivered like they wanted to smile, but weren't sure they remembered how. He blinked, his eyes warm as summer and moist as rain. There'd be no more doubts over whose baby this was. He had Buck's eyes, the same little dimple in his chin, and Buck's trademark cowlick on the crown of his head. Verna was wild for him.

"I think we should name him Buford Andrew, after you and your little brother, Buck," I said, "and then we can call him Andy. How about that?" I eyed Verna. She looked pleased. She'd brought along a dozen of her fried refrigerator donuts for the nurses, and they were fussing over how good they were and, oh my, what a fine grandbaby boy she had. I don't think it's possible to ever get over losing a child, but maybe gifting her little boy with a namesake would give her some comfort.

"Buford? You crazy?" Buck blurted out. "Why do you think I go by Buck?"

"Well, Buford is only for the birth certificate part," I said.

"Buuuford, Buuuford," Buck muttered, and shook his head. "Besides, why name him after a Jenkins? Ain't one of us had any luck in life."

Verna pinched her lips together. She crossed her arms and glanced out the window. "What we gonna call him, then?" Her head snapped around and she looked at Buck. He didn't answer. He hobbled over to the door and called out over his shoulder, the muscles in his face back in place, stretched tight as rubber bands. His enormous eyes, flat brown orbits, had lost their newfound sparkle.

"I'm tired, Ma. Take me home," he said.

Verna carefully picked up her purse. She nodded, her eyes sad and vacant, her mouth twisted off to once side. She bobbed her chin and patted my feet resting under the starched white covers as she crossed to the door. She pressed her finger across her lips and motioned for silence, her shoulders suggesting that words were now useless. I pretended not to see.

"Buck!" I called out after him. "Don't go," I said. "Please, don't go." Maybe he heard my anguish, and maybe he *cared* that he had. He turned around and dragged his crutches across the poured concrete floor back to the bed. He stood there clutching the rubber grip on one handle, his metal hook wrapped around the other. I looked down at our sweet baby boy sleeping in my arms, resting so contentedly, a tiny bubble of air perched on his bottom lip. I looked up at Buck. He touched his head gently.

"He's beautiful, Adie." He carefully traced the outline of the baby's forehead. The baby stretched and wrinkled up his brow and smacked his lips. The little bubble planted on his lip popped without a sound. "*You're* beautiful," Buck said and put his hand to my cheek. Tears flooded his eyes, ready to fall if he blinked. I'd never seen Buck cry. Not ever. His voice cracked. Verna quietly left the room.

"They ain't one thing in me comes close," he said. He lost his balance and caught himself on the edge of the bed. I had the baby in one arm and gripped Buck's with the other. He didn't pull back. He leaned into me, his shoulders heaving. Maybe this was good. Maybe this was what Buck needed, to let his grief out. To cry for what he'd lost and for what he'd never have. To be weak as a new baby, to let himself be comforted, to find that he could rebuild his life one wobbly step at a time and that I'd be there for him, that he could shoot for the moon and the worst that would happen is that he'd land in the stars, to have his slate wiped clean, to discover no matter what his past was, his future was spotless and, best of all, to believe it.

He stood up. He faced the floor and snapped his head forward, shaking his tears like they were sweat from his brow. Pride is a terrible master.

"You name him what you want, okay?" He whispered as he leaned over and kissed my cheek. Then he sniffed my skin and my hair. He nuzzled his nose back and forth against my cheek. He was so tender, like he thought I'd break. If only he knew, my heart was about to.

Buck didn't come to see me after that. When I asked Verna how he was doing she said, "Who knows? He keeps to himself. He eats the food I bring him. That's about it." Verna was being very strong. She accepted what had happened to Buck better than I had.

"Ain't nothing you can do when life slams into you, Adie," she said, "but stand up and hope it don't do it again." I thought about her little boy crushed under the wheels of her husband's truck and about Austin's head being crushed by a shovel and then Buck's limbs being blown to bits by that grenade.

"What do you do when it *keeps* slamming?"

"Pretend," she said.

"Pretend *what?*"

"Pretend you can take it," she said.

"And then what?" I asked.

"Then you keep pretending," she said, "until you get good at it." She brushed loose strands of hair off my forehead, her hand as soothing as a cool cloth on a hot summer day. A whisper of a smile rested on her mouth, her voice reverent as a prayer. I'd never seen this Verna. I loved this Verna. I vowed to remember that when the other Verna showed up.

chapter thirty-six

MURPHY BROUGHT ME AND THE baby home. Actually, not home; he drove us over to Verna's so she could help me out with Grace Annie for a few days. Murphy took care of my chickens and I took care of Sam. Verna bought a little potty chair for Grace Annie and some big girl panties while I was in the hospital. She was wild for the panties and rarely had an accident, and how she loved that little chair. The only problem was she dragged it all around the house, and as it bumped along, the contents of the bowl mostly ended up on the floor.

One evening, I had finished nursing the baby. He slept about three hours in between feedings. Sam was toddling about the room gripping the furniture to keep his balance. Verna was busy in the bathroom teaching Grace Annie how to empty her little potty bowl into the toilet bowl, but if you ask me that was making a worse mess. It was her house; I knew enough to keep quiet.

Buck was supposed to come by and have dinner with us. Murphy offered to bring him and stopped by to get him, but Buck said he wasn't hungry, so Murphy came to pick up Sam and stayed on for dinner instead. He talked to Austin like he was a regular member of the family and spoon-fed him while he was at it. Austin took to him. He mugged and grinned and smacked his lips. He was having a fine time. In fact, when Murphy picked up Sam and headed for the truck, Austin wanted to go along. He cried like a two-year-old when Verna locked the screen door and told him he couldn't.

"Time for your bath, Austin," she said. "Come on, now. I got the water running."

That got his attention. He loved splashing around in that tub—and made a mess of it—seeing as he was too big for it to begin with. I helped Verna get him in and out. He was a six-foot toddler and a handful. It made me sad to think that this was how he'd always be, his baby brain trapped inside a full-grown man. It was a sorry sight, him prancing around naked, his male parts flopping about and him not knowing or caring that they were. I did my best to act like it was no big thing, but in truth it was. Everything about him was big. I let Verna towel him off and went to check on Grace Annie. She was sound asleep in Buck and Austin's old crib, her favorite blanket curled up in a ball beside her. I checked on the baby, lingering over the cradle, reveling in the sweetness of him mixed with baby talcum and lotion. Verna gave Austin his Benadryl to make sure he slept through the night. Without it he'd wander about the rooms, tipping over furniture and banging on doors.

"Praise the Lord!" Verna said. "He'll be out for eight solid hours." Poor Verna; I had a new appreciation for what her days were like.

Soon the only sounds roaming the house were the squeaks from the floorboards as Verna busied herself tidying up, mingled with the squawks from the water pipes while I rinsed the last of the dishes from supper. The cicadas chirping drifted in through the kitchen window. It should have brought comfort, such an idyllic night, the day's work done, the babies asleep, Austin at rest. Instead, I was edgy, nervous, not able to keep my mind settled.

"You think it'd be okay if I drive over and check on Buck?"

We were resting on the front porch, Verna in her favorite wooden rocking chair and me perched on the top step.

"It's too dark for you to be meandering off in the night." That was true. There wasn't a moon or even one star perched in the black sky, but I thought maybe she just didn't want me driving her Thunderbird.

"I'd be real careful," I said. Verna lit up a cigarette, something she rarely did, and her lips curled inward as she sucked the life out of it.

"He's not answering the phone. I really want to check on him."

"He's a big boy, Adie," she said.

"I know, but—"

"You can go by in the morning if he still don't answer. Knowing Buck, he needs time to work things out in his head. Leave him be; he'll be fine."

The thing is Buck wasn't fine at all. And something inside me knew it, that strange nagging pull in the part of your brain that won't let your heart be still. You know without knowing how or why you know, but you do. Even so, I stayed put and told myself to relax, be calm, and wait until morning. I ignored the parts of myself that were sounding alarms. I fed the baby every three hours and tossed and turned in between, when I should have done something, taken the car without asking, walked if I had to, something. Anything! Maybe that's why I still carry the burden of that night and what happened, drag it around like an invisible anchor so no one will see but me. I gave up trying to sleep and started baking cinnamon rolls. It's a wonder the sumptuous smell wafting through the tiny house didn't wake Verna, but she slept through every batch.

Come morning I was ragged as a worn out sheet. At six a.m. I fed and changed the baby and started phoning Buck. There was no answer. I kept ringing the line until my nerves couldn't take any more. I peeked in on Grace Annie, then wrote out a quick note to Verna that I'd taken the car to go check on Buck. Something was wrong. Very wrong.

• • •

I knew right where I'd find him—in the chicken coop. I opened the door to the brooder coop. All the hens clucked about the same as any other day. Everything was in order. Murphy had cleaned and fed and disinfected the grounds. I could still smell the carbolineum. Buck wasn't there. And there was nothing amiss in the second coop where the hatchlings were, either. I went to the last one and snapped the door open. The growing chicks leapt backwards in one movement, like an enormous, fluffy yellow ocean wave. Their high-pitched chirps filled the coop, and the dander stirred by their panic made a heavy mist that floated upward, making it hard for me to see clearly. I coughed and waited, my eyes slowly adjusting from the bright sunlight outside to the murky dimness inside. I noticed a movement along the back wall, a gentle, twisting movement. I carefully waded through the chicks. They scattered to the opposite wall, sending another surge of dust and dander in all directions. Splashes of sunlight spilled in through the narrow windows. The patches of light drifted across the rafters in front of me, leaving a pattern of striped shadows in its wake. I looked up and there was Buck flickering in and out of the morning light. He was fully dressed, except his foot was bare. His crutches lay on the ground beneath him. A rope was knotted tightly around his neck, and his body hung lifeless before me.

"Buuuuuuuuuuuuuck!" I screamed, sending the chicks scattering to the front of the coop. I shoved an empty feed barrel underneath him and climbed up. I placed his leg firmly against my shoulder and shoved with all my might, hoping to loosen the rope from around his neck.

"Breath, Buck! Breathe!" I yelled. "You hear me?"

"Oh God," I shouted, "help him breathe! Please, please—" Buck's tongue was swollen and distorted. It rested against his chin, mottled black and purple. I stretched on tiptoes and shoved my shoulders upward as far as I could. Someone was sobbing. Their wails pierced the walls of the chicken coop, stirring the chicks to near hysteria.

"Please, please, please, Buck," I called out and realized it was me.

"Just breathe, breathe, Buck. Breathe, breathe," I crooned over and over. It was too late. *I* was too late. He would never breathe again. He was dead.

chapter thirty-seven

"Y OU CAN'T BLAME YOURSELF, ADIE," Mama said. "People do what they gonna do." Even so, I did count myself guilty. Surely there was something I should have done. I'd been busy with Grace and Sam and the chickens. I knew Buck was hurting, but I hadn't noticed how deep his wounds had festered. I was getting things ready for the new baby. Mostly, I left Buck to himself.

"We had no way of knowing," Murphy said. "Won't do us any good to hold ourselves up for punishment. We got these babies to think about." Willa Mae said, "Deys joy for you no matter all dis sorrow gwine on. You gots to takes dat joy for dat sorrow eats it clean up."

"We best not blame each other for what we shoulda done," Verna said. "I know all about blame, Adie," she said. "You let it in to visit, and it's gonna want to stay."

"This weren't your fault," Mama said. "Ain't nobody knows what's in another's head excepting the good Lord. And if He couldn't stop him, what makes you think you could?"

All the words said to me were kind and soothing on the surface. But they couldn't get near the knot in my chest, this deep ache that sucked the air out of me. My other parts, my arms and legs, my skin, were no longer connected. They moved about like usual, but the sensation was they belonged to another. I stumbled over a pull-toy left on the kitchen floor and lost my balance. I regained it by grabbing hold of the stove. My arms flew outward and my fingers on one hand ended up on the burner still hot from the last pot of coffee Mama brewed. Guess my body parts weren't as disconnected as I thought. A fierce, burning pain grabbed hold of my hand and traveled up my arm. I yanked it free; my fingertips bone white, then red as apples. Mama plunged them into a bowl of ice. The lump in my chest was still there, but it became bearable, as the pain in my hand got all my attention.

"Adie girl," Mama said, "you need to go rest yourself." She patted my wound dry, spread butter on my fingertips, and carefully wrapped them in gauze.

"Poor chile," Willa Mae said and shuffled me off to bed. My legs followed. I let Clarissa and Willa Mae do for the little ones, while Rebecca accepted the food and saw to the kindness of those who came calling. Once again, folks came with platters of comfort food. We had so much macaroni and cheese we had to send some back home with the ones who brought pies and cakes.

Verna and Mama made arrangements for Buck. Me, I curled up with Tempe's diary and traded my sorrows for hers.

● ● ●

Miz Lizabeth, that kind white woman we share crops for 'long with her husband comes calling dat week and brings sum pretty cloth for me to sews new dresses wid. She sees dat face what be mine and how longs it is and asks what be troubling me. I tells her dat Thomas be drinking and fighting agin, is all. Miz 'Lizabeth say to takes him to the revival what coming dat next week and wash him clean in da river. I say for sure dat what I do, sure nuf and I thanks her for dat pretty cloth she brings, too. Mostly I thinking dat I don't know hardly whats I gwine do.

And dat little girl baby, what be's our, you know dat little Heart, she jis playing in the wind, not a kere in the world, and da sky falling down on us and dat's a truth. Little Heart, she be's eight year old, bes' I remembers. When Thomas sober up from the corn likker I goes about and tells him the story about me branding the babies and do's he member the pattywagon takes him away all dem years go. He say what dat got to do wid dem baby's be branded? And I say, "Don't you see dat brand you gots on your bum?" And he say what of it? And I tells Thomas I puts dat brand dere. He say, "You is gwine crazy. Maybe lots a' womens put the brand on dere babies fore dey's sold."

And I say dat might could be, but den I gets him to looks in da mirror be on da wall by da bed. "Who dat cuts my hair?" he acks and I tells him I do's. "See dat mark from da cracker whip? When you's little you is hit in the head by Massah's ol' cracker. Das how I knows dat brand on you is one I puts dere." And what Thomas do den, he falls to da floor and wraps his hands right arounds my feet and den he pounds his head on da floor. He be moaning so loud he skere Heart so bad she come running in from the yard. I pulls Thomas up and sits on the bed. Thomas he put his head in my lap and he cries like he be's a baby.

"Oh Mammy," he says. "What habs we done?" Now Heart be crying and I be's, too.

"What's we gonna do, Mammy?" Thomas say. I don't say what we gwine do, eben though I knows what we gots to do. One of us gots to leave. We can't be carrying on like we don't knows what we knows. After whiles Thomas git up and go off and takes some dat corn likker. I packs a bag for Heart and me and ties it up in a bundle. We gwine have to take da wagon and da mule. Thomas, he strong and kin plow da fields wid out dat mule, but Heart and me can't walks to where we's gowing. I don't know where we be's going and when we gets dere to dat place where it be and I say, "Okay, dis be where we's going"—dat could be real far when I says dat—so we gots to hab da wagon. I cooks potatoes to eat for Heart and makes up sum turnip greens wid fatback and sum bisquits be real good, and I eats sum, too. I'm not want to eats, but I gots to hab my strength for to travel, so's I do. Den we off to bed. Fore I do I leabes a note to Miz 'Lizabeth say fore her to tell Thomas we loves him but we gots to go and he know why it be bes' and fore to tells him dat. But when the moon is high and the res' the sky be black I hears the dogs barking and da sheriff man comes pounding on da door. I gits up to open it and dey got hold a' Thomas by the arms and be dragging him and he is full of blood. His head be bashed in worser den I eber see's it.

"He fighting agin," dat ol' sheriff man say. "I should locks him up, but you bes' fix him up first. He hurt real bad dis time," he say. Dey puts him on da bed and I cleans my Thomas bes' I kin. I wash him kereful and he be moaning. "I takes kere you, Thomas," I say, "Makes you good as new, den we takes you to da river and wash you clean like Miz 'Lizabeth say and we kin habs a good life eben wif what we knows."

I wraps him in da sheets and sings all da songs Thomas always like for me to sing. I stays and pats him and sings for him all da night, I do's. But sometime come morning I falls to sleep next to Thomas and when I wakes Heart be up and playing by da bed wid da dolls I makes her wid bits of cloth.

"What be's wrong wid mise daddy, Mammy?" she acks. "He be's real cold and he hard like dem rocks be's outside. Jis stare like to skere me, Mammy," she say. And I looks and dere is Thomas jis like Heart say. I starts wailing and fore long Heart be wailing and den the dogs be barking and soon Miz 'Lizabeth come running. She see what happen and get her husband John Evans and they do's what they kin, but they like to neber gets me to stop dat wailing.

chapter thirty-eight

SECRETS ARE LIKE STORIES. THEY have a beginning, a middle, and an end. They're short, or long, or in between, and they all take on a life of their own. Some go on and on, when you'd rather they not. You can close the book anytime, but it doesn't mean you are finished. And you may think you know where they are going, but you never know for sure until you get to the end and unravel it.

I kept secrets from Buck. I didn't talk to him about what had happened between Murphy and me, just pretended it wasn't there. Buck saw through it and wrote his own ending. But he only had part of the story. He'd missed out on the chapters that were about him. If I'd been open and honest, he might have seen they were there and considered them equally important. And I'd missed the signals he sent, too. Maybe I just chose to ignore them.

You know, it wasn't only Buck's body that was different. *He* was different. His eyes were dark puddles of sadness. The sparks that used to glow in them were gone. They'd sunk like heavy rocks thrown off a bridge. All that was left were ripples of who he once was and the piercing stare of who he'd become. He looked beyond me, then into me, seeing clearly what it was I wanted, wished for, and dreamed of.

He saw Murphy. I thought I had him hidden, but he was there, firmly in my heart. How could love bring together so much sorrow?

The sheriff came by and brought a note they found in Buck's shirt pocket. He said I could read it, but I'd have to give it back. It was evidence.

"Of what?" I said.

"Suicide's a criminal offense," he said.

"You plan on having a trial?" Verna said and snatched the note out of his hand. She offered it up to me. My fingers were trembling but I managed to hold on to it. Mama took the baby. Verna picked up Sam and coaxed Grace Annie to follow. She opened the door and motioned to the sheriff.

"Be my guest," Verna said and pointed to the stoop. They each went down the wooden steps and out into the yard. I curled up on the sofa and unfolded the note. Buck's voice was there on the page as soft and gentle as it was at the hospital when he said I was beautiful.

Dear Adie,

You are the blamingest girl I know. By that I mean you always feel things is yore fault. It's your nature. That sweetness in you that always has you wanting to make things right. You got to stop doing that, okay?

This how it is: I know the baby, he's mine. But I know some other things. I know about the letter you wrote Murphy. I snooped in his truck thinking I'd find some piece of yore clothing you left behind when you two was maybe doing what I always used to be up to. All I found is yore letter telling him why you were staying with me. It ain't no secret how Murphy feels about you. A body have to be blind not to see the way he looks at you and they'd have to be double stupid not to notice you looking away and trying to hide the fact that you feel what he feels. It's him wanting you and you wanting him and me wanting things different. Like a gift we're all after, each of us hoping it's ours.

I think you found out while I was gone what it is that makes life worth something. I figured it out, too, but I found it out too late. And you found out you didn't wait long enough for what you wanted to show up. So now when it does, you won't take it. You made a promise and signed it when you married me, so now you're standing by it no matter what and won't take the gift that's there with yore name on it—Murphy's gift.

It's the one you're supposed to have, Adie. One you'd never give yoreself. It's the one I can give you. Your letter to Murhpy said some reasons you still love me. Love me for one last reason, Adie—a reason worth something. Love me for what I'm able to give you now, your freedom.

Luv,
Buck

I gave the letter to Willa Mae. She said a letter like that will break your heart, but only if you let it.

"If you thinks you can fix what a body's gwine do, you got a high opinion on yoreself," she said. "Dey's gwine do what dey's gwine do."

I knew what she said was probably true. Even so, guilt stabbed me like a spike and remorse pummeled me like a sledgehammer. It wasn't just Buck ending his life the way he did. It was this battle going on inside me. Of course, I wasn't happy over what Buck did, but once I got over the shock of it, I wasn't completely tore up over it, either. Truth be told, I was relieved. I didn't like feeling the way I did, but I couldn't hide from it. I felt like I could stand up and shoulder my future again, that I had a future worth fighting for. I could breathe in the air and not fear it would suffocate me. Buck was right. He had given me what I would never have given myself. I'm sure there are people who think he was just being a coward, that he didn't want to live with what happened to him. I think he was just being honest. For the first time in his life he was happier letting other people be happy. Still, I wondered if he would have felt the same way if I'd been honest with him about Murphy, if I wouldn't have kept my feelings secret, if we'd talked it over. Maybe he would have wanted to fight for me. Maybe he would have said, "Let's give it some time."

Maybe he wouldn't be dead. Secrets, they're very hard to keep, and even harder to hide. And you pay a price for them. I've heard folks say some secrets are best kept a secret. The dictionary says it's something unknown. How can that be a good thing? If you don't know a snake's in the grass, you might step on it. And if you are standing at the edge of a cliff and you don't know it's there, you could walk off of it. So knowing is probably always better. Except for maybe planning a party, and even then, that's not really a secret, it's a surprise. There's a difference, don't you think?

I was almost finished with Tempe's journal. After she lost Thomas, she took her little girl Heart and left Macon and traveled on up north of Atlanta. There she kept house for Doctor Harvey Beryl and his wife Loma. Tempe helped the doctor out one night when he was busy birthing a baby and couldn't get away to help birth another. The old doc said Tempe had a gift, that she could coax a baby into the world with just her voice. Soon, she traveled with Doc Harvey in his wagon when he made his rounds. Together they birthed babies, set broken bones, and tended to the sick and dying. Granny Temp they called her. Heart stuck close to home, her only playmates the doctor's son Will and his two school chums. They knew Heart was a bit slow in the head but didn't seem to mind her none or the fact she wasn't white. She played in the stream and romped in the woods with them, a nearly white-skinned Negro girl tagging along after three older white boys.

• • •

Docs and me helps all da folks what git sick and breaks bones and we helps da ladies hab's the babies. Sum Doc gots to cuts from da mama or dey's both dies. I sees him do dat and I helps him do dat, too. Heart stays home and grows into a fine young pretty gal be thirteen. Doc's lady Miz Loma teach her to read and write somes her letters and she be a pretty gal, dat Heart. Miz Loma say she look half white. And I say's, "Well she got's somes dat white blood. Dat's why she luk like dat." It not so good, neither, 'cause Heart be's a gal and sumptin' happens. She gits in a bad way and weren't no one would say who gits her dat way. I tells Miz Loma it gots to be the boys she be tagging 'long wid, but one them's be her boy Will, so she's not happy to hear dat and say, dere be no ways to know. Heart be a young woman, no telling who she be's wid. I acks Heart 'bout dat and she say, "We play's in dem woods and da boys puts a sharp poker in dis parts be right here."

"What boys?" I say.

"All dem boys."

"What kind hot poker?" I say.

"Don't know. Dey keeps it hid in der pants and I not see dat poker. Hurts me bad and dey says not to tells or dey makes dat poker hurts worser."

Old Doc Harvey say, "We don't want any trouble around here, Tempe. Best let her have the baby and we'll take care of the both of you. And no one the wiser." What's I gwine do? I makes my way in life by deze folks. Dat's how it is. Heart habs a li'l baby girl and she be white as dem sheets hangs on the line for Miz Loma's bed. We names her Rachel and she be pretty, dat li'l white baby. Fore long Miz Loma wants dat baby be hers and Doc Harvey say, "We can give her a good life Tempe, and Heart will forget all about it." What's I gwine do? I already tells you, I makes my life by deze folks. And it for sure be's true that Rachel habs herself a good live she be dere's. And when she grows she looks white and later when she talks she talks like white folks and don't nobody's know different. And she has a good fine life like ol' Doc Harvey say she do.

So they gots Rachel and I gots Heart. Ol' Doc Harvey say Heart never be da wiser, but he don't hear what Heart say. Dey's all fussing o're dat baby Rachel how pretty she be. Den, Heart and me goes home and lebes the baby dere.

"Dat shore be's a pretty baby," Heart say.

"Real pretty baby," I say.

"Da hot pokers go in and hurts dat spot and den dat pretty baby cum out dat spot and hurt worser," Heart say. "She real pretty, dat baby, dough," she say, and rock dat spot be sore.

"Don't lets no more pokers go in dat spot," I say.

"Dis spot iz broke," she say. "See dis blood? No more pokers for dis broke spot," she say. And dat was it. 'Ceptin long time later, Heart meets Ben and dey's have two little babies, but dey's married 'fore dey's do and Heart be's very happy. And I's real happy fores her. Ben he loves Heart eben if she bit slow in da head. And she be good mama to dem little babies and dat's a truth. Now Heart helps me and Doc birth the babies and she good at helping us, too.

Den dis one day when Rachel is married and having a baby be her own, sumptin' terrible happens dat none us eber counted on and dey is sadness like you kin not know. And dat's a worser truth. Dis be's what happened. Rachel married to dat nice young man what owns all the land be's round here, and she be's ready to hab dat li'l baby she gwine hab and den one

There weren't any more pages in the journal! All that was left were the ragged edges fastened in the binding of what was once there. It about drove me crazy.

"What happened to the rest of the diary, Willa Mae?"

"Dey's gone. Dey's tore out and burned," she said.

"But—"

"Best we lets it be," she said and tucked Grace Annie into her bed. I put the baby in his cradle and picked up Sam. Mama and Verna were down at the funeral home seeing about a service for Buck.

"But I just have to know what happened—"

"The words be on them pages cause lots of sorrow. Best they never be on them pages. I lost 'bout everything I had 'cause they was."

"It's driving me crazy not knowing," I said.

"Oh, dey's better things to be crazy on," she said and turned the light out. "Bes' you forgits about it, 'cause I can't be talking 'bout dat." I followed her out of the new bedroom Murphy had built onto the cabin and heard his truck pull up into the driveway.

"Don't says nothing 'bout this to Murphy," Willa Mae said and patted her lips with the side of her finger. She took Sam from my arms and walked out onto the porch.

"Your daddy be's here for you," she said and bounced him on her hip. He grinned and clapped and wiggled to get down. She walked down the steps and placed him on the gravel. He toddled over to Murphy and stretched out his arms. Murphy scooped him up.

"Where's Adie?" he said. "She okay?" He brushed past Willa Mae and bounded up the steps to the door, while I finished making up a plate of okra and tomatoes for supper.

"Adie?" He snapped the door open and we nearly collided.

"How you doing? You alright?" he said.

"I'm fine," I said, but I wasn't. Secrets, they were all around us, fixing to build walls between us. I could feel my shoulders getting heavy again. Maybe it wasn't Buck's disability that had caused them to feel that way before. Maybe it was living with lies.

chapter thirty-nine

THE CORONER FINALLY RELEASED BUCK'S body. We buried him as soon as the funeral home folks had time to fix him up proper. "He still looks awful," Verna said. "Don't look, Adie." I was glad she didn't want me to, but I was crying again and wouldn't have seen much though my tears anyway. I still felt so guilty.

"We'll have a closed casket, honey," she said and patted my arm.

I stood next to Mama as Pastor Gib read the twenty-third psalm. Grace Annie waved a dandelion Willa Mae had helped her pick. She dropped it onto the casket. It rested on top of the wreath Verna and Mama selected of wildflowers, carnations, and baby's breath. Grace Annie clapped when she dropped her flower then changed her mind and reached down trying to retrieve it.

"Mine," she said. "Mine." Willa Mae carried her over to a patch of molted dandelions, plucked one from the ground, and slowly blew tiny puffs of fuzzy pollen seeds into the air. Grace Annie reached for one, snapped it from the ground, and proceeded to mimic Willa Mae. She got the furry halo too close to her mouth. It stuck to her lips when she puckered to blow, and she gagged and brushed at her mouth with her fingers. Willa Mae dusted off the remnants she'd missed.

Murphy stood across from me, Sam sound asleep in his arms. I had the new baby in mine. He was awake, blinking at the bright sunlight. I named him Buford Andrew, hoping Buck would be pleased, even though he'd dismissed it when I first brought it up. We were going to call him Andy. Verna was very happy. She delighted in all the babies. And her and Mama got along real well. Verna was even trying to talk her into moving to Hog Gap.

"No sense you being so far away from the grandbabies," Verna said.

"Well now, I got three grandsons in Cold Rock, you know," Mama told her.

"Bring them, too. There's plenty room in this town."

"Their mama wouldn't be too happy with that."

"Have her come, too," Verna said. "And bring that Clarissa gal. We'll fix her right up with a husband."

"She'd like that. She's lost over fifty pounds. Keeping it off, too," Mama said. "Doing fine. In fact, we're all doing fine, considering."

"Life keeps gwine on," Willa Mae said. "You kins be sad or be's happy."

Murphy and I hadn't talked about a wedding date. It was too soon, but folks knew we planned on it and seemed pleased about it. I was relieved, seeing as Hog Gap was Buck's hometown, too. I thought maybe they'd all blame me for what he done.

Things seemed to be working out. We were going to be a family just like Murphy planned. The only thing is I didn't want any secrets hovering over us like a bad storm cloud. I wanted Willa Mae to tell me what was in Tempe's journal that now no longer was there and what it had to do with me not talking about it to Murphy.

"All secrets ever did for my family is cause grief," I told her. "My sister Annie died over a dirty dark one," I added. "I don't think Mama's friend Louise would have been with us that day Annie drowned in the river if Mama had known about her and my pa."

"Dat could be," Willa Mae said.

"And if she wasn't there, then Pa wouldn't have been off in the grass with her and I wouldn't have been left alone with Annie. And if I wouldn't have been left alone with Annie, she wouldn't have drowned." Willa Mae nodded. "It's like a domino game gone haywire," I said. "I want you to tell me what happened, and if it involves Murphy then he ought to know too." Willa Mae got up from her rocker and headed for the door. Now I'd really done it. Stirred up *more* trouble—and her with a weak heart.

"Willa Mae—" I called after her. "I'm sorry—"

"I gots to get Murphy," she said. "What I gwine say, I only gwine say one time and be's done with it."

Once I heard what she'd kept hidden all these years I couldn't blame her. It was a heavy load to carry indeed.

• • •

We gathered on Willa Mae's front porch, me and her and Murphy. It stretched across the front of the cabin. What fine work Murphy did. There were four large rockers resting in place. He'd crafted them out of solid oak, their hand-rubbed maple finish smooth as butter. I loved that porch and the view all around us. Murphy's porch had the same workmanship. His wrapped around the sides of the log house and had a pond with a family of ducks.

"I could sit on either one of these porches and rock for near forever," I had told Murphy while Buck was still in Vietnam.

"That can be arranged," he'd said, his eyes almost dancing.

Now they were somber and quiet, and his hands on the arms of the rocking chair were tapping like woodpeckers. Willa Mae was snapping pole beans and dropping them into a kettle placed at her feet. She cleared her throat and opened her mouth, but only silence came out. She stared off into the woods like she was in awe of what was there. I had Andy in my arms, wrapped snugly in a blanket. Verna and Mama had Grace Annie and Sam. Willa Mae took a deep breath.

"Murphy, your mama never did runs off like your pa say she do," she said. Murphy nodded, his fingers curled tightly over the ends of the rocker arms.

"She drowned up yonder in Cold Rock River wid you still inside her. My own sweet mammy cut you out her belly. Breathed da life right into you when she see'd dey was no more of it in your mama."

Murphy eyes were glassy, but he said nothing.

"Your mama drowned herself when she find out something. And she weren't never to be finding dat out. Dat's my fault."

"Maybe you could start somewhere closer to the beginning," I said.

"I be's gitting to dat."

She snapped three more beans, dried her hands on her apron, and set the bowl on the stoop.

"Murphy," she said. "Your mama Rachel be spoiled good, a prissy thing she was and real sassy, too. Treats me bad many a year, she do. And my head gets mad at her for dat. And I weren't much a grownup at dat time, eben so's I was grown. I be married to my husband Ben Satterfield. We gots two little babies, we do. One be a little girl and the other a boy. Dey's Georgia and Calvin. That before Ben is real bad with the diabetes sickness and before he dies from dat sickness. All them times I be so happy. I takes good kere of the little chillun's be ours. Now Rachel belong to Doc Harvey and his wife Loma. You members them."

Murphy shook his head.

"Sure you do's. Dey lives down the hill and den moves off while you's still in school. Members?"

Murphy continued shaking his head, his feet firmly anchored to the porch, the tips of his boots splayed far apart. He jerked the rocker back and forth with his heels. I was in the rocker next to him with Andy nesting in my lap. There was a nice breeze. It darted back and forth, catching hold of the shells Willa Mae'd brought back from Tybee and fashioned into a homemade chime. They clicked and clacked like a determined craps player eagerly rolling his dice.

"Anyways, dat not be's important. What be's important be Rachel not be's their real daughter, but don't anyone knows it but me and my mammy. Those days white ladies mostly stays confined when dey waits to habs babies, so they's no way knowing Rachel not belong to them, see? When Rachel is all grown up and 'bout the prettiest gal in deze parts ever, she marries your daddy Sam Spencer, owns all the land be here. But you knows that part. After she be married and is soon to hab the baby be you, she still treats me bad. Makes fun of me be bit slow. Say how stupid I is. Something in my head 'bout that time think how much a body can take? Den one day she say maybe now Ben gone, my little chilluns should goes and live with someone can kere better for'em. Dey's better off, she say.

"'How's about you?'" I acks her. "'You better off raised by some-one else? Is you?' And she say, 'What are you talking about, you crazy woman?' And I tells her if I is, it don't change nothing. I tells her I be her real mama and I tells her how she come to be my baby, and that my mammy gives her to Doc Harvey and Miz Loma when they see's she look like a pretty white baby and dat be's cause her daddy be Doc Harvey's boy or maybe one his friends and what dey do's to me. Rachel says I be's a liar and slap me side the head. I tells her I kin proves it and can gits my mammy's book where she has it all writ down. I do's that. I gives Rachel that book, and the words in the book be just like I say. Rachel goes crazy when she reads what be's in that book. Only we don't knows she gone crazy and Mammy don't knows I even gives her dat book. When we wakes real early dat next morn-ing—Mammy and me—the babies, the both of them, be gone. We is wondering how they gits out the house and we is running in circles looking for them little chilluns. We's near crazy ourselves and we goes to the river skeered what we find. Sure nuf, Rachel is floating in the river and Mammy pulls her out with a big stick. But my chilluns is nowhere. We habs some hope maybe they still okay and we kin finds them if'n we hurry. And Rachel be still floating in da water. And dat's when mammy grabs a rock gots a sharp point on it and Mammy cuts you from your mama's belly, Murphy. And I's standing there, thinking dis be a bad nightmare and I be skeered awake from it soon. But I don't wakes up so I knows I already awake and Mammy, she cleans out your nose and mouth and breaths air right into you! Later my babies little bodies is found further down in dat river. And dey's dead. Dey's drowned, two plump li'l raisins floating long. What habs I done? I say. I's sceaming to Mammy. Jis screaming loud as thunder and people's is coming. Now Rachel got the papers she ripped from the book stuck in her bosom. Your pa sees them papers and he reads what's on dem papers. Later, he burns them clean up. And he say mammy and me kin stay on and I kin kere for you, but never tell what happened or we haves the Klan on us.

"Your pappy say, 'You see what happened here?' And he shakes my shoulders till my teeths rattle. 'You tell folks this baby boy got some black blood in his veins, he won't have a life worth living around here. You understand that?' is what he say and I am thinking it be fore sure the truth, 'cause look what happen to Rachel and to the babies when I tells. He shakes me hard and I say I won't never tells, not never. So we stay on and Mr. Sam, your daddy, he builds us a fine little cabin and my mammy Tempe she lives many years in the cabin and we raise chickens and I keres for her and for you, Murphy, fore she dies, and then I lives there by's myself right in that cabin you lives in, Adie. I spect you figures that part out for yourself, by now."

Murphy looked at me like I was a book and he was trying to remember how to read one.

"So nows you know, Murphy. Some yore blood be in your veins is black. Folks find dat out dey's trouble," Willa Mae said. "You knows how people's is round here." She rocked her body and nodded her head.

"I don't really care what folks think," Murphy said. "But I do care about how they'll treat Adie and Sam because of it." He reached for my hand, and I held out the one nearest him. His was shaking like it had the palsy, and his eyes were brimming with tears. Willa Mae was dabbing at hers, trying to keep up with them. That was all it took for mine to sprout leaks.

"Maybe it's best we keep this to ourselves." Murphy whispered, drawing me close. "We got the kids to think about."

I nodded. Willa Mae's face brightened and her rocker jerked to a halt. "Oh, das good, Murphy. Das real good."

"But I want you to know I don't have any problem with us being blood kin, Willa Mae," Murphy said, brushing my tears away with his fingetips. "You know that?"

"You ain't told me no lies before," she said. "But we sure nuff don't needs to be telling all dis."

"What do you say, Adie?" Murphy asked.

"According to Tempe's journal, a good many plantation owners slept with their slaves. I reckon most of this town's got mixed blood and ain't none the wiser—and what of it?"

"My bloodline make a difference in how you feel about me, Adie?" Murphy asked, the concern in his eyes easier to read than a newspaper. Willa Mae dabbed at her eyes with the hem of her arpon. I looped one arm around each of their necks and pulled them close.

"Murphy, it ain't what's in a body's blood that matters—it's what's in their heart. You and Willa Mae got the best looking ones I ever glanced on."

chapter forty

THINGS SLOWLY SETTLED DOWN. MAMA went back to Cold Rock. Verna picked up Austin and they went on home, too. He'd been staying at Miz Bailey's and like to drove her nuts is what I hear from the ladies at church. Willa Mae got busy with her vegetable garden. Murphy was taking care of his chicken business and helping me with mine. He was thinking about building houses on some of the land. The carpet mills were booming.

"People are going to need homes nearby," he said. "Maybe call it Spencer and Sons Construction," he said. "Teach the boys the business as they grow. Maybe add a few more and a couple of girls for Grace Annie. What do you think?"

"I think it's too soon," I said. "Not about the business, but—"

"No rush, Adie," he said. "Take all the time you need. I got plenty to do." He motioned with his arms and directed his fingers at the vast expanse of earth laid out before us, pretty as a painting on a canvas. I watched him climb in the truck, Sam on the seat beside him, Worry in the truck bed.

"See you in the morning," he said and drove off.

I got up as the sun was creeping along the horizon. Andy was eager to nurse. I carried him out to the front stoop and marveled at how good the morning smelled. The chicken coop scent was nowhere about. It would make its way to the front of the house when the day warmed up and grew heavy. The odor would cling to the air like lint on a sweater, the way pieces of sadness cling to our hearts.

I thought about the words Willa Mae had told us her mother had given her when their world had changed forever, when their grief was raw as uncooked meat.

"My Mammy say, 'You gots to stir dat pot of sadness up real good,' she say. 'And keeps it stirred so the happy times don't git lost in dat stew. 'Cause you gwine eat dat stew for all yore life. See da good part in dat stew? Eat all dat up and keeps doing dat.' She do, she say dat. My mammy Tempe be reals smart mammy," Willa Mae said, her face full up with pride.

Tempe's and Willa Mae's English was poor, but their sentiments were richer than good potting soil. To think that the entire time I'd been poring over the diary I was reading about Willa Mae's own family. *Willa Mae was Heart.* I should have known. I mean, why else would she have the journal? I guess I was too caught up in it to take the time to wonder.

The screen door opened and Grace Annie wandered out, her nightshirt no longer covering her knees. She'd grown another two inches. Her dark hair, still baby fine, was tied in pigtails, but sleep had pulled them out of place. They dangled, lopsided, on the sides of her head. One curly little tail was ready to lose its rubber band. She had an open box of Cheerios clutched tight against her chest, an arm lost inside, her hand digging in for another handful.

Mama will get you some milk in a minute, sugar," I said. She plopped the box on the stoop and started down the steps. Murphy's truck crunched on the gravel as the sun spread a thin blanket of light on the ground. Grace Annie sailed down the last two steps but lost her footing and toppled over onto the hard clay when she reached the ground. She let out a howl and plunked down on her bottom as she inspected her knees: two angry red little bulges. One started to bleed.

"Ooweeee, oooweee," she howled. Murphy got out of the truck, plucked Sam from the interior and put him down. Sam toddled over to Grace Annie and watched as Murphy knelt beside her.

"Boo-boo," she said and pointed.

"Let me see, sugar," I said. Grace Annie's face was a picture of sorrow, her eyes pinched tight and spouting tears, her mouth twisted sideways, her bottom lip curled outward like a fat little worm inching out of the earth. She started to wail. Sam started in, too.

"I think you're gonna live, guys," Murphy said and swung Grace Annie up into his arms. He pulled out a clean white handkerchief from his back pocket, turned on the water spigot next to the garden patch, wet the kerchief, and placed it gently across her knees. Sam toddled along after him, rubbing at his tears.

"How we doing, pardner?" Murphy said and patted Sam's head. Grace Annie peeked under the handkerchief, her eyes big as cantaloupes.

"Well, would you lookie here," Murphy said. "I believe I brought breakfast on a stick."

He pulled two red suckers from his shirt pocket, each one looped on a string. Grace Annie reached for one, her skinned knees forgotten. Sam clutched Murphy's pant leg and clambered for the other. Murphy removed the cellophane wrappers and passed out the morning treat.

I placed Andy on my shoulder and patted his back. He let out two little burps.

"Hey, little guy," Murphy said and took hold of one tiny finger. "You doing okay?"

Andy's head wobbled about. He wasn't strong enough yet to hold it up on its own. I laid him back down in my lap. He curled his legs up and yawned, ready to sleep until the next feeding. Murphy smiled like a proud father, a proud husband, which was what he said he intended to be.

"If you'll let me, Adie."

He plopped one leg up on the steps and rested his arms crosswise on his knee. Our eyes followed Grace Annie. She took Sam's hand and led him to a small patch of grass next to the garden. They sat facing each other, giggly-silly with their suckers, smacking their lips and showing off their red tongues. Every few licks they'd yank the suckers out of their mouths and click them together, sometimes missing their mark, other times not, enjoying each minute, regardless. Tired of that game, Grace Annie started another. She held her sucker up like a trophy and Sam, shaking with a fit of the giggles, did the same. They turned their faces up to the sun and stuck out their tongues. By now they were redder than mama's roses.

Baby Andy was cradled in the curve of my lap, sound asleep. Murphy settled in on the step beside me and slipped my hand into his. He curled his long fingers around mine and squeezed the way a man's supposed to—nice and firm so you know it's there, but not hard enough to scrunch your finger bones.

And we sat there, me holding Andy and Murphy holding me. We watched Sam and Grace Annie, their laughter doing all the talking, red spittle dribbling down their chins, their gooey suckers and sticky faces still hoisted up to the sun, their happiness a badge for us to behold, their joy in the moment a tribute to the goodness that's there if we take it.

I laid my head on Murphy's shoulder, content with the morning, our children, each other, and the simple process of breathing.

THE END

the recipes

MAMA'S DOUBLE-LEMON MARMALADE

4   *cups fresh lemon balm, leaves and stems (about 1³/₄ ounces)*
4½ *cups boiling water*
6   *to 8 large lemons (about 3 pounds)*
5½ *cups sugar*

1. Place lemon balm in a large bowl. Add the boiling water. Cover; let stand for 15 minutes. Drain well, reserving liquid. Using a knife, peel lemons, removing yellow portion and about ¼-inch thickness of the white membranes of peel. Cut peel into very thin strips, about 1½ inches long. Measure 3 cups peel. Set aside. Remove and discard any remaining white portion of peel from lemons. Section lemons, reserving fruit and juice; discard membrane and seeds. Chop lemon. Measure 1½ cups lemon and juice; set aside. In a large saucepan combine peel and 4 cups water. Heat to boiling. Boil, uncovered, for 5 minutes. Drain; discard liquid. Cook and drain once more, using fresh water.

2. In same saucepan combine drained peel, chopped lemon and juice, and the 3½ cups reserved liquid. Heat to boiling; boil gently, uncovered, for 5 minutes. Measure 5½ cups mixture. Pour mixture into an 8- or 10-quart Dutch oven. Add sugar. Heat and stir till sugar dissolves. Bring to a boil. Boil hard, uncovered, about 25 minutes or till mixture sheets off a metal spoon or reaches 220° on a jelly thermometer, stirring to prevent sticking.

> MAMA'S DOUBLE-LEMON MARMALADE
>
> *This here jam soothes tension and helps with yore depression, if you got any. Try some.*
> Ruby Thacker

3. Ladle marmalade into hot, sterilized half-pint canning jars, leaving ¼-inch headspace. Wipe jar rims; adjust lids. Process in a boiling-water canner for 5 minutes (start timing when water begins to boil). Remove jars from canner; cool on racks. Makes about 5 half-pints.

MAMA'S CRANBERRY-PEPPER JELLY

2   *to 4 jalapeño peppers, halved and seeded*
1½ *cups cranberry juice cocktail*
1   *cup vinegar*
5   *cups sugar*
½   *of a 6-ounce package (1 pouch) liquid
    fruit pectin*
5   *small fresh hot red peppers*

> MAMA'S CRANBERRY-PEPPER JELLY
>
> Get some for Christmas. It's
> real good.
>   Ruby Thacker

1. In a medium saucepan combine jalapeño peppers, cranberry juice cocktail, and vinegar. Bring to boiling; reduce heat. Cover and simmer for 10 minutes. Strain mixture through a sieve, pressing with the back of a spoon to remove all of the liquid. Measure 2 cups liquid. Discard pulp.
2. In a 4-quart Dutch oven or kettle combine the 2 cups strained liquid and the sugar. Bring to a full rolling boil over high heat, stirring constantly. Stir in the pectin and hot peppers. Return to a full rolling boil; boil for 1 minute, stirring constantly. Remove from heat. Quickly skim off foam with a metal spoon.
3. Immediately ladle jelly into hot, sterilized half-pint canning jars, leaving ¼-inch headspace. Divide the 5 hot red peppers among the 5 jars. Wipe jar rims and adjust lids. Process jars in a boiling-water canner for 5 minutes (start timing when water begins to boil). Remove jars from canner; cool on wire racks. Jelly may require 2 to 3 days to set. Makes about 5 half-pints.

MAMA'S GINGERED PEACH PRESERVES

5   *pounds firm-ripe peaches*
6   *cups sugar*
2   *tablespoons snipped candied ginger*
1   *tablespoon lemon juice*

1. Wash peaches. Peel, pit, and chop peaches. To peel peaches with ease, immerse them, a few at a time, in boiling water for 20 to 30 seconds or till skins crack. Then quickly plunge them into cold water; use a small sharp knife to peel off the skin. Measure 11 cups chopped peaches.

> MAMA'S GINGERED PEACH
> PRESERVES
>
> Be sure and use fresh
> Georgia peaches.
>   Ruby Thack

2. In a very large bowl combine peaches, sugar, ginger, and lemon juice. Cover with waxed paper. Let stand overnight, stirring occasionally to dissolve sugar.
3. Transfer mixture to a 6- or 8-quart Dutch oven or kettle. Bring mixture to boiling, stirring frequently. Boil gently,

uncovered, about 1 hour or till syrup sheets off a metal spoon or mixture reaches 220 degrees on a jelly thermometer. Quickly skim off foam with a metal spoon.

4. Immediately ladle mixture into hot, sterilized half-pint canning jars, leaving ¼-inch headspace. Wipe jar rims and adjust lids. Process in a boiling-water canner for 5 minutes (start timing when water begins to boil). Remove jars from canner, cool on racks. Makes 7 half-pints.

MAMA'S PRUNE CONSERVE

1½ pounds prunes
1½ pounds raisins
1½ pounds dried currants
4½ cups hot strong tea
3   to 5 whole cloves
     juice of 1 lemon
2¼ cups packed dark brown sugar
1   cup whole blanched almonds
7   tablespoons brandy

1. Pit the prunes and coarsely chop them. Crack a few of the pits with a hammer and take out the kernels. Discard the rest.

2. Put the kernels into a small bowl and cover with boiling water. Leave for 1 minute, then drain, and transfer to a bowl of cold water. Drain again, then, rub off the skins with your fingers.

3. Put the chopped prunes and peeled kernels into a nonmetallic bowl with the raisins and currants. Pour the hot tea over the fruits. Cover and leave to stand overnight.

4. Pour the contents of the bowl into a preserving pan. Stir in all the remaining ingredients, except the almonds and brandy, and put the pan over low heat. Stir with a wooden spoon until the sugar has completely dissolved.

MAMA'S PRUNE CONSERVE

This one sells out ever year.
Ruby Thacker

5. Bring the mixture to a boil. Simmer, stirring constantly, for 12 minutes, or until the mixture has thickened. Remove the pan from the heat. Test for a light set. Stir in the whole almonds and brandy.

6. Pour the conserve into warmed sterilized jars, to within ⅛ inch of the tops. Seal the jars and label.

MAMA'S OLD-FASHIONED GRAPE JELLY

6   *pounds Concord grapes*
³/₄ *cup water*
3³/₄ *cups sugar*

1. Wash and stem grapes. Crush grapes in a 6- or 8-quart Dutch oven or kettle. Add the water. Bring to boiling over high heat; reduce heat. Cover and simmer about 10 minutes or till grapes are very soft.
2. Using a jelly bag or a colander lined with several thicknesses of 100% cotton cheesecloth, strain the mixture. (This will take about 4½ hours.) You should have about 7 cups of juice. Chill the juice for 12 to 14 hours. Strain again through jelly bag or cheesecloth.
3. Place juice in the Dutch oven or kettle. Add sugar; stir to dissolve. Bring to a full rolling boil. Boil hard, uncovered, till syrup sheets off a metal spoon or reaches 220° on a jelly thermometer. This will take about 20 minutes. Quickly skim off foam with a metal spoon.
4. Immediately ladle jelly into hot, sterilized half-pint canning jars, leaving ¼-inch headspace. Wipe jar rims and adjust lids. Process jars in a boiling-water canner for 5 minutes (start timing when water begins to boil). Remove jars from canner; cool on racks. Makes 5 half-pints.

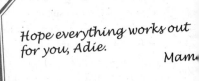

Hope everything works out for you, Adie.

Mama

MAMA'S PEACH JAM

4   *pounds peaches*
1   *package (1³/₄ or 2 ounces) powdered fruit pectin for lower sugar recipes*
¼   *cup sugar*
1   *teaspoon finely shredded lemon peel*
2   *tablespoons lemon juice*
3   *cups sugar*

1. Wash peaches. Peel and pit peaches. Finely chop peaches. Measure 5 cups.
2. Combine pectin and the ¼ cup of the sugar. In an 8- or 10-quart Dutch oven or kettle combine chopped peaches, pectin mixture, lemon peel, and lemon juice. Bring to a full rolling boil, stirring constantly. Stir in the 3 cups sugar. Return to a full rolling boil. Boil hard for 1 minute, stirring constantly. Remove from heat. Quickly skim off foam with a metal spoon.
3. Immediately ladle jam into hot, clean half-pint canning jars, leaving ¼-inch headspace. Wipe jar rims and adjust lids. Process jars in a boiling-water canner for 10 minutes. (Start timing when water beings to boil). Remove jars from canner; cool on racks. Makes 6 half-pints.

MAMA'S SWEET CHERRY JAM

3   *pounds fully ripe dark sweet cherries*

1   *package (1¼ ounces) regular pow-
     dered fruit pectin*

1   *teaspoon finely shredded lemon peel*

¼   *cup lemon juice*

5   *cups sugar*

1.   Sort, wash, stem, pit, and chop
     cherries. Measure 4 cups chopped
     cherries.

2.   In a 6- or 8-quart Dutch oven or kettle combine cherries, pectin, lemon peel,
     and lemon juice. Bring to boiling over high heat, stirring constantly. Stir in
     sugar. Bring to a full rolling boil. Boil hard for 1 minute, stirring constantly.
     Remove from heat. Quickly skim off foam with a metal spoon.

3.   Immediately ladle jam into hot, sterilized jars and process in boiling-water can-
     ner as usual.

MAMA'S SWEET CHERRY JAM

*This will help your husband
forget he wants to leave you.
Pick up a jar.*
                    Ruby Thacker

MAMA'S APPLE BUTTER

4½   *pounds tart cooking apples (about 14 medium apples)*

4   *cups apple cider or apple juice*

2   *cups sugar*

1½   *teaspoons ground cinnamon*

½   *teaspoon ground allspice*

¼   *teaspoon ground cloves*

1.   Wash, core, and quarter apples.

2.   In an 8- or 10-quart Dutch oven or
     kettle combine apples and cider or
     juice. Bring to boiling; reduce heat.
     Cover and simmer for 30 minutes or
     till apples are very tender, stirring
     occasionally.

3.   Press apples and liquid through a food
     mill or sieve. Measure 9½ cups mixture.
     Return mixture to the Dutch oven. Stir in sugar, cinnamon, allspice, and cloves.
     Bring to boiling; reduce heat. Cook, uncovered, over very low heat, about 1½
     hours or till very thick, stirring often to prevent sticking.

4.   Ladle apple butter into hot, sterilized pint or half-pint canning jars, leaving
     ¼-inch headspace. Wipe jar rims and adjust lids. Process in a boiling-water can-
     ner for 10 minutes for pints or 5 minutes for half-pints (start timing when water
     begins to boil). Remove jars from canner; cool on racks. Makes 4 pints or 8 half-
     pints.

MAMA'S APPLE BUTTER

*This here's real good on any
kind of bread.*
                    Ruby Thacker

MAMA'S PICKLED CHERRIES

2¹/₂ *pounds*
2¹/₂ *cups sugar*
¹/₂ *cup white wine vinegar*
¹/₂ *teaspoon ground cinnamon*
¹/₂ *teaspoon ground allspice*
¹/₄ *teaspoon ground cloves*

1. Rinse and drain cherries; remove stems and pits. Measure 7 cups and place in a 2¹/₂-quart casserole dish.
2. In medium saucepan combine sugar, vinegar, cinnamon, allspice, and cloves; stir to dissolve sugar. Heat to boiling. Boil gently, uncovered, for 5 minutes. Pour over cherries.
3. Cover cherry mixture, let stand at room temperature for 24 hours. Drain liquid into saucepan; heat to boiling and pour over cherries again. Cover and let stand for 12 to 24 hours. Drain again into saucepan and heat liquid to boiling.
4. Using a slotted spoon, fill hot, clean half-pint canning jars with cherries, leaving ¹/₂-inch headspace. Add hot liquid to cherries, leaving ¹/₂-inch headspace. Remove air bubbles, wipe jar rims, adjust lids. Process jars in boiling-water canner for 10 minutes. Remove jars from canner; cool. (Spices settle upon standing; stir before serving.) Makes 5 half-pints.

> MAMA'S PICKLED CHERRIES
>
> *Keep some a' this on hand fer company.*
>
> Ruby Thack

MAMA'S LEMON CURD

6 *to 8 large, juicy lemons*
1 *cup unsalted butter*
2¹/₂ *cups superfine sugar*
5 *eggs*

1. Grate the zest from the lemons on the finest side of the grater. Squeeze the juice and strain it into a large measuring cup. You will need 1¹/₄ cups lemon juice.
2. Cut the butter into small pieces. Put the pieces of butter into a glass bowl, along with the sugar, lemon zest, and juice; set over a pan of gently simmering water. The bottom of the bowl should not touch the water, nor should the water boil rapidly. Stir the mixture until the butter has melted and the sugar has completely dissolved.

> MAMA'S LEMON CURD
>
> *This here's a right nice holiday treat for yore family and company. A good stocking stuffer too, you got ones big enough.*
>
> Ruby Thack

3. Lightly beat the eggs in a bowl, but do not whisk them. Strain the eggs through a fine sieve into the lemon mixture. Simmer over low heat, stirring constantly with a wooden spoon, until the mixture thickens slightly. This will take 20–25 minutes. Do not allow the mixture to boil or it will curdle.

4. As soon as the mixture is thick enough to coat the back of the spoon, remove the bowl from the pan of water.

5. Pour into warmed sterilized jars. Place a wax paper round, waxed side down, on top. Smooth over to remove any air pockets. Leave to cool.

6. Cover with dampened plastic wrap circles. Label and store in the refrigerator.

STEWED TOMATOES

8   *pounds ripe firm tomatoes*
1   *cup chopped celery*
1/2 *cup chopped onion*
1/2 *cup chopped green pepper*
2   *teaspoons sugar*
2   *teaspoons salt*

1. Wash tomatoes. Remove peels, stem ends, and cores. Chop tomatoes. Measure 17 cups.

2. Place in an 8- to 10-quart Dutch oven or kettle. Add celery, onion, green pepper, sugar, and salt to the kettle. Bring to boiling. Reduce heat. Cover and simmer for 10 minutes, stirring frequently to prevent sticking.

3. Ladle hot stewed tomatoes into hot, clean quart or pint canning jars, leaving 1-inch headspace. Wipe jar rims; adjust lids. Process at 10 pounds pressure for 20 minutes for quarts or 15 minutes for pints. Allow pressure to come down naturally. Remove jars from canner; cool on racks. Makes 3 quarts or 7 pints.

STEWED TOMATOES

You kin freeze these tomaters fer up to ten months if you want.
Ruby Thacker

PEACH PIE FILLING

8	*pounds fully ripe, firm peaches*
7	*cups sugar*
2	*cups Clear Jel*
1	*teaspoon ground cinnamon*
$^1/_4$	*teaspoon ground nutmeg*
$4^1/_2$	*cups water*
$1^3/_4$	*cups lemon juice*
1	*teaspoon almond extract*

PEACH PIE FILLING

This here's real good pie fillin'.

Ruby Thacke

1. Wash and peel peaches. Cut fruit into $^1/_2$-inch sections. To prevent darkening, place fruit in ascorbic acid solution; drain well. Measure 24 cups fruit. Set aside.
2. In an 8-quart Dutch oven or kettle heat about 6 cups water to boiling. Add 6 cups peach slices; return to boiling. Boil for 1 minute. Using a slotted spoon, transfer peaches to a large bowl; cover. Repeat with remaining fruit, 6 cups at a time. Drain water from Dutch oven or kettle.
3. In same kettle combine the sugar, ClearJel, cinnamon, and nutmeg. Stir in the $4^1/_2$ cups water. Cook over medium-high heat, stirring constantly, till mixture thickens and begins to boil. Add the lemon juice; boil 1 minute, stirring constantly. Stir in the almond extract. Immediately add fruit, stirring gently to coat. Heat for 3 minutes.
4. Spoon hot fruit mixture into hot, clean quart jars, leaving 1-inch headspace. Remove air bubbles, wipe jar rims, and adjust lids. Process filled jars in a boiling-water canner for 30 minutes. Remove jars from canner; cool on racks. Makes 6 quarts, enough for six pies.

DILL PICKLES

$2^1/_4$	*pounds pickling cucumbers*
$3^3/_4$	*cups water*
$3^3/_4$	*cups cider vinegar*
6	*tablespoons pickling salt*
12	*to 18 heads fresh dill*
1	*tablespoon mustard seed*

DILL PICKLES

You can't buy any better pickles.

Ruby Thack

1. Thoroughly rinse cucumbers. Remove stems and cut off a slice from each end. Make a brine by combining water, vinegar, and salt. Bring to boiling.
2. Pack cucumbers loosely into hot, clean pint jars, leaving $^1/_2$-inch headspace. Add 4 teaspoons dill seed and $^1/_2$ teaspoon mustard seed to each jar. Pour hot brine over cucumbers, leaving $^1/_2$-inch headspace. Remove air bubbles, wipe jar rims, and adjust lids. Process in boiling-water canner for 10 minutes. Remove jars. Let stand 1 week before using. Makes 6 pints.

PICKLED BEETS

3	*pounds small whole beets*
2	*cups vinegar*
1	*cup water*
1	*cup sugar*
1	*teaspoon whole allspice*
6	*whole cloves*
3	*inches stick cinnamon*

PICKLED BEETS

Git plenty for Thanksgiving and serve it with the stuffing.

Ruby Thacker

1. Wash beets leaving the roots and 1 inch of tops. Place in a 4- to 6-quart Dutch oven or kettle; add water to cover. Bring to boiling, reduce heat. Simmer, uncovered, till tender, about 25 minutes. Drain and discard cooking liquid. Cool beets slightly; trim off roots and stems. Slip off the skins.
2. In the same Dutch oven combine vinegar, water, and sugar. Place allspice, cloves, and cinnamon in the center of a 7-inch square of 100% cotton cheesecloth; tie into a bag and place in Dutch oven. Heat to boiling; reduce heat. Simmer, uncovered, for 5 minutes.
3. Pack beets in hot, clean half-pint canning jars, leaving 1/2-inch headspace. Carefully add the boiling pickling liquid, leaving 1/2-inch headspace. Discard the spice bag.
4. Wipe jar rims; adjust lids. Process in a boiling-water canner for 30 minutes. Remove jars from canner; cool on racks.

CHERRY BRANDY

1	*pound cherries*
1/2	*cup sugar*
2	*drops almond extract*
2 1/2	*cups of brandy*

1. Remove all the cherry stalks. Prick each cherry all over with a sterilized needle or wooden toothpick.
2. Layer the cherries with the sugar in a large sterilized jar to within 1 inch of the top. Add the almond extract to the jar.
3. Pour in the bandy to cover the cherries by 1/2 inch. Seal the jar and shake well. Keep in a cool dark place for at least 3 months before using to allow the flavors to develop. Shake the jar from time to time.
4. Line a funnel with a double layer of cheesecloth and strain the brandy through it into a sterilized bottle. Seal the bottle and label. The brandy is now ready to use.

CHERRY BRANDY

Don't drink too much of this or you'll think yere dyin' and you'll be skeered you won't.

Ruby Thacker

PICKLED PRUNES

2	*pounds dried plums (prunes)*
1	*tablespoon salt*
2¹⁄₃	*cups white wine vinegar*
12	*black peppercorns*
12	*whole cloves*
2	*cinnamon sticks*

1. Put the dried plums into a pan of boiling water. Immediately remove from the heat and leave to stand for 2 minutes. Drain and peel. Cut them in half lengthwise, remove and discard the pits.
2. Layer the prunes with the salt in two sterilized jars to within one inch of the tops.
3. Put all of the remaining ingredients into a saucepan and bring to a boil. Boil for 1 minute, then pour the mixture over the prunes to cover them by ½ inch, making sure there are no air pockets between the prunes.
4. Seal the jars and label. Keep in a cool dark place for two weeks before using to allow the flavors to develop.

PICKLED PRUNES

Be careful not to eat too man of these prunes or you'll be livin' the bathroom.
Ruby Thac

SPICED APPLE RINGS

8	*pounds of tart apples*
10	*3-inch pieces stick cinnamon*
2	*tablespoons whole cloves*
1	*¹⁄₂-inch piece gingerroot, sliced*
6	*cups packed brown sugar*
6	*cups water*
1	*cup cider vinegar*

1. Wash apples. Peel and core 1 apple; cut crosswise into ½-inch rings. If desired, place rings in ascorbic acid color-keeper solution to reduce discoloration; drain. Repeat with remaining apples.
2. For spice bag, tie cinnamon pieces, whole cloves, and gingerroot in a square of 100% cotton cheesecloth; set aside. In an 8-quart Dutch oven or kettle, combine brown sugar, water, and vinegar. Heat to boiling, stirring constantly. Reduce heat; add spice bag. Simmer, covered, for 10 minutes.

SPICED APPLE RINGS

Git plenty and serve 'em on New Year's for good luck.
Ruby Thacke

3. Drain apple slices and add to hot liquid; return to boiling. Simmer covered, stirring occasionally, for 5 minutes or till apples are tender. Remove spice bag. With a slotted spoon, pack apple rings in hot, clean pint canning jars, leaving ½-inch headspace. Add hot liquid, leaving ½-inch headspace. Remove air bubbles, wipe jar rims, and adjust lids. Process filled jars in a boiling-water canner for 10 minutes. Remove jars from canner; cool on racks. Makes 7 pints. (56 servings.)

WINTER FRUIT COMPOTE

2   *cups cooking dates*
3   *pears*
5   *apples*
½   *cup cooked butternut squash*
1   *cup pineapple juice*

1. Soak dates, pears, apples, and squash in pineapple juice for several hours or soften over low heat.
2. Puree fruits in blender or food processor. Cook over low heat until thick, stirring frequently.
3. Ladle into jars and seal. Store in the refrigerator for up to 1 month. Makes about 4 cups.

WINTER FRUIT COMPOTE

Serve this with my Spiced Apples if you want plenty of good luck in the New Year.
Ruby Thacker

TOMATO CHUTNEY

3   *pounds ripe tomatoes*

1¹/₂ *pounds small onions*

2   *pounds cooking apples*

2   *cups white wine vinegar*

¹/₂   *cup sugar*

1   *cup raisins*

2   *teaspoons salt*

1   *teaspoon ground cloves*

1   *teaspoon ground ginger*

¹/₂   *teaspoon cayenne pepper*

TOMATO CHUTNEY

This here's real good with chunks of crusty fresh bread.

Ruby Thacke

1. Cut the cores out of the tomatoes. Put the tomatoes into a bowl and cover with boiling water. Leave 15–20 seconds or until the skins start to split. Transfer the tomatoes to a bowl of cold water. Remove from the water one at a time and peel away the skins, using a sharp knife. Roughly chop the tomatoes.

2. Peel and thinly slice the onions. Peel, core, and chop the apples. Put the tomatoes, onions, and apples into a preserving pan. Add the remaining ingredients and stir to combine.

3. Bring to a boil, stirring. Lower the heat and simmer, stirring often, for 40–45 minutes or until the fruit and vegetables are soft and the chutney has reduced and thickened. Test by drawing the back of the spoon across the bottom of the pan. There should be no runny liquid visible.

4. Spoon the chutney into warmed sterilized jars, to within ¹/₈ inch of the tops. Stir, if necessary, to remove an air pockets. Seal the jars and label. Keep in a cool dark place for 2 months before using to allow the flavors to develop.

CRANBERRY-ORANGE RELISH

1   *pound cranberries*

1   *cup sugar*

2   *oranges*

1. Chop the cranberries and put them into a nonmetallic bowl with the sugar. Stir to mix thoroughly.

2. Slice the unpeeled oranges and remove the seeds. Finely chop the orange slices and add them to the bowl of cranberries and sugar.

3. Spoon the relish into sterilized jars. Seal, label, and refrigerate immediately. The relish should be chilled for several hours before serving. It will keep for about 1 week in the refrigerator. Real tasty with sandwiches, cottage cheese, and meatloaf.

PEARS IN WINE

2	cups water or grape juice
2	cups red wine
1	cup sugar
1	star anise
1	stick cinnamon
1	teaspoon ground coriander
4	cloves
8	to 10 pears

> PEARS IN WINE
>
> Serve this before and after funerals. Folks will appreciate it and look forward to coming.
> Ruby Thacker

1. Combine water, wine, sugar, and spices. Dissolve sugar over low heat. Cool, then, strain to remove spices.
2. Cut pears in half. Peel and core. Pack in jars without bruising fruit. Cover with syrup. Seal and process 10 minutes in a pressure cooker or 30 minutes in boiling water.

BLUEBERRY MARMALADE

1	medium orange
1	lemon
2/3	cup water
4	cups blueberries
5	cups sugar
1/2	bottle liquid pectin

1. Grate peel of orange and lemon. Combine peel and water. Bring to boil, cover and simmer for 10 minutes.
2. Mash blueberries and add to peel mixture. Discard pith from orange and lemon.
3. Heat to boiling, reduce heat and simmer for 10 minutes.
4. Stir in sugar and bring to a rolling boil. Stir in pectin and bring to rolling boil again. Boil hard 1 minute.
5. Remove from heat and skim. Ladle into hot jars and seal. Makes 3–4 pints.

> BLUEBERRY MARMALADE
>
> Give 'em as gifts to yer company.
> Ruby Thacker

MAMA'S TOMATO-BASIL JAM

2½ pounds ripe tomatoes
¼ cup lemon juice
3 tablespoons fresh-snipped basil
¼ cup sugar
1 package powdered fruit pectin
2¾ cups sugar

> MAMA'S TOMATO–BASIL JAM
>
> *This is specially good on sausage biscuits.*
>
> Ruby Thacker

1. Wash tomatoes. Remove peels, stem ends, cores, and seeds. Finely chop tomatoes. Measure 3½ cups. Place chopped tomatoes in a 6- or 8-quart Dutch oven or kettle. Heat to boiling; reduce heat. Cover and simmer for 10 minutes. Measure 3½ cups; return to the Dutch oven.
2. Add lemon juice and basil. Combine the ¼ cup sugar with the pectin; stir into tomato mixture. Heat to a full rolling boil, stirring constantly. Stir in the 2¾ cups sugar. Return mixture to a full rolling boil. Boil hard for 1 minute, stirring constantly. Remove from heat. Quickly skim off foam with a metal spoon.
3. Immediately ladle jam into hot, sterilized half-pint canning jars, leaving ¼-inch headspace. Wipe jar rims and adjust lids. Process in a boiling-water canner for 5 minutes (start timing when water begins to boil.) Remove jars from canner; cool on racks. Makes 5 half-pints.

HOT CROSS BUNS

1 cup milk
2 tablespoons yeast
½ cup sugar
1 teaspoon salt
⅓ cup butter
1 teaspoon cinnamon
½ teaspoon nutmeg
4 eggs
5 cups flour
1⅓ cup currants or raisins
1 egg white

GLAZE

1⅓ cups confectioner's sugar
1½ teaspoons finely chopped lemon zest
½ teaspoon lemon extract
1 to 2 tablespoons milk

1. In a small saucepan, heat milk to very warm, but not hot. Pour warm milk in the bowl of mixer and sprinkle yeast over. Mix to dissolve and let sit for 5 minutes.
2. With mixer at low speed, add sugar, salt, butter, cinnamon, nutmeg, and eggs. Gradually add flour. Dough will be wet and sticky. Continue kneading until smooth, about 5 minutes. Cover with plastic wrap and let the dough "rest" for 30–45 minutes.

3. Knead dough until smooth and elastic, for about 3 more minutes. Add currants or raisins and knead until well mixed. Dough will still be sticky. Shape dough in a ball, place in a buttered dish, cover with plastic wrap and let rise overnight in the refrigerator.

4. Let dough sit at room temperature for about a half-hour. Line a large baking pan with parchment paper. Divide dough into 24 equal pieces. Shape each portion into a ball and place on baking sheet, about ½ inch apart. Cover with a clean kitchen towel and let rise in a warm, draft-free place until doubled in size. Preheat oven to 400 degrees.

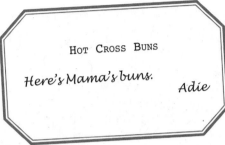

HOT CROSS BUNS

Here's Mama's buns.

Adie

5. When buns have risen, take a sharp knife and slash buns with a cross. Brush with egg white and bake for 10 minutes, then reduce heat to 350 degrees and bake until golden brown (about 15 minutes more).

6. Transfer to a wire rack. Whisk together glaze and spoon over buns in a cross pattern. Serve warm.

CHICKEN CURRY

CHICKEN CURRY

Here's Mama's recipe for chicken I told you about.

Adie

2 *pounds chicken cut in cubes*
2 *cups plain yogurt*
1 *large onion*
4 *cloves garlic, minced*
1 *tablespoon minced fresh ginger*
¼ *cup clarified butter*
4 *tablespoons curry powder*
1 *cup water*
  salt and pepper to taste
8 *ounces noodles, cooked and drained*
  fresh mint or coriander

1. Marinate chicken in yogurt for 1 hour at room temperature. Drain and pat dry. Save the marinade.

2. Cook onion, garlic and ginger in clarified butter for 1 minute. Sprinkle with curry powder and cook 30 seconds. Add chicken and stir to coat it well with spices. Add water and season to taste.

3. Cover and simmer 1 hour or until chicken is tender. Gradually add more water if necessary. Add noodles and stir gently.

4. Add yogurt marinade just before serving and heat through without boiling. Sprinkle with mint or coriander.

BLUE-RIBBON WATERMELON PICKLES

4½ *pounds watermelon rind*

6 *cups water*

½ *cup pickling salt*

3½ *cups sugar*

1½ *cups white vinegar*

1½ *cups water*

15 *inches stick cinnamon, broken*

1½ *teaspoons whole cloves*

1. Cut the skin and pink flesh from the watermelon rind (the white portion); discard skin. Cut the rind into 1-inch squares. Measure 9 cups; place in large bowl. Combine the 6 cups water and pickling salt; pour over rind (add more water if necessary to cover). Cover bowl and let stand overnight.

2. Pour the rind into a colander set in a sink; rinse under cold running water. Place rind in a 4-quart Dutch oven or kettle. Cover with cold water. Heat to boiling; reduce heat. Simmer, covered, for 20–25 minutes or till tender. Drain.

3. In a 6- to 8- quart Dutch oven or kettle combine sugar, vinegar, 1½ cups water, stick cinnamon, and cloves. Heat to boiling, reduce heat. Boil gently, uncovered, over medium-high heat for 10 minutes. Strain and return liquid to kettle. Add watermelon rind. Return to boiling. Cover and boil gently over medium-high heat till rind is clear, about 25 to 30 minutes.

4. Pack rind and syrup into hot, clean half-pint canning jars, leaving ½-inch head-space. Remove air bubbles, wipe jar rims, and adjust lids. Process filled jars in a boiling-water canner for 10 minutes. Remove jars from canner; cool on racks. Makes 6 half-pints.

> BLUE-RIBBON WATERMELON PICKLE
>
> *My girl Adie won first prize for these. Git plenty jars fore they'r gone.*
>
> Ruby Thacke

BEST EGG SALAD EVER

8 *(10-minute) hard boiled eggs*

½ *cup sweet red onions, diced*

3 *garlic cloves, finely minced*

1½ *teaspoons kosher course salt*

1 *teaspoon ground black pepper*

1 *cup mayonnaise*

¼ *cup fresh basil (cut into strips)*

1. After boiling eggs, peel off the shells. Blend all ingredients together.

2. Serve on thick-sliced homemade bread.

> BEST EGG SALAD EVER
>
> *Here's the recipe for them sandwiches I made Murphy when he went to Tybee Island to get Willa Mae.*
>
> Adie

MAMA'S FAVORITE PECAN PIE

1	*9-inch pie shell*
6	*tablespoons butter*
$^1\!/_2$	*cup packed brown sugar*
$^1\!/_2$	*cup packed white sugar*
$^1\!/_4$	*teaspoon salt*
3	*eggs*
$^3\!/_4$	*cup light corn syrup*
1	*tablespoon vanilla (yes, 1 tablespoon)*
2	*cups pecans, toasted, cooled, and chopped into small pieces.*

MAMA'S FAVORITE PECAN PIE

Here's Mama's recipe.   Adie

1. Preheat oven to 425 degrees. Place unbaked pie crust in freezer until ready to bake. Then line pie crust with aluminum foil and pie weights. Bake pie shell until set, about 5–6 minutes. Remove the foil and weights and bake 2–3 minutes longer until crust is just beginning to brown on the edges.
2. Meanwhile, melt butter in saucepan. Remove from heat; mix in sugars and salt with wire whisk until butter is absorbed. Beat in the eggs, then the corn syrup and vanilla. Strain the mixture to make sure it is perfectly smooth.
3. Place mixture in double boiler to heat. Cook and stir constantly with wire whisk until mixture is shiny and hot to the touch. Remove from heat and stir in pecans.
4. As soon as the pie shell comes out of the oven, decrease oven temperature to 275 degrees. Pour pecan mixture into hot pie crust. Bake at 275 degrees until center feels set, yet soft, like gelatin, when gently pressed, about 50–60 minutes.
5. Transfer pie to wire rack and let cool completely, at least 4 hours. Serves 6–8.

CARROT-PARSNIP COMPOTE

2   *pounds carrots*
1   *pound parsnips*
2   *cups orange juice*
2   *cups maple syrup*

1.   Cook carrots and parsnips in orange juice until very tender. Puree in blender.
2.   Combine with maple syrup and cook over moderate heat until thick.
3.   Ladle into hot, sterilized jars and seal. Store in refrigerator and use within two months or freeze for up to 1 year.

> CARROT-PARSNIP COMPOTE
>
> Here's the recipe Mama asked Willa Mae if she could have or was it a secret or something. You got to make the compote up first before you make the Souffle Pie.   Adie

WILLA MAE'S SOUFFLE PIE

3   *eggs, separated*
1½   *cups carrot-parsnip compote*
2   *9-inch pie shells*

1.   Preheat oven to 375 degrees. Beat egg yolks until fluffy. Add compote. Whip egg whites until stiff and fold into the mixture.
2.   Pour into pie shells and bake for 1¼ hours or until cake tester comes out clean. Makes 6 to 8 portions.

THREE-BEAN COMBO

2   *pounds green beans*
2   *pounds wax beans*
1½   *pounds Italian beans*
      salt to taste

1.   Wash green and wax beans; drain. Trim ends and break or cut into 1-inch pieces. Measure 12 cups of beans. Wash and drain Italian beans. Measure 4 cups. Place in an 8- or 10-quart Dutch oven or kettle.

> THREE-BEAN COMBO
>
> You can use canned beans for this recipe and it's still real good.
>
>   Adie

2.   Add enough boiling water to cover beans; return to boiling. Boil, uncovered, for 5 minutes.
3.   Using a slotted spoon, pack hot beans into hot, clean pint canning jars, leaving ½-inch headspace, Add ¼ to ½ teaspoon salt to each jar. Add boiling water, leaving ½-inch headspace. Remove air bubbles, wipe jar rims, and adjust lids.

4. Process filled jars in a pressure canner—10 pounds pressure for weighted canners or 11 ponds for dial-gauge canners—for 20 minutes. Allow pressure to come down naturally. Remove jars from canner, cool on racks. Makes 7 pints.

SPAGHETTI SAUCE

1½ *firm, ripe tomatoes*
¾   *cup water*
1   *medium onion, chopped*
1   *medium green pepper, chopped*
1   *cup sliced mushrooms (optional)*
3   *cloves garlic*
¼   *cup snipped fresh parsley*
1   *tablespoon brown sugar*
1   *tablespoon fennel seed, crushed*
2   *teaspoons salt*
2   *teaspoons dried basil, crushed*
2   *teaspoons dried oregano, crushed*
1   *teaspoon dried marjoram, crushed*
1   *teaspoon pepper*

SPAGHETTI SAUCE

You can leave out the mushrooms if you want.
Ruby Thacker

1. Wash tomatoes. Remove cores; cut into quarters.
2. Place tomatoes in a 9- or 10- quart Dutch oven or kettle. Heat to boiling, stirring occasionally. Reduce heat to medium. Cook, uncovered for 20 minutes. Press tomatoes through a food mill; return tomatoes to Dutch oven. Discard seeds and pulp.
3. In a medium saucepan combine water, onion, green pepper, and mushrooms. Cook over medium heat, stirring often, till onion and pepper are soft. Add to tomato mixture. Stir in garlic, parsley, brown sugar, fennel seed, salt, basil, oregano, marjoram, and pepper. Bring to boiling, reduce heat. Simmer, uncovered, about 2 hours, or until reduced by half, stirring frequently.
4. Ladle hot sauce into hot, clean quart or pint canning jars, leaving 1-inch headspace. Wipe jar rims; adjust lids. Process jars at 10-pounds pressure for 25 minutes for quart or 20 minutes for pints. Allow the pressure to come down naturally. Remove the jars from canner; cool on racks. Makes 4 pints.

HOT PICKLED SWEET PEPPERS

4½ *pounds green, red, and yellow sweet peppers*
1½ *pounds jalapeño peppers*
6½ *cups cider vinegar*
1⅓ *cups water*
⅔ *cups sugar*
4 *teaspoons pickling salt*
3 *whole cloves garlic*

HOT PICKLED SWEET PEPPERS

These peppers are hotter than a Georgia sidewalk in August.   *Ad*

1. Cut sweet peppers into quarters, removing stems, seeds, and membranes. Place, cut-side down on a foil-lined extra-large baking sheet. Bake in 450 degree oven for 20 minutes or till skin is bubbly and dark. Place peppers in a clean brown paper bag; seal and let stand for 10 minutes or till cool enough to handle. Using a paring knife, peel the skin off gently. Set aside.
2. Remove stems and seeds from jalapeño peppers. Slice into rings.
3. In a saucepan combine vinegar, water, sugar, salt, and garlic. Heat to boiling; reduce heat. Simmer, uncovered, for 10 minutes. Remove garlic. Place sweet and hot peppers in hot, clean pint or half-pint canning jars, leaving ½-inch headspace. Pour hot liquid over peppers, leaving ½-inch headspace. Remove air bubbles. Wipe jar rims; adjust lids. Process jars in boiling-water canner 15 minutes. (Start timing when water boils.) Remove from canner; cool. Makes 6 pints or 12 half-pints.

WILLA MAE'S STRAWBERRY MUFFINS

½ *cup butter, room temperature*
1½ *cups granulated sugar*
4 *large eggs*
1 *teaspoon vanilla extract*
3 *cups all-purpose flour*
1 *teaspoon baking powder*
½ *teaspoon baking soda*
½ *teaspoon salt*
½ *teaspoon finely grated lemon peel*
1 *cup buttermilk*
2 *cup fresh strawberries*
   granulated sugar for topping

WILLA MAE'S STRAWBERRY MUFFINS

Be careful. These are so scrumptious you can get fat just looking at them.
                    Adie

1. Grease 12 muffin cups. In a large mixing bowl with an electric handheld mixer on high setting, cream butter and sugar; beat in eggs, one at a time, beating after each addition. Blend in vanilla.
2. In a separate bowl stir together the flour, baking powder, baking soda, and salt.

3. With a wooden spoon, stir flour mixture into creamed mixture. Gradually stir in lemon peel and buttermilk until dry ingredients are just moistened; do not over-mix.
4. Scoop batter into prepared muffin pan, filling each muffin cup about ⅔ full. Evenly spoon sliced strawberries onto the center of each muffin and sprinkle each with a little granulated sugar.
5. Bake at 350 degrees for 18 to 20 minutes. Cool in pan on rack for 5 minutes. Gently turn muffins onto the rack. Best when served warm.

SNOWBALL COOKIES

4   *egg whites*
1   *cup sugar*
1   *teaspoon vanilla extract*
4   *cups crushed corn flakes*
1   *cup chopped pecans*

1. Beat egg whites until stiff. Gradually add sugar. Fold in vanilla, crushed corn flakes, and pecans.
2. Drop by teaspoonfuls onto an ungreased cookie sheet. Bake at 200 degrees (very low heat) for 1 hour.

SNOWBALL COOKIES

These are the closest thing to a snowball we got in Georgia.

Adie

VERNA'S FRIED REFRIGERATOR DONUTS

½   *cup shortening*
½   *cup sugar*
2   *eggs*
1   *cup scalded milk, cooled*
2   *packages dry yeast*
4   *cups flour*
¼   *teaspoon salt*
    Powdered sugar for coating donuts

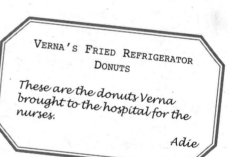

VERNA'S FRIED REFRIGERATOR DONUTS

These are the donuts Verna brought to the hospital for the nurses.

Adie

1. Cream shortening and sugar; add eggs and beat well. Add cooled milk and yeast. Add flour and salt and mix well.
2. Put in refrigerator overnight.
3. Section off dough into round biscuits. Poke hole in center, stretch hole slightly. Drop biscuits into hot grease and fry until light brown. Turn to brown other side. Remove and drain on paper towels. Put 1 or 2 donuts in paper bag with powdered sugar. Shake and enjoy.

OLD FASHIONED CINNAMON ROLLS

1	cup milk	
¹/₂	cup shortening	
¹/₃	cup sugar	
1¹/₂	teaspoons salt	
1¹/₂	packages dry yeast	
¹/₄	cup warm water	
1	egg, beaten	
4	to 5 cups sifted flour	
	melted butter	
	brown sugar	
¹/₂	teaspoon cinnamon	

FROSTING

2	cups powdered sugar
1	tablespoon butter
1	teaspoon vanilla

OLD FASHIONED CINNAMON ROLLS

These are heaven.   Adie

1. Scald milk; add shortening. Add sugar and salt and cool to tepid. Dissolve yeast in warm water. Add dissolved yeast and beaten egg. Add 4 cups flour, one at a time, beating after each addition. Dough should be soft yet firm enough to handle.
2. Knead on floured board until elastic and smooth. Avoid too much flour. Turn dough into well-oiled bowl. Let rise for 1¹/₂ hours.
3. Press dough down and divide into workable sized pieces. Roll dough out into a rectangle, cover with melted butter. Layer with a generous thick layer of brown sugar. Sprinkle on cinnamon as desired. Roll up jellyroll fashion.
4. Using scissors or a piece of string, cut off slices about 1 to 1¹/₂ inches thick. Place slices in an 8- or 9-inch round greased cake pan. Place one slice in the middle and other slices round it. Press rolls down to even out and fill pan. Let rise until the rolls fill the pan generously, about another hour.
5. Bake in 350 degree oven about 14–20 minutes. If rolls get too brown, cover with a piece of foil until the end of baking. Do not over-bake rolls.

MACARONI & CHEESE (TO DIE FOR)

8	ounces macaroni
	salt to taste
1¹/₄	plus 1²/₃ cups shredded cheddar cheese
2	tablespoons plus 1 teaspoon flour
1¹/₂	teaspoons salt
1¹/₂	teaspoons dry mustard
¹/₄	teaspoon pepper
²/₃	cup sour cream
2	eggs
1¹/₂	cups half & half

MACARONI AND CHEESE

This is the best comfort-food south of the grits line.

Adie

1½ cups heavy cream

1 teaspoon Worcestershire sauce

¼ teaspoon nutmeg

1. Boil macaroni in salted water till tender (approximately 8–9 minutes).
2. Combine 1¼ cups cheese with flour, salt, dry mustard, pepper, and sour cream. Set aside.
3. Whip eggs. Pour in half and half. Carefully blend in heavy cream. Add Worcestershire sauce. Set aside.
4. Gently fold the flour and cheese mixture into the whipped egg mixture. Add the macaroni and blend gently.
5. Place in 8½ x 11-inch glass baking pan. Sprinkle with cheese and nutmeg. Bake in 350 degree oven for 45 minutes to 1 hour.
6. Place under grill for a minute or two till cheese crust is golden brown.

SOUTHERN OKRA AND TOMATOES

1 cup okra, cut in ½-inch slices

½ cup chopped onion

¼ cup chopped green pepper

3 tablespoons bacon fat

4 quartered and peeled tomatoes

1 teaspoon salt

¼ teaspoon pepper

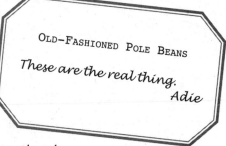

SOUTHERN OKRA AND TOMATOES

Fry some potatoes up and have yourself a meal.
Adie

1. Saute okra, onion, and green pepper in bacon fat over low heat.
2. Add tomatoes and seasonings. Cook until tender, stirring as little as possible.
3. Serve with fried chicken and home fried potatoes.

OLD-FASHIONED POLE BEANS

3 pounds pole beans, fresh

5 cups water

1 ham hock; ½ pound

2 teaspoons salt

¼ teaspoon pepper

OLD-FASHIONED POLE BEANS

These are the real thing.
Adie

1. Remove strings from beans, snap beans into 2-inch pieces. Wash beans.
2. Place water and ham hock in a Dutch oven; bring to boil. Reduce heat; cover and simmer 1 hour. Add beans, salt, and pepper; cook 30 minutes or until tender. Delicious!